ICE'S END

P. Finian Reilly

First Edition — 2025

Revised Editon.

Inquiries should be addressed to: www.pfinianreilly.com

Interior Design: Mariella Travis | www.alleiram.com
Map by Dan Kirchoff | www.dankirchoff.com
Large Print and eBook Conversion by Sam Sheng | linkedin.com/in/samsheng

ISBN
978-1-961905-47-4 (Paperback)
978-1-961905-48-1 (eBook)

12 Willows Press
Winterport, Maine
www.12willowspress.com

For my parents and grandparents.

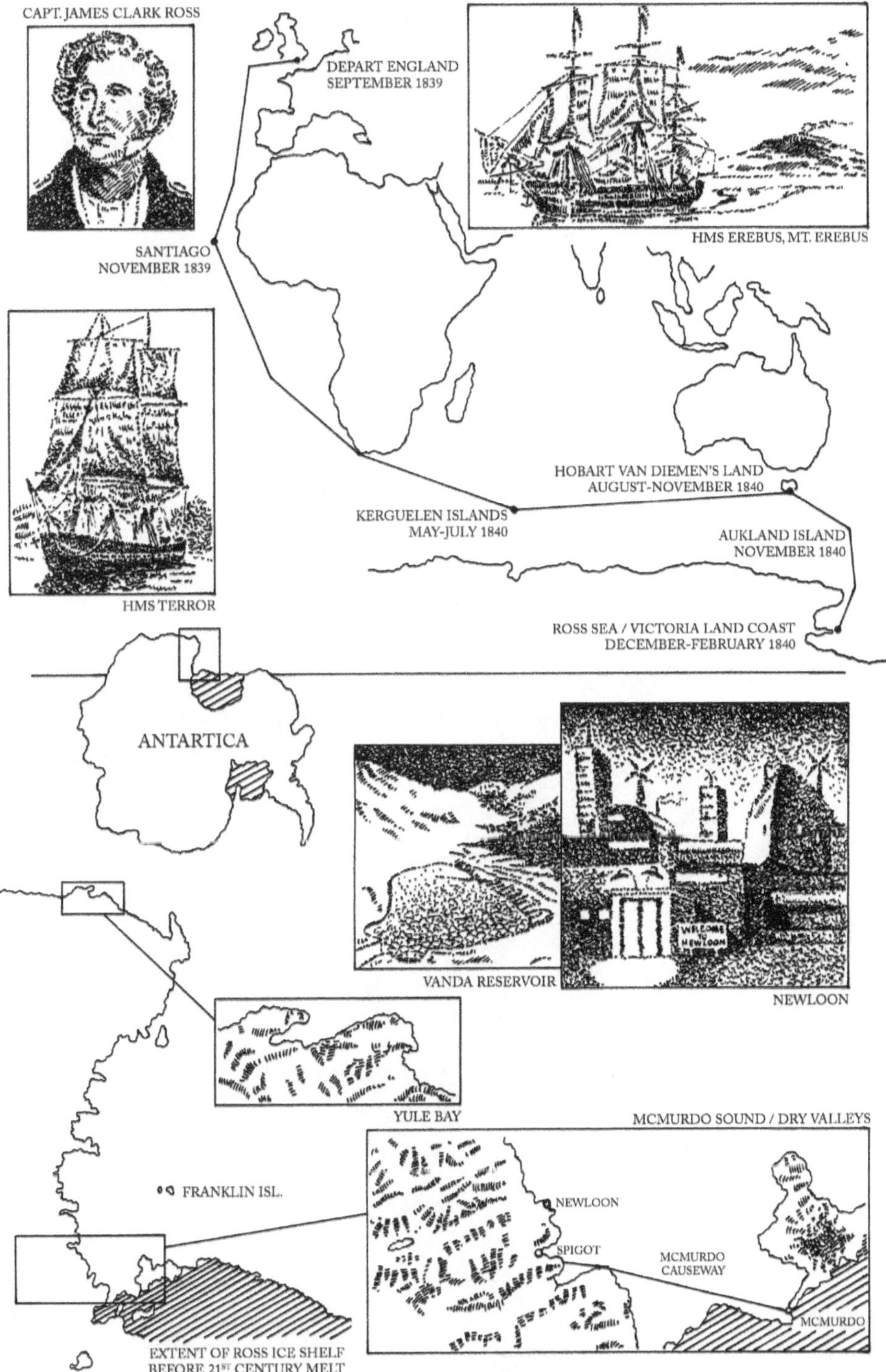

CAPT. JAMES CLARK ROSS
DEPART ENGLAND
SEPTEMBER 1839
HMS EREBUS, MT. EREBUS
SANTIAGO
NOVEMBER 1839
HMS TERROR
HOBART VAN DIEMEN'S LAND
AUGUST-NOVEMBER 1840
KERGUELEN ISLANDS
MAY-JULY 1840
AUKLAND ISLAND
NOVEMBER 1840
ROSS SEA / VICTORIA LAND COAST
DECEMBER-FEBRUARY 1840
ANTARTICA
WELCOME TO NEWLOON
VANDA RESERVOIR
NEWLOON
YULE BAY
MCMURDO SOUND / DRY VALLEYS
FRANKLIN ISL.
NEWLOON
SPIGOT
MCMURDO
CAUSEWAY
MCMURDO
EXTENT OF ROSS ICE SHELF
BEFORE 21ST CENTURY MELT

Prologue

H.M.S. *Erebus*
Unnamed Sea
February 1841

This far south, ice was an enemy.

A great frozen cliff—as high, white, and solid as the Cliffs of Dover—had blocked the two warships' progress for weeks. Now, the floes and bergs at their waterline blocked their escape.

"Swing harder!" came a shout. Yule looked over his shoulder at its source—a figure swaddled in a scarf and Welsh wig, and with the epaulets that marked him as a Captain of the Royal Navy. James Clark Ross had ordered every man not manning the sails onto the ice while he stayed on the prow of H.M.S. *Erebus*, the better to watch her able seamen and officers attack the ice at their feet with pickaxes. The ice pack had admitted the *Erebus* and her sister, H.M.S. *Terror*, through a gap in the great ice cliff they had followed for weeks. They didn't get far. The gap opened into a bay rounded by its own ice wall, as though a giant aimed to crush the *Erebus* and *Terror* like two flies between the folds of its handkerchief. Ross, in his hope that yet another gap would reveal itself, had ordered *Erebus* deeper into this bay—to the very brink of crashing into the ice cliffs. The two ships had only just escaped that fate by turning back, when the rough sheets of ice bobbing around their hulls locked into place. Second Master Henry Braddick Yule now had to hope this ice pack would yield to his pickax.

"The ship that frees herself first shall splice the main brace!" Ross bellowed. Yule glanced at *Terror*, also locked in the pack. He doubted her pickax crew had heard Ross, or that the captain's promise of a double rum ration would draw any more strength from the men. They were already driven by fear—fear that this bay at the end of the world would become their tomb.

Yule, though, had another reason to swing his pickax. It lay in his cupboard of a bunk on the *Erebus*, among the stones, potted ferns, jarred jellyfish, and boxed beetles gathered from the many ports of call on their long voyage toward the South Magnetic Pole. At the bottom of a pail, beneath a mound of basalt stones from wretched Franklin Island, Yule had hidden the papers he would need to profit from this voyage and end Captain Ross's career—along with his life.

Now more than ever, Yule smiled at the prospect.

To make it a reality, though, he needed to reach a British port alive. And so, he attacked the ice with all his might.

Chapter 1

Ross Sea Coast
Antarctica
May 2123

For the first time in his life, Roscoe felt cold.

For the first time, he wanted one of the puffy jackets he'd seen on faded posters in his internship academy, a converted ski lodge. Instead, just before the submarine hatch had been opened to the Antarctic night, a light bundle was dropped onto Roscoe's lap by a passing crewman. "Put these on," he shouted down the aisle. "Remember your safety briefing. You have three minutes!"

Stiff-necked from the jump seat, groggy from hours of sedated sleep, but grateful that the scabs he'd cut into his wrist three weeks earlier hadn't burst, Roscoe slid into the coveralls he'd been given. Drawstrings cinched the foil-thin plastic tight around his waist and closed the hood around his face, leaving just enough room for his eyes. *This* was supposed to keep him alive in Antarctica?

The sub crewman didn't seem to think so; he donned a big, puffy jacket and pants like the old-time skiers. Once the dozen bunny-suited interns lined up down the sub's aisle, he shouted, "Sorry for the inconvenience. Another sub was delayed due to a mechanical problem, leaving our slip at the port. This is the only way to get you out and keep water loading on schedule." The sedatives and the swaddling stifled any objections.

"We are going to disembark via Spigot's external pier. When you step outside, you will see a red searchlight directly ahead. Follow me down the pier, single file, toward that light. We will be outside for approximately five minutes." A few hooded heads nodded in front of Roscoe. The crewman turned and headed for the hatch. The interns followed, Roscoe bringing up the rear.

The cold sank deeper into his bones, and by the time he reached the conning tower's hatch and looked down at the pier, his toes were numb. He stared down the long, gray band stretching toward a red light glowing under a sky dense with stars. On either side of the pier, the starlight glinted off the water, which rippled between a loose, shifting quilt of dull white sheets—a frozen version of the scum that coated coastlines around the world. . In a few spots where the channels widened, chunks of the same pale hue bobbed gently. It took Roscoe a moment to recognize what he was looking at: fragments of Earth's last sea ice, floating just beneath the path to his new home.

"Get movin', we got a schedule to keep," another crew member shouted.

As soon as Roscoe stepped onto the pier, the hatch slammed behind him and wind blasted his left side. He widened his stance to brace himself. Both feet slipped, his legs splayed apart, and Roscoe fell on his backside.

He sat up and turned, just in time to see the conning tower's tip slip beneath the waves. Looking forward, he saw the line of interns shrink in the distance. He had to get moving. Roscoe started to stand—but as soon as his feet made contact with the pier's gray surface, he slipped again. None of the other interns seemed to have this problem, he noticed, as they continued down the pier. What had they done differently?

Then, he realized, they had remembered their safety briefing. He hadn't.

Three weeks earlier, as the sub sailed down Delaware Bay, the interns were warned that they might need to go out on the ice. The video said it usually didn't happen, but "sometimes water loading schedules may require disembarkation on Spigot's external pier." Roscoe knew just enough about Spigot to understand what this meant: By dropping their human cargo on this pier, the sub crews could ensure themselves enough time to flood their holds with precious water and head back north.

"In the unlikely event of a pier disembarkation, submarine crew members will distribute protective clothing," the video said. "Standard-issue intern footwear is not adequate for Antarctic conditions. For your safety, a compartment under your seat will unlock, providing ice-grips to attach to your shoes. These are essential for walking on the pier, which is often extremely slippery in winter." *It sure is*, Roscoe thought, noticing a slick sheen of ice on its surface.

A block of yellow light appeared beneath the red searchlight; the interns had reached the door, and it had opened for them. *Shit*, Roscoe thought. He had to get moving, or it would close, and he would be stuck out here. On another try, he managed to stand, take three steps, and fall again. The door closed; only the searchlight watched him now. He stood again and tried to run. He slipped on his first stride.

But this time, he didn't fall forward.

His foot slipped off the pier at the worst possible moment, and Roscoe felt gravity pull him to the right, toward a gap of open water between two ice sheets. In the split second before impact, he noticed white lights embedded along the pier about every meter, set into recesses several centimeters deep. A survival instinct, one he'd never used before, screamed *Handles!* Then, he hit the water.

The suit spared Roscoe a shock—but the numbing cold had a new weight behind it. The water wanted to get inside his suit. He knifed his left hand into the nearest recessed light and took several hard kicks to stay afloat, watching his breath cloud around the tiny bulb.

Roscoe lifted his right arm over his head, onto the pier surface just a few centimeters above the bulb. Just as he started to lift, a new pain shot up his right leg, and a new weight started to pull it down. His suit had sprung a leak.

He tried to lift himself over the pier's side, but the sedatives and cold had robbed him of the strength he needed. His leg grew heavier, and the pain was beginning to fade. Maybe this was it—the Southern Ocean would do what he hadn't managed, just a week earlier, with a razor blade on his wrist.

He looked around—maybe in one last search for help, maybe just to get a look at his final resting place. And something caught his eye: Lagrange-2. StarCross had the one sure way to distribute electricity to a storm-scoured, fire-scorched planet—beaming it through the sky—and space stations at the two best points to do it. Gravitational forces held Lagrange-2 and its sister, Lagrange-1, at opposing orbital nodes. Up there, StarCross generated electricity from city-sized solar arrays, and sent that power as microwave beams to any nation whose government had signed on to the StarCross Updated Terms of Service. If any buyer took issue with those terms, their missiles would be destroyed by StarCross long before they traversed the million and a half klicks from Earth to either Lagrange station.

Those orbiting cities, and StarCross's mining and relay station on the Moon, also promised clean air and stable weather for anyone who worked hard enough.

For the second time in as many weeks, that promise saved Roscoe. He remembered the message he received just after slicing his left wrist, the message that told him he still had a path off this dying rock and up to that orbiting city. And that path ran down the pier toward the searchlight. His parents were counting on him to keep going. *You're it! Move!*

At last, adrenaline surged through him. Roscoe hauled himself back onto the pier, taking a few deep breaths before moving again. He didn't walk. Instead, he crawled—at first dripping wet, then stiff and crusted over as the water on his suit froze.

After two agonizing minutes, the searchlight led him to flat, solid ground. Roscoe wanted to kiss the gravel under his feet, but he didn't dare stop. His limbs and face were numb, except for the feeling of new weight on his ice-sheathed right leg and the exhaustion dragging down his upper eyelids. He ran uphill, fueled by the last of his adrenaline. Beneath the searchlight, he saw a shed with a single doorway, painted with the light blue outline of a water droplet. He pounded on it with all the strength he had left.

If Roscoe had believed in God, he would have thanked Him when the door opened. He collapsed onto the floor, savoring the sudden warmth, and looked up at a startled man wearing a bulletproof vest and a shoulder patch with the StarCross logo: three white stars and one blue droplet, placed at the corners of an invisible diamond kite. Roscoe's eyes rested on the lowest point, on the droplet representing Spigot. Then, the guard jerked back and, with a "What the hell?" reached for his holster.

Roscoe, still suited and on his back, raised his hands.

"I-I-I'm an int-t-t-ern. Came f-f-from th-th-the s-s-sub."

"Let's see some ID."

Roscoe tore open his suit front, pulled back the hood, and presented the tag that had been hanging from a cord around his neck since he'd boarded the sub. The guard tapped it with his thick black wristband, then studied the shimmering screen that appeared in front of him. "Well, Roscoe Slake, why didn't you come in with the others?"

"F-f-f-forgot m-m-my ice-g-grips."

The security guard nodded, leaving his gun on his hip, and told Roscoe to strip. "Damn lucky you got here when you did," he said, handing him a foil blanket. "My shift's almost over. This door would've been unguarded for hours."

Roscoe couldn't say much more, as two medics from Spigot's infirmary checked him for frostbite and gave him a set of dry clothes. As they led him down a staircase at the shed's rear, he heard the security guard talking to an unseen superior.

"Minor incident, boss. The intern coming in from the mid-Atlantic sub forgot his ice-grips. Almost got left out on the ice." He paused. "Yeah, profile says he was a pounder. Got the height for it. Guess we'll have to tell the sub crews to watch those ones more closely." There was a chuckle. "Or leave 'em. Probably not worth search and rescue."

Reaching the base of the stairs, Roscoe heard the guard sigh. "Why do they always send us the fuckups?"

CHAPTER 2

A familiar sound jolted Roscoe awake.

Spigot's alarm was the same StarCross-proprietary one—a mechanical whir, impossible to sleep to, accompanied by a flashing blue light—that had woken Roscoe every day of his decade at Granite Gorge Internship Academy. For a moment, he thought he was back in his dorm room. Then, the ache in his feet reminded him of the night before—and his new home.

He rolled out of bed and traced the noise to a thick, black communications wristband hanging from a hook on the wall—identical to the one the guard had worn the night before. Roscoe slipped it onto his left wrist, grateful that it covered his scab. His academy wristband had been featureless, but this one had two small external hooks. As soon as he noticed them, a tiny light flickered on, projecting a notebook-sized rectangle above his palm. Roscoe read the message:

> *Good morning, interns! Welcome to Spigot! Report to Auditorium at 1000 hours for orientation. Galley is open for breakfast—map of tunnels in your wristband.*

He pecked the home-screen icon on the floating panel and pulled up a map of Spigot's tunnel network—four wide, slanted lines intersected by four, evenly-spaced narrower ones. His location was marked near the second wide tunnel from the left. The first two tunnels were highlighted white, while the other two were grayed out and marked "Restricted."

The map showed the stretch of narrow tunnel around Roscoe in light blue, while the areas across the wide main tunnel were pink. *Do they still keep genders separate down here?* he wondered.

Roscoe found a duffel bag of clothes beside his bed and got dressed, trying to recall anything from the night before, when the medics had dragged him to his room. He didn't recognize the narrow hallway outside his door, or what lay at its end: the main tunnel, all bare, tan rock, lit by overhead LEDs, as wide as a six-lane highway, and already busy. Workers zipped past in both directions, driving squat electric carts. Their clothes and vehicles all had the light blue droplet outline he'd noticed on the exterior door. Looking down, Roscoe realized the same symbol was stitched on the breast of his jacket. He was a Spigot man now.

Roscoe followed his wristband down the tunnels to the galley, served himself SynCoffee and quinoa, and took a seat near the end of a long table. He recognized a few other interns from the submarine: Ana, from an academy in North Carolina; Darren, from Vermont; and Kevin, from Wisconsin. A wavy-haired, olive-skinned guy sat nearby, but Roscoe didn't know him. None of them were talking, and Roscoe understood why.

Small talk at any of StarCross's licensed Internship Academies was a minefield. Back at school, no one had wanted to let slip where they fell in the StarCross hierarchy—which Quarterly Crosscutting Aptitude Test (Q-CAT) percentile they'd fallen into, or whether they'd been on compound. Whenever a conversation edged in on one of those topics, a mention of "StarCross Silence" sufficed to shut it down.

Roscoe wasn't complaining. After being called a "pounder" by the security asshole the previous night, Roscoe didn't want anyone else to know he had taken StarCross's now-banned, aptitude-enhancing compound.

To avoid even having to invoke the Silence, he focused on his wristband screen and skimmed through StarCross News Network (SNN). In the "Top Stories" tab, he found news about elections, legislation, and treaties—the business most governments around the world still made a show of carrying on, and SNN still dutifully reported. None of it mattered. For a generation now, StarCross had controlled the only reliable sources of electricity and water—outer space and Antarctica, respectively. To secure these two vital commodities, virtually every country had subsumed its constitution, statutes, and long-held notions about a government's proper role into StarCross's Updated Terms of Service. In the name of complying with those terms, nuclear arsenals were taken off hair-trigger alert; military hardware was either turned against refugees or mothballed; and the top-secret technologies that would have gone toward space exploration and warfare were locked away—all ready to be exchanged for more of StarCross's water and energy.

For Roscoe's entire life, and most of his parents' lives, that water and energy had kept their refrigerator full, their showers hot, and their A/C running in Pennsylvania's swampy summers. StarCross water and energy had also backed two digital currencies—Water Equivalent Certificate (WECs) and Renewable Energy Credit (RECs)—that seamlessly moved around the world, along with electricity, via the Lagrange stations. His parents and countless other small-scale generators had fed the flow, selling natural gas to a fuel cell near Scranton that beamed power up to Lagrange-2 for re-transmission. They had earned enough RECs to put Roscoe through Granite Gorge, but the Lagrange stations were the biggest producers, and governments the biggest recipients. These days, governments didn't govern so much as grovel for StarCross's water and energy. That dynamic had earned politicians and bureaucrats around the world the pejorative nickname "govellers"—but they couldn't complain. StarCross had, after all, saved their citizenries from the water and energy shortages, warfare, and financial crises that had plagued the twenty-first century.

But StarCross hadn't ended the floods, heat waves, storms, and fires that Roscoe had grown up fearing—disasters he now checked for by tapping the SNN home screen's "WEATHER" tab. The parched grass of the Great Plains and the tinderbox of dead rainforest in the Amazon continued to smolder, but Pennsylvania, for the moment, was safe.

Roscoe felt his pulse slow. He knew their prefabricated home couldn't withstand the Northeast's ever-worsening floods, fires, and landslides. He also knew his family couldn't afford one of the new, ruggedized models built in StarCross's Marius Hills lunar manufacturing facility. If their current home was lost, the Updated Terms of Service would force them into a so-called Displaced Persons Center—what everyone back home called a Femaville. These centers were supposedly disaster-proof, with strategic siting and perimeter defenses, but conditions inside bred discontent that could only be contained by razor wire, guard towers, and strict limits on outside travel. Roscoe's family had escaped that fate—for now.

Roscoe closed his wristband, slurped down the last of his SynCoffee, and reminded himself that *he* had to free his family from that fear by finding them a way off-world. *You're it*, he told himself again, trying not to think about how his family had already blown two of StarCross's three routes off-world. His parents would never earn enough WECs or RECs to purchase Resident status on the Moon or at one of the Lagrange stations. Most of the RECs they had earned siphoning natural gas had gone to his Granite Gorge tuition. Roscoe had failed to leverage that hard-earned tuition into a career-track position—one that came with family housing—off-world. The only chance left—to excel in his internship, earn a spot in StarCross's Leadership Training Program, and perform well enough there to secure an off-world posting with StarCross's Executive Staff—was now entirely in Roscoe's hands. He left the galley, letting his wrist guide him to the auditorium. *Better pay attention at orientation,* he told himself.

The auditorium lobby was also quiet. In front of the double doors, Roscoe saw one of StarCross's standard-dimension memorials to the Orbital Strike, the terrorist attack he'd learned all too much about this past year. He also saw a table and two lines of interns waiting in front of it. After a few minutes, it was his turn to face a copper-haired woman, wearing a lanyard. She sat next to a male intern with a buzz cut, also checking people in. They both looked a couple of years older than him, though they wore the same jackets as the other interns.

"Name?" she asked, barely looking up from her laptop.

"Roscoe Slake."

"Date of birth?"

"May 28, 2101."

"Happy belated birthday! Big two-two." Roscoe flinched, surprised not only by the reminder that he had turned twenty-two just two days ago—while drugged on a submarine under the Southern Ocean—but also by meeting someone this chipper. Her smile only grew as she looked up from her laptop. "You went to Granite Gorge?"

"Yeah."

"No way! Same!"

"Really? What year did you graduate?"

"In '21. Guess we never crossed paths. I'm Jen." She leaned across the table to shake Roscoe's hand. He only offered it after a quick look confirmed that the band still covered his scab. On her wristband-free hand was a bracelet—two beads shaped like black diamonds—that some of Granite Gorge's upper-class girls used to pilfer from the abandoned souvenir store in the academy building. "You're the first Gorgie I've met down here," she said, widening her green eyes.

"Really? The first one?"

Jen nodded. "Yep. Glad I can finally start a little alumni network down here."

Roscoe tried to remember if he had heard a "Jen" recognized at any of Granite Gorge's top-tenth award ceremonies; she was probably doing the same with him. The fact that neither of them had ever placed in the top tenth of the one percent on the quarterly Q-CAT exams probably helped explain why neither of them had gotten an off-world internship. "You're all checked in," Jen said as soon as Roscoe realized this. "Go on in and take a seat."

Roscoe found a seat and thought back to Granite Gorge: its cathedral-cabin main building originally built for skiers back when it still snowed in Pennsylvania, and the prefab-metal dorms, sunken into the slopes that had once been the easy ski runs. He never thought someone would smile about that place, especially when it hadn't gotten them off-world.

Looking around the auditorium, Roscoe counted fifty heads scattered beyond the front row. Everyone sat alone and adhered to the StarCross Silence. But in the front, nine interns sat clustered together. After a few minutes, Jen, and the other intern who'd been checking them in, hurried down the aisle to join this group.

The lights soon dimmed, and a screen appeared in front of them. First, StarCross's three-star, one-droplet logo came up. The graphic zoomed in on the droplet, then through its sky-blue outline to old stock footage from the mid-twenty-first century: parched riverbeds, empty reservoirs, dead crops.

"How could humanity keep feeding itself when rain no longer fell on its breadbaskets?" the narrator asked. "When every aquifer had been tapped, when rivers ran dry, brought destructive floods, or seethed with pollution? Desalination, pumping, and cloud seeding were all tried, and all failed. Then, in 2085, Rob Eatonson had an answer: Tap the last great freshwater source on Earth—Antarctica's glaciers and ice sheets—and export it around the world."

The soundtrack jumped an octave, and the video cut to a bearded, middle-aged man in a parka, safety vest, and hard hat, hunched over a machine's control panel. "Rob Eatonson's mining expertise helped StarCross source its minerals and metals from the Moon, rather than from unreliable mines on Earth. In 2085, he took that expertise to the Taylor Valley."

The camera panned over a brown sea of gravel, threaded with snow and ice. On all sides, it sloped up toward bare, craggy peaks. This was Roscoe's new home—hopefully just until he could get to either StarCross's Marius Hills facility or to one of the Lagrange stations.

The video switched to a map of the valley: a banana-shaped groove running twenty miles from ice to ocean.

"The valley had no ice itself, but it had easy access to the Taylor and Ferrar Glaciers—and to the ocean. It was the perfect place for Eatonson's vision."

The video showed a tunnel-boring machine churning through rocks the same color as the valley floor. "Under Eatonson's direction, StarCross engineers built the boldest drainage system in history. A network of tunnels to siphon the meltwater from beneath these mighty glaciers and slake humanity's thirst—and to house the hard-working employees who would run this operation."

"StarCross created a new unit of exchange, called the Water Equivalent Certificate, or WEC, to account for this water. Modeled on StarCross's energy accounting unit, the Renewable Energy Credit, it guarantees the bearer one thousand liters of fresh water."

Roscoe rolled his eyes. He'd known the difference between RECs and WECs since he was eight. He guessed Spigot showed this video to visiting StarCross Residents, whose families no longer needed to care about RECs and WECs, unless they ran some side business on-world as a hobby.

"The U.S. government lent its resources to the effort." Roscoe rolled his eyes again. *Lent?* He knew enough about StarCross's Updated Terms of Service to know that when StarCross named its price for WECs or RECs, the govellers paid. "Applying an idea first developed to export Alaskan oil in the 1970s, the American military worked with StarCross engineers to blast out a deepwater port at the Taylor Valley's northeastern end. It retrofitted its naval submarines as undersea tankers, ensuring that Spigot's water could be securely transported around the world—at any time of year, in any weather condition."

The screen cut back to the logo of StarCross's predecessor, TriStar Energy: an equilateral triangle of three stars. "TriStar Energy's three space-based energy facilities had already made energy plentiful. As the first submarine tankers sailed north from Antarctica, the water shortages that had plagued humanity also came to an end. You might say these age-old challenges were star-crossed." As Roscoe rolled his eyes yet again, the three stars shifted a bit, and a blue droplet glinted into its place well below them on the StarCross logo. *If Spigot's so important, why doesn't your logo have the droplet closer to the damn stars?* Roscoe thought.

The music crescendoed, and the lights came up. At the podium stood a balding man, slightly stooped, with cheeks that sagged like a bulldog's. A circular, red-white-and-brown pin was fastened to his jacket. Jen and the other interns from the front now stood beside him onstage. So did the buzz-cut intern who'd been sitting next to Jen out front.

"Hello everyone," said the man at the podium, his voice calm but commanding. "My name is Grei Jahnford, and I am celebrating my tenth year as the CEO of Spigot." Jahnford paused; Roscoe wondered if they were supposed to clap. After a few seconds of silence, Jahnford stretched his lips and bared his teeth. Roscoe couldn't tell if he was smiling or grimacing.

"I'm honored to welcome all of you to the Spigot family. As interns, you've been selected as some of the best and brightest in this year's internship class, and we need your skills now more than ever."

Now, Jen was the one to sneak in an eye roll; she finished it just as the CEO waved back to her and the other interns. They all looked a few years older than Roscoe. "With me are this year's Head Interns." Jen and the others gave a tentative wave. "They've just finished the two-year internship program you're beginning, and now they've entered StarCross's Leadership Training Program. With the exception of Trent here"—Jahnford gestured toward the intern who had sat with Jen at the table—"they will each be leading cohorts of you to get you situated during your first year in Antarctica. Welcome aboard, and let's bring water to a thirsty world."

Jen stepped up to the podium. "You've all had a long journey, so take the rest of the day off to get adjusted. Be in the galley at oh-eight-hundred tomorrow to get your work assignments." That did it for orientation.

The interns rose from their seats and began to file out of the auditorium, maintaining the StarCross Silence. Roscoe followed his wristband's directions back to his room. On the way, he noticed a sign at a side tunnel entrance: THIS TUNNEL FOR MALE INTERNS ONLY. VIOLATORS WILL BE DISCIPLINED. *Looks like I was right about the separate-genders thing*, he thought.

His room was small, roughly two and a half meters by three meters, with a bed and drawers set into the wall. Roscoe opened the duffel bag he'd been given and unpacked the rest of his clothes. Nothing fancy—just a few pairs of synthetic pants, shirts, and jackets with Spigot's droplet logo on the breast, along with a week's supply of socks, underwear, and some exercise shorts and T-shirts. A sign on the wall read: DISPOSE OF USED CLOTHES IN WALL CHUTE. CLEAN CLOTHES YOUR SIZE WILL BE RETURNED TO YOUR ROOM EVERY FRIDAY.

Then, his wristband buzzed. Calling up the near-opaque screen, he saw a new message:

Welcome to Spigot, Roscoe Slake!

We are excited to have your help with our mission of bringing water to a thirsty world. Please read this message as it contains important information about your cohort and job assignment.

Your cohort leader is: JEN DOIL

Your cohort leader, an intern in the StarCross Leadership Training Program, will lead you and a group of four other interns in regular discussions and social activities during your first year at Spigot. They will be in touch soon with more information.

Your job assignment is: ARCHIVES.

This job is vital to Spigot's mission of bringing water to a thirsty world. You will gain vital experience in this position over the next two years. At the end of this period, you will have the option of either pursuing a career-track position in the ARCHIVES division, or of extending your internship by two years and then entering the StarCross Leadership Training Program, which can open up new opportunities for StarCross leadership positions and transfers to other StarCross facilities later in your career.

Roscoe already knew he'd go for the Leadership Training Program. He'd made that choice a week ago, before his wrist had even stopped bleeding.

He scrolled through a few more paragraphs of platitudes probably cranked out by some algorithm, then closed his eyes. Two years of interning here, then two more in the Leadership Training Program, and *then*, maybe, he'd get his shot off-world.

A dull pain had sprouted in the center of his brain, and thoughts of his father pointing toward Lagrange-2 filled his mind. Homesickness and headaches—it was the same every time he ran out of compound. But this time, there would be no more pills. *Time to face withdrawal*, Roscoe thought, grateful he didn't have a roommate.

Even so, he had already been marked as a compounder.

"Hey, you got any extra doses?"

Roscoe looked up from his second SynCoffee-and-quinoa breakfast in Spigot's galley. The wavy-haired guy he had noticed the day before was sitting across from him, asking for drugs in an Australian accent.

After a long silence, during which Roscoe wondered what had given him away as a "pounder," the Aussie spoke again. "I got a compound for logic and geospatial reasoning," he said, snorting. "Wasn't enough to get me off-world."

Roscoe sighed and shook his head. "Mine was a coding-heavy formula. Wasn't enough for me either. Don't have any doses left. How bad are your headaches?"

"Had worse. I'll muddle through. Really wish StarCross would let us taper after graduation, rather than cut us off cold."

For the first time in Antarctica, Roscoe smiled. It was a relief to find someone in the same pharmacological bind as him—even if the compound hadn't stopped this guy from growing a dozen centimeters taller than him. When the intern extended his hand, Roscoe noticed his wrists were unmarked by suicide attempts.

"Hamza," he said.

"Roscoe."

As they shook hands, Roscoe couldn't quite place where Hamza was from—his skin and hair suggested South Asian parents, but his broad nose and thick lips seemed to point somewhere else. Roscoe spotted, on a cord around his neck, a wooden carving no bigger than two knuckles. A stylized face with almond-shaped eyes inside concentric curves stared back at him. Then Hamza leaned forward, and it dipped into his collar.

He pointed toward the gate at the galley entrance. "Think those pills they gave us will make up for it?"

When Roscoe arrived, a small hatch in the tall black box beside it had opened, dispensing a gray pill stamped T3. *Swallow*, the screen instructed. *Daily T3 doses are essential to prevent winter-over syndrome*. Once Roscoe took the pill, the galley opened.

Roscoe shrugged, uncertain what T3 was or if it resembled the compound at all.

The ceiling lights suddenly flashed blue, and everyone fell silent. Roscoe heard a disembodied voice and saw Jen, the head intern he'd met the day before, speaking into a microphone.

"Good morning, interns!" she said with vigor likely fueled by several cups of SynCoffee. "Time to head to work! Last night you should have received a message on your wristbands with your work assignment."

Roscoe and Hamza joined their new colleagues heading toward the funnel of the galley door. "Where are you working?" Roscoe asked.

"Drone Operations!" Hamza said, suddenly seeming to forget compound withdrawal. "You?"

"Archives."

"Huh," Hamza replied. "I wonder what they do there."

Roscoe shrugged again. Since last night, he hadn't figured out how Archives would help Spigot find water.

Chapter 3

He still wasn't sure by the end of the day.

Roscoe's wristband had directed him to a long, low room. A woman just a few centimeters taller than him answered the door. She looked at him through thick, circular glasses beneath a gray-streaked pageboy haircut. "Roscoe?" she asked, voice high and lilting.

"Yep."

"Karla Marmolada." They shook hands. "Welcome to the Archives."

Karla led him into a hall as wide as Spigot's main thoroughfare, and nearly half a kilometer long. Both walls were lined with grids of filing cabinets, with a row of standalone cabinets running along one side and two desks positioned near the entrance. Ceiling lamps bathed everything in warm amber. Karla swept her arm over the tunnel. "Everything you ever wanted to know about Antarctica—and lots you probably didn't."

Roscoe looked down the cavernous hall. "This is all about Antarctica?"

"It is indeed. From the first two hundred years or so of Antarctic exploration."

"What kind of stuff?"

"Depends on the era," Karla said. "From the eighteenth century, we mostly get whalers, sealers, and merchant vessels—ship captains' logs, sailors' diaries, shipping manifests, insurance records, things like that.

Not too much of it. But in the nineteenth century, then things started piling up."

Karla rapped her knuckles on a leather-bound volume lying on her desk. Roscoe read the spine: "Logbook of Capt. Josiah Creesey, S.S. FLYING CLOUD, 1851." A chip and barcode had been pasted on its spine.

"Where did we get this?"

"Let's see." Karla set the book down, tapped her wristband to the chip, and squinted through her glasses. "Looks like the old Library of Congress sent it to us when they moved to Duluth."

"Governments send us these?"

"That's right. We confirm they've purged every listing from the old World Wide Web and other databases. Under the Updated Terms of Service, they'll also have to ban all duplicates and promise to destroy any that turn up. Then they send the physical documents here. We process and look through them for anything that might help Spigot produce more water."

"How do we know when something in these books will help produce water?"

"We don't. We just pull certain information: latitudes, longitudes, weather conditions, geological observations, and various keywords. An algorithm looks through it, decides how useful it will be, then tells us how many WECs to give the sender." She slapped her palms together as if she had just swept a room spotless. "All spelled out in StarCross's Updated Terms of Service."

Karla picked up Creesey's logbook and started flipping through the pages. "This captain went around Cape Horn. Perhaps my ancestors saw his ship pass Chile. Because they didn't get too far south, this logbook won't help find water down here. We'll probably only give the gringos a WEC or two for it." With a sad smile, Karla closed the logbook. "To be valuable, it has to come from the glaciers themselves. How high was this ice in the past? How deep were the crevasses? Those are the details that will help draw fresh water from the ice. But StarCross still sees some worth in the Southern Ocean, so we have to review those records too."

"So governments trade their historical records for WECs ... and we use them to find more water?"

"Well, not us," Karla said, waving her finger between them. "Everything we collect goes to Data Processing, which uses it to figure out where Spigot should map or tunnel next."

Roscoe felt a strange thrill. History was the one academy subject he had ever really enjoyed—even after he had failed to get off-world by offering a new take on StarCross history in his senior capstone thesis. Now, in this cave under a frozen wasteland, history was useful for something—and might still be his ticket off-world. "So records from hundreds of years ago can help Spigot find water?"

She shook her head. "Not really. Since there's plenty of ice left at the inland end of Taylor Valley, the folks in Data Processing mostly want newer, twenty-first-century research on local geology and drainage. Most of that's digital and gets beamed straight to them. They probably won't touch this eighteen hundreds stuff for a long time, if ever."

The thrill fizzled. "So we just sit on it."

"Right. As long as we have it, that means the wildcatters up on the ice cap or on the peninsula don't. Every bit of knowledge we lock up keeps future WECs out of someone else's hands." Another rueful smile. "Or, at the very least, it creates a job for humanities people like you and me. They might not need us in space, but we're still good for something down here."

So it's that obvious, Roscoe thought. He'd scored ninety-eighth percentile on the lightly weighted humanities portion of StarCross's final placement exam, while failing to crack eighty-fifth on coding and logic. He didn't even want to think about his leadership aptitude score.

And that had all been with the compound, which was no longer StarCross-approved and not available down here.

Roscoe swallowed hard and blinked fast, just in case any tears emerged. Karla must have noticed. "If it makes you feel any better," his boss said, "I quit my Library Science PhD program to take this job. At least this came with guaranteed housing."

"You didn't have to go through the internship program?" Roscoe asked.

"No, it was a little looser in those days. StarCross sometimes hired people cold. That was before they realized they needed the academies and internships to brainwash people." Roscoe forced a smile. It must have been a bad one because Karla looked away and led him to the two desks. "Anyway, let's get to work."

Roscoe now saw that the Archives' two desks were mounted on rails running parallel to the stacks. "The one good thing about working for mining engineers is that they know how to make an underground workspace comfortable when they want."

Karla settled into one of the desks and demonstrated its controls, gliding smoothly along the rails. Stopping at a section, she pressed a button to select and open a case. It extended from the wall to bring its books and documents flush with the desktop. The desk's reading lamp, keyboard, monitor, and barcode-pasting equipment were all within easy reach of her slender frame.

Roscoe took a seat at the other desk, mimicking her motions as he got a feel for the system, testing the smooth glide of the controls and the way the case extended into place. "Looks like you've got it," Karla said. "We've come a long way from the old coal mines, no?"

He nodded, remembering the Mining portion of Granite Gorge's Engineering Fundamentals course, where he had learned how StarCross extracted minerals from the lunar surface—and how he could maintain the robots that did the work. "StarCross doesn't send people to the Marius Hills mining colony so they can slap on a space suit and swing a pickax," their nicotine-starved teacher had shouted at the class after a particularly bad quiz. "It has robots do that shit, and it only wants people who can service those robots. If you think they'll take you with grades like these, you're out of your ever-loving minds!"

The thought that he might be out of his "ever-loving mind" to still believe he could make it to the Moon almost tipped Roscoe toward wanting to slit his wrists again—but then the memory that sparked that thought pulled him back. "Hang on," he said to Karla. "Can't AI do this stuff?"

Karla shook her head. "It could, but it makes more sense for people to do it."

"Why?"

"You can train AI to recognize one person's handwriting, no problem. But we're dealing with stuff from hundreds of different writers, sometimes multiple writers in the same logbook. When it comes to making sense of all that, the Equation still favors humans." She smiled with pride.

"The what?"

Karla lowered her glasses and looked at him. "The Equation. They don't talk about that up north?"

Roscoe shook his head.

"It's an algorithm," she explained. "AI needs computers, and computers need energy—and water for cooling. The Equation helps StarCross decide whether it's more profitable to use AI for a given task, or to have humans do it, selling the energy AI would consume as RECs and the cooling water as WECs."

"And the Equation says humans are better for doing this?"

Karla nodded. "At least so far. And as long as it does, they need us down here." She smiled again as she sat at her own desk. "I wouldn't worry if I were you. They just added an intern position. That's a four-year investment right there. You're probably fine."

Roscoe nodded again. He pulled a folder from the box sitting on his desk, while mulling over this unspoken caveat to the promise StarCross had made to every internship academy family. *You may not be connected to anyone with a big enough Discretionary Account to get you off-world, but we can still train your kids for jobs up there—unless some secret Equation decides that it's better business for a robot to do it.*

To keep his view of StarCross from curdling any more, Roscoe turned his focus to some of the first words written in these latitudes. Then Karla spoke again. "Amazing, no?"

When Roscoe looked up, she continued. "These men wrote with quills, on sailing ships. And they outsmarted the best machines we have today."

Chapter 4

Chatham Dockyard
England
September 1839

The note reached Yule as he finished his breakfast: "Chart-boxes ready. Report to Commissioner's House."

Second Master Henry Braddick Yule complied at once. He stepped off the H.M.S. *Tartar*, the old frigate where he had been lodged, and followed the River Medway to the House.

Chatham was just starting to wake up. Yule saw the day's first puffs of smoke rise from the foundry and heard workers shouting inside the ropery as they prepared the rigging for Her Majesty's Ships. It was nothing like the old days, the older officers said. The dockyard had been working below capacity for decades, ever since Nelson drove Napoleon's fleet from the seas.

To justify his post, Chatham's current Commissioner had lavished attention on the *Erebus* and *Terror*, readying them for the voyage of discovery that Yule would soon join. The Commissioner greeted the second master himself in the brick mansion's foyer.

"Good morning, Master Yule. May I present Mister John Walker, engraver for the Hydrographic Office, who just arrived from London."

A balding man with mutton-chop whiskers shook Yule's hand. "Much obliged, Master Yule. The chart-boxes are ready for placement aboard ship." Two padlocked trunks sat beside him on the floor, one marked "H.M.S. EREBUS" and the other "H.M.S. TERROR."

Walker took the handle on one end of *Erebus*'s box, and Yule took the other. For the first time, a chart-box's weight unnerved him. This trunk held charts of every reef, shoal, and coastline between England and Van Dieman's Land, the island just south of Australia. As second master on the *Erebus*, Yule would have to navigate the ship through them—and through whatever unknown hazards lay between Van Dieman's Land and the *Erebus*'s final destination: the South Magnetic Pole. He would also have to collect soundings and surveys that would let more of Her Majesty's Ships follow in her wake.

"Your surveying skills are legendary at the Hydrographic Office," Walker told Yule. "The plainest, most digestible angle-books and remark-books we've yet seen."

"I hope I can deliver more," Yule replied, almost feeling the trunk grow heavier as they carried it across the Commissioner's front yard.

"We all wanted you to be named first master on this voyage, but the Admiralty insisted on Tucker. Second master was the best we could do."

"Well, I certainly appreciate the effort." Yule knew how the Admiralty and Hydrographic Office clashed over the choice of masters on surveying voyages. On this one, the Admiralty had prevailed. It had won the appointment of Charles Tucker—whose family had spread its breweries over several Parliamentary districts—as first master. Having inherited little beside his father's endless stories of Trafalgar, Yule would have to settle for service under Tucker as the ship's second master.

Those stories had real value, Yule told himself, as he and Walker carried the trunk through the dockyards and past the workers. When Yule had shared this voyage's route with his father, he had learned that he could return to England with enough wealth to win the Admiralty's favor.

However, a return to England was no sure thing.

"She's no *Victory*," Walker said, as they hauled the chart-box aboard the *Erebus*, "but she's tough, and that's what you'll need."

"Indeed," Yule said. The *Erebus* was no ship of the line, nor one of the great battleships like the one Yule's father had served aboard at Trafalgar. She was a bomb vessel, built short and squat to bear the recoil of launching a thirteen-inch mortar shell over an enemy's ramparts. Her heavy artillery had been removed, but the original oak hull remained. Chatham's workers had spent the summer encasing it in extra plank, felt, and copper—enough, it was hoped, to shield the *Erebus* from the ice and uncertainties of the southern seas.

The Admiralty would expose the ship's crew to greater risks, but just a few men at a time. Smaller boats had been lashed to *Erebus*'s deck. These crafts would let the crew survey and plant the Union Jack on distant shores while the *Erebus* and *Terror* bobbed at a safe distance.

Yule led Walker below decks, helping the engraver ease the chart-box down the ladder. They carried the trunk to the ship's Great Cabin, where Captain James Clark Ross sat at his desk.

He wore a look of annoyance when Yule entered, but his expression sweetened when Walker followed him into the cabin. "Mister Walker! Here with our charts, I see?"

"Indeed, Captain Ross," the engraver said, "and I look forward to revising them upon your return."

"We shall bring you much work. Magnetic observations from here to Australia, and surveys of whatever shores and seas await us from there to the Pole."

"Be sure to attend to those observations," Walker said, with a gentle smile and wag of his finger. "Having already planted the flag on one magnetic pole, you must be eager to claim the other. But all those measurements in between will let us calibrate the magnetic model and save more of England's sons from the seas."

Ross nodded gravely. "Indeed. A tilt of the compass needle can make the difference between hitting a reef and clearing it. Right, Master Yule?"

Before Yule could answer, Ross stood and led Walker to the windows set into the cabin's aft wall. Both men looked into the oily river. "With the help of Providence," Ross said, "we shall soon be able to tell a ship's location by compass bearing alone. No more need for clear skies and a chronometer." At present, Yule needed both to find a ship's longitude.

Walker nodded. "The sea's perils are receding fast." He turned to Ross and winked. "Think sailors will stop pouring good rum overboard or hunting for Jonahs?"

Ross smiled and shook his head. "We can hope, but a captain must allow his men their superstitions." He turned from the window, his voice tart again.

"Master Yule, help Mister Walker bring the *Terror* its chart-box, then report back here. We must prepare ourselves for the Lords Commissioners of the Admiralty."

"Aye, Captain."

Yule led Walker off the *Erebus* and back to the Commissioner's House.

"He's a genial one, that's for sure," the mapmaker said. "That warmth will doubtless prove useful on the voyage south."

Yule nodded but said nothing. He had seen Ross soften his voice and brighten his smile around superiors from the Admiralty or civilians from the Hydrographic Office. He dreaded the prospect of two years or more under this captain without these calming influences.

They hauled the second chart-box onto the *Terror*, leaving it in the hands of Captain Francis Crozier and First Lieutenant Archibald McMurdo. As Walker departed for London, Yule returned to the *Erebus*.

He found Ross on the top deck, and all of the *Erebus*'s officers and able seamen lined up at attention as the captain led three men down the ship. Yule winced. The Lords Commissioners of the Admiralty had arrived sooner than expected, and Ross had begun the review without him. The officers' uniforms were all resplendent; Yule would look disheveled next to them. Should he wait out of sight until the review was over? No; better a ship with a rumpled second master than a ship with no second at all. He smoothed his coat and hair as best he could, then took his place beside the other officers.

Ross led the Lords Commissioners down the line, introducing them to each officer. As Yule took his place, Ross introduced them to the ship's assistant surgeon and youngest officer, Joseph Dalton Hooker. If not for his muttonchop whiskers, Hooker would have struck Yule as a boy of twelve.

"—could identify mosses by sight at age six, from what I'm told." Ross told the Lords Commissioners as Hooker blushed. "Comes recommended from the Royal Society."

The First Lord of the Admiralty shook the assistant surgeon's hand. "We wish you many new discoveries on your voyage south, Doctor Hooker. But do be sure to place the health of the ship's crew first."

"Oh, I shall make sure of that."

The reply came not from Hooker, but from the man between him and Yule. Ross glared but kept his tone warm. "And this is our Ship's Surgeon, Robert McCormick. Joined Fitzroy's voyage on the *Beagle*." The First Lord of the Admiralty winked as he shook McCormick's hand. "Do keep an eye on Doctor Hooker. These young surgeons are known to shake the first time they wield the saw."

"I shall do my best to steady him, my Lord." Yule heard a hint of an Irish accent.

Yule's turn had come. Ross shot him another quick glare before he spoke. "May I present our second master, Henry Braddick Yule. Please pardon his appearance and placement in line. He came right from delivering the *Terror*'s chart-box."

"Master Yule. Was your father a lieutenant at Trafalgar by chance?"

"Aye, my Lord. He served aboard the *Victory*."

"Well, I hope you should uphold your family name."

"I shall do my best, sir." To Yule's relief, Ross seemed eager to move them on from his ill-dressed navigator.

Yule stood at attention, sweating in the rising sun as Ross introduced the Lords Commissioners to the remaining officers, then led them around the top deck, giving them all too much detail about each of the expedition's whaleboats. Finally, the Lords Commissioners returned to a spot ten paces before the ship's crew, facing Ross. The Earl of Minto drew a thick envelope from his pocket and unsealed it. In time-honored tradition, he read the ship's orders in a reedy voice.

"Whereas it has been represented to us that the science of magnetism may be essentially improved by an extensive series of observations—" Yule listened as the Earl instructed the *Erebus* and *Terror* to meander south down the Atlantic and east toward Australia, stopping to survey coasts, collect mineral, animal and botanical specimens, and take the all-important magnetic measurements at several ports and islands along the way. Yule smiled at the mention of one of these stops: Kerguelen Island, the knob of ice and rock Cook had found far southeast of Cape Town, where so many of Yule's hopes now lay.

His smile faded when the Earl instructed them to sail south from Van Dieman's Land, the island just below Australia. "—in order to determine the position of the magnetic pole, and even to attain it, if possible, which it is hoped to be one of the most remarkable and creditable results of this expedition. However," the Earl continued, "you are to use your best endeavors to withdraw from the high latitudes in time to prevent the ships being beset with ice."

Yule forgot the late-summer heat, and his own hopes for this voyage. Cook had been the first to venture below the Antarctic Circle, sixty-six degrees of latitude south, more than sixty years before. He had returned telling of icebergs higher and longer than any seen in the Arctic—but also insisting that the mythical southern continent, Terra Australis, could only be a myth. Yet, many still believed. The sealers and whalers who followed in Cook's wake had found many islands south of Tierra del Fuego—and glimpsed peaks and coastlines on the horizon. Was this a southern continent? Had Cook been wrong? None had dared to investigate. Once a ship filled its hull with seal pelts or whale oil, it left to escape the horrors of a southern winter.

Yule's captain had just been tasked with avoiding those hazards—but also with finding the South Magnetic Pole. Yule wondered which order Ross valued more.

The Earl's next instruction turned Yule from that dark thought back to his hopes for this voyage. He told the crews that, "in the event of England being involved with any other power during your absence, you are clearly to understand that you are not to commit any hostile act whatever." This voyage promised none of the great sea fights that had built careers like his father's, no chance for more of the prize money that had paid for him to learn navigation at the Upper School of Greenwich.

No matter, Yule had a different plan for advancement and wealth at sea, and it lay at their ship's scheduled stop in the Kerguelens—and in a years-old letter at the bottom of his trunk.

"On your return to England," the Earl continued, "you are forthwith to repair to this office in order to lay before us a full account of your proceedings, taking care before you leave the ship to demand from the officers the logs and journals they had kept, and the charts, drawings, and observations which they had made and which are all to be sealed up."

Yule and First Master Tucker would collect many of those observations. They would use the latest theodolites and sextants to survey each port in their angle-books. They would fill their remark-books with depth soundings and details of life at sea. All of this would let the Hydrographic Office update its charts and maps of these locales upon the expedition's return to England.

Yule thought that was the end of it, but the Earl had one final order. "You are to endeavor to preserve all such specimens of the animal, vegetable, and mineral kingdoms as in the course of the voyage may have been collected by any person on board either of the ships."

With that, the Earl closed the letter. "Do you accept, Captain Ross?"

"Aye, my Lord." Ross saluted. The Earl handed Ross his instructions. "Then may Providence guide your voyage." The official ceremony had ended, and the Earl shook Ross's hand. "Godspeed."

With the Lords Commissioners of the Admiralty departed, and each ship's chart-box delivered, Yule had no further duties for the day. He headed into town for a few bottles of Madeira; after all, a long voyage lay ahead. He passed two dockhands near the base of the gangway.

"Think they'll make it?" he heard one ask. "The South Magnetic Pole."

"Wouldn't bet on it, no matter how many mouthfuls of rum they toss overboard. Heard plenty o' nightmares about those parts."

"Such as?" asked the first hand. Yule slowed his pace to eavesdrop.

"Well, there was a chap at the pub once—a sealer," the second dockhand continued. "Way he put it was, 'Below forty degrees south there is no law. Below fifty degrees there is no God.'"

Chapter 5

Ross Sea Coast
Antarctica
May 2123

Roscoe's withdrawal headache throbbed all through his first day. It started soon after he opened a whaling captain's log and began deciphering the first paragraph of nineteenth-century cursive. By the time he checked the text against the list of data and keywords, he understood why the Equation favored humans for this job.

At least there didn't seem to be any hurry. When Roscoe peeked over at Karla, he saw his boss smiling to herself, flipping through the papers, and typing away.

Whatever she had pulled from the stacks must have been more engaging than the three hundred pages of weather reports this captain had dutifully noted—and slain whales he had tallied—in his log. He had decoded about thirty pages by mid-afternoon when other withdrawal symptoms—homesickness and drowsiness—joined his headache. He'd process a few sentences, enter any requested details—dates, depths, coordinates, weather, and ice observations—and then his eyelids and neck would droop. The old cursive would blur into visions of his parents scrutinizing his latest Q-CAT scores, or of scrolling through photos of life on Lagrange-2. Each time, he'd jolt himself awake and tell himself, *You're it, focus!* He finally snapped out of the cycle when Karla's footsteps approached his desk around five o'clock. If she noticed him nodding off, she didn't say anything.

"Pretty exciting, right?" Karla's accent made it hard for Roscoe to tell if she was being sincere or sarcastic. "Good work today. See you tomorrow."

* * *

As Roscoe stumbled into the tunnel, rubbing his eyes, his wristband buzzed with a new message. Jen Doil, one of the head interns, had just sent a message to him and four others. Hamza was one of them, along with Ana, Darren, and Kevin from the voyage down. He stopped to read the message:

> *Hello interns! Hope everyone's first day went well. Welcome to my intern cohort. Intern orientation group meeting over dinner at 1800. Galley, table B1. I'll be taking attendance!*

For a moment, Roscoe considered skipping, but then he remembered that Jen had gone to Granite Gorge and might know he was a compounder. He'd be wise to stay on her good side, so he headed to the galley. The tunnels were bustling with rush-hour traffic, but he noticed everyone looked about as lifeless as he felt. He didn't see a smile until Jen flashed him one from the table.

"Hey Roscoe, how'd your first day go?"

He forced a smile back. "Pretty well. No complaints so far."

"That's great! Go grab a bite and come on back."

Roscoe headed to the serving counter and filled a tray with StemSteak, quinoa pilaf, and some kind of pickled cabbage that didn't look very tasty under the galley's lamps. *One more reason to get off-world*, Roscoe told himself as he headed back to the table.

Jen started talking as he ate. "All right, now that we're all here, let's get down to business." She pecked the screen projecting from her wristband,

and read a list of bullet points in a monotone. "Welcome aboard, we're honored to have you with us as we supply the world with life's necessities. Our mission is important, so it's vital we catch problems early, yada yada yada." She pinched the screen away, leaned in, and lowered her voice. "Okay, now that that's over with, let's go to Newloon."

"Newloon?" Ana asked mid-chew, covering her mouth with one hand. She swallowed and wiped her mouth with a napkin before adding, "What's that?"

"The non-StarCross settlement up the coast. You can get everything there that you can't get here."

Roscoe rubbed his temple. The name "Newloon" sounded familiar, but he couldn't place it. Then he glanced at Hamza, whose expression mirrored his own: compound.

Hamza hesitated for a moment before speaking, his voice cautious. "We can go there?"

Jen leaned back, smiled, and tightened her ponytail. "The rules say we can't, but it's a short and easy drive and we can borrow a ride from Motor Pool anytime. They won't ask questions."

"You're sure we won't get in trouble?" Hamza pressed, the concern lingering in his voice.

"We won't. Jahnford belongs to a church that makes him ban fun in here." Roscoe thought back to the separate gender tunnels. "But he can't keep us happy with just those T3 pills. If people didn't have a place to buy drugs and booze, and a cheap motel to have one-night stands, half of Spigot would go insane, and the water supply could get interrupted." She recoiled in mock horror. "Then, he'd really have some explaining to do. The governments that buy water from us might actually be able to exercise some of their rights under the Updated Terms of Service. Can't have that."

Roscoe figured the three new interns were wondering the same things he and Hamza were. Was compound available there? If any of them were compounders, would Jen rat them out for buying? Was this some kind of sting?

Jen stood up. "Believe me, this is as much for me as it is for you guys.

I've gone way too long without a beer." One by one, they rose and followed her out.

Jen led them to Spigot's foyer: a rock portal with a row of turnstiles and security desks. Out front, a large sign with white letters on a red background caught their attention.

> **ATTENTION!**
>
> **YOU ARE ABOUT TO ENTER ONE OF THE MOST DANGEROUS ENVIRONMENTS ON EARTH**
>
> **READ CAREFULLY BEFORE PROCEEDING**
>
> Winter weather conditions on the Ross Sea Coast can cause frostbite, hypothermia, and death within hours if not minutes. Between May and September, Spigot employees and Residents may not exit the settlement without completing the following safety protocols:

- Log the journey, its purpose, expected route, expected return time, and all participants' names with StarCross Security prior to departure.
- Don a Spigot-issued survival suit. ENSURE IT IS PROPERLY ADJUSTED AND LOCATOR BEACON IS ACTIVATED.
- Only carry personal belongings in a Spigot-issued backpack.
- Only deviate from journey plans if able to contact and inform StarCross Security.
- Check-in with StarCross Security upon return.

> FAILURE TO FOLLOW THESE INSTRUCTIONS MAY RESULT IN DEATH. STARCROSS RESERVES THE RIGHT TO BLACKLIST ANY SURVIVORS AND THEIR IMMEDIATE FAMILIES.

Roscoe didn't shudder until he read that last line. Blacklisting meant getting banned from working with StarCross, receiving or selling WECs or RECs, or living on StarCross properties. It would leave someone—and their family—stranded on Earth, scratching out a life on the edge of everything StarCross offered, permanently. That threat gave StarCross's unarmored water trucks all the protection they needed as they plied the roads around Roscoe's home.

So far, StarCross hadn't blacklisted compounders, though it had barred academies from accepting new ones. And here Roscoe was, about to tempt that fate.

The other new interns hesitated in front of the sign as well, but Jen strode up to one of the security desks and smiled at the agent on duty. "Hey, Joi."

"Hey, Jen. Taking the new interns on their first driving course?" Joi answered back with a wink.

Jen returned the wink. "You know it. Standard route, up to Lake Bonney and back. We'll be back by midnight."

"Sounds good. I'm sure all your beacons will show that route," Joi said with a smirk. "Suits are in the first six lockers on the right. I'll have Motor Pool send a track up."

With that, Jen led them through the turnstiles and into the cave, where long rows of benches were positioned between rows of shoulder-high lockers. Jen opened one on the right.

Inside the nearest locker, Roscoe found a pair of boots and a hooded jumpsuit made of heavy, bright red fabric. *At least it's not a submarine suit*, he thought as he unzipped the seam and finagled his legs into the suit.

"What did you tell the girl at the desk?" he asked Jen, who donned her suit in a few quick steps and stretches.

"Oh, that's just the standard cover for trips to Newloon. Joi and I started in the same internship class. When she finished, she joined StarCross Security. She knows what's up. She'll load a decoy trip into the system, so it looks like our beacons are taking the route I gave her."

"Aren't you worried about ... blacklisting?"

"Relax, it's not gonna happen. Jahnford has to talk tough about safety protocols to keep StarCross happy, but like I said, both he and StarCross know he's got to let people have nights out."

Hamza, Darren, Ana, and Kevin all stopped wrestling with their suits' sleeves and zippers long enough to shoot Jen a skeptical look.

"And besides," Jen said, clearly unfazed as she zipped her front up, "Spigot cribbed most of its safety protocols from the old research stations years ago and hasn't updated them since. It's not so bad out there nowadays."

Roscoe felt his wristband's hooks snag on something and saw the band had aligned with a clear plastic window in his suit's sleeve. When he tapped it, its screen projected as normal. Having figured out what those hooks did, Roscoe tightened his suit's straps as much as he could. The fabric bunched up awkwardly to fit his stunted frame, making him sweat as they shuffled toward the exit.

The cave ended at a black metal wall with a low door marked "TRACKED VEHICLE PICKUP." Jen led them into another cave, and for the second time in his life, Roscoe felt cold—the temperature dropped fifty degrees as they stepped through the door. No longer sweating, Roscoe and the other interns hurriedly pulled up hoods and adjusted their goggles. Jen, unfazed, grinned. "Welcome to the South, fingies."

Someone looked at her through goggles. "Fingies?"

"Old Antarctic station slang—fucking new guys. Said with great affection."

The foyer was just a one-lane tunnel segment. Metal doors opened at one end, and a Spigot Motor Pool staffer drove in with their ride—what Jen had called a "track." It resembled the Humvees Roscoe had seen in old war movies, but it was longer, painted the same bright orange as their suits, and marked with Spigot's droplet logo on the side door. Instead of wheels, it had wide triangular treads.

The Motor Pool worker got out and left the keys in the ignition. "Keep your suits zipped up, gang," Jen said, adjusting her goggles as they climbed in. "Tradition is to drive out the first time with the windows open." Darren and Kevin got in the back row. Hamza and Ana took the middle. Roscoe was bringing up the rear, so he sat up front with

Jen, who hit the accelerator as soon as he closed the door. The tunnel sloped upward, then spat them out into the Antarctic night.

Roscoe quickly realized he hadn't properly adjusted his suit. His thighs and armpits went numb as cold leaked through the loosened straps. The wind knifed into the gaps around his goggles and facemask, and the freezing air shot up his nostrils, chilling his brain cavity and stoking a withdrawal headache. His lungs burned from the dry Antarctic air, and the ache in his scabbed left wrist returned.

He doubled over, trying to spare his face from the cold and to tighten his suit's straps; everyone else was doing the same. Jen soon took pity on them and closed the windows. She laughed as she pulled off her hood and goggles. "Like I said, welcome to Antarctica. You're not fingies anymore."

It still felt cold with the windows up, but at least breathing didn't hurt. The red searchlight dipped behind a berm and out of sight. The windows went dark. Roscoe was surprised that night had fallen so early in May, then remembered this was Antarctica, where night lasted from April to August. The windshield showed a brown path with two shallow ruts as wide as the track's treads. Small signal flags, like the ones around the overgrown golf course at Granite Gorge, marked off the route every few yards. Roscoe could make out alternating streaks of ice and rock to their left, angling upward. This road ran along a hillside.

"Anyway, guess we should introduce ourselves," Jen said, giving Roscoe a slap on the shoulder. "I already know Roscoe. He's a Gorgie like me, so he'll have a leg up in the Leadership Training Program. And rumor has it someone off-world's got executive positions reserved just for Georgies sent down to Spigot."

Roscoe's mouth barely opened to form a "What?" before Jen said, "just kidding," and flashed a grin. "No Exec or Resident's wasting their favors on a bunch of kids from the boonies. We've gotta earn our way up like everyone else."

Roscoe didn't want Jen asking more questions—questions that might force him to divulge his senior capstone topic, or who in his class *had* gotten off-world, or, God forbid, that might reveal him to be a compounder. So he turned the questioning back on Jen. "Where in the area were you from? I was outside Scranton."

"Moved around a lot," she said hurriedly, then glanced at the rear-view mirror. "Hamza, tell us about yourself."

"Hi, everyone. I'm from Hobart in Tasmania. Went to an academy there. Working in Surveying."

"Nice!" Jen said. "Don't think I've met any Aussies down here yet."

"Yeah, dunno if I'd call myself an Aussie. My mum was from Pakistan; she moved to Tasmania when it got too hot. My dad was from Rarotonga in the Cook Islands; he ended up there after his town went underwater."

Polynesian-Pakistani, Roscoe thought. That explained the carving and the odd mix of features.

"Huh," Jen said. "And they live in Hobart now?"

"Yeah, in the Naurutown."

"In what?" she asked.

"Naurutown," Hamza repeated. "For, uh, displaced persons. I think you guys call it a Femaville." Roscoe couldn't help but wonder how Hamza had managed to leave a place whose residents were usually lucky to get an outside work permit. Hamza must have known he was out of place. "I got the StarCross Cares scholarship to an academy," he added quickly.

"Oh, uh, congrats! It's so great StarCross Cares has those. Glad you're here!" Jen said.

Jen turned to Ana. Roscoe learned that she, and the rest of the cohort members, had come from internship academies in the inland Northeast and Great Lakes. He guessed they were from families who hadn't invested more of their old U.S. dollars into RECs when they were still affordable—or who hadn't found a Resident willing to sponsor them in space. They had just scraped together enough RECs or WECs to send their kids to one of the StarCross-certified internship academies, promising to rewrite their futures.

Roscoe couldn't shake the thought: How many of these families—besides Hamza's—had put their kids on compound in pursuit of off-world housing?

After a few minutes, his withdrawal headache ebbed, and the

perma-night had him pining for his shrink-wrapped bed back at Spigot. He leaned against the window. His suit's padded hood worked as a pillow—until the track lurched to a halt.

Roscoe rubbed his eyes and looked out the windshield. Jen had parked outside a floodlit sprawl of shipping containers and other battered metal shelters—Quonset huts, overturned ships' hulls, even observatory telescope domes—all connected by tarp-tube passageways. He saw a few towers where shipping containers had been stacked a dozen or more high. The structures spilled down the hillside and onto the ice-streaked sea. Jury-rigged wind turbines stood tall on the high points, harnessing the southern gale for power, while downwind, the stars flickered through a hundred chimneys' wind-whipped smoke.

One shipping container poked out of the mass, beckoning them with a set of double doors and a spray-painted sign: WELCOME TO NEWLOON.

"Woah, hold on," Hamza said. "I've seen too much sketchy construction back home to feel safe in this place."

Jen zipped up her suit. "Stay out here if you like. The people who built this place knew what they were doing. There were enough collapses along the way for them to figure out what doesn't work. Oh!" She spun around, catching everyone in mid-zip. Kevin fumbled with his suit's straps, muttering under his breath, while Darren tugged hard at his hood. "Very important errand we've got to take care of here. We need to get an XRF gun."

"A what?" Kevin asked, still fiddling with his sleeve.

"It's a thing you point at a rock to tell you what elements it has inside."

"Why do we need that?" Darren asked, peering uneasily at the WELCOME TO NEWLOON sign.

"There's a competition between all the intern cohorts coming up, and it could be what we need to win. But more about that later. Let's get some drinks!" With that, Jen hopped out of the track.

Roscoe remembered to pull up his hood and mask before stepping out. The wind hurt anyway. Kevin adjusted his hood for the third time, and Darren stamped his boots against the ground, both of them visibly trying to shake off their nerves.

"Who exactly lives here?" Ana shouted over the wind.

"Whoever wants to," Jen shouted back. "Was a temporary supply port when they built Spigot. By the time they were done, enough people were so sick of Eatonson that they decided they'd rather stay here. Been growing ever since."

Numb again from the cold, Roscoe looked up at the slapdash city and wondered why so many people would want to live in a place like this. He didn't get the chance to ask Jen—she turned back and stopped them all in front of the WELCOME TO NEWLOON sign. Roscoe now saw what Darren must have been looking at: it was pocked with small holes.

"Super important," Jen said, "no matter how hot you get inside, hold onto your suits. They're valuable commodities over here." Eyeing those holes in the sign, Roscoe's concerns grew beyond just theft.

Jen opened the door and led them down the scuffed shipping container. Even through the suit's vents, the inside air felt damp. It felt more so when Jen led them through the far door.

It opened into a long passageway, made from old shipping containers laid end-to-end and side-by-side, and linked at their ends like railroad cars. A long countertop ran down the middle, and the opposite side had been divided into stalls. Electronic signs flashed in multiple languages, advertising each stall's wares:

USED BOOKS, BANNED IN OVER 40 COUNTRIES!
CERTIFIED PRE-OWNED ADULT TOYS, UV-CLEANED JUST 4 U ;)
SALLY'S PSYCHOACTIVES
BANNED BIONICS—SEE HOW FAR AN IMPLANT CAN TAKE YOU!

Maybe that's the big draw of this place, Roscoe thought. A city with no government—no censorship, anti-drug laws, or vice squads. It was easy to see how people all over the world could feel the pull of a place like this. As the thought clicked, his eyes landed on three glowing words: WE COMPOUND ON-SITE!

Jen led them the other way and through the throng of shoppers before Roscoe could get a closer look. They all struggled to keep up, fumbling for their suits' front and armpit zippers as heat built up inside. Roscoe heard more languages and saw more races than he had ever experienced before. One guy was standing on a corner, shouting to each passerby in a different tongue as he thrust a pamphlet in their faces. A medallion swayed from his neck as he stepped in front of Roscoe and switched to English. "Jee–zis is comin' back soon, man. Repent!"

Like the other people he'd seen, Roscoe snatched the proffered pamphlet, stuffed it in a pocket, and kept walking. His headache flared back to life; his room back at Spigot seemed nicer than ever.

They turned a corner, into a row of deeper storefronts with throbbing music. Roscoe guessed they were bars or nightclubs as he read their names: SOUTHERN EXPOSURE; ETERNAL ICESTOCK; THE HOOSH PIT; EREBUS CLUB; COFFEE HOUSE 2.0; GALLAGHER'S PUB; THE TATTY FLAG; and at the far end, in glowing red neon letters with an arrow pointing to the left, SHIDURI'S.

Roscoe finally remembered where he had first heard about Newloon.

It was on graduation day. He had just bandaged his wrist and stepped out of his dorm at Granite Gorge for the last time when a shout stopped him.

"Hey Roscoe! Where ya headin'?"

Roscoe spun around to see a middle-aged Black man mowing the firebreak. He parked halfway between the dorm buildings and scraggly pines, and Roscoe's chest sank—this was someone he'd miss.

"Hey, Tim. They're sending me to Spigot, down in Antarctica."

"Antarctica!" Tim grinned. "I ever tell you I was down there?"

"No, you didn't." In all his chats with Tim, that had never come up. Tim and his parents were Gulfers; they had moved to the Femaville here when Tim was just a baby. Roscoe had always assumed he'd lived there ever since, leaving on an outside work permit to trim the firebreaks and anti-flood berms that kept Granite Gorge standing.

"Yeah. Spigot offered indentures for us Femaville folks down there back in the late nineties. Said they'd give us a place to stay after five years on a construction crew. Figured a chance like that wouldn't come my way again, so I went. Quit after six months, though. Turned out I couldn't stand the cold."

Roscoe shrugged. "We'll see if I can."

"Oh, you'll be fine. Interns like you will have it better than us indents. And I know this place trained ya well."

Roscoe didn't have the heart to tell him that it hadn't—at least, not well enough to get to one of the off-world stations he'd really wanted to go to. Luckily, the bus driver honked just then, signaling the bus' departure for the StarCross sub port.

"Keep in touch, okay?" Tim said, returning to cutting the grass. "Oh, and if you meet a lady named Shiduri in Newloon, tell her I said hi."

Roscoe hadn't asked Tim to clarify. Now, Jen kept him from this mystery lady. She stopped under the sign for Gallagher's Pub—"SERVING ANTARCTICA SINCE 1997!" it bragged in Celtic lettering. Photographs and shoulder patches from old Antarctic stations papered the walls. The whole pub had the footprint of the abandoned, cracked tennis court on the Granite Gorge campus. And it was *loud*. Electronic dance music throbbed from ceiling speakers. A few patrons hunched over highboy tables on the sides, but most flailed around in the center.

"Best nightlife there is down here," Jen said. It sure wasn't Roscoe's idea of a good time, especially now that compound withdrawal had returned. He grabbed Jen's shoulder before she dove in.

"Loud music gives me headaches." Jen gave him a look somewhere between annoyance and disappointment, and Roscoe wondered if she'd guessed he was a compounder. Then inspiration struck. "You want me to go get that XRF gun thing you mentioned?"

"That'd be great!" Jen said, smiling again. Then she raised her wrist and motioned for Roscoe to do the same. "I've been saving up my head intern stipends for this. Here's three WECs." His wristband buzzed as the transfer went through. "Get me the highest-end one you can find. And if it's more than that, tell them your boss will kill you if you can't buy one for three."

"Where should I look?"

"That area we entered through is called Skua Central. That's like the shopping district. You look hard enough, you'll find one for sale there.

If you get lost on the way back, ask for directions to Wit's End. That's the nightlife district where we are."

"When should I be back?"

"It's nine o'clock now ... definitely by midnight. But earlier if you can."

Hamza cut in. "I'm gonna go too," he said. "Learned a little bit about XRF's in my academy's hardware class. I can make sure we're not being scammed."

"Awesome! See you two later on." With that, she slipped into the bar. As soon as Roscoe and Hamza lost sight of her in the mosh pit, they headed for the compound dispensary they had seen near the door.

It turned out to be an automated stall. Hamza stepped up to the screen first. As Roscoe waited, he noticed another Orbital Strike memorial plaque on which someone had scrawled: "Inside Job." Hamza finished his turn before Roscoe could dwell on it. He followed the Machine's prompts, plugging in his weight and desired traits, then opening his wristband screen and swiping away some of his meager stipend. One-tenth of a WEC bought a ten-day supply. They each had 0.15 WECs left until the next stipend day. Roscoe wondered how Jen had managed to squirrel away three whole WECs.

Grinning, they each popped a pill. The compound would need a few hours to take effect, but the placebo effect hit fast.

"All right," Hamza said, "let's go find that XRF gun."

They retraced their steps toward the entrance. Roscoe noticed a Skua Central sign hanging from the ceiling, showing a brown bird with a ball of wire in its beak. They passed stalls selling odds and ends from all over the world. Some sold weapons, drugs, or other contraband, but plenty of their goods—patched polar gear and UV-grown tomatoes—would've been perfectly legal up north.

"Any ideas who's living here and buying all this stuff?" Roscoe asked. "Besides all the drug dealers, I mean."

Hamza shook his head. "I'm stuck on how they got all this stuff down here." Roscoe couldn't imagine. The people manning the stalls sure didn't seem likely to name their suppliers. The ones who had customers were arguing with them, mostly in languages Roscoe didn't understand. The rest just glowered.

They passed three shipping containers' worth of stalls without finding an electronics store. To get further, Roscoe and Hamza had to push open a heavy double door.

This section had no stalls, but a chill crept through Roscoe's feet and up his legs. He looked down and saw an open metal grate under his boots—below that, only blackness.

The corridor stretched another two tennis court lengths to a distant door. Plastic crates had been stacked halfway down, forming a makeshift barrier. People were being directed to the right, through a set of double doors with portholes just before the crates. Beyond the crates, Roscoe saw more people streaming out of another set of double doors, heading toward the far side.

Roscoe and Hamza followed the crowd through the first set of doors and froze for a few seconds. Then, Hamza pointed forward. "Well, I guess that's how they get all this stuff down here."

This building had no floor. Instead, boardwalks lined the sides and stretched down the center. The rest was filled with inky black water, glowing green in places from submerged floodlights. The structure was longer and taller than the Archives at Spigot or the main hall at Granite Gorge, and it had plenty of space for the two submarines lashed to the docks. Their conning towers were high above Roscoe, Hamza, and everyone else.

This was a submarine port.

It made sense. Roscoe recalled reading that twenty-first-century drug cartels had used submarines to ship cocaine. Why wouldn't today's traffickers do the same? And why wouldn't they take advantage of a submarine port StarCross had built to move Spigot's building materials underneath ice and storms? To his left, he noticed faded lettering on the sub's conning tower: KERGUELEN SHIPPING CO. Roscoe had first learned about the Kerguelens from the whaling captain's log a few hours earlier. It had been the ship's first anchorage east of Cape Town. Maybe the islands that dotted the Southern Ocean were now full of people living outside the law, trading southern contraband for northern necessities.

The sub from the Kerguelens had opened its entire top lengthwise, like a coffin lid, letting the crew lower boxes onto pallets waiting on the boardwalk. Roscoe saw labels in English, German, Spanish, Mandarin, Korean, and Cyrillic on the crates' sides, along with biohazard and radioactivity symbols on some. Once a pallet was stacked about two meters high, a forklift whisked it away through a wider set of side doors. Nearby, workers loaded undersea batteries into each vessel's stern. Those sofa-sized blocks would power the subs for days without a recharge from Lagrange-2—a recharge that would require a sub to surface. They were ideal for captains keen on concealing their coordinates from StarCross surveillance. Roscoe wondered if all the batteries stolen during the Blackout Years had ended up down here and now powered smugglers' subs.

He guessed the sub to his right was for passengers. Hamza pointed to two jet-like engines bolted to its stern. "Those must be thrusters for extra speed." Scruffy-looking people were climbing out a hatch on its bow, heading for the hangar's exit, while others lined up to board. At the front of the line, a man argued with the three crew members in matching coveralls, speaking what sounded like German. It didn't end well for him. One crew member punched him in the face while the other two grabbed him from behind, dangling his head and torso over the inky black water. The third crew member kept shouting the same question at him, over and over.

"Nein, Nein!" the man shouted back, a trickle of blood running from his mouth down his upside-down nose and forehead.

That seemed to satisfy the crew. They pulled him upright and shoved him toward the exit. As he passed by, he wiped the blood off his face and fixed his bright amber eyes on Roscoe. Then he looked away and disappeared through the doors.

Two of the sub's crew members kept taking WECs and RECs from passengers, many of whom reached into inner pockets to produce worn, possibly-untraceable wristbands. The punching crew member stepped toward Roscoe. His jacket had a faded swastika on the shoulder.

"Hey guys, how it going?" he asked, lighting a cigarette. "Ve going to New Svabia on da peninsula. You vant a free ride? Handsome boys like you make big money up there, no problem." He winked.

Roscoe and Hamza bolted under the cordon and out the exit, then out the door at the opposite end of the foyer, which led to another bustling passageway. The sign over the first stall read: WHALSTONE'S HARDWARE & ELECTRONICS.

Still panting, Roscoe looked at Hamza, who shrugged. They got in line behind a guy arguing with the owner in some unfamiliar language.

"So, uh, how'd your first day go?" Roscoe asked Hamza. Thanks to years of embracing StarCross Silence, small talk had never been his strong suit.

Hamza grinned. "Great! Subdrones are pretty easy to use."

"What does Spigot use drones for?"

"All kinds of things. You start off as what's called a flasher."

"Flasher? What's that?"

"The official name is surveyor. I didn't pick the nickname, but I'll roll with it. Flashers use lidar to inspect the tunnels, ice, and piping. Also the coastline."

"The coastline?"

Hamza nodded. "Spigot wants to know where it might put future submarine ports or look for mineral deposits. Good training for us too. Way easier to steer a subdrone in open ocean than up a glacier's backside."

"Where are you surveying?"

"Right now, we're surveying a place called Tucker Inlet. After that, they'll take the drones further north to a place called Yule Bay."

"You drive the drones up there?"

Hamza shook his head. "Nah, it's way up the coast. We've got a subdrone mothership that takes them out long distances. There's also a network of things called StarBuoys all over the Ross Sea that relays information to them."

The argument ended with the customer storming off empty-handed. Hamza approached the bearded man behind the counter and said, "Hello. We're looking for a top-of-the-line XRF gun."

The man—Whalstone, his nametag confirmed—nodded and stepped into the back room of his stall. As he rummaged, Roscoe took in the stall and noticed a display behind the counter with prices spelled out in individual LED bulbs:

1 TB Solid-State Memory: 0.5 WEC 0.2 REC

1 Drum Ice Drilling Fluid: 0.1 WEC 0.04 REC

REC Receiving Dish: 0.4 WEC 0.1 REC

He watched the sign flicker through prices in three other languages before Whalstone re-emerged, carrying what looked like an old-fashioned smartphone strapped to a pistol grip, encased in bright yellow molded plastic. "Best model we have," the man declared with an unfamiliar accent. "Barely used."

"Can you demonstrate?"

Whalstone pulled a piece of brick from under the counter, pointed the device at it, and pulled the trigger. The dark screen lit up, and a laser dot appeared on the brick. One by one, names of elements and their percentages appeared on the screen. "More accurate readings in faster times than any model on the market."

Roscoe was impressed; Hamza wasn't. His eyes darted around the stall before settling on a dark gray rock near their feet. He picked it up and handed it to Whalstone. "Scan this, too, if you don't mind."

"Smart kid. Can't say I blame you." Whalstone scanned the rock. The screen displayed a different set of elements and compounds, with different percentages. "See?" Whalstone pointed at the screen. "About half silicon—just what you'd expect from a piece of basalt like this."

Hamza nodded. "How much?"

"Three WECs."

"Just one minute." Roscoe draped his arm around Hamza's shoulders and turned him away. "That's our entire budget. Should we shop around for something cheaper?"

"Don't bother, shorty." They turned back to see Whalstone tapping a sign covered in several scripts, none of which Roscoe could read. "Lowest-price guarantee. And believe me, I know the lowest prices in Newloon. Got eyes and ears all over. If you do find a lower price, I'll match it."

Roscoe and Hamza eyed him skeptically. "Believe me, guys, there's a pretty hard floor for prices down here. New Swabia, South Shetland, and the Kerguelens have a damned shipping cartel. Anyone trying to undercut them doesn't last long."

He leaned forward. "If you're thinking a salvage sub will dock tonight with what you need, forget it. Never seen an XRF gun come in off one of those boats."

Roscoe wasn't sure what Whalstone meant by "salvage sub," but he did know he didn't want to hang around a guy who'd just called him "shorty," or irritate the growing line of people behind him. Cutting off any chance for Hamza to object, Roscoe tapped his wrist against Whalstone's.

Hamza tucked their purchase into his suit pocket. "Wonder why Jen wanted this. Dunno what kind of competition you would need an XRF gun for."

"Guess we'll find out soon enough. No weirder than anything else down here."

They hurried through the submarine port foyer and retraced their steps to Gallagher's, which was as loud as before. Electronic dance music throbbed from ceiling speakers; most of the floor was a mosh pit. Jen's red ponytail caught the lights for an instant, then vanished in the crowd.

"Looks fun!" Hamza said.

Roscoe shook his head, amazed that Hamza had recovered so soon from his compound withdrawal. "Headache hasn't stopped for me. I'll see you back here when it's time to leave." Without giving Hamza a chance to respond, Roscoe ducked out, heading down the hall toward the neon sign pointing the way to Shiduri's.

He followed the neon arrow through a second set of double doors and entered another pub—a blissfully quiet one compared to Gallagher's. Most of the highboy tables along the walls were occupied, but none of the conversations rose above a murmur. In the center, pool balls clacked around a scuffed table. In one corner stood an old-fashioned red London telephone booth. Someone inside was making a call. He seemed to be shouting, but Roscoe couldn't hear a word. In another corner, a taxidermied elephant seal watched over the room from behind plexiglass.

Roscoe checked the time on his wristband: 10:15 p.m. Plenty of time for a drink.

He headed to the bar and studied the menu. His remaining WECs would cover an Elephant Island IPA from the South Shetland Brewing Company. The bartender looked Middle Eastern—olive skin, dark eyes, silky black hair with swooping bangs. Roscoe guessed she was in her forties. When she slid him the glass, the vending machine compound had him feeling bold.

"Are you Shiduri?"

"Depends. Who's askin'?" Her Texan accent caught Roscoe off guard.

"Tim Thretson says hi."

Her face softened and her eyes sparkled. "Now *there* is a name I haven't heard in a long time. How's Tim doing?"

"Pretty good. He's working at a StarCross academy up in the Poconos."

Shiduri nodded. "I knew Tim wouldn't leave P.A. again. Our families got resettled in the Femaville there around the same time."

"Did your families know each other in Houston, before it flooded?"

Shiduri shook her head. "Never would've dealt with each other down there. But we were Texans, and we weren't crackers. That was all that counted when we got to the Femaville."

Roscoe shuddered as he remembered the refugee camp near Granite Gorge: the neat trailers with miniature southern verandas, the shipping containers flying tattered Texas Lone Stars and snarling California bears. Given the choice, he just might pick Antarctica.

"Did you come down here with him?"

"Yep. When I got an indenture with Eatonson's operation down here, it was all I could do was to persuade Tim to go with me. Parents wouldn't let me go without another familiar face." Roscoe knew that becoming an indenture, either in Antarctica or in one of StarCross's

Earth-based facilities, was one of the only ways to escape a Femaville for good. Apparently, Tim preferred the Femaville. "He couldn't stand the cold and split after three months," Shiduri said.

"But you stayed."

"In Antarctica, yeah. Couldn't stand working for Eatonson. But there were lots of other people who couldn't either and decided to try their luck here in Newloon. So I had me a captive market."

Before he could ask anything else, shouting erupted around the pool table, with voices in at least two different languages. Shiduri rolled her eyes and headed toward the commotion, pulling an electric stun gun from her hip.

Out of the corner of his eye, Roscoe thought he saw a crew member from the Nazi sub at the far end of the bar. He retreated to a side table, taking a long swig of his Elephant IPA. As soon as he set the glass down, his head started spinning. He realized too late that something in the compound didn't mix well with the beer. He was out cold before his head hit the table.

"You okay, hon?" Shiduri asked, shaking him awake.

Roscoe lifted his face off the table and wiped some drool from his mouth. "Yeah, I think so."

"Compound get you?"

Weakness kept him from lying. "Must've."

"Always happens with you first-timers from the Academies. I don't know what that machine gives you, but it sure ain't what you get up north. Oughta put up a warning sign in here. Anyway, we're closing now." Roscoe fumbled for his wristband's Pay function, but Shiduri put her hand on his wrist. "Don't worry about it. Mentioning Tim is good for one free drink around here."

He was too tired to protest. "Thanks."

Roscoe checked the time: 12:31 a.m. *Fuck!* He'd missed their meet-up time by half an hour. Adrenaline burned off the brain fog. He swiped for messages, then noticed the No Service tab up in the top left corner of the floating screen. Spigot's wristbands could move WECs anywhere, but apparently, they couldn't make calls or send messages outside the settlement.

He bolted back to Gallagher's. It was still open, its music loud as ever, but the crowd had dwindled; most of the holdouts had retreated to the side tables. Roscoe didn't see Jen, Hamza, or anyone else from the intern cohort.

They had left without him. *Fuck!*

He needed to get back to Spigot—fast. If word got out that he'd taken an unregistered trip, he could get blacklisted. Roscoe sprinted back to Shiduri's, to the closest person to a friend he had here. His heart sank as he rounded the corner and saw the neon light switched off. But then he spotted the bartender, still there, padlocking the entrance while having a heated conversation with someone.

Roscoe raised a hand to get her attention. "Hey, Shiduri," he called. "I need help."

They both turned, and Roscoe got his first good look at the stranger. It was the same guy he and Hamza had seen almost getting dunked back at the dock—wavy black hair, a five-o-clock shadow, and piercing amber eyes. His well-worn jacket had a circular shoulder patch that looked like some of the ones on the wall at Gallagher's.

"My intern cohort left for Spigot without me," Roscoe explained. "You know any way I could get back?"

She stared at the ceiling, then smiled. "As a matter of fact, I do. Chip here couldn't close out his tab because he 'forgot to activate his new credit card' and 'forgot to download more WECs before he left McMurdo'"—Shiduri said, her fingers making air quotes—"but, conveniently, he happens to have a track. Chip, give Roscoe a ride back to Spigot, and we'll call it even."

Chip gave Roscoe a quick once-over. "All right, Shid. Sounds good. Come on, man. We'd better get going."

He led Roscoe out the door, onto the ice. Too late, Roscoe realized his suit's vents were still unzipped. He struggled to close them with freezing fingers while the cold seared his lungs. He managed to close both armpits just as they reached Chip's track. It resembled the one Jen had driven them in, but was olive green and dented. The door had the same faded emblem as Chip's shoulder patch.

They climbed in, and Chip started the engine. Roscoe tried to think up the safest question he could ask this stranger.

"You live at Newloon?"

"Only when I'm too drunk to drive this thing."

"Oh."

The man gave Roscoe another look. "Relax, kid. I've just had two tonight. I've driven this road on way more."

As soon as the track lurched forward, Roscoe's stomach heaved. He flung the door open and retched, realizing too late that Newloon's compound also caused motion sickness.

"Did it freeze?" Chip asked, once Roscoe had closed the door again.

"Huh?"

"Your vomit. Did it freeze when it hit the ground?"

"Uh, no, I don't think it did."

Chip shook his head and sighed. "Back in the day, winters got so cold here that vomit would freeze as soon as it hit the ground. McMurdo gave you a pickax and you'd have to break it up yourself."

Roscoe's stomach was still in knots, and his head swirled with fear and curiosity. *Who was this guy?* All his mouth could manage was, "McMurdo?"

"The U.S. government's old research station, on Ross Island," Chip replied, slapping the faded patch on his shoulder. "A little further up the coast from Spigot."

"You work there?"

"Based there, but I bounce up and down the coast. With the weather looking like this, I'll crash at Spigot for a few hours."

Chip steered the track down the long line of flags, then furrowed his brow at Roscoe. "There's ibuprofen in the glove box if you want it."

"I'm good, thanks," Roscoe said, not wanting any other strange pills in his gut for the night.

They rode in silence for a few minutes. Just as Roscoe started to nod off, Chip cracked the window, sending a cold blast of air through the cab and jolting him awake.

His stomach settled now, Roscoe decided to satisfy his curiosity. "What do you do over at McMurdo?"

"Scientist. The only scientist there now, actually."

"Oh, what do you research?"

"Ocean chemistry and how it interacts with seafloor geology and glacial melt. Or at least, I try when Jahnford or the people at Newloon are willing to give me what I need."

"The gov—er—the federal government doesn't support you?"

Chip chuckled. "After keeping the Femavilles under control, machine-gunning whoever washes up on the coasts, and scraping together RECs and WECs from StarCross, the govellers barely have enough to keep the lights on at McMurdo. So most of the time, I just try to convince Jahnford that my work will help him get more fresh water from the glaciers."

"What were you doing at Newloon?"

He wagged a finger at Roscoe. "Not a good idea to ask people that question. Lucky for you, I don't care. I've been trying to get the sub operators to collect data for me on their northbound runs, but they aren't too keen about it."

"Why? What are you asking them to do?"

"Just stick a goddamn probe on the side of their sub!"

"A probe?"

He nodded, his tone still agitated. "No bigger than a beer can. It measures salinity, temperature, pH—things like that—and takes small samples for analysis."

"Why is that a problem for them?"

"Because that data's useless unless I know where it's from, and no smuggler wants me tracking their sub's coordinates or depth. And they don't trust me when I say I'll keep it confidential." He sighed. "Guess I shouldn't be that surprised."

The argument at the dock made sense now. "Have you tried all the smugglers that come down here?"

"All the regulars, yeah. This was my first time asking the skinheads from New Swabia to help." Another chuckle. "Don't think I'll try that again."

The scientist stole another glance at Roscoe. "You an intern or an indent?"

"Intern. Just got down here a couple of days ago."

Chip nodded. "What do they have you doing?"

Roscoe explained his work in the Archives. "Huh," Chip said. "Kind of surprised they're still feeding the models with data from the early voyages. Bet it's entertaining though."

Roscoe thought back to the barely-legible notebooks. "I'm still getting into it."

"Just you wait," Chip said. "Plenty of crazy stuff has happened down here, that's for sure. Was anyone dumb enough to put it in writing?" He shrugged. "I guess you'll find out. When your internship's done, do you want to stay on for a career-track gig or join their Leadership Training thing?"

"Leadership Training," Roscoe answered. He almost added that he couldn't wait to get off-world, then remembered that this guy had signed on for a lifetime in Antarctica.

"Can't say I blame you," Chip said. "They let me use a career-track suite when I'm at Spigot. It's all right, but for your forever home?" He shook his head. "Executive suites and Resident suites win, no contest. If you're gonna do that program, just make sure you actually get one of their positions."

"What happens if I don't?"

"You'll get classed with the indents, doing the jobs they do and living in one of their holes in the wall. Pretty hard fall for an ex-intern. Lots of them split and try their luck over at Newloon. Might as well be blacklisted."

That word drew Roscoe's attention from one grim possibility to another. Forget washing out of the Leadership Program; he might already be in too much trouble to go on. *Could this one night dash his parents' dreams for good?*

Chip passed something Roscoe had slept through on the way in—a banner, at least four meters long, flapping atop a flagpole. It read: RIP SMALLS.

"Finn Smalls," Chip explained before Roscoe could even ask. "He was an ex-indent over at Newloon, trying to organize other current and former indents. Spigot surveyors found his body by the road here a few months ago."

"What happened?"

"StarCross Security did an autopsy and said it was drugs. No one at Newloon believes it."

After several more silent minutes, Chip pulled over and parked the track. The coastal slope was steeper here. Roscoe saw a battered gray metal door engraved with Spigot's droplet logo, set into the rock. Roscoe could just make out the beam of the searchlight sweeping over the nearest slope.

"What's this?"

"Service entrance," Chip said, rummaging through his suit pockets. "Since I'm a federal employee, I don't have to go through all of Spigot's safety protocol bullshit. Of course, that means that if I get stuck out there, I'm on my own."

He fished out a key ring from an inside pocket and opened the track's door. Roscoe followed, still amazed at how little the cold seemed to bother these long-timers. Chip grabbed the door's handle, and Roscoe noticed a spark of static jump to his bare fingers. "Damn coldstatic." He yanked on the handle and cursed when it didn't budge. "Frozen, as usual."

With a grunt, he wrapped his fingers around the handle and lifted both feet off the ground. Under his full weight, the handle gave way, and Chip stumbled backward.

"You've got a wristband, right?" he shouted over the wind. Roscoe nodded. "Good. It'll work here. Just follow the directions back." Another nod.

"You're not coming?"

"No, I gotta park this thing. If I take you through Motor Pool, they might start asking questions." He turned and headed back to the track.

"Thanks for the ride!" Roscoe called, doubting Chip had heard him.

* * *

Back in his dorm room, his fingers thawed and his suit wadded up on the floor, Roscoe took a deep breath and checked for messages.

Nothing.

He scrolled through his Location History, now updated with his return to Spigot. It showed him being checked into Motor Pool at 12:48 a.m. Jen, he realized, had covered for him.

With his last spark of energy, Roscoe tapped out a quick message—just enough to let her know he'd made it back without revealing anything: *Hey Jen, thanks for the driving lesson! Made it back to my room okay. See you around!*

Having done all he could, Roscoe grabbed the survival suit off the floor and headed for the laundry chute. As he walked, he felt something in the inside pocket, reached inside, and pulled out the pamphlet he'd been given earlier. Smoothing the creased paper under his room's reading light, he saw a bizarre symbol—a crucifix, inside an atomic bomb's mushroom cloud, inside the outline of Antarctica—and a single boldface paragraph:

THE CHURCH OF THE REVELATORS

> *As Revelators, we know that God is gathering His true believers in Antarctica so that they can cleanse the world of all non-believers with the mighty power of nuclear weapons. We have dedicated our lives to this goal—and will dedicate our deaths if necessary, for we know that God will reward those who make His Cleansing Fire a reality.*
>
> *HELP US PREPARE FOR THE CLEANSING FIRE! JOIN A CONGREGATION TODAY!*

Roscoe crumpled the pamphlet and tossed it in the trash, figuring he'd be a Resident before he went to one of those services, then threw his suit down the laundry chute. Climbing into his bunk, he reminded himself to check in with Hamza. After all, Jen was a head intern—and if she knew they were compounders, they had better stay on her good side.

Chapter 6

H.M.S. *Erebus*
English Channel
October 1839

The expedition took twenty days to leave England. The Admiralty had arranged several stops for the interested public along the Medway and the Channel. The officers soon grew weary of hearing of the exotic ports where they would call, and the terrors they would face in the Antarctic seas to bring glory to Her Majesty and enlightenment to Her subjects. For Yule and Tucker, only the task of calibrating their sextants, sounding-lines, and other instruments while still in familiar waters broke the tedium.

Finally, though, Lizard Point—the knob of rock at England's southernmost tip—slipped below the horizon. With *Erebus* now in deep water, Yule had time for a proper meal.

Like the other officers, he messed in the wardroom, a space just fore of the captain's Great Cabin on the lower deck, barely large enough for two men to sit and dine. The ship's officers ate when their duties allowed. Yule had been so busy guiding the ship into open ocean that this was his first chance to meet his messmate since leaving Chatham.

"Joseph Dalton Hooker, at your service," the assistant surgeon said when Yule entered, rising from the table to shake his hand.

"Henry Braddick Yule, much obliged," Yule replied, placing a bottle of wine on the table. "Would you care for some Madeira?" he asked. "Bought it in Chatham."

"It's not Madeira," Hooker said, "but if you're offering, I'll take it."

"Beg pardon?" Yule handed Hooker the bottle to let him read the label. "This is Miles Seco. Best Madeira there is." Yule guessed that the young surgeon knew little of Iberian wine varieties.

"Regardless of what the label says, the cork tells a different tale," Hooker countered, pointing the neck of the bottle toward Yule. "See how light the cork is? How fresh it looks?"

"Aye."

"No cork trees grow on the island of Madeira. Any wines produced there must be bottled with secondhand corks. True Madeira would have a much more worn, dark cork."

Yule maintained a smile. "How about a taste test, then? Let's see who's right."

"Certainly, although the taste may be too close to call. I'm sure only a close approximation of Madeira could be passed off as such to Royal Navy officers."

Yule wondered if Hooker meant that as a slight, or if he truly did not know any better. He said nothing as he poured them each a glass, then took a sip.

As soon as the wine touched his tongue, Yule knew Hooker was right—it wasn't Madeira. The taste was close, but something was off—something Yule couldn't quite put into words and might have missed entirely had Hooker not sharpened his senses.

"You're—you're right. Well done."

Hooker blushed. "As I said, I'm sure only a very close approximation could deceive such an experienced officer." Yule again wondered if he spoke with sarcasm. "What variety would you say it is?" Hooker asked. "Port?"

"It must be. The only other wine produced in that part of the world."

"I wouldn't know. Father seldom allowed me wine. Even as he worked to place me aboard this voyage to the Antarctic, he guarded my sobriety." Hooker chuckled. "First time he can't. May I have some more?"

Yule refilled his glass, then watched this young surgeon empty it and his plate of mutton in minutes. Yule felt a stab of pity for the sailors who might go under his saw. "Well, I think I shall return to my treatises. May I have the cork?" he asked. "I may want to examine it under the microscope. Perhaps the shape of its cork cells will reveal its true origin."

"The ship's microscope has been readied for use?" Yule asked, handing Hooker the cork.

"Oh, yes, Ross has already seen to its assembly in the Great Cabin. He shows great interest in the natural sciences—we are lucky to have him as our Captain." Hooker rose and left without another word.

Yule went to the upper deck, leaned over the aft gunwale, and watched the ship's wake vanish into the darkness. At twenty-three, Hooker was just four years younger than him, yet somehow he made Yule feel long past his prime. Ross had a similar effect—he had been only four years older than Yule when he planted Britain's flag at the North Magnetic Pole. Now, at twenty-seven, Yule had no delusions of making such conquests himself—only the prospect of enduring more of Ross's lectures, the kind better suited for wayward schoolboys.

But that could all change with this voyage, Yule told himself. Each southward mile brought him closer to the wealth he needed—enough to win a promotion and escape all the indignities of being a second master in Her Majesty's Navy. His plan would work. It *had* to.

Yule looked at the last dark swig of fake Madeira in his bottle. He had never put much stock in sailor's superstitions, but if ever there were a time to appease the sea, it was now. He poured the wine overboard and tossed the empty bottle in after it.

Chapter 7

Ross Sea Coast
Antarctica
June 2123

"All right, how much did the compound fuck you up last night?"

"A lot," Roscoe admitted to Hamza. They were in the galley, downing SynCoffee and wolfing down quinoa, trying to purge their hangovers before another day's work. The only new message this morning had come from Jen: *Ok, thanks for letting me know. Glad you made it home. ;)*

Hamza had gotten an easy out. He'd been at Gallagher's with the rest of the cohort when the compound hit, so they just left him in a chair until it was time to leave. During the drive back, he'd come to prop up against the track door, with a bucket between his legs—courtesy of Jen.

"A lot of new interns get hit by that machine's compound. Jen felt really bad that she had forgotten to warn us, and that she left you, but if she hadn't gotten back in time, Security would've started a search—and that would've been bad."

So now Jen and the rest of the cohort knew that he and Hamza were compounders. *Great.*

"So ... she was going to leave me there?"

"She didn't want to," Hamza replied. "She was trying to think of some excuse to go back and look for you today, so it's good you got back when you did."

Roscoe smiled. As rough as last night had been, he'd kept things from getting worse—for both himself and Jen. At least he'd shown her a pounder could take care of himself.

"What about you, man?" Hamza asked. "How'd you get back?"

The StarCross Silence instinct kicked in—but not to cover for the compound. Who knew how useful Chip's tidbits might be? At least for now, Roscoe decided to keep them to himself.

"I found a Spigot guy who gave me a ride back. Seemed chill about it. I was half out of it in the track, so we didn't talk much." Time to change the topic. "So I'm curious. When you operate drones for Spigot, how do you use the data you get from Archives?"

"What do you mean?"

Roscoe relayed what Karla had told him, about how the Archives department culled information from centuries-old documents to guide Spigot's search for water.

Hamza blinked. "No, didn't hear anything about that. But hey, it's only day two, right? I'll let you know if it comes up."

"Sounds good." Roscoe had started to doubt his value to Spigot's mission of bringing water to a thirsty world—especially compared to Hamza's. He made a show of calling up his wristband screen and checking the time. "Well, I better go."

"Sure man, have a good one."

As soon as Roscoe stepped away, the thought hit him again—why had Jen needed that weird tool, the XRF gun? No time to go back and ask Hamza now. Roscoe followed his wrist to the Archives, where Karla was already there, her shoulders hunched and her voice tense.

"Ay, am I glad to see you, weón! I just got a message from Jahnford's office. He's hosting some bigwigs from StarCross tomorrow and wants us to supply the decor. He wants a map."

"A map?"

"Yeah," she said, exhaling through her nose, then adjusting the strap of her wristband. "An old map, from the early days. Like everyone else around here, he's insecure about doing the dirty work on Earth when StarCross sees its future in space."

"And he thinks an old map will help?"

Karla gave a small, tight nod. "I think he's hoping to convince them we're heirs to a glorious heritage of exploration and that it's something they should care about."

"Why not a photo, then?"

"He didn't say," she said with a shrug, then began kneading the back of her neck. "Probably because most of them just show old gringos trying to keep their noses or—ah—other parts from freezing off. The maps hide all the ugliness of trying to survive down here."

"Can we just look for one in the catalog?"

Karla shook her head. "These old maps don't provide anything the models using written data can't. Because the pricing algorithm doesn't assign a WEC value to them, I haven't cataloged many of them." She sighed. "If only I'd known."

Karla had lined up several of the Archives' storage bins beside Roscoe's desk. She rapped her knuckles on one of them. "These boxes are the ones most likely to have good maps inside. Look through them as a start. Once you've found one, we can frame it and deliver it to Jahnford."

"Is there any map in particular I should be looking for?"

"The Ross Sea Coast or the McMurdo Dry Valleys would be best, since that's where Spigot is, but see what you can find. Just make sure people can tell it's Antarctica. That might be hard with some of the old stuff." She returned to her desk, rolled her shoulders, and gave Roscoe a small, tired smile. "I'd help if I could, but of course this request came down on top of another deadline for me. So I'm afraid you're it."

At those words, Roscoe straightened up and hardened his voice. "I'll do what I can," he said.

Karla gave Roscoe an approving nod. "Mucha suerte," she said, before turning to her screen and whatever deadline she had.

His resolve steeled, Roscoe crouched over the first box on the floor. Instead of books, it held manila folders, each a few centimeters thick with yellowed papers.

He scanned the box's barcode with his wristband and read the entry: "Collected Letters of Sir Joseph Dalton Hooker, 1817-1911; Correspondence from Antarctic Expedition; Contains Hooker's letters from the James Clark Ross Expedition of 1839-42, as well as drawings and ephemera from the voyage. Provided by Royal Botanical Gardens, Kew, England."

The next few boxes Karla had pulled had the same label: "Records associated with the James Clark Ross Antarctic Expedition of 1839-42. Records contain blueprints, maps, captain's logs, angle-books, remark-books, and ephemera collected by the crew of H.M.S. *Erebus* and *Terror* on this voyage, as well as memoirs published by Capt. Ross and Assistant Surgeon Robert McCormick. These records do NOT contain materials associated with *Erebus*'s and *Terror*'s later unsuccessful Northwest Passage Expedition under Sir John Franklin. Provided by UK National Archives."

Roscoe pulled a folder from the first box, and found it had letters from Hooker. *Imagine going through life with a name like that today*, he thought. He turned the pages slowly, taking care not to damage any of Hooker's letters, and remembering Karla's awed voice when she told Roscoe about the men writing "with quills, on sailing ships." Roscoe guessed he'd lose Karla's reverence when he actually had to *read* Hooker's slanted script, but not today. Every so often, he found a sketch of ice-bergs, seals, or penguins—but no maps.

"Anything yet?" Karla asked, looking away from her screen.

Roscoe closed the box with the Hooker letters and checked his wristband. It was nearly noon.

"Nope, nothing."

"Well, keep at it," she said, her voice tight again. "He needs something by the end of the week."

In the next box, Roscoe found just two books, each about three centimeters thick, with reddish-brown paper. The spines had the same faded, gold-leaf label: ROSS: VOYAGE IN THE ANTARCTIC REGIONS 1839-42. One book's spine was marked "1" and the other "2."

He opened Volume 1. The first page featured a sketch of two sailing ships anchored in a U-shaped harbor beneath towering cliffs. In the foreground, a Union Jack fluttered, and on the horizon, a stone archway rose from the ocean. Turning the page, he learned that the book had been published in London by "John Murray, Albemarle Street," in 1847.

The last two hundred seventy-six years hadn't been kind to it. As Roscoe eased the book upright, flecks of paper fell onto his desk like wood shavings. Some pages clung to the binding by threads, while others had already come loose. Roscoe tried not to open the book too wide, but after a few delicate page turns, a folded sheet slipped out onto his desk.

Karla gasped and rushed over, but Roscoe's panic ebbed as he unfolded the sheet and saw that it was exactly what they had been looking for—a map.

Roscoe read the label in the lower left corner: "Victoria Land, Discovered in H.M.S. EREBUS & TERROR Under the Command of: Capt. James Clark Ross H.M.F.R.S. and Cmdr. Francis R.M. Crozier R.N., Jan'y 1841."

At the bottom of the page, between the border and the paper's edge, another note read: "London Published according to Act of Parliament at the Hydrographic Office of the Admiralty, Dec. 5th, 1846. J & C Walker, Sculp."

The coast arced across the top of the map in a solid black line and snaked down the right side, where tiny type had been used to label shoreline features: Mt. Terror, Mt. Erebus, Cape Crozier, Franklin Island, Yule Bay—the place Hamza had mentioned—Cape Hooker, and, in the top right corner, McMurdo Bay.

Roscoe realized this was a map of the Ross Sea Coast. But it was oriented with south at the top. He turned the map around, comparing it to the satellite photo of Antarctica set as his computer's wallpaper. A dotted, numbered line—the ships' voyage, maybe?—zigzagged across part of the Ross Sea. Where the satellite image showed open water, this map had a dimpled curve running down its left side, labeled with the words: "Line of Pack Indicated by Strong Blink." The ships seemed to have explored the edge but turned back. Roscoe realized that, back then, the Ross Sea had been locked in ice year-round—and, more importantly, he had found exactly what they needed.

"Perfect, weón!" Karla said after a quick glance. Squinting at the printer-paper-sized sheet, she added, "It's small, but we can work with it." She tapped her floating wristband screen. "I'm messaging the Machine Shop now. Head over there and they'll make a bigger copy and get it in a frame, so you can take it to Jahnford. I'll message them, too, so they know you're coming."

She refolded the map, slid it into a plastic sheath, and pressed it into Roscoe's hand. "Hold on to it tight. That thing's old."

His orders issued, Roscoe headed out. He was beginning to get the hang of Spigot's tunnel network; for the first time, he didn't need his wristband to navigate. The main city had been built—or rather, dug—as four slanted parallel tunnels, each eight kilometers long. Waist-high concrete walls divided each tunnel lengthwise into a four-lane central avenue with sidewalks, while additional chambers branched off on either side, bored deeper into the rock as needed.

The Archives occupied the far end of Tunnel 1, right in front of the turnaround for the city's vehicles; the machine shop was near the opposite end. Roscoe flagged down one of the passenger jitneys that ran the length of the tunnel. The few passengers aboard wore standard-issue synthetic pants and jackets, just like his. The traffic was light at this hour, so he managed to get a seat.

The jitney cruised the outside lane, occasionally pulling over to let passengers on or off at narrower cross tunnels that intersected the main one every kilometer.

Only now, after visiting Newloon, did it hit Roscoe just how sterile Spigot felt. There were no storefronts vying for his attention, no fights breaking out, no one begging for change or raving about the end of the world. And definitely no one was offering him a gig as a sex slave on another colony run by neo-Nazis. On the jitney, no one spoke or made eye contact; the few people on the sidewalks kept their heads down and their eyes on their wristband screens.

It was quiet here, but not peaceful. StarCross Silence at work.

It was also bland. Each chamber looked the same: slate-gray double doors set into an alcove. Roscoe could only tell the doorways apart by following the jitney's progress on his wrist screen, or by reading the signs set over each door frame: GALLEY, INFIRMARY, GYM, COMMISSARY, AUDITORIUM, FOYER.

Looking at the map projected by his wristband, Roscoe realized he hadn't left this tunnel since arriving, except to get to his room the next tunnel over. It looked like this one housed all of Spigot's essential services. The next tunnel over was marked "RESIDENTIAL" on the map, while the other two had the same label: RESTRICTED ACCESS.

Near the far end of the tunnel, Roscoe's wristband pinged, and the jitney pulled over. This was his stop. He walked up to a nondescript gray door marked "MACHINE SHOP." Its door handle, unlike the Archives', didn't budge at first. But then Roscoe felt an internal lock release, letting him turn the handle. It must have been his wristband.

The receptionist looked up from his wristband screen, which Roscoe couldn't make out from where he stood. "You from Archives?"

"Yeah." Roscoe drew the plastic sleeve from inside his jacket and handed it over. "We need a blown-up copy, framed for hanging. Be careful with it—it's old and fragile."

The guy nodded and took the sleeve. "Wait here, okay? It'll be twenty minutes or so." He vanished through a door.

Roscoe took a seat next to the desk, listening to the soft, rhythmic chop of Spigot's 3D printers.

Several minutes later, the receptionist reappeared, the original map in one hand and a new, framed one in the other. The map had been blown up to three times its original size, set behind plexiglass, and framed in plastic airbrushed to elegant dark mahogany. It felt bulky but light.

Roscoe's wrist pinged. He tucked the frame under his left arm to read the message: "*Access to Central Office granted. Please follow designated route.*" The screen showed a path across Spigot's four main tunnels. The two far ones were no longer grayed out or marked "RESTRICTED ACCESS." He'd been allowed into the exclusive zone; this day just kept getting better.

He headed down the main tunnel and up the nearest side street. After crossing the second main tunnel—the one where he lived—the sidewalk ended at a gray door. A floor-to-ceiling fence separated foot traffic from the vehicle lanes, making this steel door the only entrance to the next tunnel—and a sign made clear that it was for "AUTHORIZED VISITORS ONLY. TAP WRISTBAND TO DOORKNOB TO VERIFY CLEARANCE." Roscoe complied, and the door slid open.

Stepping into Tunnel 3, he did a double take. It was as wide as the other tunnels, but had a completely different layout. Vehicles only used the center two lanes, allowing for wider sidewalks—and gardens. It was just xeriscaping—pebbles and hardy succulents that wouldn't siphon too much water off Spigot's production—but it was still the most greenery Roscoe had seen down here.

Across the street, he saw a group of well-dressed people, not much older than himself, walking together. They wore jeans, sneakers, fitted shirts, and smart leather jackets—some of them sleeveless; Roscoe suddenly felt self-conscious in his Spigot-issued synthetic jacket and pants, with the bright droplet logo on the shoulder. Most people he'd seen so far wore some variation of this uniform. Would he get a wardrobe upgrade at the end of his internship? Did the career-track people live on this street, in the ex-intern suites Chip mentioned? Or was this tunnel reserved for the Residents, the Executives, and those lucky few who joined them by succeeding in the Leadership Training Program?

He didn't have time to wonder about that now. One of the group members gave him a long stare, and Roscoe scurried ahead. He followed his wristband's directions across the avenue, and swiped for entry into the fourth tunnel.

Tunnel 4 had a similar layout as the last one: two lanes for traffic, wide walkways, and pebble-and-cactus beds along the sides. Most of the people there looked to be around his age—likely Leadership Training Program interns, he guessed. Looking at his wristband screen, Roscoe saw that he stood near the tunnel's midpoint, and right in front of his destination: an alcove, twice as wide and high as all the rest, marked "ADMINISTRATIVE OFFICES—MAIN ENTRANCE."

Inside, he found another reception desk manned by a StarCross Security agent in body armor. "Name?" he asked.

"Roscoe Slake."

"Destination and purpose of the visit?"

"I have to deliver a package to Mister Jahnford's office."

The agent checked his wristband screen and nodded. He directed Roscoe to set the package down, unzip his jacket, and stand with his feet shoulder-width apart and arms outstretched. As the agent ran a wand along his torso, Roscoe found himself studying the insignia on the man's shoulder. Since leaving Granite Gorge, all the security agents he'd seen— near the searchlight, at the foyer, and now here— wore StarCross's stars-and-droplet. Meanwhile, his and everyone else's uniforms bore only the Spigot droplet. Roscoe wondered if StarCross Security people took their orders from someone other than Jahnford.

The agent swiped the wand over the map, then pressed a button on his desk. The door to his right clicked open. "Follow the hallway to the end. The elevator will take you up."

This hallway was flat-roofed, not arched like the tunnels. The color scheme was different too—granite and bronze, not the bare tan rock he'd seen everywhere else. Aides scurried between doorways along the sides. Some wore jackets like his; most were out of uniform, like the people he'd seen outside. A few gave him curious looks, like the guy in Tunnel 3 had. Once again, Roscoe felt as though uniforms like his weren't supposed to linger here. He kept his head down and bolted for the elevator.

Inside, he saw just one button: EXECUTIVE SUITE. Roscoe pressed it and felt his ears pop as the elevator shot upward. When the door slid open, he stepped into a room finished in more bronze and granite, and about as long as a tennis court, but narrower. The elevator doors opened onto its midpoint, just a few steps back from a wooden conference table that ran the room's length. To his right, the room ended in a set of wood and glass double doors. At the other end, WEC sales scrolled continuously on a screen set into the wall:

Japan—8 marine hydrophones—200 WECs

Mexico—200 tons construction-grade cement—
800 WECs

Lockheed-ChinaShip Global Sub Supply—2 tanker
subs—2,000 WECs

Roscoe barely noticed any of this. He had stepped out of the elevator and froze, transfixed by the long wall of windows—or rather, what lay beyond them: glowing curtains of green and purple, rippling from the upper window frame to the ink-black crags on the horizon. The entire valley shimmered beneath them, the snow glowing like fogged chrome under neon. The southern lights.

"Roscoe! You're a savior."

Roscoe turned to see Grei Jahnford emerging from the side doors at the room's right end. "Amazing, huh?" he said, gesturing toward the window. "We can project the lights if we need to, but it looks like God decided to put on a show for our guests." Turning away from the window, he motioned for Roscoe to lift the map to the wall. "Let's get this mounted."

Jahnford tapped his wristband screen, and the screen at the room's left end went dark. The print and frame, Roscoe saw, had been sized to cover it perfectly. He lined up the frame and pressed it against the granite until the adhesive strips on the back stuck.

"Looks good!" Jahnford said. "It'll be great to show this to our guests."

They both studied the map in silence for a moment. The copy had been touched up, and the new version seemed brighter now, the paper's tone warmer, the ancient ink sharper. Details that Roscoe had missed earlier stood out now. The Ross Sea Coast—Spigot's eventual home—was marked with a heavy black line, while the eastern coastline curled up the left side of the page in soft dimples.

Jahnford started tracing the line that zigzagged around the bay with his finger. "Looks like they entered the bay in early January 1841, then spent a few weeks exploring the western and southern coasts—right where we are."

It was the route of the *Erebus* and *Terror*, Roscoe realized. "Were these the first two ships to come down here?" he asked.

Jahnford nodded. "Under Ross's leadership, they tried to sail south but eventually were stopped by the ice. It was supposed to have looked like cliffs. All gone now." Jahnford traced the soft dimples along the map with his finger. "This is their best guess of where the shelf extended. And here," he pointed to a label, "'Blink'—their word for an optical illusion that makes ice look like dry land."

"That's amazing," Roscoe said. For the first time in a while, he didn't have to fake his enthusiasm.

Jahnford nodded. "Sure is. Antarctica's a treacherous place. Things can go wrong up on the ice. I learned that the hard way."

"When?"

"Years ago, when I was a surveyor down here, not much older than you."

"Oh, were you an intern?"

Jahnford shook his head. "This was before the internship program. Back then, you just applied for a job or an indenture." Roscoe knew better than to ask which one Jahnford had done. "They sent me and another guy up on the East Antarctic ice sheet further inland." He pointed at a spot along the coast, then lifted his finger to the top of the parchment, over the frame, and onto the wall. "Ice up there is still a kilometer or more thick. We used special radar to identify water deposits underneath—just for two weeks. Ended up being closer to two months."

"What happened?"

"Storm knocked out our comms and REC receiver," Jahnford replied, his expression darkening. "Had to travel back on foot." He paused for a moment. "My buddy didn't make it. Fell into a crevasse."

"I'm—I'm so sorry," Roscoe stammered, hoping his voice carried enough sympathy.

Jahnford nodded grimly. "Like I said, Antarctica's a treacherous place. Pretty soon after that, I got frostbite." Just then, Roscoe noticed Jahnford only had three fingers on his left hand. "Thought I was done for."

"But you weren't."

Spigot's CEO smiled. "Nope. I came back. Because I learned something incredible, Roscoe, something about why those early explorers," he said, pointing at the map again, "came down here in the first place."

As Roscoe opened his mouth to ask what the reason was, Jahnford's wristband buzzed. He called up the screen. "Ah, forgot I've got a call with the Residents' Council and some other folks in five minutes." Roscoe felt himself frown, but Jahnford smiled and clapped him on the shoulder. "Don't worry! It's not a big secret. I discuss what I learned and what it means for us every Sunday."

"Really?"

Jahnford nodded. "Every Sunday at ten a.m. in the Auditorium. You're welcome to come."

"That'd be great," Roscoe said. "I'll see you there."

"Good!" Jahnford said. "We'll be glad to have you."

* * *

On the elevator ride back down to the main floor, Roscoe remembered what Jen had told him about Jahnford's church making him "ban fun" in Spigot. Whatever Jahnford had invited him to didn't sound like a church, and Roscoe wanted to learn what Jahnford had found out there on the ice. It was up his alley, he thought on his way back to the Archives. He'd check it out.

"You delivered it to him?" Karla asked when he returned.

"Yep, it's on the wall in his suite." Roscoe took out the original map and placed it back in the box.

"Perfecto," Karla said. "Let's hope Jahnford likes it enough to keep it after the meeting. It'll remind him that we're down here, ready to help in a pinch. So what'd you think of Jahnford?"

Roscoe wasn't sure if his boss was fishing for something; he gave the most neutral response he could think of. "He makes quite an impression." When Karla raised an eyebrow, Roscoe added, "he told me about how he got stuck out on the ice. He invited me to some kind of meeting on Sunday morning to learn more about it."

Karla rolled her eyes. "Right, that's when his cult meets. He invites everyone. What excuse did you make?"

A cult? he thought to himself. "I said I'd go."

Karla opened her mouth and let out something between a sigh and a laugh. "Ay, weón," she said. "I guess it's hard to say no to the boss when you're at the bottom of the totem pole. Well, you can't back out now. Just sit in the back. He should forget about you in a few weeks, and you can slip out."

Roscoe's stomach dropped. "What exactly does his cult, or whatever it is, believe?"

"They call themselves the Revelators." Karla leaned back in her chair, looking at the ceiling. "Jahnford claims that when he was stuck out on the ice, he met the spirit of some unnamed Antarctic explorer who showed him texts etched into the ice. Of course, no one else ever found those texts. They supposedly said that Jesus is going to start a thermonuclear war to destroy the world—and only Antarctica will be spared."

Karla gave Roscoe a moment, indulging his slack-jawed stare as he remembered the pamphlet from Newloon, before leaning forward again. "This continent plays all kinds of tricks on the human mind, Roscoe. Optical illusions, terror, deprivation, hallucinations."

"Hallucinations?"

Karla nodded. "You spend hours or days alone, staring into a whiteout blizzard, listening to nothing but the wind, weighing the odds of your own death, and your brain will start playing tricks on you." She waved an arm toward the shelves. "Many of these men felt presences, heard voices, and sometimes even saw things. Often in moments of extreme peril. Shackleton once felt he was in a group of four, even though he knew it only had three." She started opening a box. "All of that's to say that even if Jahnford's not trying to trick anyone, what he says happened to him fits a pattern of people hallucinating on the ice."

"And other people believe him?"

Karla nodded. "Many of his followers are indentured workers. The ones with the tough jobs outside. Many of them have probably experienced some version of the same syndrome. Rumor has it, this religion is why he got the job."

"What?"

"It gives indents meaning for their time here. Keeps them from making too many—ah—demands. And the only way indents can afford their tithes is to ask for a WEC advance and to extend their terms. StarCross doesn't mind that."

"Tithes?" It took Roscoe a minute to connect the term to one of his history classes. "What does this church need their money for?"

"Why, to fulfill their destiny," Karla said matter-of-factly. "To build a nuclear missile that they can use to start the apocalypse." Roscoe again stared at her, too stunned to speak. "It will *never happen*," Karla continued. "Even with the tithes Jahnford collects, they will never buy the hardware needed to build an intercontinental ballistic missile. Most of that has already been traded to StarCross, and the rest is kept in reserve."

"And that's why StarCross doesn't mind," Roscoe said. "It keeps the indents in line, keeps them working longer, and keeps them chasing an impossible goal."

"Exactly," Karla said as she opened another box. "You'd have made a fine historian or sociologist, if anyone still hired those." She blew the dust off a sealing captain's log. "It doesn't hurt that this religion discourages alcohol and drugs." Roscoe looked over at Karla, but his boss had already slid into the text and begun talking to herself. "Solace without side effects. Perfect for the ones StarCross needs for physical labor."

Now, it was Roscoe's turn to lean back and stare at the ceiling. "He also said he learned about why early Antarctic explorers were here."

"Well, in the Revelators' theology, all the Antarctic explorers were sent by Jesus to pave the way for them. They read the explorers' memoirs and journals like sacred texts."

"But you said StarCross locked all that historical stuff down."

"Jahnford got them to let him keep some stuff on an air-gapped hard drive. Other congregations have bootleg copies."

"Just how many of these groups are there?"

Karla counted on her fingertips. "There are at least two or three on the Peninsula and on some of the islands further north. I think New Swabia has one. It spreads as people leave indentures to make it on their own, somewhere else under the Antarctic Circle. They have more faith in Jahnford than in StarCross." She shrugged. "With the dangers they face, they need something to cling to."

Roscoe rubbed his temples as he realized what he had signed up for.

"Take the rest of the day off," Karla said. "You've earned it."

"I can stay until five," he said, wanting to show Karla he hadn't been too shaken.

"Go on home," she said, waving him away. "I was going to finish up early too. Don't worry. I'll log your full eight hours. Besides, you've already done your share for the Archives branch today."

Roscoe headed for the door, not needing to be told again.

Chapter 8

H.M.S. *Erebus*
Off the west coast of Africa
November 1839

Many days stood between Yule and his goal, yet each one soon blurred into the next. At sea, he and Tucker tracked the voyage's progress with sextant readings, compass bearings, the chip log's unspooling rope, and the steady tick of the chronometer. These measurements yielded a latitude and longitude that—along with the warming air—confirmed that the *Erebus* and *Terror* were pressing south, toward the magnetic pole. They would call at many ports along the way, including the Kerguelens.

One day, two months out from England, Yule was watching the sun climb toward noon with his sextant, imagining it shining on the doubloons that awaited him on those far-away isles, when Hooker's shout broke through his thoughts.

"Net! Robert, bring me a specimen net!"

Yule looked between the assistant surgeon who had just dared to command his superior in this way, and the specimens Hooker aimed to collect. Schools of fish leaped alongside the *Erebus*, matching its eight-knot pace. A dolphin pursued them, gaining fast. By the time it had pulled alongside, McCormick and Hooker had already dropped a net over the gunwale. They quickly closed it around both predator and prey.

Yule joined three able seamen in hoisting the net. The flying fish thrashed atop the deck; so did the dolphin. McCormick pressed his shotgun barrel to the creature's temple and fired. It stopped thrashing.

The gunshot drew Ross on deck. He made a point of stepping in the dolphin's blood and brain matter before peering into its eye. "Well done, surgeons. The flying fish specimens from these waters will greatly interest the Royal Society. And dolphin tastes wonderful when fried. Will you need help cleaning them?"

"No, sir," McCormick said, "although a log of their location would be most useful."

"Reckon our current coordinates, Master Yule," Ross ordered. "Swab the deck when you're done."

"Aye, captain," Yule said, livid that he, a second master, had been given an able seaman's task of swabbing the deck. As he finished reckoning their coordinates, Yule wondered why Ross enjoyed humiliating him. Was it punishment for his appearance at the review? A reminder that his father's reputation meant nothing on this ship? The answer escaped Yule as he delivered the coordinates to McCormick and began mopping up the dolphin's blood.

Yule enjoyed the solitude of that night's supper, chewing on the dolphin's fried meat while Hooker and McCormick probed its entrails. Just as Yule washed the dolphin down with more ale, another round of shouting drew him to the deck.

This time, the crew was gathered at the stern. The sun had set, and the ship's wake now glowed like streaks of lightning.

"Phosphorescence," McCormick called out as the crew marveled. "Certain animalcules in the tropical seas glow when disturbed, as in the wake of a ship." As he spoke, Hooker tied a lidless jar to the end of a sounding-line. Yule watched the assistant surgeon lower the jar into the glowing foam and then pull it back on deck. The glow had faded by the time Hooker capped the jar.

Ross held a lantern to the jar. "Congratulations, Doctor Hooker. And Doctor McCormick," he added upon seeing the surgeon's scowl. "Another new discovery for our voyage." Raising the lantern, he barked

Yule's name when its light reached his face. "Get our coordinates again. We must note where this phenomenon was observed."

Yule returned to the Great Cabin for the remark-book and the chart he'd been using to track their progress across the Atlantic. As he calculated their position, he reflected on the fact that his work would be what made McCormick's and Hooker's discovery useful. It would let the Royal Society pinpoint where in the tropics this phenomenon had occurred.

But he would get no credit.

Two days later, an island broke the horizon—Santiago, under the Portuguese flag. Through his spyglass, Yule watched its low, weather-beaten hills rise over the waves. He had little desire to make landfall here, but the light winds slowed their progress, and the island barely inched closer. At this rate, Yule knew, the ships wouldn't arrive until the next day.

Approaching port tormented Yule. A ship's master proved their worth in these moments. If any of his or Tucker's figures were off, the *Erebus* could run aground. But as Tucker relieved him of his watch, there was little Yule could do besides join Hooker for supper.

The wine incident still stung Yule, but he had managed to keep things cordial with Hooker. The surgeon—or "botanist," as Hooker preferred to call himself—had yet to find Yule ignorant about any aspect of Jersey, the Channel Island where Yule had grown up. Every meal, Hooker would ask Yule about Jersey's flora: dune grasses, flowers, even the kelp that washed ashore. Whatever he said, Yule knew, Hooker would recall it to perfection years later. Yule often wondered if Hooker would remember to credit him when he did so.

But when Yule mentioned their course for Santiago, he was again Hooker's student. "Santiago!" Hooker exclaimed. "Perhaps we'll see Darwin's baobabs."

"Beg pardon?"

"My friend Charles Darwin visited Santiago some years ago on the *Beagle.* He saw baobabs there—trees native to Africa, unlike anything we have in Britain."

"How so?"

"The trunk can grow more than eight feet across, tapering to a point with only a small tuft of foliage at the top."

"And how long does a baobab take to reach such proportions?" Yule asked, hoping to maintain whatever shred of respect Hooker had for him.

"Adonson first documented them in the last century. He believed them to be six thousand years old—almost as old as the Earth itself, it was thought at the time." Hooker laughed. "But their true age and growth rate remain mysteries. Perhaps ones we can solve—if we find the same tree Darwin measured, we could compare its dimensions with his records from the *Beagle*'s visit."

At last, here was a strand of Hooker's thought that Yule could grasp. "Well, perhaps my sextant and measuring ropes would be useful for those measurements."

Hooker nodded. "Excellent idea. Darwin told me that Fitzroy allowed him to use some of the men and instruments from the *Beagle* when they went ashore on Santiago. I'm sure Ross will do the same."

Yule sipped his wine but kept silent. Ross's treatment of him suddenly made sense. To Hooker and his friend Darwin, and likely to the captain as well, Ross was just another faceless member of the "men and instruments" at their disposal—tools to be used as they studied Her Majesty's domains, names to be forgotten when the acclaim came with their published findings.

Land in the Kerguelens, find the treasure, buy some acclaim of your own, Yule told himself. He then finished his wine and stood. "I'm sure he will. I must be off—measurements to attend to."

The next morning, Yule stepped on deck to find the ships anchored a few hundred yards off Santiago's coast. To their east, crouched a smaller, rust-colored island, barren of foliage or houses. Ross stood beside McCormick, who was studying its rocky surface through a spyglass.

"Basalt, it appears," Yule overheard him tell Ross. "Known to interfere with the dip needle. Any magnetic observations collected there shall be useless."

"Very well, we shall make do aboard ship." The captain turned toward his second master and barked, "Master Yule! Find Master Tucker! Prepare the needle."

"Aye, sir," Yule replied, heading below deck to rouse Tucker from his bunk. The first master was violently hungover, having bought several bottles of fake Madeira in Chatham. He had abstained until yesterday, then indulged without restraint. Though like most Royal Navy officers, Tucker could hide his drunkenness well, Yule wasn't about to trust Tucker's unsteady hands with the Fox dip needle. This instrument needed careful handling.

The needle, encased in a brass dial wider than Yule's outstretched palm, was mounted on a metal platform. Yule carried it to a table on the *Erebus*'s deck and aligned it with the compass bearing so that the dial, and the needle inside, pointed toward magnetic north.

Ross, Yule, and Tucker watched as the needle swayed, waiting for it to settle. Once it did, Yule squinted at the dial. "Eight degrees, forty-eight minutes above the horizontal."

Ross leaned in to examine the needle himself and, satisfied, nodded. Tucker recorded the reading. They had been tasked with collecting this measurement—the angle of the invisible magnetic forces girdling the Earth—at every port of call thus far.

Finding these angles could remove much of the uncertainty from compass bearings. It might even let ships find their position using bearings alone, without needing the sun, stars, or chronometer. Yet few, besides ships' masters, would truly value this accomplishment. The public, it was hoped, would take pride in Her Majesty's ships reaching the point where the dip needle pointed straight down—the magnetic pole. Ross, as Yule had often been reminded, had already planted the

Union Jack at the North Magnetic Pole in the Canadian Arctic. Now, he had been tasked with bringing it to its southern counterpart.

In the meantime, though, McCormick wanted to explore this barren little islet.

"—prime example of an extinct shield volcano," Yule overheard the surgeon tell Ross, after he and Tucker had stowed the dip needle.

"I have no doubt, Doctor McCormick. But Doctor Hooker's father has sway with the Admiralty, and I, therefore, must indulge his desire to see these trees of his. For the crew's safety, you must remain onboard while he goes ashore."

"But could we not delay our departure by a day, so that I might go ashore while Hooker remains onboard?" McCormick's Irish accent thickened with frustration.

Ross shook his head and opened his mouth just as Yule walked in. Before Yule could give the latest noon coordinates, Ross gave him a new order. "Master Yule, go find Doctor Hooker and bring him here. See if he can collect some rocks for Doctor McCormick on his shore excursion."

Yule went off to find Hooker, checking his bunk first. It was empty. He poked his head above deck; the surgeon was absent there too. He returned to the lower deck, calling out for the assistant surgeon.

A weak reply came from the head. "In here."

Yule stood outside the door. "Are you all right?"

"No, I-I've got the bloody flux. It's my first time in the tropics. Must have been from a mosquito."

Yule winced at the familiar smells and sounds. He remembered his own bout of dysentery on the West African coast years ago.

"Will you still be well enough to go on the shore excursion?"

"No, I-I should stay here. McCormick can go in my place. I'll stay onboard but expect I can still tend to the men." Another groan and splatter from behind the door made Yule doubt this, but he took Hooker's message to Ross and McCormick.

"He'll stay onboard but expects he can still tend to the men. He also said Doctor McCormick can go ashore in his place."

McCormick smiled at this news.

"Excellent," Ross said. "Doctor McCormick, how many men do you need?"

"Just one or two to row and help carry specimens, Captain."

"We should try to keep Doctor Hooker happy," Ross said. "Did he say anything to you about studies he hoped to conduct on the island? Specimens from these boobabs or whatever they are?"

McCormick shook his head, but Yule spoke up. "He hoped to measure the height of the baobabs." McCormick and Ross both stared. "He—he mentioned that they had been measured on an earlier expedition, and he wanted to compare their growth over time. I suggested that a sextant could be used to measure them without too much trouble."

"Very well," Ross said. "Go ashore with Doctor McCormick, collect specimens, and measure the trees if you can find them. Do be careful with the sextant."

Yule had expected a direct walk to the baobabs, but McCormick had other ideas. For the surgeon, any time spent ashore was time to indulge his two great interests: rocks and birds.

"See the basalt rock above the limestone, Yule?" he asked as they walked along the beach. He swung his walking stick toward the cliffs beside them, where a dark band sat above a lighter one. "A trace of ancient volcanism. Basalt forms when lava cools." He struck the cliff with his hammer and handed Yule the resulting stone chip.

As the day wore on, Yule's pack grew heavier. McCormick stopped often to gather stones or shoot birds in the brush. To Yule's relief, a distant monkey escaped the surgeon's interest. By afternoon, Yule's heels stung with blisters, and his shoulder ached from lugging McCormick's bag of specimens. He was about to suggest they turn back when a bend in the path brought them face-to-face with a baobab.

The tree was indeed unlike anything Yule had ever seen: shaped like an upside-down carrot, tapering to a point with a tuft of waxy leaves at the top.

"Just as I remembered," McCormick said. "The first baobab we sighted with the *Beagle*'s party all those years ago. As strange and beautiful now as it was then. Ah! Look. My initials are still there." Sure enough, Yule saw them carved into the bark.

"We did prune and peck quite a few specimens from it, poor thing."

This pity for a tree surprised Yule, who had watched McCormick shoot seabirds nearly every day since Lizard Point. Still, he realized the surgeon's awe might spare him from carrying more specimens. "Shall we just measure its height and girth this time, then?" Yule suggested.

McCormick nodded with a smile. "I've laden you down enough already, haven't I?"

Yule set down his pack and stretched a measuring rope several yards out from the strange tree's base. He then used his sextant to find the angle from his line of sight to the top of the tree. Those two numbers gave him a height of thirty-eight feet, four and one-eighth inches.

"Hooker may yet be able to calculate its growth rate," McCormick suggested, gulping water from his canteen. He looked at Yule's sweat-drenched form and sighed. "Swabbing decks, measuring trees, carrying specimens for an old hoss like me." He shook his head. "Really rotten of Ross to give you such tasks."

Yule held his tongue. Though relieved to hear someone share his resentment, he knew better than to openly agree—it could easily be a test of loyalty. And so, he shouldered the pack, grimacing from its weight, as the surgeon led him back toward the ship. McCormick spoke next.

"Ross's uncle humiliated himself near the Poles," he remarked, his voice low but pointed.

Yule's curiosity got the better of him. "How?"

"Navigation error. Was scouting for the Northwest Passage on the *Isabella* back in 'eighteen. By summer's end, he thought he'd found a bay, saw what looked like a mountain range on the horizon, and marked it as 'Barrow's Bay' on his charts, before turning back and reporting it as a dead end."

"How was that an embarrassment?"

"It wasn't a bay—it was a channel. Parry sailed down it for hundreds of miles the following summer. Our own dear captain was a midshipman on that voyage." McCormick smiled. "I don't envy his position."

Yule forgot his caution. "His uncle mistook a channel for a bay? How?"

"Clouds. At high latitudes, clouds on the horizon tend to look like land. They call it iceblink. John Ross thought he was seeing mountains and didn't bother to take a closer look. The Admiralty hasn't trusted him since." McCormick laid a hand on Yule's shoulder. "Our captain may have claimed the North Magnetic Pole, but he's still trying to clear the family name on this voyage. Doesn't like being reminded of someone who doesn't have that burden."

Yule froze, digesting McCormick's words. His father's service at Trafalgar had drawn Ross's envy, yet it had brought Yule neither wealth nor accolades. In an instant, his confusion turned to fury, then to determination—determination to see through the plan he had nursed for months. Yule knew his chances of success would improve with help, and McCormick had just shown himself to harbor his own misgivings about the Navy's leadership.

Panting under the weight of the stone-filled rucksack, Yule jogged a few steps to catch up. "Wait, Doctor McCormick." The surgeon turned. "I want to discuss something with you."

Chapter 9

Ross Sea Coast
Antarctica
June 2123

Two more days passed by in a sepia blur for Roscoe.

He had barely reopened the whaling log he'd been working on when Karla got a message on a non-Spigot wristband Roscoe hadn't noticed her wearing. She looked up at him. "Some of those boxes had Joseph Dalton Hooker's letters, correct?" When Roscoe nodded, she sprang to her feet, opened one of the boxes, and took out an armful of folders. "A colleague in Data Processing wants these letters digitized as soon as possible." She gave him a brisk nod, cutting off any questions.

He'd gotten an ASAP order. It was time to hustle—and definitely not the time to leave earlier than his boss. He and Karla worked until seven that night and for ten hours each of the next two days. By Wednesday evening, Hooker's handwriting read almost as easily as a floating touch-screen message after a few beers. Roscoe had also learned one bit of Spanish slang—*weón* for "man" or "dude"—when his boss shared her collection of protest music from the 1970s South American dictatorships. Roscoe couldn't catch much else in the songs, but at least they kept his energy up without making his withdrawal headaches any worse. He wasn't about to take another chance on those pills from Newloon.

With all the work, Roscoe had no time to dwell on his bizarre night at the town up the road until Thursday, when his wristband buzzed with another message from Jen:

> *Happy Thursday, Cohort! We've got another mandatory intern meeting in the galley at 7 tonight. We're competing as a cohort in the all-intern tournament this weekend and need to strategize. Thanks to Roscoe and Hamza, I think we have a damn good shot at winning. ;) See you then.*

Roscoe read the message once, then again. He and Hamza had helped with a tournament? But how? They had gotten Jen a tool to analyze rocks. What kind of tournament would that be useful for? He still hadn't figured it out by the end of his shift.

Dread sank into Roscoe's chest as he neared the galley. It was bad enough having to face Jen so soon after his mishap at Newloon—now he might also have to answer about his weekend plans. How was he going to cover up or explain the fact that he was going to a meeting of some crazy cult? The T3 pill he swallowed to get into the galley didn't help him think of an answer.

At least this "tournament" on Saturday would spare him another invite to Newloon.

"Roscoe, one of our two team MVPs!" Jen announced as he sat down. She pulled the XRF gun out of her backpack. "By picking this up, he and Hamza might've just won this thing for us."

Met with baffled faces, Jen launched into an explanation. "StarCross is ramping up lunar mining. They don't have people swinging pickaxes up there." Roscoe realized Jen must have gotten the same tobacco-scented warning from Granite Gorge's Engineering Fundamentals teacher. "But," she continued, "they still need people with eyes for geology. So anyone who can tell one type of rock from another is someone they want up there." She pointed at the ceiling—and, high above it, the mining and energy-relay station StarCross operated in the Marius Hills.

"What does that have to do with us?" Darren asked.

"Because more meteorites have been found on Antarctica than on any other continent," Jen answered. "This isn't space, but for geologists it's the next best thing. A few years ago, the Residents up at Marius Hills started a midwinter geology tournament for Spigot interns. They gave it some fancy-ass name I don't remember. Everyone here calls it the Crapshoot."

"A geology tournament?" Ana asked, eyebrows raised.

"Mm-hmm. They get chunks of asteroids or moon rocks, one for each cohort. Then they fire clusters of them into different parts of the Dry Valleys. They try to pick a date around midwinter. Solstice isn't for another two weeks, but between the weather forecasts and orbital trajectories, this Saturday looked best."

"So they send down meteorites," Roscoe said, "and we have to find them?"

"That's right," Jen said. "Each of the ten first-year intern cohorts gets a ten-gallon bucket. We fill it with rocks we think are meteorites, then bring it back. The cohort that finds the most actual meteorites, wins."

Hamza wrinkled his nose—the first distaste Roscoe had seen on his face. "They send down meteorites and watch us run around in the cold looking for them?"

"Yeah, it's weird," Jen agreed. "But I'll sure as hell do it for the prize they're offering."

She let them all stare at her in silence for a moment.

"Executive Status. On the Moon. As soon as your internship is up."

Roscoe's spirits surged. *Off-world Executive Status.* The prize that had eluded his parents—and so far, him. But then he remembered Spigot's orientation video—the sea of ruddy rocks on the surface. "We're supposed to tell meteorites apart from all the rocks out there? In the dark?"

Jen nodded. "StarCross doesn't give spots off-world away. Lucky cohorts might get a few pebbles in a ten-gallon bucket. But"—she laid the XRF gun down on the table, then leaned back and cracked her knuckles—"I don't think any of the other cohorts have a leader who knows what an XRF gun is."

Roscoe vaguely remembered Granite Gorge offering an advanced-level

Applied Geology class. Was that where Jen had learned about these tools? His StarCross Skills Assessments had tracked him away from that class, and the thought rekindled his old loathing of those tests.

"So you're saying we'll just go out to our site and scan rocks with this thing until we find meteorites?" Hamza asked.

Jen nodded, then pointed at him and Roscoe. "There's a reason you guys are our MVPs."

"Is ... this allowed?" Roscoe asked.

She looked away. "It's ... not explicitly banned. A StarCross minder will drive us out to our site and stay with us until we say we're ready to go back. We'll just have to crouch low enough so that he doesn't see us." Jen paused, gauging the mood on the interns' faces. "Everyone good with this?"

There was only one answer to the prospect of getting off-world, especially for Roscoe. "Yes," they replied in unison.

Jen beamed, her eyes flashing as she stood. "Great! See y'all bright and early on Saturday."

* * *

Friday was another twelve-hour day. "Thanks, weón," Karla told him when they finally finished. She pulled out her wristband and sent Roscoe a bonus from her own salary. It wasn't much, but it would cover a few beers at Newloon. "You doing that Crapshoot tournament thing tomorrow?"

Roscoe nodded.

"Mucha suerte. I'll have mixed feelings if you win. I'd hate to lose the help, but they don't offer many routes off-world for career-track employees like us."

"Well, if I win, I'll put in a good word for you." He had never made an emptier promise, but Karla smiled anyway. "Much appreciated. In that case, go get some rest. We've both got a lot riding on you."

Chapter 10

Island of Jersey
English Channel
November 1820

Retired Lieutenant John Yule always told his sons that this was the last time he would tell them the story. Without fail, John Jr. and Henry Braddick got him to tell it again.

"One by one, the sails appeared on the horizon," he always began. "We got to thirty, and thought it better to stop counting."

From one telling to the next, the details never changed: John Yule's shock when he realized that his ship, H.M.S. *Victory*, would sail for miles exposed to Napoleon's artillery as she approached his fleet from the side; the cheers when Nelson spelled out, with signal flags, "England expects that every man will do his duty"; the whistling as French and Spanish cannonballs flew straight into the *Victory*'s face, shredding her sails and sending deadly splinters through her gun decks; the scurry to mend the damage and replace fallen seamen as the ship drew nearer; the roar when the *Victory* finally slipped between the *Redoutable* and *Bucentaure,* unleashing a devastating fifty-two-gun broadside into each ship. Henry and John soon learned every detail of Trafalgar's opening salvos by heart. But when their father reached the next part—when the *Victory* had locked rigging with the *Redoutable*—he always kept them rapt.

"The French cannons had stopped firing," their father would say, his voice lowering as he leaned forward. "That could only mean one thing—they meant to board us. I raced past the guns to the officer's quarters at the stern. As I went, I passed a wounded figure being carried down to the orlop deck, his face covered with a handkerchief, but I thought nothing of it. At that moment, we had to ensure every marine was on deck, ready to face the enemy." His eyes darted as if scanning *Victory*'s deck all over again.

"So I was relieved when I reached the officer's quarters and found them empty. But then, at that very moment—*crash!* A grapnel shattered the porthole, and when I reached the hole, I was face-to-face with a Frenchman! He was climbing down the hull."

"What did you do?" John and Henry always asked together, despite knowing the answer.

"Grabbed him. I only managed to grab his one wrist, the one with the grappling hook. I could have finished him off then. But for some reason, I didn't."

"Why not?"

"For one instant, I was too shocked." He smiled and shook his head. "In all my years fighting Napoleon, it was the first time I had looked my enemy in the eye with the battle still raging. But then, I saw he had a strange kit."

"What was strange about it?"

"He had no musket or pistol. Just a sealskin bag around his neck, with one sphere inside, about yea big." He made a fist. "A grenade. And where a marine would wear a cutlass on his belt, he had a hacksaw. And then I realized what a dreadful danger this man posed."

"What did he mean to do?"

"Climb down the side of the ship, down to the waterline, and cut a hole large enough to throw his grenade in."

"Why?"

"Because the ship's powder magazine lay just below the waterline. If his grenade detonated at that level—*boom!*" John spread his hands apart. "Both our ships would be lost in an instant."

"But wouldn't he die too?" Henry asked.

Their father nodded, his expression grave. "It shows the wicked cunning of Napoleon's navy. They meant to sacrifice that man—nay, sacrifice all the men on two ships—to take out our admiral. Perhaps he was told he could escape, perhaps the men on the *Redoutable* believed they could escape, but with our ships locked together there was no chance of that," he said, brows furrowed and voice firm.

"He must have seen the shock on my face," their father continued. "Before I could do anything, he raised his free hand, pulled off the bag with his grenade, and dropped it into the sea. Then he started shouting. With the roar of the muskets, I took a long moment to understand what he was saying. 'Please! I help! I help!'" John Yule always said this with terror in his voice and uncertainty on his face.

"I don't know why, but I believed him. Perhaps it was Providence. If another officer had seen me, I would have been court-martialed and probably hanged. But I heaved him onto the ship and told him to remove his shirt—most of the seamen were shirtless with the heat below decks. Then, I pulled him into the gundeck and pointed to a spot where the ship's carpenters were mending a hole in the hull. He nodded and joined them. Everyone was covered in soot—no one wondered who this seaman was, they just took his help."

Their father always spoke faster at this point. "Just then, another officer caught my eye and raced toward me. He grabbed my wrist and led me toward the orlop deck. I thought I had been found out. But when we reached the orlop deck, where the roar of the battle was dulled enough to trade words, he said, 'It's the Admiral. He's been shot.'"

Henry and John indulged their father as he recounted the rest of the familiar tale once more: his shock of realizing that the shrouded figure he had seen earlier had been none other than their beloved Admiral; the moment he was handed the captured flag from the surrendered *Redoutable* to show Nelson, proof that victory was theirs; Nelson's final words, "Thank God I have done my duty," as he breathed his last; and the reminder of the example the admiral had set for all Englishmen. Through it all, they could barely hold back their excitement for the part of the story they loved most.

"I often wondered what became of that Frenchman," their father said. "Perhaps he had been killed later in the battle, perhaps he had been found out and hanged. I thought I would never know. But ten years later, I received this letter." This was the moment they had waited for, when their father would open the envelope and read the note that held their destiny.

"'Dear Monsieur Yule,' it began. 'This is the sailor from the *Redoutable* you saved at Trafalgar. After the war, I escaped to Valparaiso and prospered from the sealing trade. Know that you have my undying gratitude for the kindness you showed that day. I cannot reveal my name nor meet in person, lest it bring shame or danger upon either of us, but I wish to repay you.'

"'In my voyages around the southern seas, I called at an island far southeast of Cape Town, discovered by your countryman Cook. Ile de Kerguelen, it is called. There is an anchorage there, shaped like a horseshoe, with a great arched rock at its entrance. Three days' walk south along the coast from that rock, there is a cave. In that cave, I have built a cairn. Walk twenty paces into the cave from that cairn, then seven paces to the left. There I have buried a sealskin bag filled with doubloons and escudos. I pray you or your family may find this bag and reap your rightful reward.'

"'Regards, a grateful sailor.'"

"How did he know who you were?" Henry asked.

"We remained at sea for several weeks after the battle," their father explained. "He must have seen me in conversation with the other officers. Not long after I got this letter," their father said, "I heard some Nantucket sealers remark about this island, and they mentioned the bay with the arched rock." His eyes crinkled. "A sailor knows to watch for omens. I'm too old to voyage to that part of the world, but perhaps one of you will someday. Something to remember if you ever do."

Yule had believed the story less and less as the years went by. But when he bade his father farewell before leaving for Chatham, Lieutenant John Yule handed him the letter.

"I really did receive this, you know," he said. "Not just something I made up to convince you and your brother to go to sea. Your voyage will take you past the Kerguelens." He winked. "See if there's something there."

Once Yule had finished telling the story, McCormick ran a hand through his hair and rubbed the Saharan dust from his eyes. They both gazed down at the *Erebus* and *Terror* in the glittering bay. For a moment, Yule wondered if he had erred in sharing such a fanciful tale with a man of science. Then, McCormick spoke.

"That is how sealers trade messages on those islands," he said. "They hide them a set distance from a cairn. And I've heard stranger sea stories that turned out to be true. When we reach the Kerguelens, it will be worth a look."

Yule and McCormick returned to the ship and resumed their tasks, neither speaking further about the Kerguelens.

The expedition pressed south; the Southern Cross constellation climbed over the horizon. The tropical sun beat down harder on the ships as the days passed. The brass fittings on deck burned at the touch. Glass prisms, set into *Erebus*'s upper deck to channel sunlight below, were now covered with cloth to reduce the glare and ease the heat below deck. Even then, most men took to sleeping on deck soon after the ships sailed from Santiago. Two weeks out from that parched island, the *Erebus* and *Terror* crossed the equator.

Every man who had yet to cross into the Southern Hemisphere was subjected to a ritual shaving. Yule watched as sailors—dressed as King Neptune and his aides—sat the first "greenhorn," a marine named Cunningham, naked in a chair on deck. The ship's fire engine blasted a jet of water against his back as King Neptune reached into a bucket labeled "LATHER."

Neptune scooped out a handful of scum dredged from the bottom of the ship, mixed with spoil from the privy. The crowd cheered as he spread it across Cunningham's cheeks and chin, then scraped it off with a razor. Yule, having crossed the equator and endured this ritual before, was only a spectator this time. He joined the applause when Cunningham, now "clean shaven," stood and raised both fists in triumph.

The *Erebus* had dozens more greenhorns on her crew. Next up was Hooker. As Neptune's aides pulled him forward and began to strip off his jacket, a shout rang out.

"No!"

Everyone turned to Ross, who was standing at the ship's stern. "His father—his father knew of this custom. He insisted we not subject Hooker to it."

The crewmen stared at one another. This ceremony was the Navy's great equalizer, one no man—no matter his rank or education—could escape. Ross broke the silence.

"Come now, get on with it!" he barked. "There are plenty more greenhorns to shave!"

Neptune's aides shoved Hooker back into the crowd as they brought forward another greenhorn, and the crew resumed its cheers.

Chapter 11

Ross Sea Coast
Antarctica
June 2123

The foyer was packed the next morning; Roscoe could see little above the heads of all fifty first-year interns, plus their Leadership Training Program cohort. He only found his group thanks to a glowing message, Jen's Cohort Over Here, that his cohort leader was projecting from her wristband over her head. Rubbing his eyes, Roscoe threaded his way through the crowd. This tournament started before the galley opened, so he would miss breakfast and SynCoffee and probably lunch too. He was too tired to care much about the tournament's prize, but not too tired to decide that "Crapshoot" wasn't a profane enough nickname. Three "cohort activities" outside work hours in one week—just how many more would there be?

He was the last member of his cohort to arrive. "All right!" Jen said. The floating text vanished as she dropped her wrist. "Opening ceremony's at 6:30 p.m. outside. "But first"—she lowered her voice and leaned in, prompting the cohort members to do the same—"I want to give you all something. Don't take these until we're out there." She reached into her pocket and pulled out what looked like five shrink-wrapped breath mints.

"CoCaffs—cocaine and caffeine, formulated to keep you going in the cold. Shackleton used 'em." She winked at Roscoe, Hamza, and no one else. "One compound StarCross hasn't cracked down on yet."

"You get these at Newloon?" Hamza asked.

"Yep. Don't worry. You can trust my supplier."

Grogginess kept Roscoe from asking more questions as Jen led them into the locker room. Suiting up didn't help his mood. He discovered he hadn't just drawn a roomy suit last time—these were all sized for people bigger than one meter, sixty centimeters, and forty-three kilos. It *almost* fit once he'd tightened the straps as much as he could.

"So do we have a plan for when we get there?" Kevin asked, giving his own straps several hard yanks.

"We'll be given a grid where our meteorites are supposed to land." Jen looked around, then continued in a hush. "Like I said, the usual strategy is for the cohort to line up and walk across it, picking up anything that looks out of place as they go. I was thinking we'd do that, but as soon as we see anything unusual, we'd scan it, and then compare it to the rocks nearby. If it has a different makeup, then we'll know we've found a winner."

Roscoe couldn't think of anything better. Then he remembered there was another head intern who might also be able to buy an XRF gun. "Is Trent leading a cohort too? Do you think he bought one of these things?"

Jen shook her head. "Trent's one of the Leadership Training Program people who isn't leading a cohort. He wants to devote all his time to kissing Jahnford's ass. Thinks that's how he can maximize his chances of getting off-world." She pulled the XRF gun from a knapsack she'd left in the locker, stuffed it into her suit, and zipped up the front. "I disagree."

Once suited up, they joined the line for the Motor Pool. The interns weren't driving this time. Roscoe watched as one track after another pulled up, collected a cohort, and pulled out with the same drivers staying behind the wheel. When their turn came, Jen climbed into the front seat next to a Spigot employee, who let them in and drove off without a word.

Their driver took a hard left outside the tunnel and parked on a flat gravel plain. The ten cohort tracks parked in a U, their roof spotlights fixed on two flags: Spigot's and StarCross's. The interns climbed out of their tracks and huddled around them.

Twin speakers sewn into Roscoe's hood beeped to life, bringing Trent's voice right into his ears. "Good morning interns!" Roscoe squinted and saw Spigot's other head intern sitting next to Jahnford in another track's driver's seat, warm enough to have his hood down.

"Welcome to the Fifth Annual Spigot Geology Competition!" The flags snapped for several seconds; Roscoe again wondered if they were supposed to cheer. He raised his swaddled forearms to clap, but Trent pressed on.

"Each year, StarCross wants to recognize interns with the skills to help identify and locate precious minerals on the Moon—and someday, beyond. On Earth, the best place to find those talented interns is right here, in Antarctica. This tournament honors this continent's long tradition of meteorite hunting. It requires perception, teamwork, and grit—the skills StarCross needs in the Final Frontier."

By now, Trent's voice had lost its pep; he rattled off the rest of the script in a quick monotone. "Each team has been assigned a meteorite landing location, which is being sent to your wristbands now." A familiar buzz ran up Roscoe's left tendon.

"Each cohort's track has been equipped with a ten-gallon bucket. Over the next twelve hours, you may fill this bucket—and this bucket only—with rock specimens from your designated survey area. . Once you return to Spigot, StarCross personnel will determine how many meteorites each team has recovered. The cohort that recovers the most meteorites will win this year's tournament—and will receive Executive Status at StarCross's Marius Hills mining, manufacturing, and energy-relay station at the end of their internship term."

One by one, the tracks dimmed their lights. "StarCross's autonomous spacecraft have inserted your meteorites from low Earth orbit. We now invite you to look overhead and watch them descend."

Roscoe raised his eyes. At first, he saw only stars—the brightest he had ever seen. Then, straight overhead, he spotted several clusters of shooting stars, a few seconds apart. Each salvo traced a different trajectory above their heads. StarCross was sending down the meteorites.

Roscoe heard gasps from the crowd, but barely noticed. Something else had caught his attention, something that made him forget his lack of SynCoffee and tell himself, *Focus, dumbass, this is your chance to make everything right.* Amid the spray of stars, he had picked out the bluish lights of Lagrange-2.

"Lagrange-2," Roscoe's dad had said, pointing his nine-year-old son's gaze toward that same bluish cluster years earlier. "You know who runs that?"

"StarCross."

"And you know what they do up there?"

"Make energy."

"That's right. Up there, they have acres and acres of solar panels. Capture the sun's energy and beam it right down to Earth." He gestured toward the folded receiver dish on the roof of his truck's cab. "And when we sell our gas to the fuel cell guys, they beam the energy up to StarCross, and they can send it somewhere else on the planet where it's needed."

Roscoe wondered why StarCross would want to buy energy beamed up from the Pennsylvania gas fields when it could make so much of it in space. He'd forgotten that question when his father continued.

"My dad told me about the Blackout Years," he said, "before StarCross figured out wireless transmission. Storms and fires always knocking out the electricity, always knocking out the gas supply for generators. Riots and shootouts almost every day. As soon as you got a solar panel up or some batteries installed, someone'd steal it." He shuddered. "Just when people were really getting desperate, StarCross came to our rescue. Energy beamed from the Lagrange stations to Earth, no matter the weather." His father's eyes caught the pinpricks of light. "And the Updated Terms of Service brought peace."

"I know *that*," Roscoe said proudly. His class had just visited the

PeaceYard a few days earlier: acres of decommissioned tanks, missiles, and even a nuclear warhead, all out of service ever since the United States had agreed to the Updated Terms of Service.

"We owe them so much," his father said. "You know what else happens up there?"

"People live up there too, right?"

His father nodded. "A whole city. Rotates to make its own gravity. Has clean air, gardens, plenty of space—it's the way Earth used to be, only better."

Roscoe's father turned from the sky to him, his expression shifting, the reverence gone from his voice. "Roscoe, your mom and I spend all day in that truck, in that stinking gas field, so we can all get up there one day, as a family."

"You mean we'll be Residents?" By now, Roscoe knew that paying StarCross a lot of WECs or RECs—or having parents who did, or doing a favor for someone who did—would buy off-world housing. He'd also heard his parents say "Rich as a Resident" or "when I'm a Resident" enough to figure that would never happen to them. Sure enough, his father shook his head and chuckled.

"No. Working our entire lives in that gas field won't get us enough RECs to go up there. But we have saved up enough to send you to an internship academy, which means you can get an internship up there. And then you'll get a job running one of those stations, or even running StarCross in the Executive Service. And then we'll get housing." His father squeezed his shoulder. "But for us to get there, you've got to study hard, do better on your tests."

Roscoe looked down at the ground. He had just gotten his first quarterly Q-CAT results earlier that day. His father's reaction had been to drive him out past the air pollution in their battered tanker truck to look at Lagrange-2. Roscoe still didn't see what the big deal was. "The tests said I'm in the seventy-fifth percentile. That's pretty good—"

"Seventy-fifth percentile will get you a dead-end job in some spaceport, or down in Antarctica, if you even get into an academy at all! You've got to be *at least* in the ninety-fifth percentile to get an internship off-world."

Roscoe jumped back as his father's voice rose. Then, his father softened his tone. "You can do it, your mom and I know you can, and when you get an internship, we'll go up there with you." He looked back up at the sky. "The air's clean up there, Roscoe. Think about that. No allergens or god-knows-what-else. No storms either. No more worrying about flash floods carrying the prefab away or fires burning it down. You want that, right?"

"Y-yeah." His dad's face showed disappointment, so Roscoe tried harder. "I do, Dad! Really!"

Finally, his dad smiled again. "Then show us on the next test."

Roscoe thought he had done just that the next quarter when he scored a seventy-eight on the Q-CAT. "I'm getting better, see?" he told his parents.

They shook their heads. "Still not enough to get off-world."

So he worked harder, drilling the most important parts of StarCross's aptitude test—logic games, leadership scenarios, math-and-coding core—late into the night for three years. Quarter by quarter, his Q-CAT scores inched up. When the email came a few weeks after his twelfth birthday, that he had been accepted into the Granite Gorge Internship Academy, he thought it had all paid off.

His parents thought so too—until they read the fine print.

"It says your scores are borderline," his mom said, squinting at her wristband screen. "They'll only admit you to the Internship Training Program on the condition that you take compound."

The next day, a nurse at Granite Gorge's infirmary explained that, under the academy's StarCross Certification, Roscoe could only attend if he took a StarCross-approved psychoactive compound that would "optimize your unique aptitudes for success at Granite Gorge."

"Are there any side effects?" his mom asked.

"Headaches upon starting and during withdrawal. And possibly stunted growth, but nothing serious."

So Roscoe swallowed the speckled beige pill placed in front of him.

The headache started within minutes and lasted for hours: a back-to-front-to-back split, like the two halves of his brain twisting apart. When the pain finally eased, he mumbled to his parents, "I can't do this."

That earned him another ride in their tanker—but not to look at the stars. This time, his dad drove him to the Femaville: a place with acres of people who had fled the South, West, and coasts, unable to afford a safe dwelling elsewhere. The Gulfers had arrived first and were given small prefabs—"trailers," his dad said. Everyone who showed up later had gotten shipping containers. The Texans and Californians still blamed each other for the disasters that had befallen their home states, and their respective sections were separated by fencing too high to throw a brick or Molotov cocktail over. Perimeter security looked tight too, and Roscoe couldn't fault people inside for wanting to escape. In the setting sun, he watched them walk the dirt lanes between their homes in varying states of cleanliness. "Most of them work at the on-site electronics factory," his father said, pointing at a cluster of smokestacks. "That's where StarCross makes wristbands and other stuff that's low-value enough to make on Earth. It's not fun work. A lot of them want to work outside. But StarCross Security or the cops can't track all of them outside. Only the lucky ones get outside work permits, and only those people get weekly shower credits. Sometimes I'll pick up one or two of them when I need help for the day."

Spotlights shone from guard towers into the no-man's-land between the two razor wire fences surrounding the Femaville. Inside, cooking fires far outnumbered electric bulbs; RECs, too, were scarce. The wind shifted, bringing a ripe stench to their nostrils.

"Not a place you want to end up, right?" his father asked. "Especially when your dad used to hire some of them."

"N–no," Roscoe said.

"Well, then you'd better take those pills."

Roscoe stared at his father, who continued. "If a flood or fire or landslide comes for our place—or really, *when* it comes for our place—we won't have enough WECs or RECs to buy a new prefab that's up to the newer standards. You know where the Updated Terms of Service say we'll have to live?" When Roscoe shook his head, his father glanced back down at the squalid camp. Roscoe's stomach dropped several centimeters. His father looked him square in the eyes. "You're the one who has to keep us from ending up there, and getting us where life's still good." He gripped Roscoe's shoulder, pointed at his chest, and tapped it twice. "You're it."

You're it, Roscoe told himself again and again in the days that followed, a mantra to confine the compound headaches to a narrow slice of his skull.

You're it, Roscoe told himself, as the visits and messages from his parents tapered off, as required by StarCross security guidelines.

You're it, he told himself, nearly each night for the next decade, as ten o'clock rolled around and his thoughts drifted away from leadership scenarios, engineering problems, and coding drills, and toward his bed in Granite Gorge's dorm.

You're it, he told himself, in the years after StarCross prohibited new compound users in its certified academies. The words distracted him from the whisper "pounder," as students and teachers glanced his way and held their palms close to the floor, clearly speculating about why he was so short.

You're it, Roscoe told himself, as he spent his final year at Granite Gorge honing the senior capstone project that he felt so sure StarCross would love—enough to give him a spot off-world.

For one instant, Roscoe thought it had.

His academy-issued wristband buzzed with a new message. The sender: StarCross Internship Assignments.

He opened it.

> *Roscoe Slake—congratulations!*

He closed his eyes in bliss, savoring the moment before reading the rest of the placement message sent to him and every other academy senior:

> *You have been selected for an internship at Spigot, StarCross's chief water production subsidiary, in Antarctica's McMurdo Dry Valleys. You were selected—*

Roscoe tore off his wristband and flung it across the room, breathing out hard. Antarctica, where StarCross pumped water. His father's voice from all those years ago echoed in his head: "A dead-end job in some spaceport, or down in Antarctica."

The compound doses hadn't just curbed Roscoe's homesickness; they had also dried out his tear ducts. He just stared at the floor, tasting the soot from some wildfire or burn pit upwind. He wondered if the Antarctic air was cleaner or if this smell would follow him everywhere, always reminding him that he hadn't made the cut for space. And neither would his parents. They had siphoned the last dregs of natural gas from the Marcellus field, sold it to a wildcat REC generator for ten years' worth of doses, and for all that effort, they'd still be on Earth. Maybe safe from the Femavilles, but still on Earth.

Roscoe's lungs were almost empty when another graduate slapped him on the back. "Hey Slake, where are you going?"

Roscoe didn't look up to see who it was. "Antarctica," he gasped.

The hand recoiled. "Oh, sorry." He heard footsteps, then, muffled through the door, "Slake got Antarctica."

Pitied sighs followed. "That sucks. Pumped full of compound and still couldn't get off-world."

"No wonder StarCross made parents and academies stop giving dumb kids that stuff last year. Even with it, they still can't make the cut for space." Footsteps carried the voices away.

Roscoe didn't know why the voices were so happy. Maybe they'd earned spots off-world fair and square; maybe their families had managed to win favors from Residents or Executives off-world, making the exams a mere formality. Maybe they had gotten less-desirable internships in one of Starcross's Earth facilities. Maybe their families could afford new prefabs if their old ones got totaled. Maybe they just hadn't cared. But *he* had cared. And now, he couldn't face his classmates—or anyone else.

He had one clean razor left in his academy-issued toiletry bag. Two trial cuts, each a couple of centimeters on his left wrist, showed they could break skin. He'd just nicked a vein, coaxing a few red beads from that wrist, when his wristband buzzed again from the corner of the room.

He picked it up and opened the screen. This latest message was from the academy's placement office:

> *Disappointed in your placement? Remember that any StarCross Intern is eligible for the StarCross Leadership Training Program—the pipeline to StarCross's Executive Service and off-world housing.*

With wads of toilet paper, Roscoe stopped the bleeding.

The air in Antarctica didn't stink—but who knew for how long? Damn right Roscoe would be on the lookout today. "You're it," he mouthed.

The tracks' lights came on, and the engines hummed. Trent opened the driver's side door just enough to point an old-fashioned starter pistol in the air. "Ready, set"—*bang!*

The intern cohorts scurried back to their respective tracks. Roscoe saw that the driver had already loaded their course into a navigation screen. Jen looked at it, then pumped her fist. "Looks like we're going to the Vanda reservoir."

"There's a reservoir here?" Hamza asked.

She nodded. "Need a reserve in case a pipe gets clogged or something. Vanda used to be a lake, so that's what they used. I think the covering's pretty light-colored, which means our meteorites will be easier to spot."

The tracks convoyed into a different underground entrance. The tunnel led to a cavern as large as Granite Gorge's lodge, bathed in the same orange glow as Spigot. It was a hub of three tunnels, each half as wide as Tunnel 1. Most of each tunnel was filled by a massive metal pipe that angled into the floor just before reaching this central cavern. Each tunnel had a space as wide as a track, with twin rails on the floor.

"What is this place?" Roscoe asked.

"Forgot you're in Archives," Jen said. "This is the hub of the drainage system. Each one leads to a glacial valley. We're right above the submarine port where each of those pipes empties."

Roscoe noticed a soft roar from below: rushing water. Earth's last glaciers, its last drops of unclaimed water, were flowing through those pipes to the submarine port for shipment north.

The track in front of theirs made a right, then parked on a metal plate at the end of the rails. The plate rose, lifting the track a half-meter or so. Then it whisked the vehicle down the rails and out of sight.

Now it was their turn. The driver steered their track toward the second tunnel on the right. Roscoe caught a glimpse of a sign overhead:

NORTHERN DRAINAGE

WILSON PIEDMONT GLACIER / VICTORIA LOWER GLACIER

EXIT TO VICTORIA VALLEY / VANDA RESERVOIR

The track stopped, then rose before speeding forward. "This tram should get us there pretty fast," Jen said. "Eatonson knew how to dig."

Roscoe watched the tunnel scroll by outside the window. At regular intervals, he saw pipe segments wider than his height running straight up from the pipe into the ceiling—or rather, into a box bolted to the ceiling. Fixing his eyes on one as they passed, Roscoe read the stenciled label: "HEATING ELEMENT."

"What do those heating element boxes do?" he asked.

"Melt the glacier," Jen said.

"I thought it was melting on its own."

Hamza shook his head. "Not this one. Most of the glaciers around here are cold-based."

"Cold-based?"

Darren nodded. "Frozen right to the ground, even now. We need the heating elements to keep the water flowing. Also, the incendiaries that the melters plant."

Just then, Roscoe felt the track slow and his seat tilt upward. The platform carrying the track came to a halt before a metal door, then dropped.

The door opened, and once his eyes adjusted to the starlight, Roscoe saw more gravel in front of the windshield. He remembered what the introductory video called this place: the McMurdo Dry Valleys. Somewhere out here, StarCross had dropped meteorites for them to find.

The track drove a few more minutes before stopping.

"All right, let's do this thing!" Jen said, throwing open her door. Roscoe's lungs started aching again; it was even dryer here. "Now would be a good time to take your CoCaffs." As he stepped out, he watched Jen unwrap her pill and pop it into her mouth. Then, she walked around to the track's bed and pulled out an orange bucket as high as Roscoe's knees.

"Anyone need to pee before we start?" she asked. Through his hood's headset, Roscoe could tell she was speaking faster. "Bottles and funnels are in the back of the track. Just tell the driver to take a hike." The track driver, still watching soccer on his wristband screen, paid no attention to them. No one needed to pee.

They followed Jen, who wove back and forth, focused on her wristband screen. They were in a valley whose walls sloped upward for hundreds of meters, finally ending in a rough ridgeline to reveal the stars. The incline was gentle on the valley floor, but Roscoe still had to keep his eyes on the ground as Jen led them down the type of loose-rock terrain Roscoe had come to expect in this bare patch of Antarctica. When he stopped and raised his eyes, he stared in disbelief.

The rocky slope's base curved away from them in both directions, just like a lakeshore. But instead of water or ice, the slope gave way to a plain of gray hexagonal tiles, each roughly two meters across and separated from the others by neat, half-meter-wide bands of frost. The tiles extended under the shoreline rocks and out of sight; there had to be thousands of them. For a moment, Roscoe felt like one of those old explorers, gazing on a landscape no human eyes had seen before. Then he realized he *had* seen this shade of gray before: on Spigot's pier. He remembered that this was a reservoir. These tiles, locked together by ice, shielded the water from the freezing cold. As he looked along the shoreline curve where the loose rubble met the neat tiles, he noticed a few lumps on the tile plain's far edge. Boulders, maybe? He couldn't tell from this distance.

Jen stopped them about twenty meters from the tiles and looked up from her wrist. "All right, where I'm standing is the corner of our search grid. Line up this way"—she swung the orange bucket to her left—"and space out maybe a meter and a half apart. Face the reservoir."

As they complied, Roscoe remembered to take his CoCaff. The cold dulled, and his veins throbbed.

"Headlamps on!" Jen told them. Roscoe pinched the light sewn into the brim of his suit's hood. A circle of rocks at his feet turned grayish-brown.

"All right, we're gonna walk forward together slowly, one pace at a time. If you see anything out of the ordinary, shout for us to stop and I'll pass the gun down."

Roscoe looked at the rocks in his lamp beam. They all looked grayish-brown. He had no clue what a meteorite was supposed to look like. He swept his beam side to side, hemmed in by Hamza's and Darren's beams. Nothing.

They took one step forward, then another. After ten minutes, each of Roscoe's limbs felt several kilos heavier. *What was happening?* Was this compound withdrawal? The CoCaff? Some mix of the two?

He grit his teeth. *This is your shot off-world, dude. You're it. Focus!*

"Stop!" Jen called.

Roscoe looked to his right. Jen had reached the ice sheet's curved edge. Bare rock still lay before the rest of the cohort.

"Is the reservoir part of our grid?" Hamza asked, maintaining his gap between Jen and Roscoe.

Jen checked her wrist screen. "Yeah, the map says it is. Like I said, that's good for us." She and Hamza swept their lamp beams across the sea of tiles, then focused on the same spot. Hamza waved Roscoe over. Remembering what had happened the last time he'd walked on this kind of surface, Roscoe waddled to Hamza's side. The tiles didn't budge.

Then the sun seemed to switch back on.

Chapter 12

Kerguelen Island
3,000 miles southeast of Cape Town
July 1840

Twenty years after hearing about it from his father, Yule finally saw the "great arched rock" for himself.

After rounding the Cape of Good Hope, the ships dipped into a latitude that sailors called the Roaring Forties—a name spoken with a shudder. Here, winds blew for thousands of miles across the southern Atlantic and Indian Oceans, not slowed by any substantial landmass. These fierce gales pushed the *Erebus* forward at speeds Yule hadn't thought possible for such a small bomb vessel. Snow and sleet crusted the decks. Able seamen shoveled coal into the Sylvester's Patent Heating Apparatus, which circulated heated water throughout the ship. It kept the temperatures below decks tolerable, though hardly pleasant.

For all the hardships these winds brought, they still had Yule's gratitude when the twin stone pillars, linked by a natural arch high enough for the *Erebus* to sail beneath, came into view.

With much effort, the crew guided the ship past these columns into a long, narrow bay whose stone cliffs walled off most of the Roaring Forties. Cook had named this anchorage Christmas Harbor. Yule pitied the sailors forced to mark the holiday here among the moss and mist, with only the penguin squawks and elephant seal grunts for music.

Yule's thoughts quickly turned back to the treasure his father had promised—doubloons and escudos, just three days' walk south along the coast. He was so close.

Yet so far.

The Navy hadn't sent him here to seek treasure, but to measure magnetism and chart anchorages. Ross picked a clifftop rock shelf for their magnetic observatory. The canvas of their tent rippled endlessly in the wind; any dropped pen or notebook would be lost. But the dip needle always sat secure in its heavy brass housing, immune to the wind, heeding only the earth's magnetism. The needle's angle grew ever-steeper the closer they drew to the pole, as *Erebus*'s officers confirmed several times each day.

Tucker grumbled as he and Yule performed this task on the fortieth day of their anchorage. "Same angle it was yesterday, and the day before that. Does Ross really think it'll change if we stay here long enough?"

"We're also surveying the island," Yule reminded him, knowing the first master would need the same reminder again soon. "We need to chart the harbor, and McCormick still hasn't returned."

"I say, if he hasn't returned by tomorrow, leave 'im for the penguins. We've suffered here long enough."

Yule remained silent. They had surveyed the island's coast all around Christmas Harbor, but the cave with his treasure had escaped him. His hopes now rested on McCormick, who had ventured into the island's interior several days earlier. Apart from the frequent gunshots signaling the dispatch of penguins and seabirds, the crew had heard nothing from him.

Yule slept worse each night. Would McCormick return with the gold coins left for his family so many years ago? His only reprieves from that gnawing question were the magnetic observations—and the surveying.

The Admiralty had charged the expedition with surveying every land they encountered, no matter how desolate, and documenting it all in meticulous detail. Yule and Tucker spent their days hauling the ship's theodolite and measuring rope around the harbor, breaking the landscape into a grid of triangles, with angles and distances all recorded in the ship's angle-book for inclusion in Her Majesty's charts.

Yule brought the sextant too. The basalt cliffs ringing the island were flat enough in some places to support thin moss beds, their green a sharp contrast to the black rock. At Hooker's request, Yule measured their height above the harbor.

Over the past six months at sea, Yule had noticed Ross and Hooker growing closer. Ross had ceded part of his Great Cabin to Hooker, and the two would work there late into the night, each logging the expedition's progress in his own way. Hooker had even gained permission to leave the ship with McCormick still deep in the island's interior. Ross now allowed him to explore the shoreline of Christmas Harbor, so long as he stayed within sight of the ship.

After Yule and Tucker had completed their tasks, they began the long, winding walk back toward the bay and the warmth of the *Erebus*. Ross insisted that the theodolite, sextant, and dip needle be returned to the ship each night, so Yule carried the tools, focusing on the treacherous terrain, black ice, and thoughts of McCormick's return. But when the base of his theodolite struck an unseen object, Yule nearly dropped it.

"Oh!" cried a voice. Yule turned to see Hooker, bent over a rock, scraping lichens into a jar. "Watch where you're going. Could've lost a new species of lichen."

Yule kept his voice flat. "Just trying to protect Her Majesty's surveying equipment."

Hooker held the jar in front of Yule's and Tucker's faces. "Eight new species of lichen from this bay alone. The captain will be pleased."

"I'm sure he will be." Yule's mealtime conversations with Hooker had dwindled to these bland affirmations. They hadn't dampened the assistant surgeon's enthusiasm for describing fungi and entrails in minute detail while they ate. "We'll see you back at the ship." With that, Yule and Tucker resumed their journey.

"No sodden lichen is worth another day on this island," Tucker muttered when they were out of earshot. "God only knows how he's getting Ross to stay this long."

Yule had no answer as they reached the shore. Elephant seals, each with half a ton of blubber and the waterproof furs that lured sealers to these sour latitudes, watched motionless from the beach as the two men shoved their rowboat into the water and returned to the *Erebus.*

"Did you see Doctor McCormick?" Ross asked as soon as they were back on deck.

Yule shook his head. "Just Doctor Hooker."

Ross let slip a smile. "He will make the expedition proud on his own, I'm sure. We shall have to pray for Doctor McCormick's safe return tomorrow."

The following morning passed like every other Sunday for the past eight months: with the crew assembled on deck, listening to Ross's Divine Service. A drizzle soaked most of the men, but an able seaman held an umbrella over Ross and his King James Bible.

"Providence has brought us here, even if it may feel otherwise." Ross opened the Bible and turned to his favorite verse for new ports. "In Genesis it is written, 'Be fruitful and multiply, and fill the earth and subdue it, and have dominion over the fish of the sea and over the birds of the air and over every living thing that moves upon the Earth.' My friends, that is what we are doing here."

Ross closed the Bible. "We are extending the dominion of Her Majesty, the Church of England, and Christ Himself over every living thing on this island"—Yule wondered if the French and their Pope had been consulted on this consecration—"and on every island yet to come. We have yet to encounter savages in these lands, but if and when we do, let this instruction be in our minds and on our lips as we—"

A shout from below interrupted him. The crew rushed to the port side to see a drenched, filthy, and unshaven McCormick waving his arms as two able seamen rowed toward the *Erebus.* The rowboat was piled high with rocks and dead birds—more than Yule would have thought three men could carry. Yule scanned the pile in vain for any sign of a chest or bag of coins.

"Doctor McCormick!" Ross shouted as the rowboat reached the ship. "I see you made good use of your bird shot."

"Aye, C-C-aptain," McCormick called back through chattering teeth. "Th-three n-new sp-species at least."

"Wonderful. Well, we shall clean them as you warm yourself." Ross scanned the deck. Yule made the mistake of meeting his gaze. "Master Yule, get Doctor McCormick's saw and other tools. Prepare to start cleaning these birds."

McCormick climbed back aboard and weakly returned Ross's handshake. A few moments passed as the crew bustled about, beginning to haul in the excursion's proceeds. Just as Yule went below decks to retrieve McCormick's tools, he locked eyes with the shivering doctor, who shook his head.

Sitting just inside the prow on the lower deck—the space that served as the sick bay—Yule numbly plucked one feather at a time as McCormick, now wrapped in a blanket, recounted his adventure. "We found a cave in about the right spot. Saw what looked like a cairn. Went twenty paces in, seven to the left. But no sealskin bag, and no coins." He smiled faintly. "Well, almost none."

Yule watched as McCormick pulled a folded swatch of cloth from his satchel and opened it to reveal a single gold coin cradled in his palm, stamped with a flared cross—an escudo.

The surgeon rewrapped the coin and handed it to Yule. "Either the sea or another sailor got to the rest first."

"Th-thank you," Yule muttered. His hopes for comfort and advancement had rested in a bedtime story, and while the story had been true, Yule had been too late. A single escudo would never buy the lavish gift that the right minister would surely expect in exchange for a promotion.

Had there been more? Yule wondered. *Could McCormick have pocketed the rest?* The surgeon seemed to sense his doubt, and dispelled it with his next act. He handed Yule the still-full satchel. Every other bag had been opened in front of Yule. This one hadn't left his sight since McCormick's return. Now, it was Yule's to unpack.

"I placed the smallest bird specimens in this bag," McCormick said. "Do be gentle with them." He sipped his tea. "These specimens are the expedition's true treasure. They may have to wait until we reach Van

Dieman's Land or even England for proper mounting, but at least we can keep them from decay."

Yule took the birds' meat to the kitchen for supper, then carefully packed their skins and beaks into padded boxes and carried them to the hold, one by one. When the last of the seagulls had been stowed away, he examined the curious rocks McCormick had gathered. Some, the surgeon explained, were pieces of fossilized wood. Another, a dark, hexagonal block, had been chipped from what McCormick proudly called "a perfect specimen of columnar basalt."

Yule, too tired to pretend interest, shook his head. "There's no space for the stones. We'll need to toss some overboard."

"Overboard?" McCormick's Irish accent thickened. "Nonsense. There's room enough on this vessel. Go up to the Great Cabin, and ask Ross if he can spare some space. He's already given Hooker a workbench in there."

Yule walked the ship's length to the captain's cabin, where the sounds of laughter grew louder as he approached. His knock was answered with a cheerful, "Yes, come in."

He entered to find the captain and Hooker seated comfortably, chairs turned to face each other, glasses of wine in hand. Ross's desk was cluttered with charts and logbooks, while Hooker's was strewn with a microscope and a small collection of pressed plants—flowers, shrubs, and mosses.

"Hello, Yule," Hooker slurred, grinning. "We were just enjoying a glass of Madeira. Real Madeira, eh? Not that adulterated port you bought in Chatham." Ross shook his head and chuckled.

"Lovely," Yule said. He turned to Ross. "Captain, Doctor McCormick was wondering if he might store some of his geologic specimens here in the Great Cabin."

Ross scanned the cabin, then shook his head. "Send the good doctor my apologies, but this space has been reserved for botanical specimens." He paused, his eyes widening with a spark of inspiration. "Why don't you see if Doctor McCormick can store his specimens in your bunk?" he suggested. "Surely a second master like you is capable of finding space."

Yule's fist clenched. Another order, delivered with the intent to humiliate him, and one he couldn't refuse. Without the funds to grease the right palms for a promotion, he was unlikely to escape such slights anytime soon. "Aye, sir." He left the Great Cabin, the laughter resuming behind him.

Yule returned to McCormick and relayed the news. "The captain said there's no space for them in his cabin. I'm to find space in my bunk."

"None? I was just in there earlier today. There's space aplenty!"

"He's already promised it all to Hooker for botanical specimens."

McCormick sighed, resigned. "Very well. If you can find space in your bunk, I'd be most grateful."

As McCormick drank more tea and rubbed his toes, Yule carefully packed each stone in a box, marking them with dates and locations, and finding some solace in the knowledge that at least one other person on this ship held both Ross and Hooker in low esteem. Within an hour, he'd stowed almost every stone under his bunk. Only a tin pail filled with coal remained. Yule picked it up and began to search for a suitable crate, but McCormick stopped him.

"Leave that here for now."

"Why?"

"So I can show it to Ross and the other officers at dinner tonight. They'll be very interested to learn of coal on this island."

Just then, Hooker opened the sick bay door, belching. "Cap'n wants to know if you're well enough for supper."

"I most certainly am." McCormick set down his tea and blanket, rose to his feet, and placed a steadying hand on Hooker's shoulder. "The question is, are you?"

"I-I think I should like to take supper in my bunk tonight, sir, if it's all right with the Cap'n." Hooker said, stumbling slightly. "He invited me for Madeira without warning me of its effects."

McCormick nodded, then shot Yule a weary look as Hooker fumbled for the door.

McCormick had returned with more than just stones and birds. He had also brought back a strange, leafy variety of cabbage that grew wild in the island's interior. "First discovered here by Cook," he explained to Yule and the other officers packed into the ship's Great Cabin that evening as they ate the vegetable, stewed with the penguins and seals McCormick had shot. "No reports of scurvy for as long as their stores lasted." Yule thought it tasted like horseradish and had more flavor than anything he'd eaten in months.

"Well, we shall need to see if some can be cultivated in England, or on Van Dieman's Land perhaps," Ross said between bites. "You set some aside for Doctor Hooker, I trust?" As soon as McCormick nodded, Ross moved on to his next question. "What else did you find in your travels? Has the great geologist Robert McCormick found a gold or diamond mine for Her Majesty?"

McCormick stood, setting the tin pail down on the table. "No, Captain, there appear to be no gold or diamond deposits here. There is, however, something else that might interest you." He passed the pail over the plates to Ross, who clutched the pail greedily as he looked inside.

"Coal—how much?"

"I could only do a brief survey, but it's a sizeable deposit to be sure. These islands could be Her Majesty's southern coaling station."

"Coal?" Tucker asked, his voice slurred from drink. "Why go all the way down here for it?"

"Aye," Yule said. "Plenty of it in England and Wales."

"Lads, lads." Ross, not much older than either of them, looked down with a smile and shook his head. "Does the Navy only call at England and Wales?"

"No," they said together.

"Well, it will need coaling stations elsewhere, won't it?" Ross said. When both Yule and Tucker failed to nod, Ross gave the other officers a knowing look and chuckled. "Gentlemen, these junior officers may not be privy to the Admiralty's long-term plans." Yule felt his cheeks redden as Ross continued. "Soon, Her Majesty's ships will need coal for more than just heating. You must know that Stephenson's locomotive engine has been modified for use at sea."

Yule knew. He had seen these steam-powered vessels along England's coasts and rivers. One had even been used to tow the *Erebus* off a sandbar in the River Medway. He had also heard of another, the *Great Western*, now steaming between Bristol and New York, built to monstrous proportions to hold enough coal for the crossing.

"How can a ship of normal size carry sufficient coal to fire an engine over such great distances?" Yule asked, but he knew the answer even before Ross responded. A ship wouldn't need to carry coal for the entire journey. It could stop at British outposts along the way, refilling at coal stations. Yule let out a simple "oh" to show that he understood.

"Perhaps you could run one of these coaling stations yourself, eh, Master Yule?" Ross said with a smirk. "If this voyage's measurements prove successful, ships could use the compass needle alone to determine their coordinates. No more need for second masters to navigate. Yule senior had Trafalgar—perhaps Yule junior can have Christmas Harbor."

The table erupted with laughter. Yule forced himself to smile along, though he loathed every moment of it. Only McCormick showed any sympathy.

The expedition returned to the Roaring Forties, where the latitudes again earned their reputation.

The highest waves and fiercest winds of Yule's naval career bore *Erebus* east. For hours at a time, every hand would be needed to man the pumps, trim the sails, and keep the ships upright. Even without a crisis, snow, spray, and fog hid the *Terror* from view. Clouds overhead hid the sun and stars for days. Unable to fix their position from the heavens, Yule and Tucker raced between the compass and chip log, striving to reckon *Erebus*'s position as best they could from her speed and bearings. Yule gripped the rigging each time he tossed the chip log off the stern, fearing that his focus on the knotted cord that unspooled behind the ship would cause him to miss an oncoming wave and be swept overboard.

But finally, a day came when Yule went above-decks to find a calm breeze and waves well below the gunwale. By the time he reached the stern, he felt sure enough in his footing to not grip the rigging as he tossed the chip log behind the *Erebus.* He turned over the hourglass, then nearly dropped it when he heard a sudden shout, followed by a splash and the alarming cry: "Man overboard!"

Yule turned to see a swinging staysail and men racing toward the stern with a life buoy. "It's Roberts!" someone shouted—the boatswain who piped them to stations. A seaman threw the life buoy overboard, then turned to Yule. "Where's the captain?"

Yule scanned the deck for Ross's epaulets amid the seamen preparing to lower a boat. The Captain was nowhere to be seen. Feeling pressed to help in some way, Yule said, "Let me fetch him," and raced below deck, his scarf and Welsh wig still on.

He reached the Great Cabin. The door was closed. Barely registering the faint shuffling sounds from within, he pushed the door open, preparing to shout, "Captain, Roberts has fallen overboard!"

The words died in his throat as his eyes registered the scene before him. He froze, closed the door softly to avoid drawing notice, and ran.

Halfway up the ladder, safely out of view, Yule blinked hard, as if it would erase the image he'd just glimpsed: Ross pressed against Hooker, both in a stance and state of undress that could only mean one thing.

Sodomy.

Thoughts swirled within Yule as the deck rocked beneath him. He knew such acts happened in the Navy. Some sailors hanged for it; others escaped under the averted eyes of their superiors. But a captain caught in such an act—especially with a well-regarded assistant surgeon—would have a terrible stain on his career. Unless, of course, he kept it hidden.

Yule had heard of captains who used bribes or flattery to keep secrets. Ross, however, struck him as someone who would turn to threats instead. Yule wondered how far Ross might go to push him and his already-dim career prospects even lower—until a shout from above broke his thoughts.

"You there! Has Ross been found?"

Yule froze for a moment, then remembered that the scarf and Welsh wig concealed most of his face. Perhaps Ross knew someone had witnessed his indiscretion, but he didn't know who. Relief surged through Yule; the scarf's folds hid his satisfied smile as he called for Ross, who soon appeared on deck, unusually disheveled, to take charge of the rescue effort.

As Yule watched the able seamen lower rescue cutters, search *Erebus*'s track for Roberts, and return with nothing but the boatswain's cap, he smiled again behind the privacy of his scarf. Ross may have cost him his treasure, but now Yule had something far more valuable: knowledge he could use against his captain—whenever the chance might arise.

Chapter 13

Ross Sea Coast
Antarctica
June 2123

A bright, white light flared up behind the interns, overwhelming their headlamps and forcing Roscoe to squint. When it dimmed enough for him to look skyward, he saw a blazing ball of light, larger than the stars but smaller than the Moon, hissing toward the reservoir. Was this a delayed meteorite? He followed its track to a point several hundred meters above the tiles, where it burst into six smaller fragments, each one headed toward one of those strange objects at the far end of the reservoir.

In the sudden light, they no longer looked like boulders. One resembled a tanker track, about the size and shape of his father's truck, painted the same grayish-brown as the rocks, and mounted on triangular treads like all of Spigot's vehicles. The other five were human figures, each dressed in the same dusty brown, motionless for the half-second each flare took to reach them. Roscoe had no time to react, let alone seek cover—not that there was any around. The five figures and the tanker track vaporized instantly, leaving a sharp glow in Roscoe's retinas. When he blinked it away, he saw only one smoldering piece of wreckage.

"Woo-hoo!" Jen shouted, splitting Roscoe's eardrums through the headset. "We know right where one of our meteorites fell!"

Roscoe blinked again at the explosion site, certain he'd seen people and a vehicle there a moment ago. But what Jen said made so much sense—what other explanation could there be for something dropping from the sky? Besides, who would come out here cloaked in brown? Spigot's survival gear and vehicles were always bright red for visibility. He wondered if he might be having a hallucination of his own.

Whatever had been there was gone now—just ash and a few dimming embers. Roscoe watched Jen draw the XRF gun, then heard something beneath the tiles. Jen took three strides before he recognized the sound: rushing water.

Jen froze. The rushing sound grew louder, and a thin fog spread over the reservoir, accompanied by a noise like birdsong. The sound and haze began at the far end of the reservoir and moved steadily toward her. As it drew closer, Roscoe saw its cause: the ice mortar between the tiles was cracking, chirping like birds as it split apart, sending up fine sprays of ice crystals with each fracture.

To his right, Roscoe saw tiles dropping into darkness, forming a ledge that stretched across the reservoir. The edge of this new cliff was receding fast; as one row of tiles fell into the blackness, it seemed to pull down the next row. The rushing sound grew louder, and Roscoe realized the reservoir was emptying. As the water level dropped, so did the protective tiles. The tiles beneath Jen were about to give away, and she still hadn't moved.

Roscoe heard Hamza's voice in his ears. "Jen, get—" but his voice faltered as a new sound erupted: falling rocks. Both he and Roscoe turned toward the shoreline, where rubble around the reservoir started sliding, following the collapsing tiles into the void. Without hesitation, Roscoe and Hamza sprinted uphill, away from the crumbling tiles, rushing water, and tumbling debris. This time, Roscoe's feet didn't betray him, and he barely noticed the snowsuit as his legs carried him higher. Dust filled the air, and the roar of shifting rock and water drowned out all else. Roscoe didn't dare glance back until the noise began to subside.

After catching his breath, Roscoe followed Hamza back toward the reservoir. He looked along the rubble berm, now seeing that it lay atop

Vanda's true edge: a concrete shell a few yards behind the berm's former edge, its upper levels now laid bare. Looking down, Roscoe saw that the tiles had gone from solid flooring to loose floats bobbing on the water and knocking against the others. Some rested half-submerged, teetering on the edge of another tile. Each tile's thick sides were linked by rubbery belts, many of them now stretched into warped, awkward loops.

"There!"

Roscoe followed Hamza's pointed finger to where Jen lay, spread-eagled and face-down on a tile. She raised an arm. "I'm okay!" she called.

Roscoe's chest loosened, but only for a moment. Jen tried to get to her feet, and Hamza shouted down, "Jen, don't—"

Too late. The tile beneath her tilted, and Jen flailed as she tipped over. Roscoe saw a splash and two tiles angle upward, then nothing.

For several heartbeats, Roscoe stood in stunned silence, remembering the bite of Antarctic water. Then he saw one red sleeve poke between the tiles, followed by the other. Jen pulled herself onto the nearest tile and managed a short crawl before collapsing, her shivers visible even through the suit.

"Jen? Jen?" Hamza called. Roscoe turned and saw his friend holding his front collar up to his mouth like Trent had. Jen didn't reply. Her headset or microphone must have shorted out.

"We gotta get her out!" Hamza said to Roscoe. His headlamp beam shined straight into Roscoe's eyes and jolted him into focus. He had no idea how to rescue a hypothermic person on an unstable floating tile, and it seemed none of the other interns did either—except Hamza. He was already sprinting back to the track, shouting as he opened the door. Hamza's collar-mic only picked up the end of it: "—a cable, or rope, or something?"

"Yeah, there's a winch in the back," the driver said with no hint of urgency. "Lemme back up to the edge."

Hamza slammed the door and waved for Roscoe to follow him. "Let's see what we're looking at here."

Roscoe marveled at Hamza's calm focus—his own withdrawal headaches and grogginess had returned with a vengeance—as they reached the reservoir's edge. The tiles lay about ten meters below them, mounded rocks and gravel along the wall. Jen was sprawled on a tile another four or five meters from the new shoreline, with two tiles between her and the edge.

"All right, as rescues go, this one shouldn't be too hard," Hamza said, giving Roscoe no time to ask how he'd come to that conclusion. Hamza turned to the track, now backed up to the reservoir's edge, where the driver had opened the bed door to reveal a cable winch with a carabiner at the end. "Oh, this is easier than back home," Hamza muttered as he locked the carabiner onto the loop on the front of his suit.

He looked at Roscoe and the other interns. "I'm gonna rappel down there, hook her into the harness, and get her out. Our Naurutown had an old quarry—sometimes kids or dogs or druggies fell in, and we had to rescue them ourselves."

Hamza faced Roscoe. "Hold the cable steady, okay? I don't want to worry about losing my mic. If I need slack, I'll give two tugs. Once I've got her hooked in and brought to the edge, I'll give three tugs. That's your cue," he said, turning to the driver, "to pull her up—*slowly.* Got it?" The driver looked surprised by Hamza's newly commanding tone but nodded.

Hamza turned back to Roscoe. "Keep her from hitting the side. As soon as she's up, get her out of the suit and warmed up."

"What about you?" Roscoe asked.

"Oh yeah," Hamza chuckled faintly. "Just send the winch back down for me too."

Roscoe gripped the cable, digging his boots into the gravel as Hamza lowered himself over the edge. His movements brought to mind an old rock-climbing poster Roscoe had once seen in the Granite Gorge basement. The reservoir wall was steep—much steeper than the rubble berm—but not vertical like that climbing wall. Its angle reminded him of a different Granite Gorge poster, one advertising an ice ramp that guests could slide down on inner tubes.

Hamza reached the bottom and gave two tugs on the cable. "More slack," Roscoe called to the driver, who tapped his wristband screen to let the winch unspool. Loops of cable gathered at their feet as Roscoe held on, watching Hamza move across the nearest tile. Face-down and crab-walking, Hamza pushed himself forward, the tiles shifting and bobbing under his weight.

After what felt like an eternity, Hamza reached Jen. Roscoe watched as he gripped her suit's collar with one hand. He waited for Hamza to give the two-tug signal for the cable to start reeling them in. Instead, Hamza raised his other arm's elbow, pressed the heel of his hand against the tile, and pushed. They slid back the length of Hamza's arm. The tile beneath them bobbed but didn't tip. Hamza raised his free arm again and pushed against the tile. They slid a bit closer to shore. Each movement rocked the tiles beneath Hamza and Jen. No wonder Hamza was dragging Jen to shore this way rather than having the cable pull them back. A sharp jerk could tip one or both of them in.

I should have gone down there, Roscoe thought. *I'm lighter and shorter than Hamza.*

Just then, the tile under Hamza and Jen—the one closest to shore—bucked, sliding them both toward the black water's edge. Jen, still held by Hamza at the collar, slid feet-first into the water, stopping only when her legs were partially submerged again. Hamza's grip kept them from sinking further—for the moment.

Flat on his belly, Hamza looked over his shoulder. His suit's headset still worked. "Need some help!" Roscoe heard him say. "Can't lift her out on my own like this, and standing up's too risky!"

"Should we try to pull her or both of you out with the cable?" Kevin asked.

"Also too risky," Hamza said. "You pull on me, I could lose my grip on her. And the loop where I'd have to clip her suit onto the cable is at waist level. I try to reach that far, I could throw this thing off balance."

The interns and the driver looked at Roscoe, clearly reaching the same conclusion that he would be the least likely to tip the tiles. Roscoe didn't wait to be asked. Remembering the old poster for Granite Gorge's ice ramp—"snow-tubing," it had said—he sat at the edge of the slope, swung his legs over the side, touched his heels to the bare concrete, and pushed off. He didn't build much speed on the way down—a survival suit was no inner tube, after all—but he aimed for a tile by the wall and lifted his heels just before landing. For a terrifying instant, the tile wobbled beneath him, but he managed to grab an edge before it could tip.

Roscoe copied Hamza's sprawled-flat stance and moved on to the next tile, feeling it bob precariously under his weight. Jen, now submerged up to her waist, shivered violently. Hamza gripped the collar of her suit tightly, but Roscoe could see his hands slipping with each lurch of the unstable tile beneath them.

This close, Roscoe heard her teeth chattering. "H-help," she moaned.

"It's okay, Jen, we'll get you out," Roscoe reassured her.

But a new clattering sound pulled Roscoe's gaze down the reservoir, where another ripple spanned the sea of tiles. This time, the tiles weren't dropping; the belt loops connecting them were vanishing. Tiles that had come to rest at odd angles began flattening out as the belts tightened, pulling the tiles into a uniform surface. Once a stretch of tiles stilled, seams of ice reappeared, and water wicked between them, freezing into place to form a solid cap over the water below. With the reservoir level lowered, the tiles had shifted closer together, leaving a hand's breadth between them. In less than a minute, Roscoe guessed, the tiles around them would lock into place—and Jen would be wedged between them.

Hamza seemed to realize this danger at the same moment Roscoe did. "We gotta lift her out now!" he shouted, even more urgency in his voice.

They pulled, but the tile beneath them tilted ominously. Roscoe peered into the water, remembering how heavy his own waterlogged suit had felt. "We gotta unzip her from the suit," he told Hamza. "Trust me—same thing happened to me. I fell in off the pier, and the water made my suit heavy. That's what's happening here."

Hamza inspected her suit, then nodded. They pulled off her hood, unzipped her front, and eased her shivering arms out of the suit. The sound of snapping belts grew louder. Roscoe looked over to see the second tile from him sliding into place and getting locked in with a rising seam of ice. He heard a grinding noise that boded ill for anyone caught between the tiles.

"As soon as the next one slides into place, we pull her out and move her onto the tile!" Hamza instructed. Roscoe nodded, barely registering that they could still tip before the next tile moved. Then, Hamza yelled, "Now!" Roscoe heaved; the tile beneath him bobbed but didn't flip. He saw Jen's waist, then her knees, and finally her feet emerge; her Spigot coveralls clung dripping to her body. They swung her onto the tile just as it locked into place. Roscoe felt his own tile shift, sliding and grinding against the others. The one beside him did too, squeezing Jen's empty suit at the waist. An instant later, new ice embedded it into the tile floor.

Once the next row of tiles had locked, Roscoe rose, but he had no time to savor his steadier footing. He knew from experience that Jen must be deep in hypothermic shock by now. He and Hamza carried her back to the reservoir's wall. Hamza clipped the cable's carabiner onto his suit, gave three tugs on the cable, and bear-hugged Jen. Roscoe realized that, with Jen now out of her suit, the winch would have to pull both her and Hamza to safety. The cable tightened. He watched, holding his breath, as the pair rose up the slope and over the edge.

The cable with the carabiner was soon tossed back over the side. Roscoe clipped in, letting himself be pulled up the hillside, away from the reservoir that had almost become his grave.

He reached the top of the ledge and unclipped himself. Hamza, Darren, Kevin, and the driver were huddled together, leaning against the track's lee side. Roscoe had just joined them when someone tapped on one of the rear windows. Hamza opened the door, releasing a blast of warm air and revealing Ana, her outer suit unzipped, and Jen, now suitless and wrapped in emergency foil blankets. Jen's teeth chattered uncontrollably.

They climbed back into the track, with Hamza taking the front seat this time. The driver offered no congratulations. "I can take you back now, or stay here until you're done searching," he said matter-of-factly. "I'm just transportation. Only rule is you gotta stay together."

The new interns exchanged glances. Did the driver think they'd want to continue the search? That finding meteorites to get off-world was more important than getting Jen back alive? It was apparently a tough question; no one spoke for a good thirty seconds—until Hamza said, "We're going back. Jen needs to be warmed up."

The driver started up the engine. Roscoe looked out the window at the sea of tiles, now as still and lifeless as when they'd first arrived. "What happened out there?" he asked, leaning toward the driver. "Did they just empty the reservoir from under us?"

The driver shrugged. "No clue. Lots of weird shit happens down here. Stopped trying to wrap my head around it awhile ago. Figured I'd be stumped until I was a Resident." Roscoe noticed the driver touch a medallion around his neck, one almost hidden beneath his shirt collar.

As the track entered the tunnel, the wind's howl giving way to the hum of the motorized plate carrying them back to Spigot, no one spoke. But Jen murmured softly, her words slurred and uneven.

"S-s-sorry mom … m-m-maybe next year. Not an-n-n-other flood, right?"

Once they had returned to the Motor Pool and Jen had been bundled off to the infirmary, the cohort parted ways, still shaken by their brush with death and lost shots off-world. At least Jen wouldn't be able to make them attend the awards ceremony. Roscoe considered going to the infirmary himself—his head pounded from the CoCaff—but didn't want to risk a nurse asking questions about drug use. Instead, he spent the next few hours in his bunk until hunger drove him to the galley.

He'd been eating alone since Tuesday; archiving those letters by Hooker kept him busy until after most of the other interns had left. He'd only seen a few bleary-eyed older adults eating, likely indents who wouldn't want to sit with him. Once Roscoe took his T3 pill and stepped into the galley, he saw that tonight was no different—maybe the interns were still out hunting meteorites, or maybe they'd gone to commiserate at Newloon. Roscoe didn't recognize a familiar face until Hamza waved him over.

"Crazy day, eh?"

Roscoe nodded. "Great work saving Jen." If not for Hamza, she might have died. Roscoe thought back to Hamza's steady movements over the tiles, a feat he doubted he could have managed, even with his lighter build. All he managed to say was, "Really, really great work."

"No worries," Hamza replied. "Growing up in a Naurutown came in handy for once. Couldn't have done it without you."

They lined up for food, reading the menu board over the serving counter: HAPPY MIDWINTER TOURNAMENT DAY, INTERNS! ENJOY THE FRESHIES!

Roscoe didn't know what that meant until he saw the food: fresh grape tomatoes, celery stalks, and baby carrots. The only vegetables he'd had all week were canned, frozen, or pickled. Except for the pickled cabbage, it had all been pretty tasteless.

Roscoe mounded "freshies" on his plate next to his StemChicken. He and Hamza savored the vegetables' crunch and juice—and the chance to talk about something other than this morning.

"Wonder where they get these," Roscoe said between bites.

Hamza shrugged. "Doubt they fly 'em down from up north. Can't count on harvests anywhere anymore, and you'd need a break in the weather to get them down here before they go bad."

Roscoe remembered the sign for greenhouse tomatoes he'd seen during their Monday night trip. "Maybe they grow them at Newloon? I think I saw freshies for sale over there."

"That makes sense," Hamza said. "Jahnford really does need that place to keep us happy. We have to go over there ourselves to get drugs. Maybe they can buy vegetables there too."

"Know if there are any trips over there coming up soon?"

Hamza shook his head. "No, seems like it's crunch time for everyone. Apparently, Jahnford had some meeting with StarCross that went really well, and they're sending another delegation toward the end of the month. So all the branch heads want their numbers looking as good as possible before then."

Roscoe nodded. StarCross Silence kept him from sharing his run-in with Jahnford. Before Hanza could ask what he was doing Sunday, Roscoe asked, "How's your job going?"

Hamza's face lit up again, in a way Roscoe had never seen when anyone else—especially another compounder—talked about school or work. "It's going great!"

"Oh yeah, not too hard?"

"Nah. The subdrones are pretty easy to drive."

"What's your work called? Scanning?"

Hamza shook his head. "Nah, we call it flashing since we mostly use lidar to make the scans. Or the fiddlers and pickers called it flashing, and we just owned it."

"What do the fiddlers and pickers do?" Roscoe asked, feeling his gaze drifting.

"Fiddlers are the repair guys. Fix valves, patch the piping." Hamza paused to chew more celery. "Pickers use boring drones to dig channels under and through the ice." He tapped his wristband and pulled up a projection. "Here's what they've done so far."

A translucent blue diagram appeared between them. The top layer was labeled "GLACIER SURFACE" and the bottom "BEDROCK." Roscoe realized he was looking at a cross-section of the glacier. Several levels of tunnels had been bored just beneath the ice, resembling the intricate chambers of an anthill or an ancient underground tomb. Each level sloped gently toward a vertical shaft that ran through meters of still-solid ice to the bedrock, where another tunnel ran to a box labeled "INTAKE" before disappearing off-screen. The tunnel and vertical shaft were lined with concrete, metal, or another smooth material, but others had a rough, dimpled look.

"You don't line all of the ice?" Roscoe asked.

Hamza shook his head. "Sometimes we can get away with leaving it in place. Pickers and fiddlers only line it when we need extra support."

Roscoe pointed at glowing dots spaced along the tunnels. "What are those?"

"Heating elements," Hamza said. "They keep the water from refreezing. Melters plant those. Sometimes chunks form anyway, so they have to use incendiaries to break them up."

"Incendiaries?"

Hamza nodded. "Also to open new tunnels. Pickers are always giving them shit, saying boring drones could do a better job."

Roscoe leaned back from the floating cutaway. "All this to melt the glaciers?"

Hamza nodded. "Like I said earlier in the track, these glaciers are frozen solid to the bedrock. Most of the old glaciers up north, like Thwaites, had meltwater running through them and under them. But the ones around here actually need some help to melt. So we use incendiaries and heating elements in the tunnels and underneath." He pointed to the intake box, which had its own glowing dot.

"But why are we mining these glaciers for water, rather than those other ones?"

"These are more stable," Hamza said through a mouthful of carrot pulp. "We can control the melting. We scan the ice, and pickers and melters analyze the data, decide where to open up a channel. Whoever makes the better case for using incendiaries or boring drones gets to do the honors. Lately, the melters have been on a roll."

So they were living downstream from the world's coldest quarry—explosives and all. "You ever seen them set off one of those charges?"

"Once," Hamza said, then swallowed hard. "You know, the flash looked a hell of a lot like what we saw on the reservoir this morning."

Roscoe swallowed too. "You think that wasn't a meteorite?"

Hamza shrugged. "Who knows?" Roscoe almost asked if Hamza had seen people on the lake before the flash, but decided against it. If he'd been imagining things, he didn't want word getting around. Instead, he changed the topic. "You doing anything the rest of this weekend?"

Hamza shook his head. "Nah, probably just study protocols some more. Gotta know that stuff if you want to make melter."

"You want to be a melter?"

Hamza closed his eyes and nodded hard. "Hell yeah, man. Planting bombs inside a glacier? Tell me that's not a cool job."

"Cooler than living off-world?"

Hamza shrugged. "Maybe not, but when you grow up in a Naurutown, there's nowhere to go but up."

“Oh, uh, sorry.”

“No worries.” Sensing Roscoe’s unease, he steered the conversation elsewhere. “What about you? Doing anything this weekend?”

Shit. Now he’d stepped in it. Roscoe paused, but Hamza was another compounder, and their career tracks were so different that he probably wasn’t a threat. He decided to drop his guard. He told Hamza about Jahnford’s strange religion and his awkward run-in with the boss, adding a bit of a spin.

“… and he was looking me in the eye, his hand on my shoulder, between me and the elevator. I couldn’t say no. Anyway, once I got back, I learned what I’d gotten myself into.”

“Sure sounds like you couldn’t say no,” Hamza said. “Hey, he knows you now, so maybe it’ll help you move ahead here. If you want, I can go with you.”

“You’d do that for me?”

“For sure!”

“All right, well, I guess I’ll see you tomorrow morning.”

They headed back to their rooms. Roscoe decided to redeem the last of his three weekly showers before turning in. As he stood under the jet of hot water, his muscles finally started to loosen. Sure, he’d spend tomorrow getting lectured about the end of the world. But at least there’d be one other sane person there.

Chapter 14

The next morning, they met outside Spigot's auditorium at 9:45 a.m. Jen and Trent were already there.

The two head interns flanked the auditorium doors, their gaze straight ahead and their hands clasped at the waist. Aside from a red nose and a slightly paler complexion, Roscoe's cohort leader showed no signs of her recent brush with an icy death. Like Trent, Jen had traded her standard-issue jacket for a black shirt with a Roman collar and a small, circular lapel pin matching Jahnford's. She'd also swapped her usual ponytail for a bun and masked any sign that she knew Roscoe and Hamza behind a friendly, professional smile that could have been AI-approved.

"Welcome," she said in a tone that also likely passed some algorithm's scrutiny. "We're happy to have you here. Will you join us as guests or as tithing members?"

"Guests," Roscoe said, more forcefully than he intended. He wasn't about to let his few precious WECs fund a nuclear missile, however impossible the Revelators' goal might be.

Jen gave the slightest nod, her eyes narrowing as if to say, *Smart move.* Then the polished mask returned, along with her even tone. "Very well." She gestured toward the door. "Please stay to the right of the cordon."

Roscoe nodded and led Hamza past the bollard just inside the double doors. They took seats in a roped-off section of seats near the back.

The few others in their section wore either sharper, more tailored versions of Roscoe's and Hamza's jackets, or non-StarCross clothes entirely. They all looked too old to be interns—likely Executive Staff or Residents. In contrast, the parishioners heading into the tithing section looked scruffier, their clothes all StarCross-issued, and all more worn than his or Hamza's. Roscoe thought he saw the track driver from yesterday's tournament taking a seat a few rows ahead.

Roscoe now recognized the Revelators' crucifix-mushroom cloud-Antarctica symbol. He'd seen it on the pamphlet from Newloon, on the medallions worn by the preacher there and by the track driver, and on the lapel pins worn by Jahnford, Trent, and Jen. Now, it was projected nearly two stories high at the front of the auditorium—but not for long.

A few minutes after Roscoe and Hamza took their seats, the screen went dark. A low tone sounded, the lights dimmed, and the crowd hushed.

With the lights still out, Jahnford's voice broke the silence.

"Lord Jesus, our world is fallen beyond repair. Bring the Cleansing Fire."

"Bring the Cleansing Fire," the crowd replied.

"Lord Jesus, we have gathered on your sacred ground and are prepared to face your judgment. Bring the Cleansing Fire."

"Bring the Cleansing Fire."

Jahnford's voice rose. "Lord Jesus, we look forward to meeting you in your glory and helping you usher in a new age. Bring the Cleansing Fire!"

"Bring the Cleansing Fire!"

The auditorium lights came up, revealing a standing audience. Roscoe and Hamza quickly rose to their feet. At the center of the stage stood an altar, while Jahnford had taken his place at the podium on the left. He wore a collar and pin identical to the ones Jen and Trent—now positioned on opposite sides of him—also wore.

Roscoe's mind jumped from the Revelators' symbol to the question of what the hell Jen was doing here. He remembered her brushing off Jahnford's church during their Newloon trip, joking that it made him "ban fun." Yet here she was, helping him officiate. Maybe she thought playing along would give her an inside track to the Executive Service.

Jahnford spoke. "Good morning, friends. Thank you for your fellowship as we await the joyful day when we shall cleanse the world of nonbelievers and usher in a new heaven and a new earth. Please be seated."

The crowd took their seats as Jahnford stepped aside, allowing for Jen to step forward. "A reading from the Wilkes Expedition log," she announced. She recited what sounded like an excerpt from one of the sailing logs Roscoe had helped archive—details about icebergs and penguins. After a few paragraphs, she stepped back.

Jahnford returned to the altar, reached underneath, and pulled out a clear, book-sized rectangle, holding it high over his head. At first, Roscoe thought it was glass—until he saw a drop of water fall from a lower corner. Ice. The altar must have a freezer built into it.

"The Sacred Revelation," Jahnford said.

"Lost on the ice, but forever in our hearts," the congregants replied.

Still holding the shard aloft, Jahnford closed his eyes. "Silence and darkness surrounded me. I thought I was alone, but then I heard His voice."

The whole congregation answered in unison. "Be not afraid. Gather your people, whom I have tasked with kindling the Cleansing Fire."

"I wondered what this meant," Jahnford said. "Then a figure pointed toward the South Pole. From there, I saw an arc of flame shoot north, saw a brilliant blaze on the horizon, heard the screams from cities turning to ash. Then"—he closed his eyes, smiled, and paused long enough for a gasp—"I learned His vision was to establish a new heaven and a new earth, in this one place unsullied by the old."

As Jahnford's words filled the room, Roscoe's mind wandered, his gaze shifting across the indents, all of whom stood ramrod-straight—clearly spellbound. Jen's and Trent's expressions, however, remained unreadable. *Did they really believe this?* Between their alter egos, the strange ritual, and the even stranger vision, Roscoe couldn't shake the feeling that he'd entered a different world.

Slowly, Jahnford lowered the ice shard, holding it out over the altar, and opened his eyes. "The ice of this Revelation has been lost."

"But He has written it on our hearts until the Cleansing Fire," the crowd repeated.

With that, Jahnford slammed the ice shard down onto the altar. Fragments scattered across the stage.

Roscoe's thoughts spun as Jen and Trent sat down, and Jahnford returned to the podium.

"Friends," Jahnford began, "today's reading from the Wilkes Expedition log reminds us that for centuries, God has been preparing this land as a refuge for His true followers—for us." He gave the crowd a knowing smile reserved for family reunions in sappy old movies. "He saved me in my hour of greatest peril so that I might deliver this message. Perhaps you have felt His presence as well."

Roscoe noticed a few nods and murmurs from the scruffier attendees in the tithing section, but none in the guest section.

"He doesn't choose anyone to come down here," Jahnford continued. "No, no. Then and now, He's only picked the strongest, hardiest specimens of humanity to populate His promised land. The first explorers journeyed here without alcohol, without drugs, without psychoactive compounds." Roscoe caught the flicker of a smirk on Jen's face and remembered her comment about Shackleton using CoCaffs.

"But some"—Jahnford's eyes swept toward the guest section, glaring hard—"have lower standards. Some see fit to defile this sacred land with these vices."

He turned back to the podium and gestured toward the tithing section. "But we are protected. For we are the hands of Christ as we prepare the nuclear missile that He will use to bring about the Cleansing Fire."

Shouts erupted from the Tithers. "Yes!" "Hallelujah!" "Bring it on!"

Jahnford's smile widened. "We are making great progress on our missile. And I have reason to think that soon, we shall have its warhead. Yes indeed. With God's grace, a nuclear bomb will soon reach Antarctic soil."

The murmurs in the Guest section turned to alarmed whispers. "What?" "Do you have any idea?" But these were drowned out by more cheers from the Tithers.

When the noise finally settled down, Jahnford spoke again. "I cannot share more at present, lest evildoers try to thwart us. Suffice it to say that we are closer than ever to making today's reading reality."

The Tithers gave a new wave of cheers. Jahnford let it reach a peak, then raised a hand. "Now, let us show God and one another that we are preparing ourselves for the glorious day of the Cleansing Fire."

Soft organ notes floated from the speakers. Row by row, the Tithers stood and formed two lines down the center aisle. Each one tapped their wristband to either Jen's or Trent's, who smiled and whispered "thanks." Roscoe saw WEC figures changing on the hovering screens. Then, each Tither stepped forward, took a small, seed-like object from Jahnford, and returned to their seats, holding it upright between both hands.

When the last of them had sat down, Jahnford raised one of the objects high. "Jesus, we take this iodine as a sign of our faith in your plans, and to protect ourselves from the radiation that the next weapon you send here may emit."

Wait, Roscoe thought, *Jesus can't protect you?*

Jahnford swallowed his pill, and Jen, Trent, and the rest of the Tithers followed suit.

"Now with one voice, let us profess our faith and joyful anticipation for the Cleansing Fire."

Jahnford led them in a hymn that, as best Roscoe could tell, re-told his so-called Revelation. The final line praised the "Final Conflagration" as Jahnford strode down the aisle, followed by Jen, Trent, and the rest of the Tithers.

At the exit, Jahnford greeted the paying attendees as they filed out. Roscoe caught a second of eye contact between handshakes. Spigot's CEO smiled.

Roscoe and Hamza headed to the galley for an early lunch. Roscoe popped his T3 pill for access, wondering why it hadn't made the Revelators' list of forbidden fruit.

No real, fresh fruit—or vegetables—appeared on the menu. They got their usual bland quinoa and took seats at the end of a table.

Hamza stopped chewing to speak first. "That was weird. So apparently they hate us."

Roscoe nodded, still trying to parse this strange religion. "And they want a nuke ... and they're going to use it to start a war ... and they think that will bring Jesus back."

"Sounds like it." Hamza stirred his quinoa. "And he thinks he's close to getting one. Wonder how? You think he's buying one with those tithes?"

Roscoe remembered his StarCross History and Operations class from Granite Gorge. Ever since StarCross rolled out its Updated Terms of Service, governments had to take their nukes off high alert to receive RECs and WECs. But they weren't required to give them up. Maybe Jahnford had found one willing to sell.

Then, Roscoe thought back to the screen in Jahnford's office—thousands of WECs, millions of liters—traded for submarines and surveillance equipment. How much would a nuclear weapon fetch? Even StarCross might not have enough water to offer. And those paltry tithes wouldn't cover it.

Roscoe shook his head. "Your guess is as good as mine. Sounded like he caught those Residents and Executive Staff by surprise too." He sipped his coffee, curiosity simmering. "Wonder what they were doing there."

"Probably same reason you were there. Same reason Jen and Trent were there," Hamza said. "Keep tabs on the boss, stay on his good side. Looks like Jen's doing a good job." He studied Roscoe for a moment, then grinned. "You gonna try to make a move?"

Roscoe shook his head. "I feel like we both blew our chance after that trip to Newloon. Besides, we're both compounders. If Jen wants to get anywhere, she'll keep us at arm's length."

"Eh, but we did save her life yesterday. And we're going to church. Maybe that redeems us in her eyes."

Roscoe finished his quinoa and felt thirsty for a beer before another week of work. "You want to go back to Newloon?"

"Can we? Like, on our own? We're just new interns."

Roscoe felt himself smile. "Let's find out."

Twenty minutes later, they stood in front of the Motor Pool counter. Hamza turned to Roscoe and lowered his voice. "This was your idea. You make the first move."

Roscoe stepped forward, trying to remember what Jen had said during their first trip. "Hi, we're interns going on a training drive."

The StarCross Security agent glanced up from his screen. "Route?"

Just in time, Roscoe remembered, "Lake Bonney and back. We should be back here by midnight."

"All right. Suits are in the first two lockers on the right. I'll have Motor Pool send a track up. All the beacons will have that route in them."

"Thanks." Hamza and Roscoe headed to their lockers and suited up, unable to believe their luck. Jen was right—they really didn't care.

A Motor Pool guy pulled up in a track. "You guys can drive, right?"

"Yeah, my academy in Hobart taught four-by-four driving," Hamza answered. "They focused on preparing us for StarCross's moon base."

The guy grunted. "Well, that's one skill that transfers." He jumped out, leaving the keys in the ignition. "Bring it back by midnight. Make sure you adjust everything before putting it in Drive."

Roscoe got into the passenger side, still trying to square the fire-and-brimstone Grei Jahnford he'd just seen with the one who let two twentysomethings take a track to a red-light zone, no questions asked.

Hamza seemed to be thinking the same thing. "Grei must really want us happy."

"I guess so. Maybe he knows most people need to drink to forget what they're doing for him."

This time, they kept the windows up when they drove out of the tunnel. The air was still cold and dry, but the track's heater and humidifier took the edge off. The clear weather offered Roscoe his best look yet at the surface, still shrouded in the six-month night. The southern lights had faded, but the stars were burning bright, and Roscoe couldn't look away from the Milky Way arcing overhead.

Somehow, Hamza managed to keep his eyes on the road. "What do you think Jahnford was talking about at church, that plan he mentioned?"

"No idea." Roscoe decided to drop his StarCross Silence. "I know he was meeting with some higher-ups from StarCross. I brought him that map so he could have some decoration. You don't think StarCross would get him a nuke, do you?"

"Maybe," Hamza replied. "I heard that when they blasted out the deepwater port down here, the U.S. Navy insisted on doing all the work themselves. They made Eatonson and his team wait in New Zealand until they were done."

"Well, I don't think any country's govellers have much leverage over StarCross now."

"True that."

Hamza wasn't flooring the track, but he seemed to be going faster than Jen or Chip had; Roscoe watched a few route-marking signal flags bend in its slipstream, then saw a red glimmer in the distance—another vehicle's taillights.

"You gonna slow down here?" Roscoe asked as they climbed a gentle slope and closed in on the taillights.

Hamza shook his head, grinning. "Nah, I got this." He eased the track into the left side of the road. There was no oncoming traffic in sight, so he tapped the accelerator. The track might not have been built for racing, but it gained on the other one, which was towing some kind of trailer.

They were side by side with the other track when lights from an oncoming track peeked over the crest of the hill. They were on a collision course. At this speed, they wouldn't get hurt, but they'd certainly return with damage they couldn't explain away.

"Pull back!" Roscoe shouted. "Get behind the slow one!" Their hood was clear of the slow track now, but the oncoming track was closing in fast. Its headlights flashed, and its air horn blared.

"Too late now! We're not gonna make it!" Roscoe's eyes darted between the passenger window and the windshield: their cab was clear of the slow track; the oncoming headlights glared like a predator's eyes; the rear bumper was just past the slow tracker; then the headlights blotted out everything else.

Roscoe squeezed his eyes shut and braced himself in his seat.

He felt the track swerve to the right and heard a soft *crunch*, but soon, the hum of the vehicle climbing uphill told him they were still moving. Roscoe opened his eyes to find the road empty in front of them. He peeked out the back window, catching sight of the two other tracks: the oncoming one and the one they passed, both at a standstill. They had both decided to stop and let Hamza and Roscoe pass. As they cleared the hill, the other tracks disappeared from view.

Roscoe sank back into his seat. "What the *fuck* was that?"

"I'm sorry, man," Hamza gasped. "We used to race four-by-four's all around our academy campus. I thought I knew what I was doing. Didn't realize how much slower these things are to accelerate."

"Damn right you didn't. Hope you learned now, after almost crashing us."

"I'm really sorry, man. When we get to Newloon, the first round is on me."

"Just drive."

Roscoe leaned against the window, letting the cold numb his panic and remaining quiet, not wanting to rattle Hamza's confidence further—he was their ride home, after all. When they passed under the RIP SMALLS banner and Hamza asked, "Do you know who that is? Jen said she didn't," Roscoe only shrugged. Hamza kept their speed at a crawl.

When they finally reached Newloon, even more tracks than last time were parked out front—some Spigot red, others olive green or black, with cracked windshields and dented bumpers. They threaded the throng at Skua Central, passing the stores and the submarine port without a word. He saw the same guy handing out Revelator pamphlets. This time, Roscoe leaned away.

His thirst for alcohol was getting dire when they reached the row of bars at Wit's End. Hamza veered toward Gallagher's, but Roscoe pulled him away. "I know a different place."

Shiduri's was just as quiet as before. The bartender locked eyes with Roscoe from across the room. "Back so soon?" she asked when they reached the bar. "Who's this you brought with you?"

"This is Hamza, a friend from Spigot." Roscoe managed a smile, his first since their near-miss, and slapped Hamza on the back. "Our drinks are on him tonight."

"Sounds good. Hon, tap your wrist to open a tab." Hamza complied, his eyes scanning the menu for the prices listed in both WECs and RECs. The thrill of revenge lifted Roscoe's spirits as he watched Hamza calculate how much of his WEC stipend he'd be sacrificing, and possibly how many showers he'd have to pawn off. They ordered seal-blubber nachos and, no longer hobbled by knockoff compound, beers.

After settling in, Roscoe took a swig of his frothy porter, Neptune's Bellows. He spotted Chip down the bar and walked over, catching the scientist already a few drinks into the evening.

"Hey man," Chip said, clearly in a better mood than the last time they'd met. "How's it going? Who's that with you?"

"That's my friend, Hamza," Roscoe said, waving Hamza over. "Hamza, this is Chip. He's a scientist at McMurdo. We met during the last trip over here."

Before Chip could divulge more about their drive together or Hamza could realize Roscoe had lied about riding with a Spigot guy, Roscoe asked, "What brings you here?"

"I'm celebrating," Chip answered, pausing to take another gulp of beer, "because I finally found a sub operator willing to collect some data for me."

"That's great! Who?" Roscoe asked.

"Group called Griqua Tierra. Just started running a shipping sub that docks in Newloon."

Roscoe raised an eyebrow. "Where are they based?"

Chip shrugged. "Somewhere in Patagonia, but I didn't push for details. They made me agree to switch off the probe when they get within a hundred klicks of their fjord's entrance. Fine by me." Another swig. "That'll still get me data from across the Ross Sea and a good chunk of the Southern Ocean."

Roscoe had heard about the wildcat water-mining settlements and even a white ethnostate called New Swabia on the Antarctic Peninsula, but Griqua Tierra was new to him. "So they're hidden away in a Patagonian fjord. Are they part of StarCross?"

The scientist shook his head. "Nah, started back in the seventies. A few research and cargo ships took shelter from a storm and decided to stay."

Hamza leaned in, looking at Chip. "Chile's govellers and StarCross don't mind?"

"Apparently not. Either no one's noticed, or they've found some way to buy off anyone who might care."

Curious, Roscoe pressed further. "What do they do there?"

Chip smirked, wagging a finger just like he had during their first drive. "What'd I tell you about nosy questions, Roscoe?" He paused, rubbed his eyes, and sighed. "Ah, what the hell, they seemed fine with sharing the basics. They've got some cooperative worker-owned businesses. Used to be all about sustainable fishing and farming. Then, they got a couple of subs and started trading. Now they're moving into higher-tech stuff, like resilient crops and agricultural robots. They thought my data might be useful, so they were happy to help."

"Wait—they're building high-tech businesses on Earth? Not even in Antarctica?"

"Crazy, I know. Even if StarCross thinks the future's in space, some people still believe in staying down here." Chip took another sip of beer. "Can I have one of those nachos? I don't know which vat Shid gets her blubber from, but it's the best I've found."

Roscoe passed him the basket before Hamza could object, figuring it was the least he could do for Chip giving him a free ride the other night. "When did their sub leave?"

"Sailed about an hour ago. I was down on the docks to bolt on the probe and make sure it worked." He chuckled. "They didn't try to chuck me in the water, so I'd say we're off to a pretty good start."

"How long will the voyage last?"

"Should be a week or so there, then about another week back."

"Think the probe'll stay working?"

"Hope so," Chip said. "A lot of these subs vary their speed so that the StarBuoys can't lock on to their acoustic signature. Don't know how that'll affect things." He shrugged. "Guess we'll find out. Whole point of a trial run."

Hamza leaned in again. "So, you're a scientist?"

"Yep."

"What field?"

"Oceanographer-slash-geologist-slash-wherever-I-can-find-funding-ist."

Chip's cynicism rolled off Hamza, who flashed one of his high-wattage grins. "Cool. I'm learning how to pilot subdrones at Spigot. It's amazing stuff."

"Enjoy it while it lasts," Chip said. "They assign you each a drone?"

"Yeah, but why?" Hamza's grin wavered.

Chip nodded knowingly. "Means they want to track you. Helps the AI learn each pilot's quirks. You're training those drones to map the seafloor and find minerals. One day, the AI will know enough to make hiring pilots like you pointless. StarCross will get more WECs and RECs out of it without you."

The last trace of Hamza's smile had vanished. "But—I'm an intern. I'm guaranteed residency and a career-track position after two years of service."

Chip shrugged. "Oh, they won't kick you out, at least not as long as Jahnford cares about StarCross rules. But as tech advances, they'll shift more over to machines wherever it's efficient, and give you work where humans still have an edge—cleaning toilets, errand-running for Spigot bigwigs, stuff like that."

"'Fraid he's right." Shiduri said, looking up from the glass she was rinsing. "Can always tell over here when Spigot's starting to automate some sector. Interns spend more of their WECs here, and, after a few months, they switch to places that sell heavier-duty stuff." She nodded toward the red-lit hallway. "After that, I only see 'em when their bosses need someone to smuggle in booze for a secret party. Just sent a track back with a load of scotch about an hour ago."

Roscoe thought back to their near miss with the other track. *Maybe that was one of them*, he thought. *Another intern or ex-intern.*

"Another option," Chip said, "is to quit the internship program and switch to StarCross Security. The Equation always favors humans for cracking heads. And you can get stationed off-world." He finished his beer, grimacing as he set the glass a bit too firmly on the countertop. "Or you could work over here. There are some legit jobs. The research stations that are left still send people over here for tech support."

Hamza stared into his empty beer glass. "Guess I'll have to go for that program."

"That thing where they promise to make you an exec, send you off-world?" Shiduri set down her glass. "Wouldn't if I were you. Got a damn high washout rate."

"Washout rate?" Hamza and Roscoe asked together.

"Share of interns who make the cut is probably in the single digits. And if you drop out, you're indent-level—with no housing for the fam."

Chip had told Roscoe this during their first drive. Hamza still sounded skeptical. "And you know this how?"

Shiduri shrugged. "Same way I know about anything else at Spigot," she said. "People come here to drink it off—at least until they want something stronger."

Shiduri looked at Roscoe's and Hamza's crestfallen faces with pursed lips. "Didn't mean to bum you guys out. Just wanted to level with you. And remember, Chip started it." The scientist's gaze shifted from his empty glass to a nearby menu. Roscoe watched him sway slightly, wondering if he'd try to drive anywhere tonight.

"Guess I did, sorry guys," he said, stumbling to his feet before slapping Hamza on the back. "Now that I'm getting data, I might need a quant person to help analyze it. If you ever want some under-the-table work as my RA, just lemme know. Might have to pay you with McMurdo-brewed vodka, but you can probably barter that somewhere around here."

Chip plunged a hand into one of his parka's many pockets, pulled out a worn-looking wristband, and handed it to Hamza. "Call me on that one. Number's loaded in there. Won't do much besides make calls, but at least you don't have to worry about StarCross knowing you're picking up work on the side. If I don't pick up when you call, just leave me a voicemail." Roscoe had just gotten over Hamza's driving mishap. Now, he felt sour again—this time, with envy.

Chip stood to leave before Hamza could thank him. "Gimme your wrist, Shid, let me settle up." Shiduri tapped her wrist to Chip's. "Think I'm gonna crash in Ye Olde Igloo Motel tonight," he grumbled.

As Chip left, Shiduri looked at Roscoe and Hamza, now the last two patrons at the bar. The few other customers kept to the sides. "You guys have a way back?" she asked.

Roscoe nodded. "We got our own track."

"Well, you might wanna get going. Weather sensors say a storm's coming in."

Hamza almost jumped to his feet, tense as he tapped his wrist to Shiduri's and prepared for another hour at the wheel. They were about to head out when a *bang,* then crashes and screams erupted from the shipping container hallway. Roscoe heard panicked cries in several languages, then one in English:

"Run! Fire!"

Shiduri reached to the back wall and flicked a switch, slamming the pub's double doors shut. A two-meter deadbolt slid into place across them.

"Everyone, follow me out the back!" Shiduri ordered, opening the gate at one end of the bar. Roscoe, Hamza, Chip, and the other patrons followed her through the kitchen and through another door into a rough rectangle of a courtyard enclosed by stacked shipping containers. In one three-high stack, Roscoe saw that the bottom container glowed orange with fire. Its interior pounded.

"I knew this would happen," Shiduri said from under her parka's hood. "Mini-meth lab in that one. They all go up sooner or later. The last time one blew up, I invested in those fireproof doors."

"Hey, Shid, we gotta get out of here!" Hamza yelled through his mask. "Pretty soon that container'll melt and the other two could fall on us."

"It'll be out in a minute, just watch," Shiduri said calmly.

Sure enough, the orange spot was already shrinking. They watched in silence for another minute. The pounding from the inside eased, then stopped. Shiduri turned to lead them back inside.

"Wait, it's out?" Roscoe asked.

"Should be," Shiduri explained. "Unspoken rule is that if you're going to add a box to this place, you've gotta put airtight doors on both ends and give 'em deadbolts on both sides. People who try to cheat on that don't last long."

Noticing Roscoe's confusion, Hamza explained, "If you close those doors, you cut off the air. The fire's isolated and goes out."

"Bingo. Works pretty well, as long as there's no ammo or fertilizer inside. They'll give it a couple of hours to cool before they open it back up. Mark my words, there'll be a new joint in there by next week."

For a moment, Roscoe admired the simple genius of this ad hoc construction system. Then, in a horrible instant, he realized what had made the pounding noise. "Wait—someone was in there, trying to get out, and they locked them in?"

Shiduri nodded, pressing her lips together. "Bet it was Earnest. Had the fish-and-chips joint next door—he'd do everything he could to save that place. But that's true of most everyone down here. They've tried everywhere else and failed. By the time they reach this place, they'd pick their corner of a box over someone else's skin. Can't say I blame 'em."

They reentered the bar, where the other patrons had already returned to their seats and drinks. Shiduri flipped the switch, releasing the deadbolt as the doors sprang back open.

Roscoe managed not to ask what Shiduri herself would pick—someone else or her own business. He didn't want to know the answer.

"Guess it's time to go before that storm hits, right, Hamza?"

"Yeah. Thanks, Shiduri."

"Don't mention it." She gave them both a sad smile.

They drove back in silence, again at a crawl. Roscoe wouldn't blame another track for wanting to pass them.

All the way back, Roscoe looked for the two tracks they nearly hit, but only the vast gravel plain stretched out before them, only stopped by a wrinkled wall of ice in the distance.

It sure would've hurt to hit that, Roscoe thought.

Chapter 15

Hobart
Van Dieman's Land
August 1840

Neither Ross nor Hooker let slip anything about their act—not during Roberts's memorial service, not over supper in the following nights, not during the days of storms and heavy seas, and not even when the Roaring Forties finally delivered the *Erebus* and *Terror* to their next port of call: Hobart.

As the ships entered the harbor, Yule saw wooded, rounded hills cradling a bustling town. Ships packed every dock in sight; Yule had not expected so many vessels would greet them at this gateway to the southern latitudes, the last port before sailors put God and the law behind them. The *Erebus* and *Terror* carefully picked their way between net-draped fishing vessels, whalers belching smoke, and merchantmen trying to outrace their competitors on the Roaring Forties. Yule recognized one vessel, an old warship with her gunports bolted shut. It had been repurposed for another use: carrying convicts. He watched a line of men in dull-blue uniforms, manacled at the ankle, step off the ship onto the dock, walled off by a line of guards.

Yule had heard stories from English sailors who had served aboard these "transportation" ships that brought thieves, murderers, and vagrants to Australia's penal colonies. Having seen Ross and Hooker's liaison, one tale came to Yule's mind.

"Start to bugger each other as soon as we slip away from dock," a sailor had said at a pub in Chatham after several pints. "Don't even bother to hide after a few weeks."

"And the cap'n allows it?" someone asked, aghast.

"Aye, keeps 'em distracted," the sailor replied, and everyone around him laughed to learn of convicts' strange freedom. They could sodomize each other in the open, but free seamen risked death if they got caught in this act. Perhaps a captain of the Royal Navy did too, Yule mused, as the *Erebus* dropped anchor.

A shout drew his attention to the gunwale. "Welcome, Captain Ross!" Yule looked down to see a round, middle-aged man standing in a rowboat, using a walking stick to steady himself against the boat's rocking. A young woman sat in the boat. Yule wondered if she was the man's daughter.

"Governor and Lady Franklin!" Ross shouted back. "Thank you for greeting us in person!"

Yule blinked. *This* was Sir John Franklin? Yule's father had often mentioned Franklin in the same breath as Nelson, as another British hero for his sons. The governor had led three expeditions to chart rivers in the Canadian Arctic, with one reaching the brink of starvation and leaving Franklin known as "the man who ate his boots." He was clearly well-fed now, and enjoying the company of a wife half his age. The stout governor steadied himself with effort while Lady Franklin remained seated.

"Whalers brought word of your approach weeks ago," Franklin called. "Naturally, we prepared some hospitality on shore."

They had indeed. The able seamen were granted shore leave that night and scattered into Hobart's pubs and bordellos. Meanwhile, the officers were invited—or in the eyes of some, condemned—to dinner at the Governor's House.

"The South Magnetic Pole!" Franklin exclaimed when they had seated. "You know we had some Yankees here a few months back, also reconnoitering the southern latitudes. Some of them believed they would find a hole leading into the center of the Earth. Holes in the Poles!" The officers laughed.

Ross, ready with his wit, grinned, "Well, that superstition should keep them from getting too close."

As the officers around him laughed again, Franklin gulped down more of his wine. A servant in a dull-blue dress—one that matched the male convicts' uniforms—rushed forward to refill his glass. Yule guessed she was one of the female prisoners who had been assigned to the Governor's House.

"Indeed." The governor belched. "Still, they returned from their first summer in the South saying they had seen a coastline."

Ross's smile vanished. "A coastline?"

The governor nodded, also serious now. "At sixty-five degrees south. They said it had the look of a whole continent. French chap named d'Urville was also leading a few ships down there last summer. Said he found a wall of ice that looked like it rested on land. They followed it south, trying to find the pole."

The officers fell silent, leaving Ross to ask more. "And ... and how far south did they get?"

"Dunno, but not past seventy-five degrees south." Yule saw Ross relax, only to tense again when Franklin added, "D'Urville was dead-set on reaching the magnetic pole first. Promised every man a hundred francs if they made it to seventy-five south, and more for every degree of latitude after."

Yule liked this promise of prize money for scientific achievements rather than for martial conquests, but Ross's face only showed disgust. "And yet they turned back?"

Franklin nodded again. "Too cold. Ships couldn't break through the ice. And scurvy started picking the men off."

"How many?" McCormick asked.

"Wouldn't say. But for a fleet that size, seemed about a dozen men short. Would've been more if they'd spent much longer at sea."

Ross spoke with a tone Yule had only heard when wives asked about husbands missing at sea. "Did they say anything else about the seas to the south?"

Franklin shook his head. "All I can say is that none were too eager to leave port again. When it came time to go, they were falling over one another to find good luck charms. Midwives made a pretty penny selling them satchels filled with what they said was caul."

The officers finally laughed, Yule with them, at the mention of the old wives' tale that carrying caul could save a sailor from drowning. Ross also chuckled, voice slack again. "British sailors are not so easily spooked by the Roaring Forties."

"Hmm," Franklin said at last. "I wouldn't be so sure. Man by the name of Aspley arrived here a few months ago. Thinks there's money to be made selling life insurance to crewmen on the sealing and whaling ships."

The officers laughed again. Yule knew that several of the older officers, the ones with wives and children, insured their lives like Lloyd's insured ships, but he had never heard of ordinary seamen buying such policies.

"Does he have many customers?" Ross asked.

Franklin nodded. "Always a queue of them before a ship leaves, especially on a Friday." This drew another laugh. "Probably helps that he includes a 'caul purse' with every purchase. Warns 'em not to open it, though, or the luck will vanish." Away from their men, the officers cackled again at their crew's possible superstitions.

Yule, though, remained silent. The idea that had come to him during that dreadful day east of the Kerguelens flared back to life. But before he could stoke it further, Ross spoke once more.

"We shall put our faith in Her Majesty's reinforced bomb vessels. And we made sure to collect Cook's antiscorbutic cabbage at Kerguelen Island."

"Oh yes, I have no doubt you will be able to press farther south—to the pole itself!" Franklin toasted, draining his glass in a single gulp. "But remember your uncle's error, dear Captain. I'd rather be known as 'the man who ate his boots' than mistake clouds for land!"

Franklin laughed; no one else dared. Yule saw Ross scowl for just a second, enough to quash more talk of his uncle's mishap or of the hazards that awaited them. With the mood subdued, the captain began formal introductions. As he had with the Lords of the Admiralty in Chatham a year earlier, he mentioned that Hooker could identify mosses by sight at age six, that McCormick had joined Fitzroy on the *Beagle*, and that Yule's father had served with Nelson at Trafalgar.

"The ovicers on *Victory* 'ere famous!" Franklin exclaimed. It had taken the governor several introductions—and gulps of wine—to reach Yule.

"Oy, some of the seamen lost their way after the Peace, got transported down 'ere. Maybe you can find some of 'em, tell 'em who yer father was, tell 'em they owe you a 'South Seas Handshake.' They all know how to give those down 'ere!" Franklin cackled. "Just don't let Ross 'ere see you." He slapped the stony-faced captain on the back. "Navy still hangs for buggery and sodomy, last I 'erd."

Lady Jane Franklin, standing beside him, blushed. Yule felt himself do the same, and he noticed the other officers casting uncomfortable glances between him, Ross, and Franklin, their eyes widening in disgust. Yule didn't dare look at Hooker.

For once, Ross's curt tone brought Yule some relief. "Indeed it does, and that penalty will be enforced on any ship I command."

Then, McCormick's voice broke in. "Captain, I believe Master Yule has some measurements to attend to onboard ship."

Ross held McCormick's gaze briefly before speaking. "Ah, yes, Doctor McCormick, thank you for reminding me. Governor, if you would be so kind as to excuse Master Yule, he must return to *Erebus*."

The governor, finally settled down, waved him off. "Very well, very well, thank you for your company, Master Yule." Yule stood, saluted, mouthed "thank you" to McCormick, and headed for the door.

Alone in the street, Yule again recalled the idea that had first come to him the day he had seen Ross and Hooker. But then, he recalled how time and again on this voyage, McCormick had risen above the officers' boorishness and set aside any personal greed to help him. Now, Yule decided that his idea was a poor way to make use of that help.

For all of Ross's impatience, there was little the expedition could do but wait.

Sailing further south in summer would be dangerous; sailing south in August, the depths of the southern winter, would be suicidal. The expedition would remain in Hobart until November—but Yule and Tucker had much work to occupy them before then. The Admiralty had directed them to update the survey of Hobart's coast and shoals—and, of course, to continue their magnetic observations.

Lady Jane, rather than the governor, met Yule, Tucker, and several officers the next morning to guide them to their observatory site. "Governor Franklin has taken ill after last night's affair," she said, which did not surprise Yule. "I am well acquainted with the site and can answer any questions you may have." Before any of the officers could respond, she led them into the town.

Most of the streets lay quiet at this hour. A man in a top hat and frock coat stood holding a sheaf of papers at the first corner. He called out to them as they passed.

"Expedition members? Got special rates for you! Safeguard your wives' and children's futures in case the worst—" Lady Jane's icy stare cut him short. Realizing who glared from beneath the bonnet, he fell quiet, tipped his hat, and scurried away.

"Who is that?" Yule asked.

"Lunk Aspley," Lady Jane said, not looking back. "My husband mentioned him at the banquet last night. I doubt his insurance policies are worth the paper they are printed on."

They continued in silence until they reached a sandstone quarry. "Our understanding is that sandstone does not interfere with your instruments." Yule and Tucker both nodded. "Good. Please do not hesitate to call at the Governor's House if I can be of further assistance." With that, she turned and left them to their work. Tucker made a crude face at Yule, who rolled his eyes.

The dip needle worked as well here as it had in Christmas Harbor, Santiago, or England. With the other officers handling the magnetic work, Yule and Tucker focused on surveying Hobart's coasts and harbors. While carrying their sextants and theodolites along the shore, Yule passed through forests denser than any he had seen in England, filled with trees unfamiliar to him, including one that Hooker called "eucalyptus."

"A Frenchman first defined the species some decades ago," he had explained over supper one night. Yule noticed that Hooker seldom smiled anymore, even when discussing plants. He wondered whether the captain had prevailed upon him again. If he had, Hooker still had no qualms about relaying his commands. "Captain Ross suggested you might help with surveying them tomorrow."

"Very well," Yule replied, recognizing the thinly veiled order. "We shall leave after breakfast."

"Excellent!" Hooker said, rising to leave. "Oh, I nearly forgot, a letter came for you while you were out."

He handed Yule an envelope addressed to "2nd Master Henry Braddick Yule, H.M.S. Erebus," before leaving him alone.

Yule turned the envelope over in his hands. Exchanging mail between England and Her Majesty's ships was a scattershot business, especially over vast distances. Family and friends often sent multiple copies of a letter with different ships bound for a known port of call, hoping at least one would reach its intended recipient. This one, sealed with a crest from Jersey, had made it all the way to Van Dieman's Land.

Yule returned to his bunk and broke the envelope's seal. He recognized his mother's angled script—the writing she had passed on to him—on the page within.

21 January 1840

My dearest Henry,

It is with great sadness that I write to tell you that your father passed away of pneumonia today. In the months before his death, he spoke often of wanting to learn the results of your voyage, the new lands you would help the Navy find in the South, and whether there was any truth to what the Frenchman he met at Trafalgar told him. Regardless of what you find, I trust you will conduct yourself in a manner that does your father's memory proud.

Your loving Mother.

P.S. Your father's Navy pension did not cover the full cost of his interment and funeral. Please do not be surprised to find his service mementos and furniture gone—selling them was necessary to cover this expense.

The next day, Yule was numb as he followed Hooker through the eucalyptus grove, unspooling measuring tapes between trees and marking angles so he could later compute their height. While he measured, Hooker brought his net down on one beetle after another, only stopping when he exhausted the supply of specimen jars from Yule's pack.

"Whatever is the matter, Yule?" Hooker asked as he tucked away the last specimen jar. "You seem dour."

"My father died yest—well, I learned yesterday that he died," Yule said. "Pneumonia."

"Oh," Hooker replied awkwardly. "I-I'm sorry to hear that." Apparently, no amount of botanical knowledge had equipped Hooker to handle death.

They started back to the ship in silence. Yule's fury rose with each step. His father had served the Royal Navy in its hour of greatest need, had comforted its greatest hero on his deathbed, and had given it a son to carry on that service. How did it reward him? With a pension too meager to even pay for a proper funeral. When a church steeple appeared as they neared Hobart, Yule wondered if some divine justice was at work here. Was this his father's due for aiding the enemy at Trafalgar? Was it his own punishment for seeking to profit from that act? He shook the thought from his head. Neither he, nor his father, had betrayed their country. Instead, it was the Admiralty—those small, petty men who denied John Yule a dignified funeral, and now moved his son around the seas like a chess pawn.

Near the dock, Yule and Hooker passed Lunk Aspley again, still hawking his insurance policies with little success. They then passed a row of newly arrived convicts, their guards jeering about buggery. Hooker seemed out of earshot—the weight of Yule's pack slowed his pace.

One convict returned the guard's taunt. Yule froze, his mind returning to the dinner with Franklin, the evening when a dark idea had first formed. It was stronger than ever—and no longer countered by any moral scruples. He knew his idea was wicked, but unlike McCormick or his father, Yule also knew the Navy was wicked.

Chapter 16

Ross Sea Coast
Antarctica
June 2123

Roscoe didn't talk to Hamza at all the next week.

He saw him in the galley but chose to sit alone, letting bits of other conversations drift by. He learned about Food Production's troubles in trying to nurture a new stem cell line for goat meat, Filtration's new system for removing glacial till before shipping, and even rumors of StarCross's lunar base bribing FIFA to tilt soccer rules in favor of its low-gravity, moon-based team. He also heard about the intern cohort that had won the geology tournament. "Five meteorites in eight hours," someone said. "Defective gloves, two fingers lost to frostbite, lots of frostnip. And the fly of one guy's suit jammed. Can't imagine what he lost." The group of guys winced. "Guess that's what it takes to get off-world."

What Roscoe didn't hear was any talk of his and Hamza's—well, mainly Hamza's—rescue of Jen. Maybe no one believed it, or maybe StarCross Silence kept the other cohort members from spreading talk of heroism too wide; promoting someone else's good deeds too much could mean they got off-world instead of you. No one asked Roscoe about the Archives either, and he didn't have much to share. He wasn't getting far at work.

Karla knew that Roscoe hadn't won a spot off-world from the tournament, but she didn't pry. On Monday morning, she simply told him to catalog the rest of the Ross Expedition records. The Updated Terms of Service didn't require them to prioritize any particular submissions for WECs, she explained, but Britain's govellers had stepped up their WEC orders to support their so-called Armed Lifeboat Britain Initiative, and processing their submissions quickly might encourage more.

The books that held the map had been printed, so Roscoe was glad for a break from nineteenth-century handwriting. Even if reading had gotten easier, concentrating hadn't. He'd catalog for about twenty minutes before his mind would drift. To Granite Gorge and the promise he had clung to through the tedium of classes and the terror of exams: *You work hard, your parents give us whatever we demand, and we will get you off this shit planet.* To the greater-than-ever distance Lagrange-2 seemed from him now. To the classmates and the security guard who'd called him a "pounder" and a "fuck-up." To the hard lesson he'd learned after his finely-wrought senior capstone project failed to get him off-world, a lesson he'd been reminded of during Chip's talk with Hamza at Newloon: that being good with words counted less than being good with numbers these days. To Hamza, who had surpassed him in that skill and managed to pull off a fucking water rescue, despite growing up in a refugee camp. To the regret that he hadn't just told Hamza to leave Jen in the track and resume hunting for the meteorites that could get them off-world. To the realization that maybe the best he really could hope for was a cave with some rocks and cacti out front, shared with parents who'd been expecting better, and a boss who wanted the whole world blown up. To wondering whether the razor blades down here could break his skin.

"Hey Karla, I'm not feeling so good," Roscoe finally said around noon on Friday. "Mind if I head out now and come in early on Monday?"

Karla looked up from an old Lloyd's registry. "Of course, weón. Hope you feel better."

Roscoe headed back to his room and changed into his standard-issue exercise shorts and T-shirt. The sneakers looked sturdy enough for running. He'd run more klicks than he could count on the old ski trails around Granite Gorge. When the air was clear and the humidity low, it got him away from the grind of exam prep. Now, he needed an escape from archiving—and from pretty much everyone.

Jogging down the sidewalk to Spigot's gym, he found it empty. Having beaten the after-work rush, Roscoe hopped on the treadmill, where a curved screen wrapped around his head. VR exercise gear had been another of Jahnford's perks for the workers; for now, Roscoe was happy to take it. He scrolled through the course options and chose Chicago's Lakeshore Trail. The sky was clear blue, the lake turquoise, the fall foliage bright red. The treadmill's vents blew at a crisp sixty degrees. This footage must have been decades old. Half an hour later, his heart pounding and endorphins back up, Roscoe stepped off the treadmill and started to think he should do this every day.

On Saturday morning, eager to see what the Rockies looked like before the snow melted and the fires got out of control, he selected the course for Montana. Again, he found the gym empty. He was just skirting another virtual lake, wind in his face and snowcapped peaks to his right, when his wrist buzzed with a call from Hamza.

Roscoe ignored it. Two minutes later, Hamza called again. Sighing, Roscoe paused the course and picked up.

"What's up?"

"I need help, man," Hamza whispered, sounding tense. "I beached Rangiora near the road to Newloon."

"Beached what?"

"Rangiora—that's what I named my subdrone. I need someone to help me recover it."

"Does anyone else know?"

"Don't think so. Pretty empty around here. I wasn't on my shift. I—I just wanted to get in some extra practice."

"Extra practice?"

"Yeah, driving the subdrones. You're not supposed to work off-hours, but everyone does it. It's pretty much the only way to learn what they expect."

"You call your pal Chip yet?" Roscoe asked, not bothering to hide his scorn. "He's got a track."

"I dunno if it's got space to carry a subdrone." Hamza sighed. "And yeah, I tried calling Chip, but he didn't pick up. Must be out."

Before Roscoe could say anything else, Hamza cut in again. "Listen, man, I fucked up driving last week and I get that you're pissed, but I really need your help. Tell me what you want, and I'll make it happen once we get back."

Hamza only had one thing that mattered much to Roscoe. "I want two showers."

"What?—Yeah, sure. I'll give you two of my showers. So you'll help?"

"Sure. I'm on my way. Meet me by the foyer."

"Thanks, man."

Roscoe hung up, sighed, and gave himself a quick sniff. He hadn't worked up enough of a sweat to justify one of his weekly showers. As he headed for the door, he found himself face-to-face with Jen Doil.

"Hi," he said.

"Hey." Jen, in spandex shorts and a sports bra, still wore her double-diamond bracelet from Granite Gorge. "Thanks for helping save my life last week. I wanted to tell you in person—sorry I didn't get a chance sooner."

Roscoe felt his cheeks flush. *Relax*, he told himself, *she'll chalk it up to exercise*. "Um, no worries. Hamza did most of the work. Sure you'd do the same."

Jen leaned against the door, scrolling through her wrist screen. "I saw you and Hamza at church last Sunday. You guys getting ready for the Cleansing Fire?" Before Roscoe could answer, she lowered her wrist and rolled her eyes. "I'm sure as hell not. But hey, gotta suck up to the boss somehow, right?"

Roscoe felt his shoulders drop and chest loosen. "Yeah, for sure. I was delivering a package to his office last week and he invited me. Couldn't exactly say no."

She shook her head. "No, you definitely couldn't. I appreciated seeing you guys there. You have no idea how tough it is for me and Trent to stand up there while Jahnford's working his crowd of indents."

"So that's who they all are? None are former interns?"

"Far as I know. Some of the Residents and Executives just go to suck up too, or in case Jahnford drops any hints about what he'll do next." Jen sighed. "As smart as Jahnford is, he's too dumb to see that none of them care."

Roscoe nodded, burying the questions he had about this church and trying to think of something witty and erudite to say. "Yeah, funny how that works," was the best he could do. "I was going to be there again today, but Hamza, uh, wanted to play blackjack." *Blackjack? Where did THAT come from?*

"Oh, don't let church get in the way of a good bromance." She smiled, and Roscoe's cheeks flushed again. "Actually, there is something I wanted to talk to you about. Do you have a minute?"

Spigot's drone was still sitting out there. Sooner or later, someone would notice it was missing.

"Yeah, I've got a minute."

"I'll keep it short. StarCross's trying something new with the Leadership Training Program. A special transfer division. Selectees will get to alternate between their subsidiary and others. From what I've heard, they'll also have way better odds of making Executive Service. I'm already on the shortlist, but Jahnford asked me to choose a shortlist candidate from my cohort. You interested?"

Was this for real? "That'd be great. Thanks for asking."

"You bet. Least I could do for the guy who saved my life."

"What about Hamza? He really did most of the work that day."

Jen sighed, closing her eyes briefly. "Look, if I could name you both, I would. But, I mean, Hamza's from a Femaville—or Naurutown, or whatever the hell it's called in Australia. I'll be a Resident before StarCross lets someone from one of those camps off-world. Frankly, I'm surprised they even let one down here."

"What would the big deal be?"

"If one person from one of those camps gets off, other people in them will start getting ideas. Might want more education, more than just the bare minimum. Who knows where that might end?" She shrugged, then smiled again. "Besides, you're a Gorgie. That counts for something in my book."

Roscoe's face wasn't getting any cooler. "Well, great, thanks, I really appreciate it."

She grinned. "Awesome. It's still in the early stages, but I'll keep you posted. Who knows, if we play our cards right, the off-world posting could be permanent."

"Sounds good. I gotta go now, but I'll see you around."

"See ya!" She raised her pointer finger to her mouth and whispered, "Keep the StarCross Silence up on this one."

Roscoe gave her a thumbs-up and jogged away, hoping Jen would think he was cooling down.

He didn't stop until he had reached his room, where he changed into his standard-issue pants, undershirt, and jacket before heading to the foyer. Hamza was already there, leaning against the wall with a bulging backpack slung over his shoulder. Relief washed over his face when he saw Roscoe.

"Thank you so much man, I really—"

Roscoe raised a hand. "Let's just go take care of this."

They gave StarCross Security their "training drive" route—Lake Bonney and back—then got suited up and secured a track, with Hamza making sure to ask for one with a cargo bed. Roscoe didn't speak until they exited the tunnel.

"So what do you need me for?"

"Those drones are heavy. It'll take two people to haul it off the ice and into the track." Roscoe wondered what he'd gotten himself into.

After several minutes of silence, Hamza's wrist projected a navigation screen onto the windshield. Wrist-to-wrist communication might not work outside Spigot, but StarCross Navigation did. Roscoe watched as their dot grew closer to a blinking red one on the coast. Only a blinding white flare above the snow-dusted crags of the Asgard Range could pull his gaze from the screen. He'd seen that kind of light once before. It was enough to make him drop the silent treatment.

"Shit. Is that another meteorite?"

Hamza shook his head. "That wasn't a meteorite we saw before the lake caved in."

"What was it then?"

"Missile."

"A missile?" Roscoe asked, incredulous.

"Yeah. Overheard some Security guys talking about the launch."

"For what? Is StarCross worried someone will try to repeat the Orbital Strike down here?"

"Not exactly." Hamza explained that wildcatters, having given up on Thwaites Glacier and other glaciers on the peninsula, had moved closer to Spigot, trying to drill into its water supply. "StarCross considers it a big contamination risk. When satellites pick up wildcatters, they take them out with a missile strike."

So those really had been people, Roscoe realized. People like his parents, desperate to wring something of value from this frozen continent—and StarCross had incinerated them before the interns' very eyes.

"Those StarCross Security guys you overheard—did they say anything else about what happened the day of the tournament? Did they know we were out there?"

"Yeah, they'd been on duty that day. They'd placed bets on how accurate the missiles would be. The guy who guessed none of us would get hit won."

"They launched a missile strike when they knew we were nearby? Does Jahnford know?"

Hamza shook his head. "I don't think so. Pretty sure Security reports straight to StarCross. Jahnford's not in their chain of command." Roscoe recalled that the Security staff all wore StarCross's full stars-and-droplet, rather than just Spigot's droplet. Hamza continued, "Not sure why they cut him out."

Because all StarCross cares about is keeping the water flowing—not who manages it. StarCross Silence kicked in and kept Roscoe from saying that out loud. Instead, he asked, "What about the reservoir level dropping? Did they say anything about that?"

Hamza paused. "I dunno. One guy was watching a surveillance-camera video of the reservoir level dropping, and he sounded surprised. Said he'd never seen the reservoir 'Goldilocks' that fast. Dunno what he meant by that."

Just then, their position dot converged with another on the screen. "We're here," Hamza said, pulling the track off the travel lane, but still within the line of flags marking the road's edge.

Roscoe adjusted his mask, turned on his headlamp, and got out of the track. They had stopped on a hillside. In the cone lit up by his headlamp, Roscoe saw patches of brown mottled with white sloping down to the sea; Antarctica had a solid collar of sea ice, a few meters wide, by this point in the winter. There was no drone in sight, and Roscoe wondered how they'd get it back.

Hamza was already outside. Roscoe followed him around to the back of the track, and found him pulling what looked like a thick, rolled-up, rubber mat, the same shade of red as the track.

"I'm not the first guy this has happened to," Hamza said over the headset. He unlocked the track's winch, clipping the cable's carabiner to a metal loop on the mat. "We call these things grabbers. C'mon, we gotta get it down to the ice."

Roscoe looked up and down the road, wondering how much traffic to expect between Spigot and Newloon on a Sunday morning. For now, the coast was clear. Taking one side of the mat, he and Hamza picked their way down the rocky slope, the cable trailing behind them.

They reached the ice's edge and set the grabber down. Hamza unrolled the mat, pinning it flat against the ice with his feet. "All right, watch this." He began tapping the screen projected through his suit's clear band with gloved fingers. The grabber hummed to life and started sinking into the ice. Hamza stepped off once it was flush with the frozen surface. As it kept sinking, Roscoe realized this strange mat was melting the ice beneath it. In less than a minute, it had burned a dark pool into the frozen sea and sunk out of view, pulling more winch cable into the abyss.

A minute passed in silence, as Roscoe watched the cable sweep across the hole, probing the depths like a fishing line. Finally, Hamza spoke. "All right, we're locked onto the drone." A few taps on the controls, and the winch cable went taut. Moments after, the grabber bobbed to the surface, wrapped around a torpedo-shaped drone.

The meter-wide pool seethed as the subdrone lurched out of the ice, just onto the edge of the hole. Roscoe could now see that it was a little shorter than he was tall, with a bulbous front made from some kind of Plexiglas and a lime-green body. Spigot's droplet had been stenciled on the back fin.

Hamza punched the air. "Almost there! Now we just gotta walk it up to the track."

"Wait—this thing got itself out of the ice. Can't we just fly it back up?"

"Nah. The grabber doesn't have enough power for that. The thrusters are really only good for underwater steering and lifting it out of the water. C'mon, let's get under it and pick it up."

Positioning themselves on opposite sides of the subdrone, Roscoe and Hamza squatted down, wrapped their arms around the underside, and stood. To Roscoe's surprise, the dripping cylinder they held at their waists was light. Hamza looked at its tail. His headlamp illuminated a clump of gray netting hanging from the fins, with flecks of blue, yellow, and red glinting in the plastic strands. "Guess that's why I couldn't steer it. Damn microplastics."

The net held something else: a small but heavy cylinder. Roscoe barely had time to get a good look at it when Hamza led him back up the slope. They were almost to the track when Roscoe felt an odd tightness around his ankles. Looking down, he saw both he and Hamza had gotten their feet tangled in the winch cable.

He opened his mouth to speak, but before he could, they tumbled onto their sides, the cable binding their feet. The subdrone rolled from their grasp, down the slope and onto the ice, coming to rest about two meters from the hole.

Then, Roscoe heard a puff.

Hamza's wrist had been pressed into the ground when they fell, activating the grabber's thrusters. Unable to lift the subdrone, the air jets scraped it across the ice. The subdrone swung back and forth like a wayward compass needle. Each sway yanked on the winch cable clipped to the grabber, pulling Roscoe and Hamza further downhill. The subdrone moved toward the hole in the ice, toward the water that could kill in seconds.

Roscoe's trussed-up feet pointed uphill, preventing him from digging his boots into the ground like he had at Vanda. Here, he could only shout at Hamza. "Turn it off! It's gonna pull us under!"

Hamza raised his wrist, but no shimmer of a screen appeared. "Shit! Suit band's messed up!" Roscoe watched helplessly as his friend tugged his suit's zipper, struggling to free his sleeve. Through his headset, he heard Hamza mutter "No fucking voice commands on this thing?" as the subdrone edged back toward the hole. One swing sent it onto the ice; the next had it teetering on the hole's edge. Then, with a *glug*, it plunged beneath the surface.

For a moment, their descent halted—then, they were moving faster than before. Hamza had said the thrusters were for underwater maneuvering. Now that they were submerged, they were firing hard. Roscoe watched the gap between them and the ice close. He squeezed his eyes shut and waited.

He felt himself slide another meter, then stop.

Roscoe opened his eyes to see Hamza's face lit by the wristband screen; he had freed his left arm, letting his wristband project again.

Still pinned on his side and tangled in the cable, Roscoe watched as Hamza made a few stiff taps on his wristband screen. Moments later, the tightness around his ankles eased. Hamza had reactivated the thrusters and reversed the grabber's direction. Within seconds, the subdrone rose, tail-end first, out of the hole.

"We gotta pull it out!" Hamza shouted. He shoved his arm back in his sleeve and started wriggling downhill. Roscoe followed his lead. A few more minutes later, the subdrone was back on the ice.

They spent several more minutes wriggling downhill, unclipping the grabber, and untangling themselves. Once they were free, Hamza tapped his wristband screen again. The cable that had almost killed them slithered back uphill to the winch and the track.

Hamza lowered his wrist, and Roscoe felt his grudge slip away. "Damn good sailing, or driving, or whatever the hell that was."

"Thanks. They told us how to use those things, but never said to unclip them."

Now free of the cable, they walked the subdrone back up to the track.

"All right, I guess we're even," Roscoe said, surprising himself with his own humor.

"Still want those showers?" Hamza asked.

"Oh yeah, I might even want a third." With the subdrone's body no longer wrapped in a grabber, Roscoe noticed lettering on the side: RANGIORA—HAMZA T.

"So you guys name your drones?" he asked as they climbed back in the cab.

"Yeah," Hamza replied. "It's a tradition since each of us is assigned one. Maybe it also helps their AI spy on us."

"What's Rangiora?"

"A Polynesian story my dad told me," Hamza said as he searched his suit's pockets for the key. "Hui Te Rangiora was a navigator from Rarotonga in the Cook Islands, just like us." He gave his carved wooden necklace a fond squeeze. "He and his men traveled far enough south to see icebergs, all in an open canoe, following the stars, wind, and currents. Real badass."

Roscoe was about to ask Hamza if he believed the story when his friend found the key, slid it into the ignition, and turned it. The electric motor hummed briefly, then fell silent. One by one, the cabin's lights flickered off. The battery was dead.

Chapter 17

"Try again, dammit!"

Hamza jammed the key a second time. Still nothing.

"If the battery's dead," Roscoe asked, "why can't we download electricity from Lagrange-2? Does this thing have an energy receiver?"

Hamza sighed. "It might get us into trouble, but I don't know what choice we have." He tapped a few buttons on the dashboard. Something whirred in the trunk and then fell silent.

They both turned and saw the REC receiver dish, motionless in its cradle. They were cut off from StarCross and its energy, as if they'd been thrown back to the Blackout Years.

"Shit," Hamza muttered. "I've heard about this. Portable receiver dishes are tricky in the cold. Their electronics freeze up sometimes."

The heavy realization sank in: they were stuck. Roscoe's heart pounded out a few hard beats. Just then, a pair of headlights crested the next hill.

Hamza pointed. "We could flag them down and see if they'll tow us."

"Worth a shot," Roscoe replied. "If they're heading from Newloon to Spigot, we're probably partners in crime. Let's just say we're out for a day trip."

They lowered their goggles and pulled up their masks and hoods, and stepped into the headlights' growing glare, waving their arms. The track ground to a halt, and as Roscoe stepped closer, he saw that it was olive green, not Spigot red. A figure rolled down the window, and Roscoe's heart jumped when he recognized the driver's piercing amber eyes.

"Chip?"

The amber eyes squinted from behind the goggles. "Roscoe? Hamza? What the hell are you guys doing out here?"

Roscoe stumbled around to the passenger side, climbed in, and explained their predicament. When he finished, Chip nodded and asked, "Any chance you saw a little probe out here? About the size of a beer can?"

As Roscoe gasped, Chip immediately climbed out of his track and moved to the back of their disabled one, popping open the door. Moments later, he returned clutching the net. Through it, Roscoe got a clearer look at the cylinder, which had several pinhole openings on one end. On its side was an emblem: a yellow wedge like a pie slice, with three spikes on the curved side.

Chip pointed at it. Roscoe realized it was a wedge of the Sun. "That's the Griquas' symbol," he explained. "Built this for them. They wanted to test a few monitoring ideas and sent specs with some WECs for parts. I broke through the ice and dropped it here a few days ago, then figured I'd check on it when it stopped sending data. I'm heading back to McMurdo—I can drop you guys off on the way."

Ten minutes later, Roscoe and Hamza were squeezed into Chip's track, inching forward while their disabled track rolled behind them, clipped to Chip's winch. He made sure they knew his track's capabilities. "When you're on your own down here, you gotta invest in your ride," he said, patting the dashboard. "Doubt one of your Spigot models could pull this load."

Roscoe wasn't impressed. Chip's track could only pull theirs at a slug's pace. As they inched down the row of signal flags, he wondered if their absence would be noticed in the time it took to reach Spigot. His mind raced for something to distract itself.

"How are the other probes doing?" Roscoe asked.

"Working like a charm all the way north. Turned around today, should be entering the Drake Passage right about now. The Griquas have a second sub that takes a longer route around Antarctica, trading with all the settlements along the coast. It docked at Newloon today. I was just there setting a probe up on that one."

"What do they want the data for?" Hamza asked.

"Nothing specific for now. Earth Science funding's been pretty much dry for fifty years, ever since StarCross convinced everyone that the future's in space. So no one knows what the Southern Ocean's like these days. That's a problem if you're trying to make a living down here without selling WECs or RECs to StarCross."

"The Griquas don't sell anything to StarCross?" Roscoe asked.

"Oh, they definitely sell something," Chip replied. "They were buying sub parts with RECs, so they must be cranking out energy that StarCross will take. Got no shortage of wind or tidal power in Patagonia, that's for sure. But they want to do more. They're hoping research like this can get them a clearer picture of what's out there."

"What else could they do?"

Chip tapped the brakes, slowing the track even more as it rattled over a patch of uneven ground. "Fuck if I know. Like I said, they started out with fishing but now they want to move into biotech, aquaculture, other higher-tech stuff. Whatever they want, they seem to think a washed-up scientist on Antarctica will help, so I'm not complaining."

Hamza leaned forward, bracing himself as the track jolted. "Hey, Chip, you ever done much work around Yule Bay?"

Roscoe's ears perked up. *Yule Bay*—the place from Ross's map.

"Yeah, I did my dissertation research up there, just before the NSF stopped sponsoring Earth-based PhD students. What about it?"

Hamza paused, glancing at Chip before continuing. "I was surveying the seafloor there last week and picked up something weird on sonar. Some kind of structure that kept changing shape with each sonar sweep."

Chip's eyes narrowed. "Where was it?"

"Right at the mouth of the bay."

"How big was it?"

"A-a meter or two long and a meter high," Hamza answered. "I didn't get the exact dimensions, but I remember it changed with each sweep."

"Did you tell anyone?"

"No."

Chip kept one hand on the wheel and thumbed the console to dim the track's dashboard lights. "Good," he exhaled, looking relieved.

"Do you know what it was?" Hamza asked.

"It was a freshwater plume." Chip gave the accelerator a gentle tap as the road smoothed out. "Changes in ocean salinity affect sonar. That plume's not on any charts, so the software doesn't correct for it. That's probably what you picked up."

Roscoe's mind spun as he processed what Chip was saying. "There's fresh water down there? How did you find out about it?"

"I picked it up myself during my dissertation research. After I finished my PhD, I asked Jahnford for help researching it."

"What did you think it was?"

Chip eased the track around a sharp bend, his eyes flicking between the road and the rearview display. "My hypothesis was that some kind of fissure in the seabed channels meltwater away from Taylor Glacier, all the way under the seafloor to Yule Bay, where it finally bubbles up."

"From Taylor Glacier to Yule Bay?" Hamza asked, incredulous. "That's hundreds of kilometers!"

"It's strange, sure, but not unheard of." Chip adjusted the heat, clearing the fog forming on the windshield. "There's a river that flows underground for a hundred and fifty klicks in Mexico. Based on the chemical makeup of the water, Taylor Glacier seemed like the most likely source. And if I recall correctly, you guys have been melting lots of water from that glacier and shipping it north. That means the bedrock underneath suddenly has a lot less weight on it. Things can shift. Cracks can open up."

"Did you have a way to find out for sure?"

Chip nodded. "Wanted to run a dye test."

"How so?" Roscoe asked.

"You'd get a ton of dye—biodegradable, nontoxic—all that good stuff. If there is a fissure, I have a pretty good sense of where it starts—under one of the meltwater channels Spigot's melters have opened up on the underside of the glacier. A subdrone takes the dye there and lets it fly. Meanwhile, another subdrone's camera is trained on the plume site near Yule Bay watching for the dye to show up."

Chip slowed the track as they hit another stretch of uneven ground. The suspension creaked under the load. Hamza braced himself against the door while Roscoe gripped the handle above his seat; he could swear this low speed made the jolting worse.

"And if the dye shows up there," Hamza said, leaning forward as the track jolted, "then there is some kind of connection, under the seafloor, between Taylor and Yule Bay."

"Bingo." The road smoothed out, and Chip added speed.

"But Jahnford wasn't onboard with doing this. Why?" Roscoe asked, checking the time on his wristband again. "His job is to keep the water flowing. Wouldn't he want to know if he's losing a bunch of it out a fissure?"

"Not exactly," Chip chuckled, shaking his head and adjusting the rearview display. "In retrospect, I was stupid to even ask for his help. Put yourself in Jahnford's shoes. When I came along, he'd just gotten the job on Eatonson's recommendation. He was not the Residents' first choice, but Eatonson convinced them that his cult would keep the indents in line. Now how do you think he'd look if it turned out he was losing the water from one of Spigot's main glaciers? He'd look incompetent, even if he was just the messenger."

Chip had cranked up the track's heat again to clear the windshield, while Hamza wriggled out of his suit's sleeves. "But wouldn't he want to locate the fissure anyway, rather than letting you or someone else discover it by accident?"

"Maybe, but my guess is that Jahnford doesn't think so. He must be praying that he can retire and leave someone else holding the bag before that happens."

"Do you think you could do the test without their permission?" Hamza asked. "Maybe drill a hole straight through some untunneled section of the glacier to release the dye?"

Suddenly, another fireball lit up the Asgard Range. Chip chuckled again, bringing the track to a stop. "Not if I don't want to meet one of those up close," he said. Together, they all watched as the rocket arced into the sky, away from the coast.

"How far are they striking?" Hamza asked, watching the contrail fade.

Chip squinted at the horizon. "Looks like that one was meant to take out wildcatters south of the glaciers, out on the East Antarctic ice sheet."

"Why do they care about people drilling for water so far away?"

"Because it's not just about theft. They've gotta make sure no one else produces too many WECs."

"Why?"

Chip put the track back into gear. The tow cables groaned as they resumed their crawl toward Spigot.

"Think about it, kid. You're supplying reliable, fresh water to the world, and they trade you whatever you want—missiles, data, scientists, raw materials—"

"Old manuscripts," Roscoe added.

"—to get it. And you're starting to get your hands on the good stuff—orbital rockets, classified space-station designs—the stuff you'll need to escape to the Moon, or Mars, or wherever when what's left of this planet goes to shit. Then, someone decides to open up an ice quarry or drill into one of the subglacial lakes to produce their own WECs, someone who doesn't make buyers follow StarCross's Updated Terms of Service."

He shot Roscoe and Hamza a knowing look. "You think the govellers will want to trade the good stuff with StarCross then?"

They shook their heads.

Chip continued. "They don't mind the wildcatters up on the peninsula or Thwaites. Those glaciers are shifting too fast these days to produce much. StarCross isn't worried about the West Antarctic ice sheet. It's breaking up so fast that a crevasse will swallow up any wildcatters who try to drill it before a missile takes them out. But the Ferrar Glaciers? The East Antarctic ice sheet? Those are stable. The ice itself isn't moving, and it's sitting on top of giant freshwater lakes. Together, that's *oceans* of fresh water waiting to be bottled and shipped north. StarCross will do whatever it takes to protect them. Rumor had it Finn Smalls wanted to tunnel under them, give people an alternative to StarCross, and reduce their leverage. You saw what happened to him."

Noticing a confused look on Hamza's face, Chip recounted the story of Finn Smalls and his suspicious "drug-related" death.

"So they're killing people to keep water scarce," Hamza said, stunned. "How do they get away with that?"

"Lie about it," he said, turning the heat down just as Roscoe had started peeling off his own suit. "Whenever some government asks StarCross Security about a missile strike, they just say they had intel suggesting the target was about to threaten Spigot's glaciers—risking contamination of the water supply or whatever. Any fool with a map can tell it's bullshit, but no one can call StarCross on it."

"Or they could get blacklisted," Roscoe added, zipping his suit back up as the cabin cooled.

"Right again." Chip gave a grim nod.

"But—but they need water," Hamza said, getting back into his own suit. "Everyone in the world needs water. Why don't governments call them on it, or support a wildcatter who can do it cheaper than StarCross?"

"Because StarCross works pretty well, at least as far as water goes," Chip replied. "Spigot keeps people happy."

Roscoe watched the road's signal flags slowly scroll by the side window, thinking back to Pennsylvania—the constant fear that a fire or flood could send him and his parents to a Femaville. "Happy?"

Chip nodded, risking a bit more speed as he did so. "Happy enough to go along with StarCross. If you're up north, and you're not in a refugee camp, you've got five or six showers a week, uninterrupted energy from Lagrange, and a constant food supply from StarCross-network greenhouses. You've even got a good old-fashioned flush toilet and maybe even a green grass lawn, just like your parents knew and loved. Sure, a flood or fire might get you, but you've at least got a shot at getting off-world through your kid." He elbowed Roscoe just as the track bounced, making them both rock. "That's the challenge for Jahnford, or whoever's in charge of Spigot. Send up just enough water to keep people comfortable, keep StarCross trusted, and make everything else look like too big a risk, but little enough water that governments will still trade real valuables—space tech, military tech—to get it. There's a narrow range of water production rates where that's possible. Jahnford's got to keep water production in that Goldilocks zone."

Both interns jolted again as the towed track thudded over a ridge. Roscoe steadied himself, listening as Hamza relayed what he'd overheard from StarCross Security—how, after the missile strike took out wildcatters, something had "Goldilocksed," causing the Vanda reservoir's level to drop.

Chip nodded, reducing speed and eyeing the tow line in the side mirror. "So, what's the official line for that place? Backup storage when they have to do maintenance?"

"Pretty much."

"Well, it's bullshit," Chip said, scratching his stubble. "When wildcatters cause too much trouble or production overshoots, they store water there to create scarcity. Then, once the wildcatters are dealt with or the problem's fixed, they release some from the reservoir to keep production in that Goldilocks zone."

Hamza's expression darkened. "StarCross almost killed us for some stupid number?" But then skepticism crept into his voice. "This all sounds like some conspiracy theory. I don't believe it."

"I do," Roscoe said without hesitation. "They did the same thing with energy."

Chip and Hamza turned to him, and he launched into the story of his senior capstone.

You're it, Roscoe had told himself nearly every night during his last year at Granite Gorge. Nine years after hearing those words from his father, he believed them more than ever. So when it came time to write the final essay that carried heavy weight in StarCross's internship-assignment process, he chose the one topic he felt he could master without compound: history.

While his classmates proposed new uses for alloys in lunar gravity or better systems for prioritizing energy relays between Lagrange-1 and Lagrange-2, Roscoe had devoted fifty pages to reinterpreting the tragedy memorialized at every StarCross facility: the Orbital Strike. That was when Earth-launched missiles destroyed the original solar arrays and relay satellites placed in low orbit by StarCross's predecessor, TriStar Energy. His classes at Granite Gorge, like the plaque out front, framed it as a tragedy that claimed hundreds of lives and nearly ended TriStar's dream of space-based energy.

But after hours of combing through Granite Gorge's StarCross Info service, Roscoe found signs of something more in the attack's aftermath. TriStar's pre-Strike press releases and shareholder reports had always described its maximum operating range to be a few hundred kilometers above Earth. Transmission from the Lagrange points—one and a half million klicks farther—had been framed as little more than a way to burn their excess R&D budget. Yet, once the attack threatened a return to the Blackout Years, it took only a few months for governments to supply TriStar with the hardware and manpower it needed to move all operations to the Lagrange points.

Yes, the Orbital Strike had been a tragedy, Roscoe wrote, but one that forced progress, driving humanity's push into deep space in ways that might never have happened otherwise. "The Black Death led to the Renaissance," he concluded, "World War II nurtured computers. And the Orbital Strike drove humanity to the stars."

"It was a total suck-up to StarCross," he confessed to Chip and Hamza as Spigot finally came into view, "but I thought it was the kind of thing that would strike a chord with them and land me a spot off-world. But the whole time I was writing it, I kept thinking how good it had turned out for StarCross. After all, Lagrange-2 is so far away that you need super-precise targeting to send or receive electricity, and under the Updated Terms of Service, governments had to grant TriStar—or StarCross now—a monopoly on that technology and shut down ground-based grids in exchange for REC deliveries. People were desperate; they couldn't say no."

Hamza looked between Chip and Roscoe. "You're saying StarCross staged a terrorist attack to move production further away from Earth and keep RECs scarce?" Their silence was enough of an answer. Roscoe recalled the graffiti on the memorial at Newloon: "Inside Job."

Chip eased the track around a bend and nodded slowly as if both motions helped him gather his thoughts. "Like I said, same mindset as with water. RECs meant reliable energy from space—no worries about storms or fires knocking the power out. Governments wanted those badly. They could allow some independent energy production—and actually needed some to get people to buy into the whole REC system. But too much energy would tank the value of those RECs. So StarCross figured out how to keep production in check. Fake a security threat, then move production so far away that energy's guaranteed to be scarce."

He tapped the dash as to emphasize the point. "They don't have that luxury with water. A few people will retire enough WECs to become Residents, but they can't compensate for all the wildcatters. So they just blow up anyone who tries to produce water themselves. Or, if you're Finn Smalls, they'll say it was an overdose. And the next person who points out that there's another source of WECs off their beach free for the taking?" His pitied laugh told Roscoe and Hamza everything they needed to know.

"So yeah," Chip continued, "with all the sonar sweeps and surveying, that freshwater plume turns up from time to time. Whoever sees it will ignore it if they're smart." He fixed Hamza with a hard look. "I think you're smart. Don't prove me wrong. If anyone tries to bottle it, they won't last long. It'll be game over for whoever's in charge of Spigot too. Jahnford's just praying it isn't him."

Roscoe didn't feel any better about his work down here, and he could tell Hamza didn't either. Before Chip could sink their mood any further, he parked next to Spigot's battered service door.

"You guys stash the drone here for now. I'll tow your track back to Motor Pool so you can check in."

Hamza and Roscoe hefted the torpedo-shaped drone from the track's cargo bed, placing it just inside the doorway. As Roscoe kept checking the horizon for headlights, he remembered their cover story. "We told them we were going to Lake Bonney Hut and back. Just in case they ask."

Chip shook his head. "So that's the cover story for Newloon trips these days? Lake Bonney. Guess I'll tell them I was collecting samples—though nothing much is worth testing up there, unless it's a reservoir now too."

Roscoe and Hamza carried Rangiora, the rescued drone, to the empty drone control room and onto a cylindrical metal cradle. Hamza pressed a button, closing a sliding door over it. "Dumbwaiter," Hamza said. "It'll take the drone down to the port."

They both sighed. "Thanks again, man," Hamza said, again scrolling through his wristband screen. "I'll credit your showers now."

"Thanks." Even if Hamza had just saved his life, Roscoe wouldn't say no to those showers.

Finally back in his room, Roscoe crashed on his bed, too tired to sleep. He lay there, replaying the events from the last few hours: StarCross's Goldilocks zone for water production, the drone recovery, the run-in with Jen, StarCross's new exchange program, and the realization that he just might get a shot out of this cave. *How could he not blow it?*

Roscoe didn't have an answer to that question that night, or at church on Sunday, as Jahnford dropped no new hints about his nuclear weapon, but did predict that God would spare compounders' immediate incineration at the start of the Cleansing Fire, so as to prolong their suffering. The off-world spot stewed in his mind on Monday as he returned to Ross's book.

He had just followed Ross and his crew out of the Ross Sea and back to Tasmania, then skipped ahead to their second Antarctic summer. Roscoe was starting to doze off—this particular compound withdrawal symptom always hit worst midafternoon—when Karla's wrist buzzed.

"Jahnford wants us to take the map back." She scoffed. "Guess it was too much history for the gringos to handle. Mind going to pick it up?"

Roscoe hopped on the jitney toward the Residents' district and Jahnford's penthouse office. He remembered Jahnford's prophecy of how Spigot would soon gain the tools to start the Cleansing Fire, and Hamza saying something about Jahnford having meetings. Then, inspiration struck.

This was a golden opportunity.

Striding through the Residents' tunnels, Roscoe summoned his courage and rehearsed what he'd say. He entered the elevator and steeled himself with a few deep breaths. *Don't fuck this up.*

Chapter 18

H.M.S. *Erebus*
Unnamed sea south of Van Dieman's Land
November 1840

The austral summer had arrived—and with it, the time to make for the pole.

Hooker arrived late to supper their first night back at sea, explaining to Yule, wearied, that he and McCormick had administered one final round of mercurous chloride to the seamen who had visited Hobart's bordellos one too many times.

At first, Ross also seemed relieved to return to sea, but his impatience flared quickly. A few weeks south of Hobart, they anchored off a rock marked "Auckland Island" on the charts.

Hooker eagerly set off for its thickets of ferns. Yule, meanwhile, carried out magnetic observations on the ship and then onshore. Hooker returned from his first day in the thickets with three potted ferns, the largest of which measured at least four feet from base to tip. Yule watched the botanist brace its pot between his legs and grip the stalk with both hands while two able seamen rowed him back to the *Erebus*.

"Surely a new record, if an unexpected one!" Ross called out when the fern was hoisted aboard, sounding more affectionate than he ever did with the crew. The captain and assistant surgeon carried the swaying plant into the Great Cabin, finding just enough space for it among the specimens that Hooker had gathered from points further north.

"Where shall we put the other ferns, then?" Hooker asked the captain. The other two, shorter ferns swayed at Yule's side.

Ross scratched his head. "No more space in the cabin. The hold, perhaps?"

Hooker shook his head. "There's no space. And besides, these specimens need sunlight and protection from the elements. If the Great Cabin's full, an officer's bunk would be ideal. Master Yule has space in his. The prism set into the deck there should provide adequate sunlight."

"Excellent!" Ross said. "We appreciate your dedication to the expedition's scientific inquiries, Master Yule. Please show Doctor Hooker to your bunk, and be sure to follow his instructions on tending them to the letter."

Yule carried the pots below, gritting his teeth and watching Hooker arrange and rearrange his tiny bunk until the two ferns caught the prism's light. The surgeon found the space ideal, but not Yule's caretaking skills. "I shall come by every few hours to check on them, and perhaps to water them." Before Yule could protest, Hooker returned to the Great Cabin.

He looked at the ferns, deciding now was as good a time as any to advance the idea that struck him in Hobart. Yule took a piece of paper from his notebook, recalled the date when Roberts had died and he had seen Ross sodomize Hooker, and began to write.

> *July 30, 1840*
>
> *On this date I, Second Master Henry Braddick Yule, witnessed Captain James Clark Ross of H.M.S. Erebus engaged in grossly indecent conduct with Ship's Assistant Surgeon Joseph Dalton Hooker.*

Yule paused. Was it fair to bring Hooker into this? As much distaste as he had for the young surgeon, he was just that—young—and unable to resist a captain's advances, especially when that captain had given his scientific work every possible support. Hooker was unlikely to be punished, at least by the law, so Yule continued to write. He spared just one sentence on the carnal details, then added the facts that would surely damn Ross in the eyes of the Navy.

> *Captain Ross engaged in this act during our passage from the Kerguelen Islands to Van Dieman's Land. Erebus had encountered unusual calm for those waters, and Ross's absence from the deck was unlikely to draw notice. It was only by chance that I discovered Ross in the Great Cabin, as I attempted to inform him that our boatswain, Mr. Roberts, had fallen overboard. To the foregoing, I am prepared to attest in any court-martial against Captain Ross.*
>
> *Signed this 2nd of July, 1840.*
> *Henry Braddick Yule*
> *2nd Master, H.M.S. Erebus*

He folded his attestation, then slipped it into an envelope beside the life insurance policy he had purchased from Aspley and Sons Insurance Co., guaranteeing the bearer's designated beneficiary a five-thousand-pound payout upon the death of Captain James Clark Ross.

Aspley had thankfully not asked what Yule's relationship with Ross was, or any other questions one might expect from such a salesman in England. In a land of convicts, standards were lower. Yet Yule knew the grave risk he was taking; he could not testify that Ross had committed sodomy, a hangable offense, having taken out a life insurance policy on the captain in his own name. And so, he had waited until his last night in Hobart to make the purchase, spoken to Aspley in a rasp with a hood over his head, named his mother as the beneficiary, and given his name as Dalton McCormick. Yule's single gold escudo had convinced Aspley to waive his usual requirement for proof of identity. Time would tell if the ruse worked.

Yule felt another qualm as he looked at the names he had stolen from the kind Irish surgeon and his brutalized, if insufferable, assistant side-by-side on the certificate. Yes, he had wanted to return from the voyage with money, but would he go this far to make it?

Yule fought the question back. He was not going far at all, he reminded himself, simply enforcing the law and ensuring accountability on the high seas. And besides, he alone would not benefit from this plan; his mother, already shortchanged by the Navy, would too. He slipped the envelope back into the pail and stared into the pinprick eyes of the beetles Hooker had gathered in Van Dieman's Land. "Another secret for you to keep."

Hooker had found more than ferns on barren Auckland Island. The next morning, Ross took Yule, McCormick, and several other officers ashore to a spot the assistant surgeon had designated. They found two boards sticking up from a pile of stones. One had a message written in French, a second language for every Jersey native. Yule translated it for Ross and the others: "Left by French expedition, led by Dumont d'Urville, after successful charting of the southernmost seas, 1840. Expedition achievement: from 19 January to 1 February 1840, discovery of Adélie Land and the South Magnetic Pole!"

"A hoax," Ross scoffed. "Franklin told us scurvy turned them back. I trust his word over that Frenchman's any day."

"What about this other one?" McCormick asked, reading the message written in English on the second board. "Left by an American ship last summer. U.S.S. Porpoise. Part of a squadron led by Commodore Charles Wilkes."

Ross snorted. "Ah, yes. Did the Yankees find that hole in the south pole they were looking for?"

McCormick looked again at the message scrawled on the wood. "Ah, no, Captain. Says an ice barrier turned them back before the pole."

The captain nodded again, his lips pursed. Neither the French nor the Yankees had reached the South Magnetic Pole, but they had come close. And what was this "Adélie Land" d'Urville mentioned? Had he discovered a southern continent? Yule knew these questions would light a fire under Ross.

"Master Yule, return to the ship and bring the dip needle here at once. Gather what observations you can before nightfall."

"But we were to collect observations for at least—"

Ross cut him off. "We're cutting our observations short. Our instructions are to reach the pole. All else is secondary." He turned to confer with the other officers.

Once again, Yule had no choice but to comply. This wasn't how he remembered the instructions they'd received back in Chatham. For the world magnetic model to function effectively and guide ships reliably, far more than the pole needed to be charted. Observations had to be conducted systematically and continuously, on fixed days and at specific points around the globe. But he knew that work would bring little glory to the nation—or to Ross.

The expedition pressed onward, each day colder than the last. The Roaring Forties brought more rain, then sleet and snow. The able seamen shoveled coal into the heating apparatus. Three weeks out from Van Dieman's Land, Ross directed the ship's purser to distribute foul-weather gear: padded trousers and jackets, long underwear, Welsh wigs, boots, and thick gloves, all packed for them in England more than a year earlier. Yet the seamen refused to wear gloves in the rigging—high above the deck, a tiny snag could prove fatal. Yule watched them descend the masts, fingers ghost-white and bleeding, and scurry below deck.

Their sufferings were not for nothing. By mid-December, the ships emerged unscathed from the Roaring Forties. The seas calmed, the skies cleared, and the sun stayed above the horizon. Whales breached for air, unbothered by the two ships, and icebergs glistened at a safe distance like diamonds on velvet. Perhaps superstition placed them beyond God now; they were surely beyond man, in waters few other ships had plied before. Yule could only hope the worst was behind them.

On New Year's Eve, when Yule reckoned their latitude, his mouth fell open. He double-checked, then triple-checked his calculations, and noted the time and temperature before heading to the Great Cabin. He knocked.

"What is it?" Ross asked when he entered.

"We've reached sixty-six thirty south, Captain. The Antarctic Circle."

"Excellent! We'll splice the main brace." A double ration of rum for every man. Time-pressed though they were, the *Erebus* and *Terror* had reached a latitude few vessels ever had. No captain would deny his crew a celebration at such a moment.

The ships pressed southward; the sun soon ceased to set. Through his sextant, Yule watched it roll a tight, endless circle above the horizon. With each degree of latitude, the dip needle sloped steeper, and the compass needle veered further off the bearing that the sextant and chronometer showed. The magnetic pole was getting closer—and the ice was thickening.

One day, the *Erebus* could avoid it no longer. Almost two months out from Hobart, a whistle summoned Yule above deck. He pulled on his trousers, jacket, gloves, and Welsh wig, and climbed into the Antarctic's eternal sunshine. Blinded as he stepped onto an icy deck, Yule slipped and fell on his side.

No one noticed. The able seamen continued their dance with the rigging, undeterred by the ice. The officers, meanwhile, had massed along the port bulwark, shielding their faces from the sun and staring straight ahead. Yule climbed to his feet and gasped. A quarter-mile ahead, bergs and floes choked off all open water. A scab of ice stretched to the horizon—directly in front of the *Erebus*.

He scanned the deck, looking for a pair of captain's epaulets. Ross was nowhere to be seen. So he shouted, through a taut jaw and ice-crusted scarf, to the figure ahead of him on the gunwale. "Aren't we going to turn?"

The figure shook its head. "Cap'n ordered us to ram it head-on."

"At this speed?" They'd hit the ice pack at six knots or more.

The capped figure nodded. "Wants to be sure we'll break through and come out the other side. Says this hull can take it."

Yule thought back to Chatham, to all the armor its dockhands had given the already-tough *Erebus* and *Terror*. It had all been for this moment, he realized—a moment that few ships or sailors had faced, and even fewer had survived.

Ice would pierce a normal hull at this speed. Could the *Erebus* make it?

As the gap closed, Yule gripped the gunwale tighter. He couldn't tell if the other officers were fazed; the able seamen seemed undaunted, trimming the sails with their usual speed. Their shouts were no less clear under their scarves; their bare grips on the ropes seemed as sure as they had been in the tropics. Yule's hands were gloved, but he had lost all feeling in his fingers.

They were thirty yards away now. Then twenty, then ten. "BRACE!" came a shout. Yule crouched low, wrapping his arm around the gunwale.

The impact jolted them, but the sound was worse—a dull thud, then a screech like the devil grinding his nails along the hull. A few more thuds followed, yet the deck under Yule's feet stayed level, and the ship's pace barely slowed. The *Erebus* and *Terror* were pushing the ice aside. The able seamen cheered; both they and the ships had passed their biggest test yet. The expedition remained on course for the South Magnetic Pole.

And Yule might yet live to achieve his plan.

Chapter 19

Ross Sea Coast
Antarctica
June 2123

Roscoe caught the end of a sentence as he stepped off the elevator: "—store the warhead in the Ferrar Glacier drainage tunnel, that would give us—" The conversation halted as he entered the room.

There were no southern lights outside the office window this time. The table had been draped with relief maps and technical drawings. More had been projected on the wall screen, where Roscoe had helped Jahnford place the map. It went blank a second after Roscoe walked in, but not before his eyes caught the boldface word Argus-3 in one corner. Roscoe saw Jahnford, Trent, and three men with StarCross logos on their jackets studying the printouts.

"Roscoe, thanks for coming up," Jahnford said. "Map's right over there." The frame had been taken down and now lay flat on the conference table.

Roscoe had hoped to have another private moment with Jahnford to broach his idea. Should he risk it with other people here, or abort the mission? But seeing the two-hundred-seventy-year-old map and recalling the hardships of those early explorers gave him courage.

"Mister Jahnford, if I may, there's something on this map I think you and your guests might find interesting." Not giving Jahnford time to respond, Roscoe placed the frame over the printouts and pointed to a spot labeled "YULE BAY." "I heard Drone Operations recently picked up a big freshwater plume coming from the seafloor there." Now, time for the lie that would let both him and Jahnford save face: "None of their past surveys in the area picked it up, so it must have emerged recently. It could be a valuable new source of WECs for Spigot and StarCross."

The StarCross men raised their eyebrows, clearly interested.

"Anyway, just thought you wanted to know," he said, careful not to overplay his hand. "I won't waste any more of your time."

"Th-thank you for letting us know, Roscoe," Jahnford stammered, looking to the StarCross representatives. "We appreciate it."

Roscoe gave them a respectful nod, picked up the map, and headed for the door. As he waited for the elevator, he heard them whispering but didn't try to listen—he felt good enough as it was. He'd just handed both his boss and StarCross a vital piece of information about a new WEC source—one that happened to have emerged too recently for Jahnford to have missed. So what if Drone Operations had done all the work? Roscoe had been the face of it, so he figured he'd get the credit—or at least, be at the front of the line when StarCross was picking candidates for that intern exchange program. He might get off-world after all.

Roscoe couldn't think about much else the next few days. When he was cataloging or pounding the treadmill, the prospect of a ticket off-world was never far from his mind. Then, on Wednesday, his wrist buzzed.

He was heading to work when he received the message: *URGENT: Meeting with Trent Hale. Report to Administrative Offices Immediately.* Roscoe forwarded it to Karla with a note—*Just got this; I'll be a little late today*—and headed to headquarters.

Once again, his wristband opened all the doors. He almost rolled his eyes when he saw the succulents in the Residents' section and imagined how pitiful they would seem next to the trees on La Rambla Nueva, Lagrange-2's pedestrian promenade. The StarCross Security agent on duty at the Admin Offices pointed him to Trent's office, an unmarked door near the elevator. As Roscoe neared the end of the hall, he grew sure that his gambit was paying off, that he was going to be congratulated—and maybe rewarded—for cluing StarCross in on the WECs just outside Spigot's doorstep.

Or maybe not, Roscoe thought, when he saw Trent's expression.

This head intern seemed a bit older than Jen—late twenties, maybe—with his hair buzzed to the scalp. When Roscoe had seen Trent before, this cut's severity had been offset by a smile. But now, the haircut made Trent's ashen face even more unsettling.

"Roscoe, sit."

He obeyed. Trent leaned across his desk. "I want to flag you on something. You had one job on Monday—to pick up a map from Mister Jahnford's office. Grei and I were having a meeting with StarCross officials—Residents' Council reps, higher-up Executives—important stuff. No one asked you to interject with something you'd just heard through the grapevine."

"I-I'm sorry. I thought Mister Jahnford and StarCross would want to know about a new source of WECs nearby."

Trent's voice stayed flat. "We have channels through which information about new water sources is supposed to be collected, analyzed, and acted upon. The only way this whole system works is if everyone works through these channels."

"Like I said, I'm sorry. It won't happen again."

Trent nodded, eyes widening. "You're right—it won't. StarCross takes security and respect for protocols very seriously." Roscoe knew what that meant: one more slip-up, and he'd be blacklisted. "Have I made myself clear?"

"Yes, sir."

"Good. Around here, we have a saying. 'New interns should be seen and not heard.'" Trent leaned in to meet Roscoe's sinking gaze. "Don't let me hear from you again."

"I won't."

"Good. Now get out of here."

As Trent's office door closed, Roscoe heard him mutter something about pounders. Dodging curious looks, he scurried from Trent's office, his throat tight with dread. How did he fuck up this bad?

A few days ago, he had been on a shortlist for getting off-world. Now, he was one misstep away from blacklisting. He replayed that moment, those few sentences he'd said to Jahnford and the others. He was so sure they'd appreciate a plucky new intern clueing them into another supply of the very resource that was this place's reason for existing, somewhere else they could mine and sell—or at least lock down.

Instead, they put a target on his back—but why?

Pacing the tunnels, he thought over what Chip had told him and Hamza about how StarCross kept the water supply in the Goldilocks zone: scarce enough to be worth trading high technology for, but plentiful enough to keep a lot of people's lives comfortable up north. He'd just told Jahnford and the execs where the water was. What they did with it—whether they tapped it, ignored it, or plugged it with concrete—was up to them. StarCross and Spigot wanted to know where fresh water was—they were shopping for archives and sending out subdrones to find every drop of fresh water around this rock, either to sell it or kill anyone else who wanted to. So why didn't they want to know?

Roscoe hadn't thought of an answer by the time he reached the Archives. When Karla asked what Trent had wanted, he answered, "Just thanking us for the map. Said we should keep it handy in case they have any other meetings." It was a lame excuse—nothing Trent couldn't tell Karla in a message—but once again, his boss didn't press further.

Roscoe popped open Ross's memoir, returning to the decks of the *Erebus* and *Terror*. He muddled through the rest of the week, thanks in part to Karla's steady playlist of protest music. On Sunday, he did the one thing that might lift Jahnford's opinion of him. He went back to church.

He thought about asking Hamza again, but figured they needed a break from each other for a while. And on the off chance Jahnford wanted to bring up their last meeting—well, he'd rather face him alone.

Jen robotically welcomed him to the guest section. Roscoe once again studied the Revelators' logo and overheard the Executive Staff in the guest section trade whispers—whispers that included the word "nuke." For the first time in this long, hard week, Roscoe began to question what Jahnford had meant about a nuclear weapon in his sermon two weeks earlier.

The indents filed in, and the service began with its usual call-and-response. Trent read an account of a flogging during the Wilkes Voyage to Antarctica, followed by Jahnford's now-familiar retelling of the Revelation. When Jahnford returned to the podium to deliver his sermon, Roscoe's curiosity had sharpened with urgency.

"Friends, today's readings remind us of the importance of vigilance. There have always been evildoers among God's chosen people—when they did God's work in charting Antarctica, and even today, here at Spigot. As the Cleansing Fire draws nearer, they grow desperate, eager to thwart our just ends and escape their just punishment."

Jahnford gripped the edges of the podium and leaned slightly forward, scanning the congregation as if weighing their resolve. Then, with a measured breath, he straightened and continued. "Two weeks ago, I shared that we had moved closer to fulfilling our destiny, to bringing a nuclear bomb to Antarctic soil in fulfillment of the Sacred Revelation. I regret to inform you that evildoers in our midst, and beyond, have thwarted those plans." He paused, letting prayers and murmurs ripple through the Tithers. In the guest section, the Executive Staff shifted in their seats, their whispers sharp and urgent. Jahnford waited until the noise settled, then raised his voice. "I pray that they will face God's judgment, and trust that God will soon present us with a new opportunity to achieve His plans on Earth. In the meantime, let us stay vigilant, even in the dark of midwinter, for any threats to our shared destiny."

As the Tithers took their iodine pills in preparation for the Cleansing Fire, something clicked.

Two weeks earlier, Jahnford had preached that Spigot would soon have a nuclear warhead. On Monday, Roscoe had overheard his meeting with StarCross representatives where they spoke of a "second warhead."

Jahnford had been close to obtaining a nuke—but now it seemed he wasn't.

Was it something I said that day? Roscoe rolled his eyes at the very thought. He didn't see how that could've happened. Maybe Trent really had just been angry at him for going around the chain of command. As he left, he avoided Trent's gaze—and everyone else's.

That night, Roscoe sulked to the galley to find Hamza chatting with some of the other interns. When Roscoe sat down with his tray, Hamza turned, his usual grin flashing.

"You all right, man?"

"Yeah, uh, no. Not really. I fucked up."

Roscoe unloaded everything—Jen's offer, the internship exchange program, the chance of getting off-world, the map, his meeting with Jahnford, Trent, and StarCross officials, and the fallout with Trent.

When he finished, Hamza's response surprised him. "That sucks, man. I'm sorry."

"I know I was a dick to tell them about the plume. That was your department's work. I just wanted the credit." *Even though you grew up in a refugee camp and needed a scholarship, I was willing to take it,* Roscoe thought, again wondering how sharp Spigot-issued razors were.

Hamza sighed. "I get it, man. Fuck, if I had a one-on-one with Jahnford, I might want to bring it up too, especially if it meant getting off-world."

"Yeah, maybe Jen'll give you my spot," he lied. "Pretty sure I'm not in the running anymore."

"Don't be so sure, man. She still seems to like you."

"We'll see."

Hamza stood up, giving Roscoe a sympathetic nod. "Sorry, but I gotta go now. I'm working evening shifts now."

"What?" Roscoe knew some divisions had night shifts, but he hadn't heard of interns working them before.

"Yeah, gotta do more surveying work before Argus-3."

"Argus-3?" Roscoe asked, remembering the name he had seen for an instant on the screen in Jahnford's office.

"It's a codename." Hamza leaned in, lowering his voice. "Don't ask me how, but StarCross got itself a nuke. They're planning to test it down there."

"You mean—near the freshwater plume?"

Hamza, halfway to standing, froze and looked up. "Now that I think about it—yeah. Same coordinates. Damn, man, maybe Chip was right about that stuff."

"When's the test?" Roscoe asked.

"Not for a month or so. They're waiting for better weather, even though it's at the bottom of the ocean. Look, I gotta go, but I'll message you soon."

With that, Hamza was off, leaving Roscoe alone and stunned.

CHAPTER 20

H.M.S. *EREBUS*
UNNAMED SEA
JANUARY 1841

When he heard the shout "Land ahoy!" Yule raced onto the deck. A snow-crusted cone rose from the haze on the horizon. Was it real, or an illusion? Yule remembered McCormick's warnings about iceblink, where clouds and ice could resemble land at these latitudes.

"We shall inspect at closer range," declared a flat voice beside him. Yule turned to see Ross standing close by. "Reckon our current position, Master Yule." The second master went below deck to consult the bearings and log readings Tucker had gathered overnight.

When Yule stepped back on deck, he had no doubt: they had reached land.

The peak pierced the sky before them, its thick, flat bands of ice and rock rising high above the sea. Even at this distance, Yule could hear waves crashing and sea ice grinding against the mountain's base, which stretched across the horizon in both directions. Could this be the southern continent, Antarctica, long whispered of by sealers and whalers? Even if it was merely an island, it was a significant find.

And one made of basalt, McCormick told Yule before the second master had regained his breath.

"Never have I seen such fine columnar jointing," the surgeon declared, holding a spyglass to study the coast. Yule wondered what scientific observation could take precedence over sheer wonder at this moment. "Look here," McCormick said, passing him the instrument.

The spyglass let Yule pick out an odd feature of the coastline. Its cliffs were not quite sheer. As they sloped into the sea, their bases took a curious form: packed black pillars of perhaps six sides.

"Same as the Giant's Causeway in Ireland, or what we saw on Kerguelen," McCormick observed. "Certain varieties of basalt form this shape. Watts has proposed that molten lava solidifies around isolated centers, creating large balls that press together to form this hexagonal symmetry. We shall have to gather some specimens, and perhaps compare them to those gathered from the causeway and Kerguelen." He clapped Yule on the back. "Good thing we didn't toss them overboard, eh?"

Yule did not bother to answer, as yet another feature of this coast held his interest. These pillars were hardly barren; thousands of birds covered them, their squawks nearly as loud as the waves. None took flight; they resembled the penguins they had seen on Kerguelen, but fatter.

Only Ross's command could tear him away.

"Master Yule! Do you have our coordinates yet?"

"Seventy-one degrees, fourteen minutes south, one-hundred-seventy-one degrees, fifteen minutes east, Captain."

"Good. Gather soundings and estimate the height of these cliffs. We shall survey this coastline as best we can on our voyage south."

"Are we not going to make landfall, Captain?" McCormick asked, incredulous. "Add this new land to Her Majesty's domains?" Yule caught a note of sarcasm in the surgeon's Irish tone, but Ross failed to pick it up. If one thing could convince the captain to pause their race to the pole, it was the renown of being the first to plant the Union Jack on a new shore.

"Ah, yes, of course," Ross said, clearly embarrassed by his oversight. "Master Yule, consult with Master Tucker and the other officers. Find a suitable place for us to make landfall."

Even at a glance, Yule saw that landing on this coast would be suicide—waves would splinter even the sturdiest whaleboat against the stone pillars. But the spyglass revealed a small island off the ship's prow with gentler shores. The officers agreed; they would attempt landfall there.

Twenty minutes later, Yule sat behind McCormick in the *Erebus*'s whaleboat, rubbing shoulders with the able seamen heaving them toward the island. With each stroke, a foul tang from the island grew stronger.

"Guano, judging by the smell," McCormick shouted. "There must be thousands of these birds."

Indeed there were. The island teemed with fat birds packed so closely they covered the ground. When the boat reached shore, it stopped not with the familiar grind of wood on sand, but with a soft thud, accompanied by the strongest wave of the guano stench yet.

Yule wanted to retch, but Ross wasted no time becoming the first Englishman to set foot on this new island—and the first to slip on it. He grabbed the boat's gunwale as he fell.

"Why—the ground itself is guano!" he shouted, regaining his balance. "It must be several feet thick! It will make a fine fertilizer source for our Australian colonists. Franklin will be pleased."

The birds' squawks deafened Yule as they waddled around the boat, pecking its sides and each man as he stepped onto shore. Yule was grateful for his padded trousers.

They waded through the crowd of birds, taking several spongy, fetid footsteps before reaching firmer ground. There, two dozen crew members from both the *Erebus* and *Terror* gathered in a knot around Ross as he planted the Union Jack, claiming the land for Queen Victoria and naming the coastline "Victoria Land" in Her Majesty's honor.

"And what shall we name this island, Captain?" asked Archibald McMurdo, the *Terror*'s first lieutenant, as able seamen gathered stones to fortify the flagpole. "Chatham Island, perhaps, for the dockyards whose work got us this far?"

Ross shook his head. "We need a name befitting the British Empire's first landing in the Antarctic." He pointed skyward. "Possession Island! Master Yule, add that to the remark-book on our return."

A gunshot rang out, scattering all the penguins but one, which now lay lifeless on the rocks, its feathers bloodied. McCormick aimed his pistol overhead and fired again, and a large brown bird fell at their feet. He bent down to examine it. "Some type of skua, it appears," he said, placing both birds in his rucksack.

"Well, Master Yule," Ross said, "quite a busy day for you—a coastline to survey, an island to name, and now two new specimens to clean."

"I'm quite capable of doing it myself, Captain," McCormick said, hoisting the bloody rucksack over his shoulder. "My hands are not quite so frozen this time. Yule's are not needed."

"No, I *insist*, Doctor McCormick. No attention should be spared on your precious specimens."

The sun shined bright as the whaleboat returned to *Erebus*, but a deep chill sank into Yule's bones. For all the menial tasks Ross had assigned him, this was new. Making an officer assist a surgeon over the surgeon's refusal of help? Yule had never seen the captain do such a thing, though both McCormick and Hooker had given him plenty of occasions to. Both were loath to take help from a nonsurgeon.

Yule decided Ross wanted to remind him who was in charge. Did the captain suspect it was Yule, wrapped in foul-weather gear, who had seen him with Hooker?

The question lingered in Yule's mind as he daubed blood and guano from the bird's feathers and handed McCormick each scalpel and tool he requested.

"You're even quieter than usual, Yule," McCormick noted as they lowered the bird into its padded crate. "Something on your mind?"

Yule froze. Did McCormick suspect something? Just then, a bump from an ice floe nearly made them drop the crate lid. Muffled shouts and curses came from the upper deck.

"No," Yule replied, as they closed the crate. "Just taking it all in."

Chapter 21

Ross Sea Coast
Antarctica
June 2123

Roscoe's wristband buzzed the next day. It wasn't Hamza. It was a message from Jen to the entire intern cohort:

> *Hey guys! Hope everyone's first few weeks have been going well. Planning another "driving lesson" tonight ;) Tomorrow's the official solstice—and midwinter at Newloon is EPIC. Meet at 7pm at the foyer if you're interested.*

Great. Another night of grinning and bearing it with someone who knew he was a compounder—and who had offered him an opportunity that he'd thrown down the toilet. Roscoe started wondering about the razors here again when his wrist buzzed with another message from Jen, addressed only to him:

> *Hey Roscoe! Hope you're doing well. Really hope you can make it to the "driving lesson." Was planning some one-on-one time when we could talk about the exchange program.*

He was still in the running for the exchange program? *How?* he asked himself. Had Trent not told Jen about his slip-up? Was it not as big a deal as he thought? Was it a second chance? Or was this the "good-cop bad-cop" routine they talked about in old TV shows?

He didn't know, and for now, he didn't care. He still had a shot out of this hell hole.

Roscoe reported to the foyer that evening. Hamza wasn't there—probably working another night shift—but Jen was. "All right, guys, I'll have you driving like pros in no time."

She made sure Joi, the StarCross Security agent, had loaded the course to Lake Bonney into their locator beacon. They suited up, picked up their ride, and headed out onto the ice with the windows closed this time.

"You know where Hamza is, Roscoe?" she asked from the front seat.

"Yesterday, he told me he's working the late shift." Roscoe remembered the way Hamza had lowered his voice and didn't share more.

Jen didn't seem to mind. "Yeah, Drone Ops are slammed getting ready for Argus-3—the nuclear test."

"A nuclear test?" Ana asked.

"Yep," Jen said. "The whole project's actually pretty cool. Or maybe insane."Here, I'll show you." She flicked her right wrist, and her wristband projected a screen onto the windshield. Keeping one hand on the wheel, she used her other hand to position the display so everyone could see it from the back seat. Then, she said, "Navigation."

A map of the area appeared. Their track's dot hugged the Ross Sea Coast, moving away from a point labeled "SPIGOT." Inland, a swirl of brown-and-white streaks indicated the Dry Valleys and the glaciers pierced and underlaid by Spigot's piping. Jen traced a finger along one of the white streaks.

"Right now, Spigot's draining meltwater from these glaciers," she explained, "but they don't melt on their own, so we have to warm them from below and inside. Remember the heating elements we saw during the geology tournament?" Roscoe had tried to forget that awful day, but here was Jen, of all people, bringing it up. "Heating them takes energy, which is bad for business."

She shifted the map inland, bringing the East Antarctic ice sheet into view. "Down here, though, beneath all this ice, are oceans of fresh water, as much as the Great Lakes combined, and way cleaner. If Spigot could tap into *that*, we wouldn't need to keep melting glaciers."

Roscoe remembered Chip mentioning the "giant freshwater lakes" under East Antarctica's ice sheet. "So Spigot will bore a tunnel there?" he asked, not sure how a nuclear bomb was part of the plan.

Jen's ponytail swung as she shook her head. "Not at first. That water's super-pressurized from the tons of ice pushing down on it. If we tunneled straight from Spigot into the ice sheet, the pressure would wreck our filtration system and probably any sub that hooked up to it."

Roscoe still didn't see where Jen was going, but Darren did. "You need another reservoir," he said matter-of-factly.

Now, the ponytail bobbed as Jen nodded. "Vanda's not big enough. We need another one, and we're not messing around with a tile covering this time. The new one'll be an underground cistern, with a tunnel connecting it to the ice sheet. Then, we'll stick a pipe into the cistern from above, which will let us fill our subs safely."

It clicked for Roscoe. He couldn't tell whether the water-pressure explanation was true. But it sure made a good excuse for what he guessed were StarCross's real goals: keeping those hidden oceans permanently out of the wildcatters' reach—or creating another Vanda-like reservoir to regulate supply and keep production in the Goldilocks zone. "And you're going to blast out this reservoir with a nuke?"

"Been done before." Jen tapped her wristband again. "Show me an image of Project Gnome."

The map switched to a black-and-white photograph of what looked like a cave, with no stalactites or stalagmites. A figure wearing a hard hat with a miner's lamp stood on the rubble-strewn floor, dwarfed by cragged walls and a domed ceiling high above.

"The U.S. government blasted out this cavity under New Mexico back in the 1960s," Jen explained. "The govellers up there still have plenty of nukes, and thanks to the Updated Terms of Service, they don't need them for much else."

"Has StarCross ever gotten a nuke before?" Roscoe asked.

"Not since they used one to blast Spigot's port out," Jen said. "I think it's actually in the Updated Terms of Service that StarCross won't ask for any decommissioned nukes." She shrugged. "Makes 'em look more peaceful, I guess. They worked out a side agreement to get this one."

Darren, who had been assigned to Filtration, had another question. "Won't the reservoir be radioactive?"

Jen dismissed the question with a wave, then pointed back to the photo. "The one in New Mexico didn't stay radioactive for long. And I'm sure you guys in Filtration can handle any contamination that's left over."

"And they're planning to create this reservoir under Yule Bay?" Roscoe asked, knowing it was far from Spigot's sub docks.

"No, the actual reservoir will be closer to Spigot. Yule Bay is just a proof of concept. Originally, the idea was to establish a stockpile down here and let StarCross run some blast simulations whenever the Equation indicated. But now, they want to do a live test. And, for whatever reason, they picked Yule Bay."

Jen swiped the projection away and returned her focus to driving.

"Jahnford was pissed. You know that, right, Roscoe? He's been talking about it at church." She lowered her voice to mimic Jahnford's, "'With the grace of God, a nuclear bomb will soon reach Antarctic soil.'" She held her thumb and pointer finger just barely apart. "His prophecy was *so close* to coming true. But then some 'evildoers' came along. A nuke slipped through his fingers."

Roscoe bolted upright, nerves kicking in. Did Jen not know what he'd told Jahnford, Trent, and the others about the freshwater plume under Yule Bay? Or did she know and simply not care? Did he still have a shot at this exchange program, or was she just playing with him? And if she was, why?

He hadn't figured it out when they stepped into Newloon. It looked just like he had remembered: repurposed lights bathing the packed stalls and passageways in countless shades of white and amber. It smelled the same too: sweat, weed, and whatever approximations of ethnic food could be cooked down here. Only the sounds were different—music from Wit's End throbbed over everything else as the row of bars and nightclubs celebrated midwinter.

Together, they made their way to Gallagher's. "You guys go in, get me whatever their midwinter special drink is," Jen shouted over the music. To Roscoe's mortification, she added, "I gotta help Roscoe find some decent compound. Won't be too long." His fellow interns shrugged and headed inside, while Jen cast Roscoe a quick look and waved for him to follow. "C'mon, let's talk."

They weaved back through the crowd to Shiduri's, where most of the dance music stopped at the door. Chip was at the bar, chin in one hand and a beer in the other. He shot Roscoe an impressed look when he saw him with Jen.

They found an empty table and ordered beers.

"So, how's it going?" Jen asked. "How'd I do with the readings at church this week?"

"You were good," Roscoe said. "Put the fear of God in me, that's for sure."

She rolled her eyes, then sighed and rested her chin in her hands. "As long as Jahnford thinks I give a shit. Sometimes I feel bad faking it, but I also feel like I have to do it to get a shot off-world. What do you think?"

"I-I don't blame you."

"Really?" She cocked her head, eyebrows raised. Jen didn't seem so confident. She seemed desperate for someone to confirm she was on the right track—and that someone was Roscoe. He snuck a deep breath in through his nostrils.

"Yeah, you definitely have to do it," he said. She still didn't look reassured, so Roscoe added, "I'd do it."

"You'd fake it?"

"Totally—especially if I thought it'd get me a shot off-world."

"Thank you. That's so reassuring." Jen's shoulders relaxed. "I think a lot of people would. And those Residents know it. Did you hear about all the frostbite the winners of the geology tournament got?" Roscoe nodded. "Rumor has it the Residents make sure things go wrong in that tournament. They don't care about geology. They just want to see who will push through and do what StarCross tells them." She leaned forward. "What do you think about that?"

"Wouldn't put it past them," Roscoe said, loosening up. "Not after the way they fucked over the compounders."

She toyed with her bracelet, looking down at the table. "Roscoe ... I'm ... I'm a compounder."

His mouth fell open. "So am I." Feeling foolish, he muttered, "But you already knew that."

Her eyes met his. "Those headaches are the worst, aren't they? I had to tough 'em out. My parents were recyclers, but StarCross's push to expand lunar mining and move manufacturing off-world killed their business." She forced a smile. "Can't beam plastics to space. So we could only afford floodplain housing, had to move every couple years." Roscoe thought about what she had moaned, delirious, the day of the tournament. Pennsylvania's empty riverbeds didn't flood often, but when they did, no prefab nearby stood a chance. He and his parents had managed to dodge the storm surges—so far.

"I'm sorry to hear that," he said. "That was always the big worry for my family too."

Jen nodded. "So you know what it's like, to *have* to tough it out to get a spot off-world. I got off compound about a year ago," she said, "but there's always this doubt if I'm really good enough. Never got a top-tenth award my entire time at Granite Gorge." Her eyelids flexed as if she were crying—but she couldn't, Roscoe knew, because of compound.

"And on top of that, I have to deal with StarCross telling us we're no good and Jahnford saying we're the spawn of Satan. I've been here almost three years, and I'm just desperate to get out. Do you ever feel that way?"

Roscoe nodded, and Jen gave him another pleading look. *You're it, dammit,* he told himself. *She's counting on you. Try harder!* "Sure I do. I've only been here a few months, but that's been enough to make me want to go anywhere else." He forced a small smile. "I can't imagine having to deal with Jahnford's bullshit every day." Jen still didn't look convinced, and Roscoe remembered what she faced if she washed out of the Leadership Training Program. He leaned in. "Jen, I know you can get off-world. We compounders are as good as anyone else."

Finally, Jen smiled, reaching over to take his hand. "Thank you, Roscoe. That's just what I needed to hear tonight." She released his hand, then downed the last of her beer. The confident Jen had returned; her tone was businesslike again. "Anyway, I've picked the other shortlist candidate for the Leadership Training Program transfer division. You're it."

Roscoe froze, unsure if he'd heard her right. "Me? That's ... great!" Caught off guard again, his mind raced for the right words. "Anything I should do to get ready?"

She shook her head. "Not right now—just don't break rank again."

Roscoe's stomach dropped. She knew.

"Relax," Jen said, her voice warm but steady. "Trent's pissed, but he'll get over it—he's just a hard-ass. Jahnford's pissed because StarCross has decided to use the nuke to destroy that freshwater source instead of leaving it here for his cult. In StarCross's book, *that's* worth nuking."

"Gotta keep it scarce somehow, I guess." Roscoe was grateful that Chip had explained the fundamentals of WEConomics, so Jen didn't have to.

She nodded and fiddled some more with the bracelet on her wrist, twisting the two diamond beads as she spoke. "Look, it showed you had your eye on what StarCross wants: locking up fresh water. It didn't hurt you in their eyes, and they have a say in this decision too—not just Jahnford."

"But Jahnford has a say too."

She nodded, frowning. "There's no getting around the fact that he's mad at you. Keep your head down for now and hope it fades. He might block you this selection round, but maybe not the next one. Just keep showing up at church."

Roscoe nodded. He could take it.

Jen leaned back, stretching her arms over her head before standing up and placing a hand on his shoulder. "Well, I'd better be going. Can't keep the others waiting. See you at eleven?"

"Sounds good."

"All right. And stay away from the compound machine this time." She winked, then turned and headed for the door.

Roscoe drained his Elephant IPA and moved to a stool at the bar to order another, savoring the buzz after the turmoil of the last few days. He barely noticed when Chip sat down on the stool next to him.

"Damn, she an intern too?"

"Yeah. Just work-related."

"Whatever, man. I don't care. Happy Midwinter. If I get some nachos, will you help me out? I'm celebrating again."

"Yeah, sure, thanks. Just for Midwinter?"

Chip nodded and waved Shiduri over. "Seal-blubber nachos and another round for both of us."

Shiduri raised an eyebrow as she took the order. "Midwinter and nachos—classy. Got something to celebrate?"

Roscoe shrugged. "Just Midwinter."

"Uh-huh." Shiduri rolled her eyes and walked off.

A few minutes later, she returned with their food and drinks, setting them down with a grin. "Don't party too hard. I'm not hauling either of you out of here." She left before Roscoe could respond.

Chip scooped some quivering blubber with a chip. "Anyway," he said, "it's not just Midwinter. Successful first sampling run. Got some good data. Even found a backer in the Griquas."

Roscoe took a swig of beer and reached for a chip. "Congrats. Learn anything useful?"

Chip shook his head, chewing. "Still analyzing it. Some of their people are helping me out. We'll see where it takes us. They also said they'd back the dye test."

"The one to prove a fissure runs from Spigot's glaciers and Yule Bay?"

Chip nodded, reaching for another chip. "They've been breeding bioluminescent algae. Been using it to refine their DNA sequencing and incubation techniques, but they think it'll work for this. Only lights up in fresh water."

"They want to dump glowing algae under a glacier?"

"Yep." Chip wiped his mouth with a napkin. "They'll tweak the DNA so it won't reproduce, won't throw the local ecology any more out of whack than it already is. Said they'd give me a batch to release where the fissure probably starts."

"But you'd still need Jahnford and StarCross to go along with it, right?"

Chip nodded. "Told them that too. Said we'd still need Jahnford to open the glacier's tunnels—and how bad he'd look if the test worked. They told me to try persuading him. I said we'd see." He sighed, staring into his beer. "Maybe one day they'll let me do my dye test. And maybe one day I'll be a Resident."

"No way around Jahnford?"

Chip started to shake his head, then steepled his fingers and stared hard across the bar. "Well," he said, "I could find an inside man."

Roscoe fell silent, fully aware that he or Hamza could be that inside man—but also aware that Chip couldn't ask them to do it outright. He drained his beer and flagged Shiduri over to settle his tab.

"Gotta get my ride back to Spigot. Thanks for the nachos and beer."

Chip stared at the counter. "Don't mention it."

Roscoe left and headed back to Gallagher's, where he found Jen and the other interns. This time, Ana rode shotgun; Roscoe figured Jen wanted to keep him at arm's length around the other interns. The ride was quiet—they were all too tired and fucked up. As they rolled along the rocky coast, there were no explosions rocking the mountains. But the wind blew hard all the way back.

Chapter 22

H.M.S. *Erebus*
Unnamed Sea
January 1841

"Ready the whaleboats!" an able seaman shouted. "We have an opening in the pack!"

Yule closed the remark-book and climbed the ladder. He had spent three weeks charting this alien shore, sounding depths and plotting peaks as the *Erebus* and *Terror* inched along the coast. Their gradual plod let Yule and Tucker gain at least a rough sense of these waters for the Admiralty and Hydrographic Office. The work had toughened Yule against the cold, but not against his captain. The South Magnetic Pole, where Ross so fervently hoped to plant the flag, still lay ahead, even as summer waned.

Since Possession Island, Ross's teasing had given way to curt orders and angry tirades. On January 23, they had surpassed Weddell's record of seventy-four degrees South, reached in another open section of the southern seas. This achievement—and the double rum ration it justified—brightened the captain's mood, but by the next morning, it was as foul as ever.

To make matters worse, they had yet to land on the Antarctic mainland. So far, they had only seen sheer rock, thick pack ice, and high white cliffs calving into the ocean. Providence seemed to have fortified this entire continent against human settlement. But now, four days after passing Weddell's record, they had found a landing point.

A small one, Yule noted as he looked through the spyglass. This latest knob of land seemed like all the rest—waves crashing against cliffs and caverns, ice sloughing into the sea, snow—or was it ice?—lining every crevice and slope. But on the peninsula's southern side a gentle, sandy beach offered a place where a whaleboat could land. It was time to claim the mainland for Her Majesty.

The able seamen heaved to, turning the *Erebus* and *Terror* into the wind and dropping anchor. As Yule watched Hooker, Ross, and other members of the landing party board the whaleboat, a familiar tang wrinkled his nostrils.

"More guano," McCormick said, attempting to sketch the island with gloved fingers. "There must be more penguins there, thousands of them, perhaps new species." He sighed, breath clouding in front of him. "They will escape my collection."

Yule nodded, recalling Ross's order that at least one surgeon stay on board at all times. "A terrible loss to science," McCormick muttered as they watched the able seamen lower the whaleboat toward the waves. "Leaving the first impressions of this land to such an untrained eye."

Again, Yule felt the urge to share his secret with McCormick, but before he could speak, Ross called his name. "Master Yule! We need one more to balance the boat."

"I'll get you what I can," Yule whispered.

McCormick clapped him on the shoulder. "Good lad."

By sheer luck, Yule noticed an empty pail beneath the gunwale nearby. He brought it with him onto the boat.

He and the other officers sat, backs to the wind, as the able seamen rowed toward shore, oars thunking against bergs while the guano stench grew stronger. Every few strokes, Yule peeked over his shoulder. The beach appeared as before, but the ice-sheathed slopes and cliffs to its left revealed something odd: several hundred yards were shaded, but past a certain fold in the ice, they gleamed.

Ross noticed it as well. "Take us around that outcropping before we land," he shouted. They skirted the shore, and as they moved, the same fold in the ice separated shadow and light. The boat passed it, and Yule noticed the ice nearest them turning northward. To his left he saw ... open water.

This was an island, not part of the mainland. The bright shoreline remained miles away. Ross's uncle had mistaken clouds for land, and now Ross had mistaken water for it.

"Turn around!" the captain barked, his fury clear through the scarf. "Let us land and claim the island, at least."

The able seamen turned the boat back toward the beach. Yule now saw that their intended landing spot, too, was not as it had appeared from the ship. It was not a beach at all but a steep, rocky slope that leveled out several yards above them. From the flat, higher ground, penguins gazed down at the intruders.

Yule knew landing here would be dangerous. Captain Crozier of the *Terror*, who had joined the landing party, agreed.

"Perhaps you should lay your hand on the ground and christen it without endangering yourself," Crozier suggested. They had reached the shore; waves lifted the whaleboat up and down, surging several feet beside the rocks.

Yule watched Ross slap Crozier on the back. "Ah! Old boy," Ross declared, "if I put my hand on it, the body must follow." Another wave lifted the boat, and Ross leaped from the prow, wedging his gloved hands and booted toes between the stones, before scrambling up to the flat ground. Crozier followed on the next wave. On the third, Hooker attempted the same leap.

The young surgeon tried to match Ross's and Crozier's steps, but his boot slipped on the gunwale, sending him into the waves. Yule sat fixed to his seat as the able seamen sprang to the side, leaned over the gunwale, and braced one another while plunging their arms into the icy water. Several waves rolled past, drenching them with spray, before they pulled Hooker back into the whaleboat.

"Get him warm!" Ross shouted from the top of the slope, an unfamiliar panic in his voice. "No one else out!"

Hooker said nothing as the crew on the boat stripped off his soaked clothes and cocooned him in their outer jackets. Yule started to remove his own coat, but a seaman stopped him. "That should do until we get him back to the ship."

The whaleboat was filling with frigid bilge. "Does anyone have a pail?" someone shouted. Yule grabbed the one he'd brought and started bailing, tossing several pailfuls overboard as Ross and Crozier leaped back into the boat.

The captain's scarf hid his expression as he looked at Hooker's silent, china-doll face, but his voice trembled. "Back to the ship at once."

Yule tossed out one last pailful, then remembered why he had brought the bucket in the first place. Bracing himself, he ordered the nearest seaman to hold on to him. Timing his move with a wave crest, Yule stretched toward the slope and plunged the bucket into the rocky edge, filling it with gravel and smooth, dark cobbles for McCormick. He held it between his legs as the able seamen shoved off.

The crew rowed in silence, with the penguins' squawks and the crash of waves drowning out Hooker's whimpers. Several oar-strokes away from the island, a tiny Union Jack, tied to a dowel, came into view atop the slope.

"What did you christen it, Captain?" Yule asked, adding, "so I might record its name when we return."

"Franklin Island," Ross replied. "Something to make that oaf of a governor happy."

No one spoke the rest of the way back.

Chapter 23

Ross Sea Coast
Antarctica
June 2123

The day after the Newloon trip, Roscoe was back to the Archives. His fears assuaged by Jen, he turned his focus to a handwritten log from the *Erebus*, labeled "Remark-Book." Nineteenth-century handwriting had gotten a little easier to decipher. But in early afternoon, Roscoe's wrist buzzed with an all-employees message, breaking his concentration.

The sender's address was a meaningless string of numbers and letters. Surprised it had slipped past the spam filter, Roscoe opened his inbox to delete it. But as soon as he tapped on the message, a video started to play. When Roscoe realized what it showed, his wrist almost dropped.

Jahnford, Jen, and Trent were sitting around a table, passing a compound bottle, each taking a few pills before the clip ended.

Roscoe heard the video play from Karla's wrist as well. He watched her lean back in her chair and mutter, "Ay."

Karla had never hinted that she knew Roscoe was a compounder, so he feigned shock. "You—you think it's real?"

Karla took off her glasses, wiping them with her jacket. "Jahnford will say it's fake, but who can know for sure?"

Roscoe thought back to what he'd seen of Jahnford: the earnest look, his sincerity in his church invitation, his conviction while preaching the end of the world and the incineration of all evildoers, especially compounders. "He really seems to hate us—I mean—those compounders in church."

Karla replaced her glasses, not seeming to have heard his slip-up. "So? As long as there's been religion, there have been religious hypocrites. You don't believe me, go to a used media store in Newloon—yes, I know you visit that place. Ask for a book on Jim Bakker or Frank Sandford, or the Catholic Church in—well, pretty much anywhere. Jahnford would be heir to a long, fine tradition."

Roscoe was nearly as stunned by her response as he was by the video. If Jahnford heard what Karla had said, it might be a serious risk—but maybe she was confident he wouldn't or didn't care. Jahnford tolerated trips to Newloon and any pre-ban compounders in Spigot. Why wouldn't he overlook someone saying what everyone was thinking?

Roscoe's productivity was once again shot. He managed to catalog only three more pages in the remaining four hours of work. As he closed the book, his wrist buzzed again with a message headed by StarCross's stars-and-droplet.

Good evening,

Earlier today, an unidentified individual sent a video to all Spigot employees and residents. It depicted Spigot CEO Grei Jahnford engaged in prohibited conduct with two interns. THIS VIDEO IS A FORGERY. StarCross Security has opened an investigation into its source. StarCross will initiate blacklisting proceedings against any individual(s) involved in the production and release of this video. Spigot residents and employees with information on these individual(s) may submit anonymous tips to StarCross Security at tips@segurity.sc.

The video has been removed from Spigot servers. StarCross will initiate blacklisting proceedings against any individual(s) found to have saved a copy of it on a wristband, computer, or external storage device. As a reminder, all such devices within Spigot are subject to search by StarCross Security. These measures are necessary to ensure Spigot's stability and water production.

A further reminder: While individuals who received doses of IQ-enhancing compound prior to StarCross's 2120 ban may reside in Spigot, continued possession of these substances is prohibited. StarCross Security reserves the right to search the living quarters, workspaces, and personal effects of any Spigot resident for prohibited compounds.

Thank you for your cooperation in this matter. Spigot management and StarCross Security wish all residents a pleasant evening.

Just as Roscoe finished reading, another message came through, this time from Jahnford.

Dear Spigot Family,

I'm sure you have seen the false and obscene content shared earlier today. I am at a loss to understand why someone would want to slander me and two hard-working interns in such a way, and to sow discord and mistrust in this godly community. I pray that StarCross Security will soon locate the evildoers responsible for this act, and that they will face StarCross's discipline and God's judgment. I humbly ask that all employees and residents provide whatever aid their investigation may require.

Thank you for reading. I am sorry that you have had to face such obscenity, and I pray that we can put this disruption behind us and continue bringing water to a thirsty world. If you were subjected to experimentation with compound in your youth, please know that you are always welcome to attend the Revelator Church in the auditorium on Sundays. Christ always helps those who return to His path.

All my best,
Grei Jahnford

Roscoe rubbed his forehead. He didn't feel up to running—it might mean another encounter with Jen. Instead, he headed to the galley, where speculation about the culprit swirled around him.

"Maybe it was StarCross Security themselves," someone suggested. "They're tired of Jahnford and want a pretext to get rid of him."

Another intern shook her head. "It was one of Spigot's customers. They want to take Jahnford down a peg, make it look like he doesn't have his shit together. They're hoping whoever comes next will give them a better deal, cut them some slack from the Updated Terms of Service."

"Or maybe some disgruntled Executives decided they'd stage a coup."

"Naw, it was the Revelators. They're sick of waiting for Jahnford to get his hands on a nuke and think someone else can do the job better."

"You're all overthinking this. It was someone at Newloon."

"Newloon?" several people at Roscoe's table asked at once. "What they'd get out of it?"

"Lots of things. Maybe there'll be mass blacklistings because of this, which'll mean more people going over there, desperate for work and willing to sign on to whatever god-awful venture someone is cooking up over there."

Roscoe ate in silence. He felt a little sorry—not for Jahnford or Trent, but for Jen. She didn't deserve this. He thought about sending her an it's-okay message, but decided against it. This was *not* the time to call attention to himself.

More speculation filled the galley in the following days. Besides Karla, everyone seemed to take for granted that the video was fake, that there was just no way Spigot's Bible-thumping CEO would use compound with two interns. The tunnels were patrolled by more StarCross Security agents, now in body armor, some armed with assault rifles. All this over a drug video? Roscoe was puzzled, but he wasn't worried.

Until Friday.

He and Karla were in the Archives, cataloging old files, when the door swung open. They both looked up to see three StarCross Security agents—masked, armored, and packing.

Karla shot Roscoe the briefest glance, her eyes sharp with warning, before she stood. "May I help you?" she asked the three agents.

"We're here to do a search pursuant to our investigation into the network breach incident," the lead agent, a woman, announced. The eyes between her helmet and balaclava darted from Karla to Roscoe, who had just remembered the "subject to search" bit in the all-employees email when the lead agent said, "Both of you, up against the wall."

Roscoe rose from his desk and followed Karla's lead, placing his palms against the wall and biting his tongue through a minutes-long frisk. Finally, the agent released him and ordered, "Stay against the wall while we search the premises."

They had no choice but to comply. One agent—the one with the largest gun—stood by, watching them closely. Roscoe risked a quick look behind him and saw the other two agents seated at his and Karla's desks, tablets plugged into each of their computers.

A couple of minutes later, the tablets dinged, signaling the scan had finished. The agents unplugged their devices and headed for the door.

The head agent motioned to the one standing guard over Karla and Roscoe to follow. "Thank you for your time. As you were," she said as the door closed behind them.

Karla and Roscoe traded a look, then they both exhaled deeply and sank into their chairs.

"They ever done that before?" Roscoe asked.

"No, never. Guess they're cracking down."

Roscoe stared at his page, but unease tugged him back toward Karla. He toggled his desk alongside hers and whispered, "You think they're listening to us in here?"

"Maybe," Karla said, just as hushed. "Guess we should both be more careful."

The weekend passed without incident, and Roscoe didn't bother going to church. On Monday, another three-person crew from StarCross Security showed up. Whether they were the same agents as before, Roscoe couldn't tell—the balaclavas made sure of that. This time, though, the frisk was rougher. Their gloved hands pressed higher up his thighs than before.

They didn't stop at the computers this time. After scanning the systems again, they dumped the cabinets he and Karla had been cataloging, fanning books and letters across the floor.

"Be careful!" Karla snapped, glaring right past the agent keeping her and Roscoe against the wall at gunpoint. "Some of those records are centuries old."

"Just following our orders, Miss Marmolada," one of the agents said. He flipped through Ross's log like a deck of cards, bending the spine as he rifled through the pages. *What was he looking for?* Roscoe wondered. *Compound? A hidden chip with a copy of the tape?*

Whatever it was, the agent didn't find it. He set the book down on Roscoe's desk, motioned to the others, and left.

"Is this still about the video last Tuesday?" Karla called after them. "I can assure you—"

"We are just following orders, Miss Marmolada," the head agent interrupted, turning back to face them. "StarCross has classified this investigation as a top priority. And I remind you both"—his eyes locked on Roscoe—"that all Spigot facilities, employees, residents, and interns are subject to random searches by StarCross Security at any time, for any reason."

With that, they left.

That evening, after another unproductive afternoon, Roscoe headed to the galley. The place was quieter than usual. Even whispers felt risky. An armed StarCross Security agent paced the wall. Roscoe got a tray of food and sat down next to Hamza.

"Hey."

"Hey," Hamza said, barely raising his eyes. "How's it going?"

"Oh, you know, the usual."

They ate in silence. Hamza looked like he might say something, then stopped, eyes dropping to his tray. He wolfed down the rest of his StemSteak and stood. "Gotta go. More surveying work tonight."

That night, Roscoe lay awake, letting his mind fill the dark ceiling with the last few days' events—the messages, the searches, the frisks, the endless theories, and what he'd seen in that video: Jahnford, Trent, and Jen, each taking compound. It all kept leading him back to the same question: What the hell was going on down here?

A buzz on his wristband jolted him upright. "Visitor at the door," the floating screen informed him. He held his breath, hoping it was a glitch, but it buzzed again. Roscoe checked the security feed on his wristband—just a hood. Then a hand pulled the hood back. Hamza. Roscoe exhaled. He could trust Hamza—as much as anyone down here.

"Hey," he said, opening the door.

"Hey, listen," Hamza whispered, stepping in quickly. "I gotta make this quick in case they're watching. They questioned me about you."

"Questioned? Who did?"

"StarCross Security." Hamza leaned in close, his forehead nearly touching Roscoe's. Roscoe glanced around his room, realizing all the places where it could hide a camera or microphone.

"What'd they ask?"

"They wanted to know about our trips outside Spigot. They told me I wouldn't get in trouble for going to Newloon or anywhere else, but they needed to know the truth. They asked the dates of those trips, where we went, and who we talked to."

"What you'd tell them?"

"Everything," Hamza said, making Roscoe's jaw drop, "except our conversations with Chip." That was a bit of relief. Hamza added, "I didn't say we'd met him at Newloon. I told them he gave us a ride when we picked up the drone but said he was on a satellite call with people in the States the whole time and didn't talk to us."

"Thanks," Roscoe whispered. "I mean it."

Hamza nodded. "Sure thing. Look, I don't want to be out too long, but just wanted to let you know so our stories line up in case they question you." With that, he slipped out the door.

As Roscoe lay back in bed, he realized he'd forgotten to ask Hamza why he thought StarCross was acting this way. But he didn't get the chance for the next few days.

Karla nodded when he arrived at work; so did some of the other regulars in the galley. But StarCross Security had put a damper on things. Conversations had dried up entirely—not just the big stuff, but even the usual chatter. And with the wrong word in the wrong ear carrying the risk of blacklisting, no one seemed eager to break the StarCross Silence.

To Roscoe's own surprise, he couldn't take the quiet anymore. On Wednesday, he decided to go to Newloon, alone. Maybe Chip or Shiduri could shed some light on what was happening. But when he arrived at the Foyer, ready for another "practice drive," he found another sign placed out front, next to the one listing all the safety protocols.

ALL NON-ESSENTIAL TRIPS OUTSIDE SPIGOT ARE SUSPENDED UNTIL FURTHER NOTICE

Spigot employees and residents wishing to travel outside the settlement must submit their travel plans to StarCross Security for approval at least 24 hours in advance. StarCross Security will only approve trip applicants who consent to the presence of a security agent in the vehicle. Participants in any unapproved trip will be blacklisted.

The StarCross logo—but not Spigot's standalone droplet—appeared at the bottom of the notice board.

Roscoe returned to his room, annoyed at the lost beer. He remembered what Jen had told him and the other interns during their first trip to Newloon, about how Jahnford had to look past all those excursions. They were the only thing keeping everyone in this cave from snapping. Now, StarCross Security had closed that pressure valve—but why?

Roscoe was no closer to an answer by Friday, as he pretended to study a whaling captain's log, pecking at his keyboard often enough to look busy. He only looked up when StarCross Security walked in.

"Roscoe Slake?" the masked head agent asked. "We need to take you in for questioning."

Roscoe looked between the agents and Karla, who said nothing. Seeing no choice, he let the agents escort him out.

They led him to the back of a walled, covered jitney—a rare sight down here—and sat him between two agents. Narrow metal armrests separated Roscoe from them. "Grip each one," the agent on his left ordered. As soon as he complied, his wristband snapped to one armrest, like a magnet had switched on. When he tried to move, the band tightened until he relaxed his arm. The ride passed in silence.

Roscoe gasped when the jitney drove through the Motor Pool vehicle entrance. Were they about to toss him out into the cold? But then the driver stopped outside a pedestrian door.

The agent on Roscoe's right opened the door and pulled him out. "Through here."

He entered a room no bigger than his dorm: a desk down the middle and chairs on either side. The agent pointed to an empty chair. Roscoe took a seat, facing a StarCross Security agent with a bald head, clean-shaven face, and gray eyes—so nondescript he might as well have been masked.

"Mister Slake, we're investigating the recent network security breach. We want to ask you a few questions."

Roscoe nodded.

"First, I'd like you to share your reaction when you first saw the video that was sent out."

"I-I was shocked. I thought it had to have been a fake."

"What led you to that conclusion?"

"I had met Mister Jahnford a few times, had seen him at church, and just couldn't believe he would use compound or provide it to interns. I was relieved when I learned that it was a forgery." The agent raised an eyebrow. "But not surprised."

"You were reprimanded for insubordination following a recent interaction with Mister Jahnford, correct?"

"I was told by Trent Hale that it was wrong of me to share certain information with Mister Jahnford."

"How did you feel about that interaction?"

In the second of silence that followed, Roscoe noticed that this room wasn't quite featureless. A grid of small, dark circles studded each wall and the ceiling. He guessed they were cameras, microphones, or some other kind of sensor, all trained on him. He felt his chest tighten, pulse quicken, and mouth turn dry.

"I, uh, was very disappointed in myself. I had only wanted to provide information helpful to Spigot's mission. I realized it was a grave breach of protocol on my part and resolved not to do it again."

The agent nodded; Roscoe noticed he had an earpiece, likely supplying him with all kinds of information. The agent extended his wrist. "You left base with Hamza Tetuanui on the evening of June Thirteenth, correct?"

Roscoe nodded.

"Please state your answer verbally."

Roscoe flattened his voice as best he could. "Correct. We did leave the base on that day."

"What did you do on that excursion?"

"We recovered a drone that he had beached by mistake."

"Did you interact with anyone else during that excursion?"

"Our track broke down, and a scientist from McMurdo named Chip Erskin towed us back. He was on a satellite phone call on the way back, though, so we didn't really talk."

Another nod. "Have you had any other interactions with Doctor Erskin since then?"

"No."

The agent tapped his wrist screen. "Please listen to the following audio." A hidden speaker beeped to life.

Roscoe heard a crowd talking; the crowd at Shiduri's. Then, he heard Chip.

"Maybe one day they'll let me do my dye test. And maybe one day I'll be a Resident."

Roscoe heard himself ask, "There's no way you could go around Jahnford?"

"Well," Chip said, "I could find an inside man."

As Roscoe remembered it, that had been the end of his talk with Chip that night. But the audio kept playing. "I'd do it," Roscoe heard himself say. "I'd fake it if I had to. I can't imagine having to deal with Jahnford's bullshit every day. StarCross fucked over the compounders, but we compounders are as good as anyone else."

The audio stopped. The agent leaned forward. "Would you like to amend your previous answer?"

Roscoe fumbled for his words, knowing that what he said here—and how he said it—would be dissected. "I-I did have that conversation with Doctor Erskin, but I don't remember saying that last part, about offering to do the dye test and not wanting to work under Mister Jahnford. I never said that to Doctor Erskin. I-I don't know where you got this recording."

As soon as the words left his mouth, Roscoe realized they hadn't gotten it anywhere—they had made it up. He might not have said the last bit to Chip—but he had said it to Jen. Roscoe's eyes widened, and sweat beaded his forehead, both of which the sensors would undoubtedly pick up. It had all been a setup—Jen's "private" one-on-one talk with him, the drug video, maybe even the conversation with Chip. Security had gotten him to make incriminating statements, spliced together into the conversation he'd just heard, to build a case against him. For all Roscoe knew, StarCross might be preparing to dole out its harshest punishment: blacklisting. Once again, all Roscoe could think was—why?

The agent cut off Roscoe's spiraling thoughts. "Have you had any further communications with Doctor Erskin since that evening?"

"No."

"Have you taken any steps toward the dye test you discussed in that recording?"

"No."

Roscoe braced himself for more evidence they might have fabricated, but the agent simply closed his wrist screen. "Very well, Mister Slake. Thank you for your time. We will review your responses and let you know if we have any other questions."

Roscoe rose and stepped out of the room; the agents were waiting to escort him. "We'll give you a ride back to the Archives."

Once again, he sat wedged between two agents in the back of the jitney, cuffed to the armrest by his wristband, trying to process it all. Was he unlucky, stupid, or both? He'd walked into that room so sure—sure that pointing to the bay with fresh water on the map would get him rewarded for helping Spigot supply water to a thirsty world—or at least control that supply.

Instead, he'd cost his boss a nuclear weapon—a weapon his religion might have used to achieve its goal. Because of what he'd told StarCross, Jahnford's bomb would be set off underwater to eliminate the freshwater plume. That was all the reason Jahnford needed to want him gone, and the video gave him a pretext—and everyone else a damn good distraction.

The jitney pulled up. Roscoe stepped out, and the irony sank in. He may have just saved Earth from a nuclear war. Instead, it would run out of water, and he wouldn't have a way off.

Chapter 24

Roscoe really hated being right.

The next Monday, he had just sat down for another day's cataloging when a single StarCross Security agent opened the door. This one had no gun—just a manila envelope.

"Delivery for Roscoe Slake."

This seemed like a bad time to speed his desk toward the door on its rails; the Archives hall felt longer than ever as Roscoe walked forward. The agent handed him the package and projected a wrist screen that faced him, requesting his signature. He scrawled it out, and the agent left.

Roscoe felt a sheaf of papers inside the envelope; if someone was sending him a message on paper, it had to be important. He opened the envelope, and Karla joined him in looking at the first sheet, topped with the StarCross logo:

SUMMONS FOR ADMINISTRATIVE DISCIPLINARY HEARING

Defendant: Roscoe Slake; First-year archival intern

Alleged offense(s): Libel; Fabrication of obscenity;

Distribution of obscenity over StarCross IT network; seditious conspiracy

StarCross Security's requested penalty if found guilty: Prohibition from StarCross employment and contracts (aka "Blacklisting"); expulsion from all facilities owned by StarCross and/or its subsidiaries

Date: Friday, July 16, 2123

Time: 0900 hours

Location: Hearing Chamber, Spigot Administrative Office

Dear Mr. Slake,

You are hereby ordered to appear at the time and place designated above for an administrative hearing conducted pursuant to StarCross Disciplinary Code 4.7. StarCross Security and Spigot officials will present evidence for your guilt of the offenses listed above. If you wish, you may present any evidence and/or witness testimony that you believe demonstrates your innocence, and/or warrants a downward departure from StarCross Security's requested penalty. Once all evidence is presented, a panel of three StarCross Examiners will determine your guilt or innocence by majority vote. If found guilty, you will be permitted to appeal that decision to the StarCross Disciplinary Review Board.

StarCross's case against you is included with this summons. If you wish to present evidence or witnesses to testify on your behalf at the hearing, contact the Office of StarCross

Examiners at defendantinfo@examiners.lg no later than July 9, 2123.

Sincerely,
Office of StarCross Examiners

Karla barely had time to react before Roscoe turned over the summons, revealing a ten-page packet, titled "SUMMARY OF DEFENDANT'S INFRACTION." He flipped through it, bile rising as he read StarCross's case against him—how, sensitive about his compound dependency and dissatisfied with his internship posting, he had sought to undermine Spigot's mission by sending StarCross employees on "a wild goose chase" for a nonexistent freshwater source on the ocean floor. How a reprimand from Chief Assistant Trent Hale had only enraged him further. And how he had decided to retaliate by hiring one of Newloon's digital animators to produce a video showing Spigot's CEO using the compound he so reviled. The full transcript of the doctored conversation from the interrogation room was also included.

> Mr. Slake's actions tarnished the reputation of Spigot CEO Grei Jahnford and threatened to undermine Spigot's technical and economic viability. Interviews with Mr. Slake's associates indicate that he is unrepentant and poses an ongoing threat to Spigot. For this reason, StarCross Security recommends expulsion from Spigot and prohibition from all further dealings with StarCross.

Behind the summary, Roscoe found another section labeled "REPORT OF STARCROSS IT SECURITY INVESTIGATION"—too technical for him to understand but likely meant to show that he had fabricated and distributed the video. Behind that was a third document marked "AFFIDAVIT OF JEN DOIL, SENIOR INTERN AND SUPERVISOR OF MR. SLAKE'S INTERN COHORT." Roscoe dreaded what he'd see, but read on:

First, as it unfortunately seems to be a recurring feeling, I want to express my disappointment in Roscoe's performance. Although this should hardly come as a surprise. Time and again, he buys into lies and propaganda from disgruntled indentured workers at places like Newloon, casting doubt on Mr. Jahnford's leadership and the importance of Spigot's mission. In my discussions with him and in our intern cohort meetings, not once has he spoken positively of his position or of Spigot's work. I was also shocked to learn that, in his senior capstone thesis, he interpreted the tragic deaths of StarCross employees in the Orbital Strike terrorist attack as a positive development for humanity.

If Roscoe chooses to hold and share these unhelpful thoughts, so be it. However, Spigot and StarCross must punish his actions of the past few weeks—the effort to distract Spigot from its search for water and his role in sharing of a fake video depicting Mr. Jahnford, Trent, and myself using compound.

Just to give a sense of the damage that Roscoe's actions did to my personal life, last week I ran into a fellow member of the Revelator Church, whose teachings I and Mr. Jahnford both hold dear. "Even if it was fake, that video might have hurt you a lot," he said. In my shock and grief, all I could think to say was, "It sure didn't help me."

Roscoe is a dangerous, infantile young punk. StarCross cannot condone his behavior.

Respectfully submitted, Jen Doil.

Roscoe sank into his chair, exhaling. Karla also sat back and gave him a sad look.

"Ay, weón," she said softly. "I'm sorry. I don't believe what they say, but you've ticked them off. This is what they do. When they want to get rid of someone, they build a case against them." Karla turned back to her work as Roscoe stood, stepping over to Karla's desk. He kept his voice low, more mindful than ever of hidden microphones.

"It's a lie. They made that video, and now they're trying to pin it on me." He dropped his voice even further. "I know why they want to get rid of me. There really is a source of fresh water on the bottom of Yule Bay. I heard that Drone Operations found it. I told Jahnford and three StarCross people about it when I went to pick up the map from him. The StarCross people were here to discuss storing nuclear weapons in the tunnels."

Karla's hands froze mid-scribble. "You mean ... like the Revelator goal?"

"Right. Now, instead, they're going to use the nuclear bomb to blow up the freshwater source I showed the StarCross people. I cost Jahnford his nuke."

Karla leaned forward, pressing a fist to her mouth. "Wow. Getting rid of you is a lucky break for Jahnford."

"How is that lucky?"

"Keeps the Revelators united," she explained. "If an atomic bomb ever does get stored down here, a schism will open up."

"A schism?"

She nodded. "Some Revelators will want to take that bomb. Some will want to build it from scratch. And some will start to think that maybe blowing up the world isn't the best idea, that maybe the whole thing is symbolic."

"And losing one nuke is better for Jahnford?"

"It gives him a story that'll make all the Revelators happy: they almost had a nuke, but some 'evildoer' cheated them out of it at the last minute, and Jahnford took swift and decisive action to remove that individual from the community. He's still their best man for the job, and he needs their support. And StarCross doesn't have to worry about religious fanatics stealing their nuclear bomb."

"So, it's good for him—but a drug video?"

Karla shrugged. "It keeps people distracted and makes you look as bad as possible. Also, remember StarCross Security has a lot of former Spigot people. Once Jahnford told them to get rid of you, it was their chance to toy with their old boss while getting away with it."

Roscoe rubbed the back of his neck, staring at the floor. "Do you think I have any chance of beating the charges?"

Karla shook her head. "If they bring a case, they will win. I can take the stand if you want, tell them what a fine Archivist you are. But to beat a disciplinary hearing, you need rock-solid proof they lied."

Roscoe stared at the wall, then grinned. "I think I know where to get it." Karla stared at him, incredulous. "You mind if I skip work for a few days? I've got to work on my defense."

"Of course."

Roscoe bolted for the door; there wasn't a moment to lose. Just before it shut behind him, he heard Karla say, "Mucha suerte."

Chapter 25

Roscoe ran down the tunnel, avoiding eye contact until he reached the door marked "Drone Control Room." It was locked, and his wristband couldn't open it. Time for Plan B. He tapped the Knock button on his wristband screen and waited. An older intern, stick-thin with short black hair, answered.

"Package for Hamza Tetuanui," Roscoe told her, lifting up the manila envelope with his summons and hoping his friend was on duty now. When the intern reached for it, Roscoe pulled it back. "I need him to come out here and verify receipt."

She nodded and held up a "just a minute" finger, letting the door close behind her. A minute later, Hamza stepped out.

"What's up man? I thought—"

Roscoe stopped him by putting his hand on Hamza's shoulder. "I'll make this quick. I need the wristband that Chip gave you."

"Um, sure, why?" Hamza asked, reaching into an inner pocket.

"Long story short, I might be blacklisted unless I can get ahold of him."

Hamza had just pulled out the worn, government-issued wristband and started to hand it over. "What the—" he began, but it was too late. Roscoe snatched the wristband and took off, barely remembering to shout "Thanks!" behind him.

Adrenaline carried Roscoe down Tunnel 1, up the spindly metal staircase near its end, and to the service entrance where Chip had dropped him off after that first night at Newloon. He figured this would be the safest spot in Spigot—the place where he'd be least likely to be watched or overheard.

For all he knew, Chip might be in on this whole thing and planning to testify against him at the hearing. But maybe he wasn't. Roscoe had nothing to lose by reaching out.

He leaned against the metal door; its chill seeped through his jacket as he tapped through the screen's icons, finally finding Chip's number. Raising his wristband to his ear, he waited. It rang. And rang some more. Roscoe's heart sank a bit with each tone, but he didn't dare hang up. Finally, on the tenth ring, the line clicked to life.

"Hamza?"

"It's Roscoe."

"Oh." Chip sounded disappointed but quickly covered it up. "What's up?"

"Why do you want me blacklisted?"

"What the—I don't—what the hell are you talking about? I don't want you blacklisted!"

It wasn't solid proof, but Roscoe would take it. The fact that Chip had even answered was a good sign StarCross Security hadn't gotten to him.

"All right, then I need you to prove it. I might get blacklisted unless you help me."

"What?" Chip sounded confused, and Roscoe's spirits lifted. McMurdo's last scientist didn't seem in on this.

"Listen, I can't talk here, it's not safe. I need you to pick me up at that service entrance you dropped me off at the night we met."

"Roscoe, I'm sorry, I can't just drop everything. I just started running some numbers—"

"Chip, help me on this"—Roscoe cupped his hand around his mouth—"and I'll find a way to do the dye test for you."

After a few agonizing seconds, Chip replied, "I'll be there in an hour." The line went dead.

Roscoe spent fifty-eight minutes on tenterhooks, when someone pounded on the door. He turned the handle and opened it, only then remembering he wasn't wearing a suit. Chip didn't hesitate. Wrapping an arm around him, he walked Roscoe ten numbing paces to the track and shoved him into the passenger seat. Then, he started driving.

"All right, talk," Chip said once Roscoe's teeth had stopped chattering. Roscoe brought him up to speed. When he finished, Chip pulled over to think.

"So you ticked off Jahnford by keeping his prophecy about a nuclear bomb from coming true. He had StarCross Security build a case against you. They recorded our talk at Shiduri's the other night, and the hot intern there goaded you into saying some other, incriminating stuff. Then they edited all of that to make it sound like you'd do the dye test?"

"Right. They also said I helped produce and distribute that fake video of Jahnford using drugs."

"And ... now they're using all this to blacklist you, and you want me to testify that they're lying."

"Yeah," Roscoe said as Chip gave him a sideways look. "Just about the talk at Shiduri's. Don't know how I could disprove the thing about the video."

"And you told me on our call that you would do that dye test. I'm guessing that was just to get my attention?"

"Yeah, pretty much."

Chip tapped the wheel with his thumb, then eased the track back into drive. "Look, you're a good kid, and the position you're in sucks. But even if I were to testify—and I'm not saying I will—the decision's already made."

"Is it?"

"Yep. StarCross's hands are tied. They want nukes to make reservoirs, and nukes are one thing governments still care about holding onto. StarCross probably had to promise the govellers five years' worth of water, minimum, to get the firecracker they're sending down now. They'd have to promise decades' worth of water to get H-bombs. StarCross also needs to show they're reliable. As long as Jahnford keeps the water coming, they've got to keep him happy—which means blacklisting whoever he wants gone."

By now, Roscoe knew enough to connect the dots. "Meanwhile, StarCross can falsify the readings of the freshwater plume so governments don't catch on, then nuke it anyway to say it's for their reservoirs."

Chip nodded. "You catch on pretty fast, dude."

The last of Roscoe's fucks had gone. "Pretty convenient for you, huh? If my hearing's already decided, you don't have to testify and risk pissing off anyone who might support your research."

Chip leaned back in his seat and exhaled slowly, eyes fixed on the road. "Yeah, maybe I'm a coward. Doesn't mean I'm wrong." He drummed his fingers on the dashboard, then let his hand fall to his lap. "All right, you guilt-tripped me. I won't testify, but I can take you on as an RA at McMurdo—or see if the Griquas will take you in. It's warmer up there, and you'd get to see more of the sun."

Roscoe thought of his parents back up north. He hadn't seen or talked to them in years, but he'd always known they were counting on him to get off-world—not to Antarctica or some other place he'd only just heard of. He was still it for them, and he wasn't ready to give up.

"You know anyone who's appealed a blacklisting and won?"

Chip shook his head. "It takes years. The StarCross Appeals Board is based on the Moon, and you'd be at the end of a long list of cases already queued up. If you go that route, you'll need a place to live in the meantime. And I hate to break it to you, but holing up with me or the Griquas won't look good to them."

Roscoe rested his head against the window. "If it doesn't mean water, energy, or hardware, they don't care, do they?"

"Welcome to reality, kid."

As Chip drove, Roscoe realized they were heading south of Spigot, not north toward Newloon as he'd expected. The road stayed level, but the land around them fell away. About two meters beneath them, he saw ice floes like the ones around the pier. He realized they were on a causeway of some kind. No longer having to account for the vagaries of gravel, Chip hit the accelerator. Soon, they were outpacing any other track Roscoe had ridden down here.

"What is this bridge?"

"McMurdo Causeway. Sound'll be frozen solid pretty soon. Brits thought it was a bay when they first charted it." He pointed ahead. "And that is Ross Island, home of McMurdo."

The road ahead curved onto an island of peaks. Most were low and rounded, but one cone trailed wisps of smoke, its summit glowing a faint red. He recognized it from the Ross Expedition records: Mount Erebus, still active after all these years, its smoke just escaping the crater before getting scattered by the gales.

"Do any other countries have bases here?"

"Nope. Kiwis used to have Scott Base, but they pulled out when the U.S. helped StarCross come down here."

"Why?"

"Said they wouldn't work with us as long as we were exploiting this place in violation of the Antarctic Treaty. Some countries still give a shit about that stuff—or did. Pretty sure New Zealand's signed onto the Updated Terms of Service by now."

After a few more coast-hugging curves, the remnants of the U.S. government's Antarctic research station came into view. Even at high speed, it took several more minutes to reach the causeway's far end and to turn onto the island's road. McMurdo looked smaller than Newloon, but no more appealing. Roscoe saw a cluster of prefab housing and Quonset huts huddled against a hill. A flag-marked road ran downhill to more above-the-ice platforms—docks, probably, for ships to unload in the summer. Roscoe thought he saw a cross atop a nearby hill.

"You're the only one here?"

"In the winter, yeah. There was a small support team when I started, but now they just give me a few WECs and tell me to buy what I need at Newloon. Crew's not much bigger in the summer, and it gets smaller every year. Gallagher's Pub moved to Newloon maybe fifteen years ago. Since then, everyone's known this place's days are numbered."

"Not a great sales pitch."

"Hey, it's your call whether you want to stay. Just givin' you the unvarnished truth."

Chip stopped the track outside the complex's largest building: a two-story block of wind-dulled aluminum. The scientist gave Roscoe another one-armed bear hug and pulled him inside.

The building's foyer was dim and dingy. A dull metal drum sat on the concrete floor, painted with a yellow wedge of sun and the words "Bioluminescent Algae / Algas Bioluminiscentes." A barcode had been printed on the top. The bottom let out a fish-tank gurgle.

"Griquas gave that to me the other week," Chip said as he unzipped his suit.

"I thought you told them that Jahnford wouldn't greenlight the dye test."

"I did, but hope springs eternal for those people. They said to hold onto it, in case the opportunity arises." He freed an arm from its down sheath and gave the drum a wistful pat. "They've just started breeding this stuff, and want to test it at scale as much as they can to see if there's fresh water down there."

"Any reason to think you'll get to test it before they nuke the site?"

"Nope. Even if we drove a drone up the underside of the glacier, it wouldn't do much."

"Why not?"

"Say the test shows there really is a fissure leaking fresh water from the seafloor. You'd need StarCross people to see it, so that they realized Jahnford was either a fuckup who'd missed it or a liar who'd tried to hide it. And you'd need the outside world to see it, so StarCross couldn't say the video was faked or make other excuses for nuking a freshwater source they're promising to provide."

Chip finished peeling off his suit and stared at Roscoe. "You know a way to get those three groups in a room together?"

After a moment, they both grinned, each realizing they were thinking the same thing.

"You mean, like a disciplinary hearing?"

Chip hung up his suit and opened the door. "Come on, kid. We've got ten days. Let's get to work."

The next morning, Chip dropped Roscoe off at Spigot's service entrance. Running on an hour or two of sleep and a weak brew of McMurdo's SynCoffee, Roscoe knew he could count on adrenaline to carry him through—that, and Hamza.

Chip had made sure to drop him off just as the night shift was ending. Roscoe found his friend in the galley, eating alone. He stopped chewing when he saw Roscoe.

Roscoe leaned in close and whispered, "We need to talk—not here. Remember that service entrance Chip dropped us off at?"

Hamza nodded.

"Meet me there in an hour—we shouldn't risk being seen together."

Roscoe waited twenty minutes against the cold service door before hearing Hamza's feet clang up the metal steps.

"Hey," Roscoe whispered, leaning close, again all too aware that a microphone or camera could be hidden nearby. "I have a disciplinary hearing on the sixteenth."

"Disciplinary hearing?" Hamza repeated.

"Yeah. Remember the dye test idea Chip told us about after we got your drone? They're trying to stick me with conspiring to do that, and with sharing the video. They want me blacklisted."

Hamza gasped. Roscoe continued, "Chip and I think there's a way I can beat the charges."

"How?"

"StarCross Examiners will preside over the hearing. We use it to show them Jahnford can't be trusted, that he's been sitting on this fissure that's leaking their precious water."

Hamza squinted. Again, all he could manage was, "How?"

Roscoe explained for several minutes, terrified to see how his friend would react. Hamza knew the engineering here, knew the technology they'd need—or knew it better than Roscoe, at any rate. He was the closest thing they'd get to a second opinion. If Hamza had doubts, Roscoe knew his own would worsen.

Hamza nodded through most of it, asking Roscoe to clarify a few points, but never once saying it couldn't be done. When Roscoe finished, Hamza simply asked, "Chip thinks it'll work?"

Roscoe nodded.

"And it'll show Jahnford's trying to smear people like us?"

Another nod.

"All right, I'm game."

Roscoe handed back the wristband with Chip's number. "He'll want to hear it straight from you."

Hamza opened his wrist screen and dialed Chip. This time, he answered on the first ring.

He whispered, "Hey, Chip, Roscoe told me your plan. Sounds crazy, but fuck it. If you think there's a chance it'll work, I'm in."

That was all Roscoe needed to hear.

Chapter 26

H.M.S. *Erebus*
Unnamed Sea
January 1841

Hooker kept moaning and chattering.

Yule only discovered this when Hooker failed to meet him in the mess for supper. Hooker's absence did not trouble him at first—if anything, Yule savored the silence as the steward set a plate of seal steak, potatoes, and pickled Kerguelen cabbage in front of him. He had taken a liking to these peppery greens, and was eager to learn how they paired with Antarctic fare. He only wished the mess were warmer. The heat seemed to have drained from the ship over the past day. Yule had only gained a few degrees when he went belowdecks for supper.

"Has the heating apparatus been fired with coal?" he asked the steward as the food was brought in.

The steward shook his head. "Cap'n ordered us to cut back. Says we need to conserve our coal for the final approach to the pole, and our return to Hobart." He set the two plates on the table and looked at the empty seat across from Yule. "Where's yer mate?" he asked. "Wasn't here yesterday either. Still getting over his dunking?"

"Not sure—let me check." Yule cursed himself as he stepped down to the lower deck. Why was he, a second master, taking orders from a steward? And what concern was it of the steward's, anyway?

Yule stood outside Hooker's bunk, listening to the moans coming from within. A knock drew no response, so he cracked the door open just enough to see Hooker's face—almost as lifeless as when he'd been pulled from the water.

He closed the door and made his way to McCormick's bunk, even more annoyed that he had let this responsibility fall on his shoulders. He found the surgeon wrapped in a scarf, pasting a label on a vial of seawater. "He's still not better," Yule said.

McCormick followed him back to Hooker's bunk, where he placed the back of his hand to his assistant's forehead and pressed an ear trumpet to his ivory chest.

"It's not warm enough for him here. We'll have to put him in the boiler room."

Yule held Hooker by the ankles, while McCormick wrapped his arms under the young surgeon's armpits. Together, they carried Hooker to the orlop deck and laid him beside the heating apparatus. Finding it cold and quiet, Yule told McCormick about Ross's order to conserve coal. It was hardly any warmer here than in Hooker's cabin.

McCormick pressed his lips into a line, then turned to Yule. "Ask the captain if he'll reconsider for this purpose."

"If he asks how serious it is, what should I tell him?"

"Tell him ... tell him it's Hooker's best chance at recovery."

Bundled in his padded jacket, trousers, gloves, and Welsh wig, Yule climbed to the deck, taking in the contradictions of the Antarctic. It was late evening and well below freezing, but the sunlight was blinding. Ice dotted the sea and cloaked the peaks onshore. His eyes had barely adjusted when the able seamen began shouting and pointing at one of the peaks.

Yule could scarcely believe his eyes. The tallest peak seemed to be getting taller—sprouting a pillar as gray as ash. It really was ash, Yule realized, as the column sent red-hot coals onto the slopes below, melting steaming rivers into the snow. This volcano was belching lava—the source of McCormick's basalt—onto this newly charted land.

Nearby, Yule found Ross studying this latest wonder through a spyglass.

"Yes, Master Yule, what is it?" he asked without lowering the scope.

"It's Doctor Hooker, Captain. He still hasn't recovered. Doctor McCormick says we need to fire the heating apparatus with more coal to warm him."

Ross kept his gaze fixed on the mountain. "We *need* to, do we?"

"Doctor McCormick thinks it will give Doctor Hooker his best chance at recovery."

Ross collapsed his spyglass and motioned for Yule to follow him to the stern. The ship was hove to, sails drawn and bow pointed into the wind so the crew could observe the shoreline. The stern afforded them the most quiet and shelter.

"Tell me, Master Yule, by your estimation, how many miles separate us from the pole?"

"About three hundred, Captain."

"At our current rate, how long before we reach it?"

"Two or three days—assuming open seas and steady winds, of course." Neither, Yule knew, were guaranteed in these waters.

"Two or three days to the pole, two or three days back to our current location, then two months back to Van Dieman's Land—assuming open seas and steady winds, of course," Ross said, with a tone that hinted at a smirk beneath his scarf. "Tell me, Master Yule, with sixty-three men to keep warm during this journey, and no certainty as to how much more the temperature may drop, would you have me expend our limited coal to warm one of our two surgeons?"

Yule gave Ross the answer he wanted. "No, sir."

"Then you have your answer." He nodded for Yule to return below decks. Just before Yule descended, Ross called out to him again. "When you're finished, mark those peaks' locations. Label the erupting one Mount Erebus." He pointed to another, shorter, silent cone beside it. "That one can be Mount Terror."

"Aye, sir."

Yule returned below decks, fuming at Ross's condescension and questioning his motives. Perhaps his decision not to burn more coal was a prudent, if bloodless, one to sustain the expedition on the way to its main prize, the South Magnetic Pole. But perhaps Ross, who had panicked for Hooker's safety after he fell, now hoped that this witness to his crime would vanish. Yule's resolve to disgrace him only hardened.

When he relayed Ross's decision, McCormick glared but said nothing. Fifty years after Bligh's debacle on the H.M.S. *Bounty*, the Admiralty still placed Royal Marines aboard every expeditionary vessel; speaking ill of the captain could end very badly.

McCormick slipped his arms under the other surgeon's. "Take his feet, Yule. We will carry him to the galley."

"What for?" he asked, complying.

"Do you remember the coal I collected on the Kerguelens? The specimens I asked you to store in your bunk?"

"Aye," Yule said, inching backward down the pinched passageway.

"We'll fire the cookstove with it. Perhaps that will suffice to warm him." The surgeon looked at his young charge again and slowly shook his head. "His odds are not good."

Yule's mouth opened, but the words stuck. "Do ... do you think he'll survive?"

"I truly cannot say. That coal is his best chance, however." They set Hooker down beside the stove.

Yule fetched the pail from his bunk, careful to remove his attestation and insurance papers tucked among the lumps. He studied the envelopes in his hand. Now, more than ever, he wanted Ross to hang. But was that goal worth the shame it could bring Hooker, a man who might not survive the night?

Yule shook that question from his head. He slipped the papers into the pail of basalt he had gathered from Franklin Island and hurried back to the galley. *Erebus*'s one healthy surgeon filled the stove. The heat gradually built in the tiny space; Hooker's shivers eased. "I shall keep watch over him for now," McCormick said, loosening his scarf and unbuttoning his coat. "Yule, do be so kind as to gather his papers. If the worst happens, I can see they are returned to his family and the Royal Society. The Admiralty is not always reliable with these things.

If we cannot bring him back, at least we can record some of his work for the ages."

Yule turned to leave, but McCormick laid a hand on his shoulder. "As insufferable as Hooker is at times, he really has a great deal of respect for you, Yule." Yule nodded, not convinced, and headed to the Great Cabin, now as cluttered with specimens as his own bunk. Thankfully, Ross remained above deck. Yule opened Hooker's desk and found it piled high with papers. The top page read "Notes for letters to Mother—to write upon return to Van Dieman's Land."

He must have been collecting observations as he went, Yule realized, to compile them on their return to Hobart. Several short paragraphs ran down the page, and near the bottom, Yule spied his name. Hooker had written:

> *Your former letters have doubtless told me all about Jersey. I hear a great deal of that Island from one of my messmates, Yule—a most worthy fellow—whose father was one of Nelson's Lieutenants at Trafalgar, & a retired Commander. He has since died, I believe, since his son left England, & so, I believe, has the mother too, though Yule has had no letter announcing it & is, of course, ignorant of the fact. His family has left Jersey, but he is constantly talking of it & describes the climate as very beautiful & the scenery delightful.*

Feeling hollow, Yule returned to McCormick and recounted what he had read. "Did Hooker tell you my mother had also died?"

McCormick nodded. "Learned of it through helping Ross with his correspondence. He was concerned how you would receive the news. We agreed it would be best not to tell you so soon after you learned of your father's passing, as we entered such perilous seas." He put his arm around Yule. "He wanted what was best for you, and so did I. We tried."

Yule shrugged off McCormick's arm, retreated to his bunk, and buried his head in his hands.

Chapter 27

Ross Sea Coast
Antarctica
July 2123

"Please state your name for the record."

"Roscoe Slake."

"Date of birth?"

"May 28, 2101."

"Role at Spigot?"

"Archival intern."

The Lead Hearing Examiner gave a small nod. The Examination Room's high-definition screen and dedicated satellite link relayed every subtle gesture made by the Examiners, joining remotely from their base in the Moon's Marius Hills. They all looked bored.

"To the first charge, libel of a Spigot employee, how do you plead?"

"No contest." Roscoe almost clenched his teeth. Chip had convinced him to take this approach—don't waste their time and attention bickering over the tape, he had explained. Just focus on the dye test.

"Fabrication of obscenity?"

"No contest."

"Distribution of obscenity over StarCross IT network?"

"No contest."

"Seditious conspiracy?"

"Necessity."

The Head Examiner blinked. "Beg pardon?"

"The necessity defense," Roscoe repeated, reciting the legal encyclopedia entry Chip had found. "Used when an illegal act is necessary for survival in the circumstances. Accepted by some courts during prosecutions of environmental terrorists in the early twenty-first century. In this case, I decided that assisting Doctor Erskin's research was necessary to ensure Spigot's continued productivity and hold its present leadership accountable."

The Examiners scrolled through their wrist screens, trading glances and whispers. Then, the Head Examiner spoke, "Mister Slake, This ... necessity defense, as you call it, is not permissible in StarCross disciplinary hearings. Please plead guilty, not guilty, or no contest."

"No contest." Chip and Roscoe had anticipated this response, but at least the seed had been planted in the Examiners' minds. So far, so good.

"Thank you. Please be seated."

Roscoe stepped down from the Hearing Room's podium, set about a meter back from the screen displaying the Examiners. He sat in his designated front-row DEFENDANT seat next to Chip, his only witness. Two StarCross Security agents, masked and armed, guarded the door to the Hearing Room, a stark white chamber in Spigot's Administrative Offices. A viewers' bench ran along the back wall, where Jahnford, Trent, Jen, and two employees sat. Roscoe didn't recognize them, but he knew who they were: Drone Operations employees Hamza had tipped off. Their plan would have two uninterested witnesses as it unfolded.

The Head Examiner spoke, drawing Roscoe's focus. "We will now hear the testimony from Inspector Jay Smailer, lead investigator in this case." A buzz-cut man in a StarCross Security jacket took the podium. "Thank you, Examiners. StarCross Security's complete case against Roscoe Slake is contained in our Summary of Defendant's Infraction and accompanying materials, which we trust you have already reviewed. We feel nothing requires elaboration, but I am happy to answer any questions you may have."

"I have none," said the Head Examiner, looking to his colleagues, who shook their heads. "Thank you, Inspector Smailer. Please be seated."

With that, StarCross had rested its case. There would be no cross-examinations or closing arguments like in the old courtroom dramas. The week leading up to the hearing had been free of the pretrial filings and motions Roscoe understood had been common in old criminal trials. The civil rights and legal traditions that had once required these rituals did not burden StarCross disciplinary hearings, even if they doled out punishments worse than prison.

At least StarCross lawyers wouldn't be shouting "objection!" like in the old days—that would tank their plan fast. As Roscoe, Chip, and Hamza had prepared this gambit, they'd become acutely aware of how desperate it was.

"Mister Slake, please step forward." Roscoe obliged. "Do you wish to call any witnesses?"

"Yes, Examiner. I call Doctor Chip Erskin, head scientist at McMurdo Station."

Roscoe returned to his seat, and Chip took his place at the podium. For the first time, Roscoe saw the scientist groomed and shaven.

"Thank you, Examiners. Mister Slake has pleaded no contest to conspiring to undermine Spigot's water production by fabricating evidence of a freshwater source on the Yule Bay seafloor. I intend to demonstrate that his actions were not fabrications and were necessary to reveal serious shortcomings in Spigot's environmental knowledge."

The Head Examiner lost his boredom. "Please proceed, Doctor Erskin. I remind you that each witness is limited to ten minutes at the podium." They'd known that too. As Roscoe and Hamza got things ready, Chip had practiced his speech, sanding it down to the key points.

"Thank you. As you all know, Spigot drains meltwater from the Taylor Glacier's underside for exports." The Examiners nodded. "It stands to reason, then, that any leakage of meltwater into the open ocean could threaten Spigot's business model—and its viability." A few more nods followed. A few eyebrows went up too.

Chip tapped his podium screen, activating a two-sided presentation display showing the same images to both the Examiners and the Drone Ops employees in the back. They could all see Chip's first slide: a satellite view of the Ross Sea, with Spigot, Yule Bay, and the freshwater plume labeled.

"In 2111, I detected a freshwater source on the floor of the Ross Sea, near the coast of Yule Bay. It had not been detected in any previous surveys of the area."

"What do you think caused it?" asked one of the Examiners, a woman, leaning forward.

"I hypothesized that some kind of underground connection had opened up between Taylor Glacier and this site near Yule Bay."

"You mean, water was flowing underground from one of our glaciers and bubbling up into the ocean?"

"Yes, water can flow dozens or even hundreds of kilometers through underground channels. Based on local geology and the chemical makeup of the water, I surmised that some combination of underground erosion and shifts in the Earth's crust had opened up such a passageway for water to flow from Taylor Glacier to Yule Bay."

The three Examiners stiffened. They processed the implications quickly—every day, they dispensed with StarCross employees, but now its water was at stake.

"Only StarCross has the technology to test this hypothesis," Chip continued. "Over the years, I have asked Mister Jahnford for the technology and manpower to conduct a seismic survey of the bedrock in the area. He has refused. I have also asked him to secure StarCross Security's permission to release dye into Taylor Glacier's meltwater stream, then monitor the freshwater site to see if this dye surfaced. He refused this request as well."

The Examiners' expressions hardened. Unlike with Roscoe, Chip didn't need to explain why Jahnford might want to ignore this place, or why StarCross should care that he had.

Chip had been honest up to this point, but the time had come to stretch the truth. "I informed Mister Slake of this situation when we met on the twenty-first of June. He had recently learned of the freshwater plume from a friend who worked in Spigot's Drone Operations department. When he learned of Mister Jahnford's failure to conduct an experiment, he became gravely concerned that StarCross would lose a valuable water source and struggle to fulfill its obligations under the Updated Terms of Service." The Hearing Examiners flinched at this reminder that StarCross—like its customers—had obligations under the Updated Terms of Service.

"At great risk to his future, Mister Slake attempted to inform Mister Jahnford of this freshwater source himself, presenting it as a recent discovery to ensure Spigot's CEO would not face repercussions for failing to act on it sooner." Roscoe didn't dare look at the Examiners or Jahnford, but he savored the knowledge that they were within each other's sight. *You had your chance, Grei*, he thought. *I tried to help you.*

"Mister Slake didn't just inform Mister Jahnford. He also offered to use his inside access to Spigot to conduct the dye test and determine if such a freshwater source existed."

Roscoe couldn't stifle a small smile. Chip had just confirmed StarCross's accusations regarding the dye test as true. But with the way he'd framed them, the Examiners didn't seem to care.

Chip tapped the podium again, playing a ten-second video loop. Rippling ice filled the top third of the screen, with tan silt at the bottom and floating particles in between, all illuminated by an unseen light.

"This video was taken from the camera of a drone recovery device known as a grabber. The day after my conversation with Mister Slake, he piloted this device up Spigot's tunnel network to the underside of Taylor Glacier."

Chip was outright lying now—Roscoe hadn't done any of this. It was Hamza who'd pretended to be practicing tunnel maneuvers with the grabber, secretly positioning it beneath Taylor Glacier while carrying the Griquas' bioluminescent algae canister. "They'll notice if an open-sea subdrone goes missing," he'd explained to Roscoe and Chip, "but no one keeps track of the grabbers."

Another tap brought up a second video, taken from a camera mounted on the back of the grabber. It showed a milky spray hitting the murky water, turning electric blue a few centimeters out from the camera. The glowing stream lit the underside of the glacier as it drifted out of view—hopefully toward the fissure that Chip believed lay somewhere nearby.

The algae were working perfectly. Chip had shown Roscoe and Hamza how the dye worked by turning off the McMurdo galley's lights and adding some dye to his SynCoffee press. "It only activates in fresh water, under pressure." He pressed down on the piston, and the dye, initially cloudy, came out glowing blue. His National Science Foundation mug cast an eerie sheen onto the ceiling.

"How long does it glow like that?" Hamza had asked.

"Indefinitely, as long as the freshwater concentration's high and there are enough nutrients in the water," Chip had answered. "I've calculated that the journey from the glacier to the plume site should take nearly a week. So if we release it soon, it should reach the plume by the time the hearing begins."

Hamza had gotten the dye in place. Now, the Examiners saw the same eerie glow on the glacier's underside. "One week ago," Chip explained, "we released bioluminescent algae from the grabber into Taylor Glacier's meltwater stream."

"And any dye that flows into this fissure," the Examiner said, "would survive and illuminate the site of the freshwater plume at the bottom of Yule Bay."

"Couldn't have said it better myself, Examiner." Chip seemed to be enjoying himself now. It was time for the kicker.

"As it happens, StarCross itself has eyes on the site. StarBuoy-18 monitors this region of the Southern Ocean at all times. One of its cameras is near the seafloor, so it should capture the test results. Using my research credentials, I requested a time-lapse video from the past week. This footage comes directly from StarCross. I'm viewing it for the first time myself. You're welcome to inspect the source code to confirm its authenticity. Spectral analysis of the dye's light will confirm the presence of fresh water." Roscoe didn't quite understand what that meant—other than that it was the moment of truth.

Chip tapped the podium and pressed Play. The Examiners leaned in. So did Roscoe. Everyone seemed to have the same question: What would this video show?

Nothing.

For eighteen seconds, the screen stayed a deep, inky black. The progress bar stretched across the bottom of the screen, then started again as the video looped. Roscoe silently willed the video to change, for even a spark of light to appear, but each loop was the same as the last.

"Um, is this it, Doctor Erskin?"

"Er, I believe so, Examiner."

"What exactly are we looking at? Where's the freshwater plume?"

"It's down there somewhere. But ... the dye doesn't seem to be there."

The Head Examiner waved to someone off-camera. The back of an aide's head appeared on the screen. "Patch us into a live-stream from StarBuoy-18," he instructed. "Yule Bay in the Southern Ocean." The aide disappeared. "Let's take another look, Doctor Erskin, just to be thorough." If nothing else, Chip had certainly won their interest. Two agonizing minutes passed in silence. Finally, interference filled the screen, then cleared to show another black screen. "STARBUOY-18—LIVE," the caption read, followed by coordinates.

"Doctor Erskin, what would it suggest if no dye is visible at this site?" the Head Examiner asked.

"It ... it would suggest that whatever is the source of this freshwater, it isn't a fissure. Or, maybe there is a fissure, but water takes more than a week to flow through it. Remember, we only released the dye one week ago. Longer-term monitoring may be necessary to conclusively establish a connection, or lack thereof, under the seafloor."

Roscoe nearly slapped his forehead. Nervousness was bringing out the techno-speak in Chip. That wasn't going to help here. *Just tell them we need to give it more time!*

"Is that all you wish to present, Doctor Erskin?"

"Yes, Examiner, unless you have any questions." Each of the Examiners shook their heads before the Head Examiner spoke again.

"Mister Slake, are there any further witnesses?" he asked.

"No, Examiner." Roscoe told himself that there was still a chance, however small, that they'd decide to prolong the proceedings, giving the dye more time to reach the site—if it *could* reach the site.

"All right, thank you for your presentation. Please wait in the Examination Room while we deliberate." The speakers went dead; the screen switched back to the StarCross logo.

Chip hunched in his chair, cupping his hands over his mouth, then dragged his fingers down his face. "Christ, I'm sorry, man. I really—"

"Don't worry about it," Roscoe replied. "You did all you could."

Chip leaned back. "It's just—sometimes, when you're doing science, you're just certain you'll be right. You forget it's just a test."

"We don't know you're wrong," Roscoe said. "For all we know, there is a fissure, and it'll just take the dye more time to travel through it. Maybe they'll give the experiment more time."

"Maybe." Chip tapped the table lightly, his jaw tight. "The simple fact that they're even deliberating might be a good sign."

Just then, the ceiling flashed blue, and a recorded voice asked them to rise. The Examiners appeared on screen again.

"We find Roscoe Slake guilty of all charges as presented by Inspector Smailer. We further find that Mister Slake's witness testimony has not established any mitigating circumstances or other compelling reason to deviate from StarCross Security's recommended punishment. We therefore prohibit him from employment with all StarCross subsidiaries and from residence in any StarCross properties for life. He is to be transferred to the custody of StarCross Security until transportation away from Spigot can be arranged. StarCross Security is instructed to provide Mister Slake with a transcript of this proceeding, all associated documents, and instructions for the StarCross appeal process if he chooses to pursue that option. This hearing is adjourned."

Roscoe felt gloved hands clamp on each bicep as the two masked and armed StarCross Security agents pulled him to his feet, cuffed him, and marched him out of the Examination Room. They had made it ten paces down the hall when a voice called from behind. "Wait! Turn him around."

The agents spun Roscoe around, bringing him face-to-face with Grei

Jahnford. Without a word, Spigot's CEO punched him in the gut. As Roscoe doubled over, Jahnford grabbed his shoulders and slammed him chest-first onto the floor.

He lay there a moment, bracing for another blow, but instead, the agents pulled him upright. Jahnford and his two head interns were already heading to the elevator. Jen stole one quick look—Roscoe could swear she looked pained—before following Jahnford and Trent away. None of them spoke.

The agents took Roscoe to his tiny dorm to collect his single duffel bag of clothes, then back to the StarCross Security office. This time, they rode in an open jitney. An intern, handcuffed, bruised, and shell-shocked, wedged between two armed agents. StarCross couldn't send a clearer warning to anyone else considering defiance. The driver turned on the siren and drove slowly. Heads turned as they passed, but Roscoe kept his eyes on his lap the entire way. By the time they reached the holding cell, the lump in his throat had shriveled from rage.

"Mister Slake, do you wish to appeal this decision?" the booking agent asked after Roscoe had surrendered his wristband.

Roscoe paused, thinking of his parents up north. Sequestered by StarCross, he hadn't seen or talked to them in years. Still, he knew they were counting on him to get off-world, and if he refused to appeal, they never would. Even now, Roscoe couldn't forget the feeling of his dad's finger on his sternum as he said "You're it," and looked back up at Lagrange-2.

"Um, I—"

The booking agent, still staring at his computer screen, cut him off. "You are aware that your parents exchanged their future intern family housing in Antarctica for a third party's gas lease? If you are blacklisted, they will have to forfeit that lease—and possibly other assets."

Roscoe froze, the words sinking in. His parents hadn't even wanted to see him after his internship? All they had ever cared about, he realized, was getting off-world. To do that, they'd been willing to drug him for years, and when he failed to deliver, they took what they could and ran.

Was he supposed to start crying right now or something? Compound had dulled so many reactions he'd read about in old books and seen in movies. Instead, all he said was, "Fuck them, then."

The agent flinched.

"I won't appeal," Roscoe added. "I'm done with StarCross—and with them. Just let me call my ride."

Chapter 28

H.M.S. *Erebus*
Unnamed Sea
January 1841

Yule entered the galley the next morning to find both surgeons still there. "Morning, Yule," McCormick greeted him. "Doctor Hooker here is on the mend."

"M-m-morning, Yule," Hooker stammered. "Th-th-thank you for your help."

"And ... and thank you for yours," Yule said. "Doctor McCormick told me of your concern with the letter." Hooker managed a weak smile and sipped his tea.

McCormick leaned toward Yule. "Return his papers to his desk," he whispered. "They won't need a custodian."

Yule returned to his bunk. Just as he was about to open the drawer where he had placed Hooker's papers, the grinding of ice and shouts for depth soundings drew him above deck.

* * *

The *Erebus* and *Terror* had left Franklin Island and Mount Erebus behind. Ross no longer sought to touch the mainland. February had arrived; the expedition had a shrinking window to reach the magnetic pole and escape the advancing winter ice.

Yule reckoned their location—they had reached seventy-six degrees, six minutes south. The dip needle stood almost vertical now, but he estimated they still had three hundred miles to go to reach the pole. This distance was not to Ross's liking.

"Damn this wind, and this crew!" Ross shouted through his scarf. He waved his arm at the able seamen. "I offer them all I can: an extra brace of rum and a bonus upon our return to Hobart, if they can maintain a speed of at least nine knots."

To Yule, this sounded much like the French captain's strategy Ross had scorned back in Hobart.

"I would not want such speed in these waters, Captain," an officer said from behind Yule, nodding forward. "Look at what awaits us."

A thick white band lined the horizon.

"Perhaps it is the iceblink, or more pack ice," Ross said. "We shall proceed at full sail for now."

It soon became clear, however, that this was no trick of the light. Through his spyglass, Yule saw the band sharpen into a towering ice cliff—an unbroken wall, hundreds of feet high.

Ross lowered the spyglass. "We may as well try to sail through the Cliffs of Dover." He convened his officers in the Great Cabin, then was rowed over to the *Terror* to confer with its crew. When he returned, he announced a plan: they would sail east in hopes of finding a passage through the ice shelf.

"The pole is at hand!" Ross proclaimed to the crew. "Providence has brought us this far. Let us trust that it shall provide a passage for us!"

The officers and able seamen managed a weak cheer, their zeal for discovery dulled by the Antarctic chill and ceaseless sun glare.

At least no one has developed scurvy yet, Yule thought as two more plates of Kerguelen cabbage were set before him and Hooker that evening. McCormick stepped in as soon as the steward left.

"Evening, gentlemen. The Captain has asked each officer to sign this note." Yule and Hooker read the slip of paper placed between them.

February 3rd, 1841

On this date, Her Majesty's Ships Erebus and Terror, tasked with reaching the South Magnetic Pole, encountered a barrier of ice at 76 degrees south, 195 degrees east. This barrier measured several hundred feet in height and blocked further passage to the south. The officers have determined that this obstacle will not deter the Expedition from pursuing its goal. The ships will proceed east, in the hopes of finding a channel through this barrier that will lead to the Pole. We trust that Providence will provide this channel and ensure our reaching the Pole. Should a safe return prove impossible, we trust that Providence will deliver this message to a civilized nation capable of recording our achievements for the glory of Her Majesty, Queen Victoria, and for posterity.

Ross and several other officers had signed the note already. McCormick did the same, then handed the quill to Yule.

"What's he planning to do with this?" Yule asked as he signed.

"He's instructed me to collect signatures from all the officers, then place it in a cask and throw it overboard." McCormick said. "He wants some record of our voyage to survive, even if we don't—and he wants it to look like we were all in agreement, even if we weren't."

Yule instantly regretted signing. That old dread he had first felt in Chatham over a year ago crept back. Their lives had become secondary to Ross's thirst for glory.

"Does he truly think we might not return?" Hooker asked.

McCormick shrugged. "He sees it as a possibility. Time will tell."

Yule pressed the paper flat and slid it across the table toward Hooker. The assistant surgeon's hand hovered above it before McCormick placed a reassuring hand on his shoulder.

"Sign, lad. Our best hope of getting out alive is by keeping our

Captain confident. And the best way to keep Ross confident is to have him believe that all the officers support him."

"Even if we really don't?" Hooker asked.

Yule's gaze held steady on Hooker as he gripped the quill tighter.

"Aye," McCormick said. He lowered his voice. "Even if we really don't."

Chapter 29

Ross Sea Coast
Antarctica
July 2123

Chip picked Roscoe up and pointed the track toward Newloon. They both needed a beer.

"Maybe we didn't use enough dye," the scientist wondered aloud. "A couple of kegs' worth of dye dumped into a fucking glacier's meltwater stream."

"Yeah, I don't think we're gonna get a do-over," Roscoe said. "Any word from Hamza?"

"Nope. I invited him to come for a beer but haven't heard back." Roscoe figured the outside travel ban might still in place—or that Hamza just didn't want to take any chances.

As Newloon came into view, Roscoe thought it had shrunk—looking about two-thirds as big as last time. Then he realized that the other section was still there, just dark. No exterior bulbs lit the trailers and shipping containers, and no light leaked out from inside. The whole area sat black and empty on the ice.

"What happened there?"

"Fire," Chip said. "Bad one. Traveled too fast to contain. That entire section got torched before they managed to close the bulkheads and seal off the rest of the settlement."

"Any idea what caused it?"

"No one's sure, but everyone has an idea. Burned hot enough to melt straight through containers. Last time anyone saw something like that here was a few nights after Smalls died."

"They think StarCross started it?"

"Can't prove that they did, but it sure sends a message, doesn't it? 'Don't cross us, and don't harbor people who do.'" Roscoe was suddenly glad Chip had brought him a suit from McMurdo—he wouldn't stand out as an ex-Spigot guy.

Chip parked. "Anyway, I think a beer is worth the risk. Come on, let's go to Shiduri's."

White-hot rage flashed through Roscoe. "I'm never going to that shithole again. Let's go to Gallagher's."

Chip gave him a startled look, so Roscoe elaborated. "She was in on it, Chip. She let StarCross Security hide a mic in there, record us, and doctor our conversation to use as evidence against me."

Chip unzipped his suit, reached into an inner pocket, and pulled out a mashed wad of plastic and wire, no bigger than a raisin.

"While you and Hamza were getting things ready, I went over to Newloon and told Shiduri what happened. She closed up early, and we swept the whole place for bugs. Found eighteen of these."

Roscoe sank into his seat, feeling even shittier. "Oh. Thanks."

"Don't mention it." Chip pocketed the dead bug. "Now, let's get that drink."

They stepped into a packed Skua Central. Many of the booths had been subdivided since Roscoe's last visit, making space for an extra tenant.

"So are all the people from the burned section just doubling up?"

"Yeah, subletting counter space by the centimeter."

"Are they gonna rebuild?"

"Someone will—not until summer, though. Even around here, no one's desperate enough to try winter construction."

They reached Wit's End and made a beeline for Shiduri's.

"We lost," Chip told Shiduri. She brought them two Neptune's Bellows porters and leaned across the counter, giving Roscoe's hand a squeeze.

"I'm sorry, hon. Really, I am. I've seen StarCross fuck over a lot of people, but no one this bad." A tear ran down one of the nicotine wrinkles around her eyes.

"Thanks, Shid." Roscoe said. "And thanks for helping. Chip told me what you did."

She nodded. "She looked nice, the gal you were talking to. Used to think I could spot a sweet-talker a mile away, but I never would've guessed she was pulling one over on you. Guess I was wrong."

"Well, that makes two of us," Roscoe replied, trying to push Jen's anguished gaze, the brush of her fingers, out of his head. She was lying the whole time, he told himself.

Shiduri went into the kitchen and returned with a basket of corn chips, piled high around the bowl of trembling vat-grown seal blubber. "On the house. I don't know if this'll fix anything, but maybe it'll take the edge off."

"Thanks, Shid," Chip said, already reaching for a chip.

Shouts erupted from the pool table. Shiduri rolled her eyes, drew her stun gun, and stepped away.

"If there's one thing Shid takes a hard line on, it's privacy," Chip said, using a chip to scoop a sliver of blubber into his mouth. "If people know they're getting listened to in here, well, she won't last long."

Roscoe nodded and took a long swig of beer, drowning his guilt in porter. He'd drained the bottle by the time Shiduri returned and ordered a Blood Falls Red Ale.

Desperate to shift topics, Roscoe looked up at the menu. "Blood Falls ... Neptune's Bellows—where the hell do they get these names?"

"South Shetland names all their beers after places in Antarctica," Chip explained. He took another bite of blubber and chewed before continuing. "Neptune's Bellows is a channel in the South Shetlands. Cliffs on either side. When sealers first discovered it in the eighteen hundreds and heard the wind howling through it, they named it Neptune's Bellows—and the name stuck."

"And Blood Falls?" Roscoe asked, studying the label, which showed a glacier face oozing red streaks like a giant's bloody nose. "Don't tell me that thing's real."

"Oh, it was," Chip said. "Near the McMurdo Dry Valleys."

"What was it?"

"Millions of years ago, that glacier trapped a pool of liquid seawater, microbes and all. Some of them managed to survive, using iron compounds for nutrients. At some point, the glacier couldn't handle the seawater's pressure anymore, and water started pouring out. The iron reacted with the air, forming iron oxides, better known as rust. That was Blood Falls."

"Is it still there?"

"Nope," Chip crunched another chip. "StarCross prospected up there—maybe thirty years ago. The microbes survived down there but couldn't make it on the surface. It's all gray now."

"So microbes survived without sunlight but couldn't survive on the surface?"

Chip nodded. "Millions of years in a sealed-off petri dish, living off iron. No reason to adapt to anything else."

"That's amazing," Roscoe said, drinking more and forgetting how little he knew about science. "You don't think microbes caused the freshwater plume?"

Chip toyed with his beer tab, spinning it between his fingers. "Maybe. Back in the early twenty-first century, they developed microbial desalination cells—colonies of microorganisms, basically, that made seawater drinkable."

Roscoe ate another bit of blubber and washed it down with a swig of Blood Falls. "You mean we didn't need Spigot?"

Chip nodded. "There were other options too. The Israelis and Saudis had desalination technology. But that all took lots of energy, which was already becoming a pretty precious commodity. The microbes they used in the desalination cells, called geobacter, were pretty low-maintenance by comparison."

Roscoe ate a chip straight. "So they had these desalination cells using microbes—why haven't we heard of them? Why does everyone need Spigot?"

"Because the cells don't work anymore," Chip explained, pausing to sip his beer. "They got some pretty big ones up and running all over the world, but by the fifties, they broke down one by one."

"Why?"

Chip leaned back and wiped his fingers with a napkin. "No one's really sure. The oceans were pretty acidic by that point. Maybe it was more than the geobacter microbes could handle. Or maybe all the microplastics building up in the oceans finally did them in."

"No one researched it?"

"Nope." Chip scraped the last bit of blubber from the bottom of the bowl. "Once Spigot opened up, they flooded the market." He rolled his eyes. "Pun intended. No one was going to make a buck researching how microbes could do it—or how we could help them do it. Governments wouldn't gamble on that kind of research either, not when they had a ready water source and people were getting desperate."

"Maybe the microbes in Yule Bay—if there are any down there—found a way to desalinate the water anyway."

Chip nodded. "But even if they did, we have no way of knowing right now. We'd need to collect a sample from the seafloor and get it to someone to study it."

"You mean, like the people who gave you a bunch of algae to run a test even after you told them it wasn't going to happen."

"Yeah, like them." Chip paused and knocked back the last of his beer. "But don't forget, whatever's down there is going to get nuked to hell in a month or two. We'd need to do it before then. And ideally, we'd need to show the rest of the world that there's fresh water down there and force StarCross to explain why they're about to destroy what they're supposed to be providing."

They grinned in unison.

"All right," Roscoe said, brushing crumbs off his lap. "Sounds like we have our work cut out for us."

Chip waved Shiduri over and ordered another round, then grabbed a nearby napkin and clicked a pen.

They spent the next hour sketching out plans, pausing only to drink beer and pick at the chips. Once they were both satisfied, Chip headed over to the red London-style telephone booth in the corner. It was, he explained, a privacy phone—soundproofed, with calls encrypted and relayed north on a string of non-StarCross pirate satellites.

Chip emerged after twenty minutes and flashed a thumbs-up. They were on.

Chapter 30

H.M.S. *Erebus*
Unnamed Sea
February 1841

The ships sailed alongside the barrier, their hulls holding firm against the pack ice. Yule and Tucker tracked their progress and sounded the bottom, pulling up soft green mud, stones, and clay from the seafloor. McCormick busied himself studying the bird life; using nets and snares, he and Hooker lured a penguin from the pack ice onto the ship's deck, where the great bird met its end at the barrel of McCormick's shotgun. After one kill, the surgeons deemed the penguins' meat too fishy to warrant future harvests.

None of this improved Ross's mood. Mile after mile of ice cliff stretched before them, and no southward passage appeared. Ross emerged from the Great Cabin less and less. Hooker, Yule noted, had started avoiding it.

But the sight of a gap, six days after they tossed the cask overboard, drew Ross on deck within minutes. "Hand me your spyglass, Master Yule," he said. After a quick look, Ross turned to his crew. "We have our channel! Set a course for the opening at once!"

Taking the spyglass back, Yule could see that the ice cliff ahead curved inward. Their angle of approach hid the opening's width—and whatever might lie beyond.

The ships ground through the pack ice toward the point where the wall curved in. Yule again felt the dread of being crushed—not crushed from below this time, but from above. Stalactites like tree-trunks and slabs like houses hung from the shelf's edge, poised to break free and splinter any ship venturing too close.

The *Erebus*, then the *Terror*, rounded the bend. The ice overhead held firm, and the able seamen kept the ships under open sky. But when the prow swung hard to starboard, Yule grabbed the gunwale for balance. Ahead lay more ice.

This was no channel; it was a bay. The ships could proceed a mile at most before encountering another ice wall.

"Shall we turn back, Cap'n?" an able seaman asked Ross.

"No. Let us sail closer to the ice. Perhaps another gap will reveal itself."

The crew trimmed the sails and raised signal flags. Yule looked at Ross and bit his lip. Any channel leading onward from this bay would be narrow, forcing the ships directly under the overhanging ice—and Ross would doubtless order them to enter it. Yule looked back at the open water, unsure if he'd leave this bay alive.

The ships pressed forward. Yule again got the sense that the Antarctic had fortified itself against human intrusion. Frozen spray slicked the decks, and the hulls groaned as pack ice ground harder against them. Ahead, rising higher than any rampart Yule had ever seen, loomed the ice wall.

It stood perhaps half a mile ahead now. No channel appeared. The ships were running out of space to turn around.

"Are you mad?" shouted an officer, muffled by his scarf. "There is no channel here, Captain! Turn around!"

Ross said nothing. His hooded figure stood fixed, spyglass in hand, as though he could will a passage into existence. The officer ripped it away from Ross's hands.

"Captain! Your crew will die!"

Ross lowered his scarf, raised his whistle to his lips, and ordered the *Erebus* to turn around. The able seamen, as sure-footed as ever, complied. Little by little, the prow shifted away from the ice wall, and the fearsome barrier moved to starboard, then astern. The *Erebus* and *Terror* were on their way out.

But not for long.

This deep in the bay, the wind had dwindled, and the pack ice thickened until the ships could barely move. The able seamen could not coax enough strength from the sails to break through, and soon the *Erebus* and *Terror* ground to a halt, trapped in the ice.

Ross blasted on his whistle. "Every man not manning the sails, out on the ice! We shall break our way through."

And so, Yule found himself beneath *Erebus*'s prow, swinging a pickax and wondering who might be the next to suffer Hooker's fate. By some miracle, none did. After an hour of picking and digging, the ice yielded. With a mighty crack, the *Erebus*, then the *Terror*, lurched forward. Yule followed the others up a rope ladder, his boots slipping against the frozen rungs as ice stung his face like wasps.

No one cheered when the ships emerged from the bay. They had known their vessels could withstand crushing by pack ice. Now they understood that this ice could still entomb them, and that a chunk of the cliffs could destroy them from above.

As the ships resumed their eastward course, another sharp crack drew the crews to their sterns. Yule watched an ice slab, just visible inside the bay, tumble into the icy water, sending a wave of ice toward the ships. Only the bay's lip shielded them from disaster.

"No God below fifty degrees south, that's for sure," Yule heard one able seaman mutter to another. "This can't end well."

The expedition's man of science agreed, Yule learned that evening.

"We can't go on like this," Hooker said at supper, huddled over his soup for warmth. "Ross will get us all killed."

Yule nodded but said nothing. He still hoped to see Ross hang, but for the moment he dared not speak ill of the captain.

"Could the officers somehow override his decision?" Hooker asked.

Yule didn't answer, just shook his head and pressed his finger to his lips. He rose from the table, stepped quietly to the doorway of the officer's mess, and glanced out. No one lingered nearby; he sat back down.

Hooker lowered his voice but kept on. "Come now, there must be some way—"

"Silence!" Yule hissed, leaning in as Hooker flinched, trembling. Yule decided against telling him they both could hang for taking this talk much further. Instead, he reminded Hooker what their mutual friend had told them. "Remember what Doctor McCormick said. Captain Ross must believe we all support him."

Hooker nodded, staring down at his plate. "Aye. But then why would he place that note in a cask and throw it overboard?"

"So that a record of our voyage might survive, even if—" Yule paused, catching Hooker's eye, unable to finish.

"Ross wants the world to think we all consented to continuing along the ice shelf."

"Aye. He wants to be remembered as a good captain, not—" Yule bit his tongue.

"A good captain?" Hooker muttered, eyes fixed on the table, shaking his head. "I know better—"

His voice faltered, and Yule, desperate to distract Hooker from Ross's abuse, started listing the captain's failures, one by one, consequences be damned. "He certainly isn't a good captain. No good captain would have sailed into that ice bay. He's neglected our magnetic observations in his mad quest for the pole. He's out to please the Admiralty, but he's treated me like an ass every day since leaving England." Little by little, the pain left Hooker's face as Yule stripped Ross of the aura that had surrounded him as a Captain of the Royal Navy.

Before Yule could continue, a commotion drew them out of the officer's mess. It was Cunningham, one of the Marines, rummaging through Tucker's bunk.

"What's this?" Yule demanded.

"Searching all the bunks on the Captain's orders," Cunningham replied. "Captain Ross suspects a mutiny is afoot."

Chapter 31

Ross Sea Coast
Antarctica
July 2123

Roscoe and Chip helped Shiduri close up that night, then crashed in a cramped room at Ye Olde Igloo Motel, the tallest building in Newloon at fifteen stories. Roscoe awoke to a pounding headache and a mouth like sandpaper. He rolled out of his hammock and headed back to Shiduri's. His job was to stay there—specifically, inside her privacy phone. He was expecting a call soon, Chip had told him as he emerged from the battered red box the night before.

"Griquas are on board," he'd said. "Sub's leaving tomorrow morning; should be here in six days. They've got an incubator on board to cook up more algae that'll light up in fresh water."

They wouldn't just be brewing algae on the way down. They'd also be hammering out the details of the plan's next steps: using the Griquas' sub to collect a sample from the seafloor at the freshwater plume's source, releasing the algae, and broadcasting the glowing stream to the world.

All of this was going to take hardware. The Griquas were finalizing a shopping list, Chip had told Roscoe, and would give it to both of them soon. To boost their chances, they would split up the search for supplies.

Chip would head back to Spigot and ask Hamza if he still wanted to screw over StarCross. If he did, they would steal as much hardware from Spigot as they could. Meanwhile, Roscoe would shop in Skua Central. But first, he would need the list—and for that, uninterrupted access to the privacy phone. Shiduri had agreed, with the promise of discounted beer and blubber shipments on the Griquas' sub.

"Those discounts had better be steep, Chip," Shiduri had said, voice oozing doubt, as they draped the booth with a tarp. "This thing drives a lot of business."

"The Griquas' word is gold, Shid," Chip assured her. "That discount will more than cover a few days' dip in business."

So Roscoe spent the morning on the floor of the phone booth, which Shiduri had equipped with tortilla chips, a water bottle, and a bucket. He hadn't touched any of it when the phone finally rang.

"Hello?"

"Hola, is this Roscoe?" asked a tinny voice with a roll on the "R."

"Yes. Tell me what you need." Roscoe jotted down the list: an underwater camera with long-range Bluetooth, an underwater floodlight, the toughest, highest-pressure spray nozzle he could find, and instructions to call back once he'd found them.

"Sounds good." Roscoe hung up, cracked the door, checked that the bar was empty, and slipped out. He walked Skua Central's passageways, hood up, shopping cart draped with a tarp, looking like just another trash picker or drug dealer plying their trade. He eyed the signs, passing two food stalls and a VR brothel before finding Whalstone's, the hardware-and-electronics dealer who'd sold him the XRF gun. That felt like an eternity ago.

Chip had given him a low-end wristband, his entire NSF annual discretionary stipend—one whole WEC—and the same advice Jen had given him for haggling in Skua Central: "Whatever price they give you, tell them you can't afford it, and that your boss will kill you if you ask for more money."

Roscoe pushed his list toward the scrap dealer without a word, hoping silence would make him seem more serious. Whalstone looked it over, nodded, and disappeared, reemerging several minutes later with each of the requested items. That was a relief; even if Hamza and Chip managed to find some of the same equipment, they'd have backups. The nozzle had a disturbingly fleshy hue, but if it worked, Roscoe didn't care.

"One-point-five WECs, or one-point-eight-five RECs," he told Roscoe.

"I can't afford that," Roscoe replied. "Max budget is one WEC. My boss'll kill me if I ask for more."

Whalstone rasped—or was he laughing? "Kind of amazes me how bosses down here can get away with killing their workers. If I had a WEC-cent for every time I heard that line, I'd be a Resident."

Roscoe cursed Chip, Jen, and their outdated haggling advice. He tried another angle. "Well, I guess I'll have to go somewhere else." He pushed the cart back a step, just enough to make it look like he might leave.

"Good luck with that. I remember you, shorty. XRF gun, right? What'd I tell you then?" He tapped the sign with its unreadable lettering.

"Lowest price guarantee."

He nodded. "Ironically, you could've gotten some of this stuff off a salvage sub. One just 'found a new wreck'"—Whalstone made air quotes—"and came in with quite the haul. But it's all gone now, sold off to other subs that'll probably end up wrecks themselves. Anyway, one-point-eight-five is the best you'll get unless you find a way to break this damn shipping cartel."

"I have, actually," Roscoe said, his tone steady and assured. Whalstone raised his eyebrows. "You heard of the Griquas?"

"Who?"

Roscoe's chest swelled. As he described the Griquas—a group now operating a sub out of Patagonia—Whalstone leaned further over the counter, intrigued. "This is for them," Roscoe explained. "Help me out, and I bet they'd find some space on their sub for you."

Whalstone stroked his beard thoughtfully, then narrowed his eyes. "Sounds good—if it's for real. Lotta people make promises around here. Not many keep 'em."

"If you'd like, I can put you in touch."

Whalstone gave his beard a few more strokes. "What the hell. I've got a burner wristband with some juice left on it." He scrawled a number on the back of a receipt. "Make it quick. If I don't hear from 'em by closing, I'm smelting this burner. Not a good idea to have a contact number floating around too long down here."

Roscoe nodded and raced back to Shiduri's, slipping into the phone booth to dial the Griquas' sub, grinding his teeth with each ring. Finally, the tinny, accented voice answered, and he relayed Whalstone's terms.

"Sounds like the cost of doing business down there," the voice said, flat but resigned. "I'll call him."

Returning to Whalstone's booth, Roscoe saw the shopkeeper had his wristband to his ear. He hung up and gave Roscoe an approving nod. "Good outfit you're working with there, kid," he said as Roscoe swiped over a WEC. "Said they'll be docking here in six days, and we'll work out the details then."

Roscoe called the Griquas' sub again. The tinny voice agreed to daily check-ins so Roscoe wouldn't be tied to the phone. Shiduri let him stash the cart in the pub's back room. He spent the next six days lying low in the Igloo Motel, watching whatever English-language shows its pirate satellite dish picked up—mostly nature documentaries about extinct species. It took him hours to separate the sounds of animal mating rituals from the sounds of the one-night stands coming from the next room over.

On the sixth check-in, Roscoe finally heard the words he'd been waiting for: "We're docking in an hour," the tinny voice informed him.

Roscoe pulled his hood low and retrieved the cart. "It's time," he told Shiduri, giving her a grateful nod. "Thanks again."

"Anytime," she said, looking up from the cocktail she was mixing to smile. "Just don't let Chip forget those rates."

Roscoe eased the cart through the throng, careful not to bump the wrong person or lose any of his precious cargo. He gave Whalstone a quick nod as he passed. The vendor casually looked away.

The cart clattered over cold metal slats as Roscoe pushed it into the port section. He passed through a door marked "STEVEDORE ENTRANCE—SUB CARGO ONLY" and entered a Quonset hut the size of several tennis courts. Along one wall, propped-open double doors every few meters let in the orange light of the submarine port. Roscoe realized he'd seen forklifts shunt cargo in and out of this space his first night here.

It wasn't bustling like that now. A few Newloon roughnecks had parked crates and carts on the floor, leaving plenty of space between them. Most leaned against their loads, smoking, their eyes fixed on their cargo. Roscoe did the same, staring at the slice of green-black water where submarines surfaced. He jumped when another cart rolled up next to him.

"It's me," Chip said from under his hood. "Got what I could from McMurdo."

"Sounds good," Roscoe replied. "Where's Hamza? Did he get anything from Spigot?"

Chip closed his eyes and sighed heavily, but the water started to churn before he could answer. "We'll talk about that later. C'mon, let's get this stuff onto the sub."

They wheeled their carts through the double doors as the Griquas' sub broke the surface. Before them rose a long, tubular craft. On its conning tower, Roscoe saw the Griquas' emblem: a wedge of yellow sun pointing straight down, as though glimpsed between a fjord's slopes. Beneath it was the word "LAUTARO." A deep groove ran the length of the vessel a meter or so above the waterline, curving over the top in front of the conning tower and continuing along the other side. It marked where a surface ship might have a deck.

Chip and Roscoe watched as this section rose from the sub's body: first an outer hull, then a lattice of metal struts, and finally an inner hull. The two parallel segments slid away, revealing a bay maybe seven or eight meters deep.

"Chip, Roscoe, down here!"

Looking down, they saw a man waving to them from the base of the conning tower. He had a long, gray ponytail and a stubbled goatee, and wore jeans and a gray fleece vest with the sun-wedge logo on the breast. Roscoe recognized the voice from over the phone. It no longer sounded tinny.

"That's Ricardo, our main contact," Chip said, returning the wave as the hull's top section clicked into place on the sub's port side, leaving the bay fully open. A narrow ramp unfolded from the hold and tapped the dock not far from where they stood.

Chip pushed his cart onto the ramp and down into the hull. Roscoe followed his lead. He turned a corner and started down another ramp that ended at the base of the conning tower. Inside the hold, Roscoe saw more algae drums, a two-person hovercraft, and a strange, curved object under a blue tarp. A crane-like machine stood just inside the prow.

Just as Roscoe started down the main ramp into the hold, shouting erupted in several languages. Roscoe made out just one word: fire.

Turning, he saw pillars of flame rise from the dock's far end, their heat already bending the walls and ceiling. The blaze sucked in air from every corner of the vast, hangar-like space. Wind blasted Roscoe's face while heat blistered the back of his neck.

"Chip, move!" Roscoe shouted. The scientist was still easing his cart down the ramp.

"I'm trying!" Chip yelled back, carefully maneuvering the cart. "This stuff's fragile! Can't move too fast."

"I can't seal the hull until you guys are down!" Ricardo called. "The ramp is part of the mechanism."

Chip was almost at the base of the ramp when Roscoe ducked below the gunwale, finally shielded from the heat. The fire was growing fast, its flames licking at the dock. The roughnecks and other workers had vanished. The shouting had stopped. Everyone else had bolted.

Chip finally reached the floor of the cargo hold. Roscoe cared less about saving his cart; he let it careen down the ramp. As it neared the conning tower's base, he dug in his heels and leaned back with all his might, stopping the cart just before impact.

His breath came short and fast as he looked up. The outer ramp—the part touching the dock—was already folding in, its end drooping from the inferno. The hull's top section started to roll back into place above them, narrowing the glowing orange strip of ceiling. The sub's lid had less than a half-meter to go when a tortured groan filled the air—the walls were starting to buckle.

"Shit, the port's coming down," Chip said. "If we're not clear of this place when it collapses, we'll be trapped."

Finally, the hull's top section sealed shut with a metallic snap. Roscoe heard water rush in all around them. "Ballast tanks are filling," Chip explained as the sub began to sink. Above them, the groaning from the port's walls became a thunderous roar—and then nothing.

Roscoe let out a long breath. The sub was still moving. Ricardo pulled an old, gray smartphone from his pocket, a relic from before wristbands. "We're clear," he told Chip and Roscoe. "We've got external cameras on the conning tower. Bridge says roof came down right on top of us, but the dock supports held."

"Damn," Chip muttered. "StarCross really wanted to send a message with that fire. Port'll be out of commission for months. Don't think you guys will be welcome in Newloon again."

Ricardo looked at Roscoe. "How could they—" the question died on his breath as his eyes met Roscoe's. Together, they brightened with recognition. "Whalstone."

"Who?" Chip asked.

"The guy I bought this stuff from," Roscoe said in a small, hard voice. "Either StarCross scared him, or they paid him, and he talked."

Chip pinched the bridge of his nose and closed his eyes. "You told him what we were doing?"

"No," Roscoe said. "I just told him the Griquas would give him a shipping discount if he sold me everything for that one WEC you gave me." With every word, he realized, his voice had gotten more defensive—which was not the tone to strike when he'd just messed up this badly. "I-I'm sorry."

"It's not just your fault." Ricardo rubbed his eyes. "I should have seen it coming. Soon as I talked to him, he asked too many questions—who the Griquas were, when we'd be docking, if we were hiring crew. Said he wanted a shipping deal." He kicked at one of the submarine's metal ribs. "I should have known. He was fishing for more. Last time I let my guard down."

Chip slumped against the wall, scratching the stubble along his jaw. "Well, fuck. Now StarCross knows we made it out, and they'll be looking for our sub down here. Just when I thought this plan couldn't get any more off the rails."

"What do you mean?"

Chip tapped his wristband, projecting a screen for Roscoe:

ATTENTION ALL MCMURDO EMPLOYEES

ARGUS-3 NUCLEAR TEST SCHEDULED FOR 1200 HOURS ON SATURDAY, JULY 31

BE READY TO ASSIST

StarCross will detonate a nuclear warhead under the Ross Sea Coast, near the opening to Yule Bay, for research purposes at noon on Saturday, July 31. Although this blast, codenamed Argus-3, is too distant from McMurdo to pose any threat, the U.S. government's agreement with StarCross requires it to provide any requested assistance with this test. Please respond promptly to any StarCross requests for aid.

Thank you for your cooperation.

U.S. Antarctic Program

"They're going ahead with their nuclear test now? In the middle of winter?" Roscoe asked, incredulous.

"Yep. Guess your disciplinary hearing got them scared," Chip said, still scratching his jaw. "They don't want to leave that freshwater plume sitting out there for long. If someone else finds it and proves what it is, StarCross'll lose control. Must've promised the govellers enough WECs to last decades to get them to go along with this."

Roscoe checked the date on Chip's wristband: July 23. Eight days.

They had planned on at least a month—enough time to work in secret, without StarCross hunting them.

Chip was right. This plan had completely derailed.

But Roscoe didn't feel the sharp stabs of worry in his chest like he had back during Q-CAT exams or during the last few days before his senior capstone deadline. The past few weeks had dulled his nerves. He was past panic.

"All right, well, I guess we need to get working," he said. "Where's Hamza?"

Chip drew a slow breath, then looked at Ricardo, who stood nearby. They both looked down, their expressions tight. Then, Chip placed his hand on Roscoe's shoulder. His eyes had the same intensity that had hooked Roscoe so long ago, but when he spoke, his voice had a rawness Roscoe hadn't heard before.

"Roscoe," he said, "Hamza's dead."

Chapter 32

H.M.S. *Erebus*
Unnamed Sea
February 1841

The Marine finished searching Tucker's bunk. He placed a hand on the door to Yule's—the door that concealed a pail full of basalt, hiding both the life insurance policy on Ross and the attestation to his crime against Hooker.

Words failed Yule—but not Hooker. The assistant surgeon stepped forward and rested a hand on Cunningham's shoulder.

"You're not going in there."

"What?"

"Yule is storing specimens that I and Doctor McCormick have gathered throughout this voyage in his bunk. They're fragile."

"And what would Ross say to that?" Cunningham challenged.

"Go ask him. Take a good look at all the space he's already given up in his Great Cabin for my specimens, and then get his permission to go rummaging through more of the expedition's scientific proceeds."

The three men stared at each other. Then Cunningham brushed Hooker's arm aside and moved on. Hooker shot Yule a quick look—sharp and knowing, the sort of look one pickpocket might give another in a crowd—then turned.

Yule returned to his bunk, closed the door, and remembered that he still had Hooker's papers. He lifted them from the drawer. Underneath lay his mother's last letter, the one that had informed him of his father's death. Unfolding the paper, he read again her final assessment of John Yule—and of him.

> *In the months before his death, he spoke often of wanting to learn the results of your voyage, the new lands you would help the Navy find in the South, and whether there was any truth to what the Frenchman he met at Trafalgar told him. Regardless of what you find, I trust you will conduct yourself in a manner that does your father's memory proud.*

Yule's father had looked his sworn enemy in the eye and let him live. Now, Yule held papers in which Hooker—who had spared Yule the grief of losing both parents at once and who cared enough for Yule's privacy to take a great risk in stopping the search of his bunk—had called him a "worthy fellow." In the pail at his feet sat papers that would disgrace the young surgeon for profit. Yule's profit.

Shame smoldered in his chest as he dropped Hooker's letters back in the drawer. He needed air. Donning his coat and Welsh wig, he stepped out into the bracing cold and blinding sunshine. The deck was unusually quiet, manned only by the officers of the watch and a few able seamen. Despite the sunshine, it was late.

The *Erebus* maintained her course along the ice cliffs, which stood high and solid as ever. Ross remained undeterred. Yule stared at the cliffs and tried to console himself: no matter how vile his plans may have been, they mattered little now. Ross's thirst for glory seemed certain to deliver them all to an icy grave, with the world believing his men had loved and trusted him to the end. None dared speak ill of him in their letters home, while the currents now bore another false vote of confidence northward in a cask.

Only Yule had documented Ross's true nature. He had the only proof that his men questioned his skills.

And only to make a profit at Hooker's expense, Yule thought, unable to avoid the shame. Ice grinding and wind whistling around him, he stared into the patch of calm, inky water just aft of the stern—the one place his eyes could escape the sun.

You are no better than Ross, he thought bitterly.

Oh, I doubt that, another thought answered.

Yule pushed himself back from the gunwale in surprise. He hadn't spoken, and he was quite sure no one had spoken to him. The thought wasn't his; it seemed to belong to someone else.

Why? Yule wondered, hoping this other strain of thought would reply.

A ship is only as good as her masters, the voice replied. Yule gasped; his father had often said the same thing. Undeterred by Yule's shame or his doubts about superstitions, ghost stories, and tales of unseen "presences," the thought pressed on. *You and Tucker have guided the Erebus around the world, into waters no vessel has plied before. These men owe their lives to you.*

They may not for much longer, Yule thought grimly, his gaze returning to the dark water. *Ross seems driven to carry us to our deaths. He only cares for his legacy.*

Aye, the voice conceded, *but you left something in Hobart that could tarnish it—unless Ross gets back alive.*

The realization knocked him back like one of the Roaring Forties' waves. Yule steadied his feet, raced to his bunk, pulled the shroud off its prism for light, and yanked the insurance certificate from the pail. With his penknife, he cut out the fictitious name he had given himself and his mother's name on the line marked "BENEFICIARY." It now showed only that the policy was to be paid out in the event of James Clark Ross's death.

He underlined the part of the certificate that read, "Copy kept by Lunk Aspley & Sons Insurance Co., Hobart, Van Dieman's Land," and reached for a fresh sheet of paper. Then, he wrote, "Your men bet against you, Ross—prove them wrong. Turn back now."

He placed the note and the altered certificate in an envelope, slipped it under the door to the Great Cabin, and hurried away.

Chapter 33

Ross Sea Coast
Antarctica
July 2123

Roscoe closed his eyes and sank against the wall, the sub's dim hull spinning around him. "How?"

Chip crouched down, placing a steadying hand on Roscoe's shoulder. "When I didn't hear back from him for a few days, I reached out to a contact in Drone Ops. He hadn't shown up to work since—since your disciplinary hearing. Then an email went out. He—he's gone."

"What did the email say?"

"Roscoe, I don't—"

He pushed away Chip's hand. "What did it say?" he demanded.

Ashen-faced, Chip tapped his wristband, projecting an email with a StarCross-logo heading:

> *Dear Spigot Family,*
>
> *With a heavy heart, we write to inform you of the death of first-year intern Hamza Tetuanui. Hamza's body was found near the track route south of Spigot. An autopsy revealed a fatal level of non-approved psychoactive*

compounds in his blood, as well as self-inflicted cuts on his wrists. It is not clear which was the cause of death.

Spigot CEO Grei Jahnford offers his condolences to Hamza's family in Tasmania and his friends here at Spigot. "His death is a loss to all of us, and a tragic reminder of what can happen when we lose focus on our mission of bringing water to a thirsty world," Jahnford said. "I pray that we can all find the strength to continue with that mission."

The StarCross Cares Wellness Team will offer video counseling to all those—

Roscoe stopped reading and stared at the floor. "You think he did it?"

Chip took another long breath, then let it out. "I don't know. Maybe he did. Or maybe StarCross did him in like they did Finn Smalls to send a message. Or maybe—" He stopped himself and gripped Roscoe's shoulder. "It doesn't matter. He's gone now."

Roscoe couldn't cry. He cursed the compound for that. "Hamza's dead because of me," Roscoe said, each word more bitter than the last. "Fuck. It's my fault."

"No," Chip said firmly. "This isn't on you. It's Spigot's fault. It's on StarCross. They made you, Hamza, and every other intern in that hole think that pleasing them is the only thing that matters. They trained you to believe your work was the only way to do that."

He paused, looking down. "You take someone raised to think that way, have them make a move against StarCross, then fail—well, it's not surprising," Chip's voice softened. "If anything, it's my fault too."

Their eyes met, heavy with shared guilt. Finally, Chip spoke again. "You don't have to keep helping with this test if you don't want to." He nodded toward Ricardo, who was studiously keeping his eyes on his phone's screen. "He says the Griquas can find a place for you up north. Or you can come back with me to McMurdo. It's your call."

Roscoe stared at the floor. Neither choice meant anything to him in that moment. "I gotta sleep on this," he said quietly.

Chip nodded but let slip an impatient wince. "That's fine." He turned to Ricardo. "Show our guest to his bunk."

Ricardo pocketed his phone and gave Roscoe's shoulder a reassuring pat. "Certainly. Follow me, amigo. Watch your step—mind your head."

The crewman led him through the sub's cargo hold to a hatch at the stern. It opened into a long, low-ceilinged compartment lined with workbenches covered with test tube racks, beakers, and electronics spanning a century of manufacturing dates. Along a far wall, a computer glowed beneath a framed painting of the Sacred Heart of Jesus. An old man with white hair typed away at the station without looking up.

"That's Padre Petí," Ricardo said as they passed. "The brains of our operation. Great guy. He doesn't like to be disturbed when he's working though."

They climbed a steep set of stairs to a second level lined with sleeping berths, some with privacy screens drawn closed. Ricardo guided him to an open bunk at the far end of the hall. Its sheets were crisp, and a knapsack lay atop the pillow.

"Here you are, señor," Ricardo said with a gentle smile. "Luxury accommodations on Griqua Cruise Lines. Clean clothes and a toothbrush are in the bag. Face the stairs when you go down them. Head's at the end of the hall," he said, pointing to a hatch. "Get some rest."

He turned to leave, then stopped. "I almost forgot—the shower shuts off after three minutes. Water's precious down here too."

"No worries, I'm used to it," Roscoe muttered, collapsing onto the bunk.

He woke a few hours later and stared up at the ceiling. He didn't know what to make of the Griquas—whether they could pull off the test, whether he wanted to try his luck with them, or whether luck even mattered anymore. All he knew was that he still had a chance to strike back at StarCross. After all they'd put him through, he wasn't about to let it pass.

Fuck it, he thought, rolling out of the bunk. He pulled on his shoes, felt the stiffness of his legs, and stumbled down the hall. Yawning, he climbed the stairs to the top level. The first thing he saw a was monitor and control panel crewed by a female Griqua with Asian features. The bridge, he guessed.

Roscoe looked over his shoulder and almost lost his grip. The top deck was about as long as the sleeping berth, with a long table down the middle, ending in a serving counter and a narrow kitchen. But none of that held his attention.

Unlike the dull-gray metal, wiring, and piping he'd seen so far on this sub, the walls around the serving counter were alive. Rows of lettuce, herbs, tuber sprouts, vegetables, and berries erupted from pots mounted on the walls, glowing under purple-hued grow lights. Tubes snaked around each pot, feeding the plants like veins feeding organs. In seconds, Roscoe saw more fresh food than he had eaten in months.

Chip sat alone at a table, sipping coffee.

"What is this?" Roscoe asked, gesturing at the greenery.

"Hydroponic garden. Keeps the sub running longer without resupply, takes pressure off the CO-two filters, and gives Evangelina here"—he nodded toward a figure trimming lettuce at the back—"a way to test the latest grow lights and plant varieties."

Roscoe stared harder at the plants. "They have WECs and RECs to spend on all this?"

"Not quite. Evangelina works for Griqua Tierra's Civil Service. By letting her use this space for research, the *Lautaro* co-op offsets its WEC and REC contribution to Griqua Tierra's general fund."

"Besides her and us, how many people are on this sub?"

Chip ticked off five fingers. "Gabriel, Wangari, Petí, Ricardo, and Yongchen. The Equation tipped in favor of computers for running most sub functions decades ago. Even with secondhand parts, they only require a small crew."

Chip set his coffee down. "Don't want to pressure you, but—"

"I'm in." Roscoe interrupted. "Let's do the test."

Chip grinned. "Good. It really was your call, but I'd be lying if I said I didn't want to hear that. Grab some food, and let's get to work."

Roscoe ate the most flavorful quinoa he'd had in months. While he ate, Chip fetched Ricardo. Over coffee, the scientist started talking through their options.

"We've got a tighter schedule now, but in principle, there's no reason we can't pull this off. We'll reach the freshwater plume in a few hours. Padre Petí and the crew are already assembling the parts, and we have the dye ready to go."

"What we don't have is secrecy," Ricardo added, his face grim.

Chip nodded. "Right. StarCross plans to nuke this place in a few days, and they already know it's got fresh water. They're going to be on guard. Roscoe, that's where you come in."

"You ... think I can get past StarCross?"

"Maybe—with one of the Griquas' toys," Chip said. "Let's go down to the hold."

Roscoe followed them through the dim sub, passing Petí's empty lab and stepping into the hold. Welding sparks cast silhouettes of three visor-clad figures—two with torches and one with a fire extinguisher.

Beside the algae drums and hovercraft, the tarp had been pulled back, revealing a bizarre, dull-gray craft. Roscoe thought it looked a bit like a football, squashed flat and stretched at the ends. About four and a half meters long, two meters high, and one meter wide at the middle, it balanced on a pair of black struts.

A nearby table was draped with a printed vinyl map. Chip pointed at a small blue tick mark near its center. "The freshwater plume's source is a one-meter streak of seabed near the mouth of Yule Bay," he said. By now, Roscoe recognized this stretch of coastline at a glance. A hand-drawn red arc spanned the bay's mouth and extended far out into sea. Chip traced it with his finger. "StarCross Security's set up a no-sail zone around Yule Bay." He tapped the red arc. "If we sail this sub in there, they'll blow us out of the water."

Roscoe folded his arms. "That's a problem."

"It is," Chip replied. "But we've caught a break. This new deadline means they didn't have time to redeploy many of their naval assets. So they only have the StarBuoys for surveillance and one sub for enforcement."

"How does that help us exactly?" Roscoe asked.

"We have an inside source," Ricardo said. "Hacked their system. That's how we know all this. The buoys monitor radio traffic, sonar waves, and disturbances from sub propellers inside the zone. We need a way to get in that avoids all those."

Chip turned to the strange craft. "And that," he said, "is where you come in."

Ricardo led them to the craft. Roscoe now noticed two large fiberglass fins folded flat against its side. He realized it wasn't shaped like a football. It looked more like a fish.

"This is an underwater kayak," Ricardo explained, "developed by our Inuit friends in Greenland."

"Greenland's the only other ice cap of any real size left on the planet," Chip said. "Naturally, StarCross was interested. But after a few years, they decided it wasn't worth the effort. Subdrones kept vanishing, piers collapsed, and a few subs had 'accidents.'" He made air quotes with his fingers.

Roscoe examined the vessel more closely. "You're saying the Inuit attacked StarCross with these things?"

"They've been kayaking around Greenland's coasts for thousands of years," Chip said. "Didn't take 'em long to adapt kayaks for underwater ops. Once they did, they had the upper hand. Far as we know, StarCross still hasn't figured out what hit 'em."

"It took some careful diplomacy," Ricardo added, "but we convinced them to give us a model to test down here. If it works, we'll talk about setting up a licensed manufacturer at Griqua Tierra."

Roscoe tilted his head. "And how does it handle?"

"We don't quite know yet," Ricardo admitted. "We only picked it up two months ago. Inuit kayaks are custom-built for their users, and this one's too small for anyone on the sub." He smiled. "Until now."

Roscoe understood what they were getting at. He looked at Chip. "That's why you need me? Because I'm small enough to fit in this thing?"

"Hey, no one said outsmarting StarCross would be good for your ego," Chip said with a shrug. "You can still back out if you want."

Roscoe exhaled sharply, forcing himself to focus. "You need me to take this thing to the freshwater plume, get a sample, and get out."

Chip nodded. "That was always the plan. This sub's too big for tight maneuvering. So initially, we planned to get close to the site and have you go down in this to drop the dye and collect a sample."

Roscoe's lips tightened. "Except now, you need to send me in from—how far out, exactly?"

"Thirty-five klicks, give or take," Chip answered. "That's the shortest distance from the no-sail-zone boundary to the plume."

Roscoe stared at the kayak. "You want me to paddle this thing thirty-five klicks?" The thought alone turned his arms to rubber.

"Relax," Chip said. "The Inuit figured out a way to make these things go long distances without motors."

Chip stepped over to the kayak's elongated end, gesturing at two circular vents pointing backward. "These are compressed air cylinders," he explained, slipping his fingers into a groove in the hull. A section popped open, revealing a cramped space with a reclined seat.

"This is a range meter," Chip said, pointing to an eye-level dial. "It shows you how far your compressed air will take you. When you're running on air, you hold these fins out to the side and flat, like airplane wings. When your compressed air runs out, the fins work like kayak paddles, and you can maneuver short distances."

"And the StarBuoys won't pick me up?"

"They never caught these things in Greenland," Chip said. "Shouldn't down here. Sonar signature's tiny."

Roscoe exhaled, the plan clearer to him now. "So you put me in this thing, point me in the direction of the freshwater plume, and off I go."

"That's right." Chip pointed to two screened circles on the kayak's underside near the front. "These are gills. They extract dissolved oxygen from the water and remove carbon dioxide from the inside. So your breathing air supply won't be an issue."

Roscoe paused, his fingers brushing the edge of the kayak. "And once I'm at the plume, how do I get down there?"

"Gravity," Ricardo interjected. "The dye and sample collector mounted beneath you will weigh the kayak down gradually on the voyage over." He moved his palm left and right, keeping it level at first, then arcing it downward. Roscoe watched, his chest tightening, as Ricardo's palm turned vertical.

"Don't worry, weón," Richardo added quickly, turning his palm flat again. "It's balanced to stay level even as it sinks. We'll calculate the trajectory, buoyancy—all of that—so that when you run out of compressed air, you'll be right on top of the plume."

Chip noticed Roscoe eyeing the kayak's thin hull. "This can handle the depth," he said reassuringly, rapping it with his knuckles. "We'll be near the coast. It's only a few hundred meters down."

Roscoe nodded. "Okay ... so assuming it holds, how do I get back up?"

"You drop the dye," Chip said. "That's your ballast. Once you drop that, the weight loss will bring you to cruising level—just a meter or two below the surface. Then you paddle around to find a clear patch."

"And then?"

Chip pointed to a button beside the seat, a red one with white lettering in one of the strange scripts Roscoe had seen on Whalstone's sign. "You push that. It flushes the internal ballast tank with hydrogen electrolyzed from the water. You'll rise to the surface."

Aside from these features, the kayak's interior was sparse—just a few dials, no touchscreens or LED panels.

"How do I collect the sample?" Roscoe asked.

Ricardo nodded to the welders at the far end of the cargo hold. "That's what they're working on—rigging this up to scoop some sediment from the seafloor." He gestured toward the kayak. "In the meantime, take a seat inside and get a feel for it."

Roscoe climbed into the kayak, more worried than ever about what he was getting into. The kayak fit his slender frame, if not his sense of comfort. Ricardo closed the hatch, leaving just a few centimeters on either side of his ears. Roscoe felt like he was inside a peapod—or a coffin.

"How does it feel?" Ricardo's voice came muffled through the hull.

"Uh, I fit," Roscoe called back.

"Perfect!" Ricardo opened the hatch again. "Like I said, we'll calculate the trajectory to position you directly above the plume. Once you're there, all you'll need to do is pull a lever to collect the sample and release the dye."

"Okay," he said hesitatingly. *They know it needs to be idiot-proof, right?* Roscoe thought.

Ricardo pressed on. "After you drop the dye, the kayak will lose weight and begin rising. It'll weigh enough to stay one or two meters below the surface." He gestured toward the side of the kayak. "That same mechanism triggers the incendiary buoy. It's one of Petí's inventions—it'll melt a hole in the ice large enough for the kayak to surface. Once you find that hole, paddle to it."

Ricardo pointed to the two rubber grips on either side of Roscoe's seat. "These are your paddles. Pull them back when you're ready to move."

Roscoe saw plate-sized disks above his lap on either side, dark black against the orange hull. A rubber cylinder spanned each disk, bulging inward. Leaning forward, he grabbed the ends of the cylinders and pulled. They swung back on hinges, locking into position perpendicular to the hull. They looked a bit like sawed-off scooter handles.

"The blades are perpendicular to the side in this position. Push one forward, pull the other back—same as a kayak."

Roscoe followed the instructions. The handles spun the disks, producing a rhythmic click with each push and pull. A few strokes later, he had the hang of it.

"Good!" Ricardo said, grinning. "Those Inuit builders knew what they were doing. All bicycle mechanics—pretty impressive."

Chip and Ricardo continued to guide Roscoe through the basics: turning, slowing down, reversing, and locking the paddles into a wing-like position for when the kayak was running on compressed air. It all seemed manageable—at least in the sub's dry interior.

"How will I find the hole in the ice?"

"Quite easily," Ricardo replied. "See those strips?"

Most of the kayak's interior was an orange, sodium-vapor glow, except for the handles, two portholes in front, two more overhead, and three long black strips running the kayak's length. One ran along each side at eye level, and the third stretched overhead and curved down in front of his face.

Roscoe nodded.

"Those will point you toward the clear patch," Ricardo explained. "They glow when they detect light wavelengths from the Moon and stars shining on open water. If one side lights up, paddle in that direction. If the ceiling lights up, you're under the opening."

Roscoe shifted in his seat. "And if they don't light up? What if the incendiary buoy doesn't work?"

Ricardo rubbed the back of his neck. "If that happens, head north. Winds and currents are more likely to create openings in that direction. Just follow the compass bearing."

Roscoe glanced around and saw a compass between his legs. "Aren't we too far south for compasses to work?"

"Most compasses, yes," Ricardo said. "But this is different. It's designed for high latitudes. Inside, there's a dip needle that measures the Earth's magnetic field. Gears and clockwork calculate true north and south. No electronics required. Like I said, these guys know what they're doing. Once you find the opening, push the red button to surface."

Roscoe wasn't reassured. Relying on the same tech polar explorers had used nearly three centuries ago wasn't exactly comforting. Neither was Ricardo's answer to his next question.

"How do I get back to the sub?"

Ricardo exchanged a glance with Chip.

Chip crouched down to meet Roscoe's eyes—a gesture that now meant only bad news. "That's the tricky part." He gestured toward the small craft parked beside the kayak. "We'll send the hovercraft."

"On the surface?" Roscoe asked, thinking back to Ross's journal. The *Erebus*'s crew had faced life-threatening dangers even in summer. This was still winter.

"This time of year? How?"

"Pray that it's calm enough to get through."

Roscoe's stomach churned. "And if it's not?"

Chip looked askance. "Then we've got a bigger problem."

"What about StarCross satellites?" Roscoe asked. "Won't they detect the hovercraft?"

"Yeah, that's another risk. We're betting its small size and surface speed will help it slip through."

The word "betting" stuck with Roscoe. If they were willing to risk the hovercraft in one direction, why not risk it both ways? "Couldn't we just use the hovercraft to take the kayak out, drop the dye, and collect the sample?"

Chip shook his head. "We looked into that. The kayak and dye barrel wouldn't fit." The explanation did little to raise Roscoe's hopes for a safe return.

"Like I said, Roscoe, it's your decision. You can still back out."

Just then, two welders walked up. One pulled Ricardo aside, speaking rapid-fire Spanish. A third figure approached Roscoe. He looked about seventy, with thinning white hair, thick-framed glasses, and a Roman collar—Padre Petí, the "brains of the operation."

Petí shook Roscoe's hand. Roscoe thought of Jahnford and steeled himself for some unwanted proselytizing.

"Señor Slake, Juan Petí," the priest said, his English soft but clear. "My condolences on the loss of your friend." He laid his hand on the underwater kayak—the tiny craft meant to challenge a superpower. "We thought we might name this in his honor—the *Hamza.*"

Roscoe felt something odd on his face, then realized it was a tear. "I'd like that. Thank you."

Turning to Chip, he managed to recall something from Cultural History—cursing around priests had been taboo. He kept his answer clean. "I'm still in. Let's do it."

Chip had apparently missed that lesson. "Fuck, yeah." He turned to the welders, who were lugging a bulky, metal apparatus down the hold. "All right, they still have some modifications to finish. Let's let them do their thing."

While Petí and the welders worked to convert the *Hamza* into a proper research vessel, Chip and Roscoe headed to the galley for a meal of sub-grown potatoes and StemSteak that Roscoe never would've guessed had been frozen.

"Patagonians know what they're doing with this stuff," Chip said.

Boots thudded on the stairs, and Ricardo popped his head into the galley. "Señores, the modifications are ready."

They followed him back to the hold, where Ricardo directed Roscoe to stand on a cargo scale. He pecked the result into his phone. "We need to account for every gram to finalize things," he explained.

The kayak remained mounted on struts, leaving just enough space underneath for the team's attachments. A dye barrel, now outfitted with a camera and the fleshy nozzle Roscoe had procured, hung beneath the kayak's tiny prow. Behind it was a mechanism resembling a miniature, old-fashioned railroad hopper car. Painted neatly on the side were the Griquas' sun-wedge logo and the word "HAMZA" in black lettering.

Roscoe's throat tightened, but the welding team brought him back to the task at hand.

"This is the entire apparatus," explained one of the welders, a woman with dark skin, waist-length braided hair, and an unplaceable accent. She opened the kayak's hatch, revealing a gnarled plastic rod angling up beside the seat, its top wrapped in duct tape.

"This is your release lever. Sorry about the rough shape—our three-dee printer draws microplastics from ocean water, and sometimes the viscosity is off. It's not perfect, but it should work fine. Once you settle on the ocean floor, pull this to drop the dye and collect the sample."

She demonstrated, pulling the lever. The hopper car-like box slid downward on springs, spreading open to scoop a few pounds of sediment from the ocean floor. Once it closed and retracted, clamps released the algae barrel, which dropped onto a rubber pad beneath the hull. Simultaneously, a metal arm swung out from the kayak's side. A claw on its end popped open.

"That will release the incendiary buoy," she explained.

"Thank you for the demonstration, Wangari," Padre Petí said. "Simple enough, no?"

"I think so," Roscoe replied, though uncertainty crept into his voice. "But are we sure it'll still reach the plume with all that added weight underneath?" He caught himself, surprised at how much the question sounded like something Hamza might have asked. *Maybe they should paint "Rangiora II" on the barrel*, he thought, *in honor of Hamza's subdrone.*

Wangari nodded and tapped two large cylinders welded to the top of the kayak. "We've accounted for the extra weight. These will be filled with more compressed air to balance it. They should compensate for the attachments below."

Roscoe nodded, his initial wonder souring into terror. Forget painting something on the barrel. Adding an ounce of extra weight felt like tempting fate as he considered the entire operation. The kayak, the dye, the sample collection, and his safe return all relied on springs, gears, secondhand parts, and plastic strained from the ocean.

Could they really beat everything at StarCross's disposal?

He had a full day to grapple with that question on the voyage to Yule Bay.

Chapter 34

The *Lautaro* had no TV, no books in English, and no treadmill where he could blow off steam. Roscoe tried pacing the hold, but every glimpse of the *Hamza* reminded him that he would soon squeeze into that tiny space, possibly never to return. He stepped into the conning tower stairwell, considering whether to ask Petí if he needed help in the lab. Music and prayers floated up from the lower deck—familiar sounds from his Cultural History class. A Catholic Mass. It was Sunday. Roscoe had no interest in church after the Revelators, so he climbed to the next level.

Wangari was off-duty and asleep, so he couldn't pace the berth. He kept climbing. Another flight of stairs brought him to the top level. The only people there were Yongchen at the control panel and Evangelina tending to the plants.

"Mind if I help?" Roscoe asked.

She turned, startling him with her resemblance to Hamza. Roscoe remembered that Hamza's father had been from the Cook Islands. Perhaps the rising sea levels that sent Hamza's dad to Australia had sent Evangelina's parents to Griqua Tierra. She studied him briefly, then nodded. "Hold the reeds apart, will you? I need to change a pH sensor."

Roscoe stepped closer, parting a wall of greenery with his palms. The hydroponic garden had more than food. Behind the vines and roots stood thousands of reeds, each as wide as an old-fashioned fountain pen and as tall as the deck itself. Roscoe held the plants aside, watching as Evangelina popped one bolt-like sensor from the wall and slide another into its place.

He stared at the stalks. "What are these? They're not vegetables, are they?"

Evangelina shook her head. "Totora reeds. From my parents' home on Rapa Nui—Easter Island. We're testing varieties that can tolerate brackish water."

"What for?"

"To cultivate them on Griqua Tierra for building materials."

Roscoe eyed the delicate-looking stalks skeptically. Zip ties pinned their tops against the hull. "Building material? This stuff?"

"The Rapa Nui bundled these reeds together to make canoes and floats. But totora also grow on Lake Titicaca, in Peru, and the Uros people who lived there did us one better." Evangelina handed him a smartphone. On the screen, Roscoe saw a village of huts with thatched roofs and women in bright dresses and bowler hats walking beside a lake—no, not beside it. He blinked. They were on it. The huts rested atop a mat of thousands of reeds, bundled together several meters thick.

"They built *islands* out of this stuff?" Roscoe pinched one of the reeds.

Evangelina nodded. "The Uros lived on them for thousands of years. Kept them from being conquered by the Incas." She turned back to the reeds—each one tagged—and started measuring them with calipers, one by one. She typed the data into her phone.

"And you want to build mats out of these reeds in Griqua Tierra?"

Evangelina nodded, looking at the reeds with the kind of focus the interns had as they watched the meteorites descend during the tournament. "Not to build houses on, but to use as gardens, docks, space for solar panels. Maybe we could even make a river walk like the ones cities up north used to have. If nothing else, totora mats like those will be a good buffer against storm surges."

Roscoe nodded, impressed with the slender stalks' potential, but only able to think of one possible customer. "What do you think StarCross will want it for?"

Evangelina paused, lowering her calipers. She turned to Roscoe, disgust on her face. "I don't know, and I don't care." She continued measuring. "StarCross can have their space colonies. This is for the people staying on Earth."

Roscoe remembered he was one of those people now, and he was less sure than ever what that meant. "Sorry," he mumbled.

Her expression softened. She reached into a bush and handed him a fruit. "Here, try this." It looked like one of the strawberries he'd seen in old photos, but with ghost-white flesh dotted with red seeds.

"What is this?"

"Chilean strawberry. We're developing varieties that can grow in Griqua Tierra."

Roscoe took a bite and froze. He had never tasted a piece of fruit so sweet or juicy—not in Antarctica, and not up north. Not anywhere. He couldn't imagine anything this good growing on La Rambla Nueva, the pedestrian strip on Lagrange-2, or even in the lunar gardens. Evangelina smiled at his shock.

"Earth isn't all bad, weón. Come on, let's get to work."

He helped her tend other berries with stranger names—maqui, murta, and calafate. They all tasted good, but none quite as sweet as that first strawberry. Each fruit had a label: a small rectangle that fit in Roscoe's palm, with the plant's common and scientific names penned in unique calligraphy. The script for "Chilean strawberry - fragaria chiloensis" reminded him of the letters on an old Paris metro station. "Maqui / Chilean wineberry - aristotelia chilensis" had arabesque curls with thick, slanted strokes. "Calafate / Magellan barberry - berberis microphylla," looked like something straight out of the antique polar journals he had read. Each tag had been crafted with care but had just enough flaws—a stray pen stroke here, a tiny inkblot there—to show they had been written by hand.

"Who made these?" he asked, holding up the calafate tag. "They're beautiful."

"Upper-form art students," Evangelina replied, scanning more totora tags with her phone. "Co-ops give them design work when they can. Gives them a chance to practice—and keeps things less dull down here."

"You guys still teach art?" This surprised Roscoe almost as much as that first bite of strawberry, but Evangelina just nodded. "Mmm-hmm. Hold these reeds apart, will you? I need to change another sensor."

As Evangelina popped one bolt in and another out, Roscoe's gaze drifted to the thicket of plants swaying gently from the vibrations of the sub's engines. "You grow all these in Griqua Tierra?"

"Most of them," she said without looking up.

"Is it warm enough up there for all these?"

She smiled. "It is if you have greenhouses." She pecked her phone and then handed it over, giving him his first glimpse of the *Lautaro* crew's home: a broad, flat valley ringed by jagged peaks. Roscoe stared, awestruck by the mountains—sharp and wild, biting like fangs into the Patagonian sky. Compared to them, the mountains near Spigot looked like worn-down molars.

He thought the valley floor in the foreground was strewn with gray boulders. Zooming in, he saw they were some translucent material, treated to barely gleam.

He swiped to the next photo and saw a three-story dome with a circular floor divided into garden plots, all centered around a small pond. A skylight at the dome's apex scattered shards of light and shadow around the space. Zooming in, Roscoe saw the skylight was actually one of the boulders. Zooming back out, he saw a few people kneeling among the rows, pulling tubers from the soil, while a spindly robot arm picked berries. Around the perimeter, others lounged by doorways, reading, chatting, or playing cards.

"People live there too?"

"Well, *someone* has to take care of those plants," Evangelina replied as if it were obvious. She held out her hand for the phone. "These plants are counting on us," she added, taking the phone back, "so let's get back to work."

As they changed more sensors and logged pH readings, Roscoe asked about how things worked in Griqua Tierra. At first, Evangelina humored him, explaining how the households surrounding each garden shared responsibility for plant care and divided chores on a rotating schedule. She described how the plants under each dome, along with the animals in the pens and ponds, were carefully selected to ensure a balanced diet for each resident.

"Specialty Food Co-Op handles some delicacies, like StemSteak," she said. "We pick up people's junk food orders in Newloon." Her tone clipped, she leaned into the murta bush. Roscoe bit back more questions.

No one said much at dinner. Roscoe ate without really tasting anything, his mind already fixed on what lay ahead. When he returned to his bunk, his thoughts spiraled. He tried to measure his mission against what little he knew of engineering.

What if he hit something on the way down? What if the dye didn't drop or the scoop turned into an anchor, snaring him on the ocean floor? He thought about the clicking noise while testing the paddles. "Bicycle mechanics," Ricardo had explained.

Those paddles were connected to gears. What if they jammed? What if the gills clogged, or the hull wasn't as strong as Chip thought, and the pressure crushed him? What if the buoy didn't release? What if he couldn't find open water to surface, or the hovercraft couldn't reach him? Worse yet, what if StarCross found him and blew him out of the water?

What if... what if... what if...

The question spun endlessly through Roscoe's mind, retracing the same loop that had haunted him before—when he'd stared down his own self-inflicted end. Soon enough, the repetition wore thin, leaving him bored. The sub's electric hum, steady and soothing, began to lull him, the polar opposite of StarCross's grating proprietary alarm. Sleep began to creep in ...

A tap on his bunk post drove it away. He pulled his curtain aside to see Chip standing there. "Time to go."

Roscoe went to the head, splashed cold water on his face, dressed, and climbed to the galley, only to find the serving counter closed. Chip stood waiting with an apologetic look. "No food or water—not before launch. Don't want to throw the weight off, and you're gonna have to hold it for a few hours at least."

Roscoe nodded, annoyed but understanding. Together, they descended to Petí's lab, now empty, and stepped into the cargo hold.

Ricardo was there, along with Petí, Evangelina, Wangari, and Gabriel.

"Yongchen's at the controls. She sends her best," Ricardo said. "Mucha suerte—you've got this." He handed Roscoe a red button on a lanyard. "This is a locator beacon. It transmits short-range on a secure frequency. Once you make it to the surface, just stay inside and press the button. It'll help Chip find you in the hovercraft." Roscoe nodded, slipping the lanyard over his neck.

Ricardo led the group to the far end of the hull, where the modified *Hamza* sat atop the forklift-like contraption Roscoe had seen before. The machine's prongs plugged into the kayak's compressed-air cylinders. It had been readied for launch, and someone just needed to pull the trigger.

Wangari opened the kayak's hatch and pointed to a saucer-shaped attachment atop the oxygen tanks. "This is a searchlight. Once you surface, turn it on. It'll help Chip find you." As Roscoe studied the locator button around his neck, she added, "When it comes to safety, redundancy is essential."

Petí stepped forward, laying his hands on the kayak. He mumbled a Latin prayer and flicked holy water over the vessel and the crew. Gabriel and Ricardo made the sign of the cross when the drops hit them. Evangelina, Wangari, and Chip bowed their heads. Roscoe rubbed the damp spot where the holy water had hit his sleeve, uncertain whether to feel comforted or unnerved. Would Petí offer him a blessing? No. The priest only shook his hand. "I look forward to seeing you upon your return."

Now, it was time. With knees knocking, Roscoe climbed into the *Hamza*, which felt even more like a coffin.

"We've swept the route with sonar," Ricardo said. "You've got a clean shot to the plume. Just lock the paddles in wing position, then sit back and enjoy the ride. Once you reach the plume, pull the lever."

Roscoe forced a grin and gave him a thumbs-up. The hatch closed, leaving him bathed in the interior's orange glow. His breathing quickened, his headache roared back, and the hull seemed to close in around him. He reached for the handle to abort—

A fist pounded on the hatch. Ricardo's muffled voice called out, "Weón—get those paddles locked into position."

"Sorry," Roscoe called back. "Just a little nervous." He pulled the handles, locking them at the angle that kept the paddles outstretched at the kayak's sides. Somehow, the *click* reassured him. *Relax*, he told himself. *You've got this*.

The *Hamza* thrummed from underneath and began to drop. Through the portholes, Roscoe watched as the hull cargo deck slid away, the kayak descending steadily. The front viewports showed metal scrolling upward before giving way, with a soft gurgle, to a spray of foam and then ink-black water. The hum stopped. The *Hamza* now dangled from the sub's prow, resting on a platform lowered to its limit. Then came the release—a pop, a lurch, and suddenly, he was falling.

Foom!

The kayak surged forward. In the glow of the *Hamza*'s external LED, a flurry of plankton and other floating specs streamed past like snowflakes against a track's windshield.

Not much to do now, Roscoe realized. Chip had said the trajectory would take him to the plume in under an hour. Roscoe lost track of time watching the ocean's darkness slip past him. His eyelids dropped, his head slumped forward ...

A jolt ran through the seat, snapping him awake.

He was no longer rushing forward through the floating specs. The viewports had gone tan and cloudy. He had reached the bottom—and if the Griquas' calculations were right, he had also reached the plume. Roscoe shook himself.

The gnarled plastic drop lever stuck up beside him, waiting to be pulled. To further idiot-proof the mission, Wangari had taped a handwritten note to the handle: "Push in Paddles Before Pulling." Roscoe complied, positioning the kayak's handle grips against the hull. Now flush with the outer hull, the paddles wouldn't slow his ascent.

His trembling fingers wrapped around the handle. If this were a movie, he knew, this was the moment something would go wrong. Some unforeseen crisis would demand every ounce of the hero's strength and ingenuity to survive.

Roscoe had no clue what he would do in that situation. He'd just die—alone down here. His body, the plume, and whatever microbes created it would stay hidden until a nuke obliterated it all in a week.

Despite everything, a wry smile crossed his face. His eye caught the faint end of his wrist scar, gray in the interior's orange light. *That's what you wanted, right?* he thought. Time to find out just how dark the universe's sense of humor was. He pulled the lever.

A water-muffled *thump* shook the kayak. A jolt ran up his spine. He heard the grind of metal against metal—a sound he hadn't heard from this contraption last time. *Shit!* Something had gone wrong.

Or maybe not.

Cloudy swirls cleared in front of the viewport. Plankton and silt began rushing downward. The kayak was rising. Whether it had successfully collected the sample or if the barrel of algae had deployed was still to be determined. Roscoe felt his heartbeat slow—then race again as light flashed through the portholes from above. It was just the incendiary buoy, he realized, melting a gap in the ice for the *Hamza* to surface.

He lost track of time again, watching the specs out the porthole. Then, they slowed. The kayak bumped against surface ice. Bending his head forward, he peered out the porthole to see a white ceiling stretching away into the void. He was bobbing beneath the ice. It was time to find the opening.

Roscoe unlocked the grips and repeated the motions Ricardo had taught him to turn the kayak. On his first spin, he only saw more white ceiling. On the second spin, though, the strips in front of him lit up. Roscoe started paddling. The front strips kept glowing green, then the ceiling strips did too. He now sat under open sky.

He flicked the tab covering the SURFACE button and pressed. A loud *fizz* shook the kayak as hydrogen was pulled from the water, lifting it upward. The viewports showed black, then a rush of sea spume, then more black studded with stars. It was a clear, calm night; the odds that he'd get found were good.

Roscoe switched on the overhead light and pressed the locator beacon button, hoping its frequency was secure and short-range enough that StarCross wouldn't pick it up. He leaned back, letting the kayak rock him to sleep.

Once again, a noise from outside startled him awake. Someone pounded on the hatch.

"Hey Roscoe, you in there?" came Chip's muffled voice.

"Yep," Roscoe called back.

"All right, brace yourself."

The hatch opened, blasting Roscoe with subzero air. The snowsuited scientist leaned in, shoved a bundle into Roscoe's lap, and said before slamming the hatch shut, "Get yourself into this, then come on out."

Roscoe spent several minutes contorting himself into the survival suit. He lifted a few centimeters off the seat to slide his legs down into the pants, then hunched forward to shove his arms through the sleeves. Finally, he donned the gloves, mask, and goggles, and tugged the hood over his head. Suited up, he opened the hatch, only to have another bundle dropped in his lap.

"Life jacket," Chip hollered through his face mask. The Griquas' suits apparently didn't have built-in headsets. "Didn't think you'd have room to put it on in there." No longer stuffed into a peapod, Roscoe buckled the vest over his suit.

Chip had pulled the hovercraft alongside the *Hamza.* Lighting the way with a headlamp, he steadied Roscoe as he climbed over its rubber skirt. "All right, now let's get the goods."

Inside the hovercraft lay a two-meter metal pole with what looked like an oversized pipe wrench on the end. Roscoe watched Chip dip the wrench behind the *Hamza*'s stern and poke around.

"Come on, come on," he muttered.

With a *click*, the pole locked into place, jutting from the water at an awkward angle. Chip dislodged it with a shove, and pulled out the wrench end, now clasped around a dripping metal box: the sample scoop. Maybe—just maybe—it held microbes capable of turning ocean water fresh. Roscoe didn't dare to hope after the last dye test. Chip placed the scoop in a cooler bolted to the hovercraft's floor. So far, so good.

Chip pulled a small cylinder from beneath the hovercraft's steering wheel, twisted its two ends, and tossed it into the *Hamza* before slamming the kayak's hatch shut.

"What's that?" Roscoe asked.

"Bacterial culture for recycling. It digests plastic and metal, then dies. That should be enough to take care of the *Hamza*. It'll only leave a lump on the ocean floor."

"You're gonna destroy it?"

"Can't tow that thing back to the sub, and we've gotta cover our tracks." Chip shouted over the hovercraft's hum. "Griquas have the blueprints, and thanks to you, we know it handles well in the Southern Ocean." Keeping one hand on the wheel, he turned back and gave the bobbing kayak a final salute. Roscoe did the same. "How long does it take?" he asked.

"A few minutes."

Not waiting to watch the *Hamza* sink, Chip steered the hovercraft through the icy leads. In the starlight, Roscoe saw icebergs towering in the distance and chunks no bigger than golf balls at his side, all moving with the gentle waves.

"You ever seen it this calm?" Roscoe asked.

The scientist shook his head. "Never. Southern Ocean's not as bad as it used to be, but this is unusual for winter. Guess we got lucky. Or maybe there really is a God, and Petí got Him on our side for once."

Chip steered around a small node of ice, making the smooth ripples fizz with spray.

"Oh, by the way, when we get back the Griquas are going to present you with their highest honor."

"What's that?"

"A five-minute shower."

"I'll take it."

Roscoe suddenly realized he wasn't craving his return to a warm interior. Maybe he was finally toughening up, or maybe Antarctica's night wasn't so bad when he wasn't trying to escape imminent death or plot some path off-world. Looking up into the dense dome of stars, Roscoe couldn't even pick out Lagrange-2 anymore.

But he could spot another familiar sight, almost right overhead.

"Hey Chip, is that a constellation?" He pointed to a group of four stars, metal-grate steps.

"Yeah, that's the Southern Cross," Chip said.

"They just copied a constellation for their logo?"

"Yep. How creative did you think they were?"

Chapter 35

Soon enough, the *Lautaro*'s blue searchlight blinked on the horizon. Its beam swept across their path as the submarine rose, guiding Chip closer. Hooded figures wearing headlamps grasped the railing outside the conning tower.

As Chip pulled alongside the sub, pride surged through Roscoe, tingling in his fingertips and toes. Antarctica had given him his first taste of cold; now it had delivered the first thrill of cheating death. He had been launched through the fiercest seas on Earth, beneath tons of ice, past who knew how many sensors and torpedoes—and lived to tell the tale. He had done it. He had fucking *done it.*

"Did you get the sample?" a figure shouted. Roscoe recognized Ricardo's voice.

"Hell yeah we did!" Chip shouted back, raising the cooler overhead. Roscoe's exhilaration spiked even higher.

"Quick!" Ricardo shouted, more urgency than triumph in his voice. "Put it in the net!" Two other figures tossed a nylon net over the side. Chip slipped the cooler inside and pulled the drawstring tight. The two figures hoisted it up.

"Now climb, quick!" Ricardo yelled.

"What about the hovercraft?" Chip called back.

"Forget it! Something's come up. We need to go—now!"

Chip started up the cable ladder slung over the sub's side. Roscoe followed.

"Move, weón!" Ricardo shouted once Chip was halfway up. "We need to get out of here!"

Roscoe scrambled to the top, his pulse racing. What had gone wrong? Had StarCross found them? Were they being pursued? Ricardo said nothing, just hit a button on his phone to spool the ladder into the sub's side and hurried Roscoe into the conning tower. He arrived just in time to look down the stairwell and see, through the ladders' slats, Wangari and Gabriel rushing the swaddled cooler into Petí's lab as though it were a kidney headed for transplant. As soon as Ricardo slammed the hatch, the engines hummed. The *Lautaro* began to dive.

Chip gripped a handrail. "What's happening?"

Ricardo, still catching his breath, pressed a finger to his lips. "We've got company. Keep quiet."

Roscoe followed them to the sub's bridge, where Yongchen gripped the throttle. Ricardo pointed to the sonar screen, which showed a blip creeping closer. It didn't have the long lozenge shape of a StarCross tanker sub or the skinnier profile Roscoe would've expected of an attack sub. Rather, its shape reminded Roscoe of a gothic letter "t," some kind of balloon animal, or—in his giddy, still-adrenalized brain—one of the obscene drawings that got teenaged boys everywhere in trouble.

"We think that's the *Dönitz,*" Ricardo whispered.

Roscoe bit his cheeks to stifle a laugh. The shape clearly wasn't amusing anyone else. "*Dönitz*?" he repeated.

"New Swabia's flagship sub," Chip explained under his breath. "You're probably right. I think they docked in Newloon a few days ago, and that shape's, ah, pretty distinctive." Roscoe remembered the two giant, jet-like engines he and Hamza had seen on the back of the Nazi submarine.

"But isn't that just a passenger sub?" Roscoe asked. "They don't want trouble, right?"

"I dunno," Chip muttered. "Most of the time, Antarctic shipping cartels respect each other's routes. But we just burned down their dock in Newloon. They'll be pissed."

"And they've been heading straight toward us for twenty minutes," Yongchen added.

"Do we have torpedoes?" Roscoe asked. "You know, to fight them off?"

Ricardo shook his head. "Griqua Tierra's Council has a strict non-armament policy," he explained. "Weapons draw too much attention. Even that kayak was a stretch."

They fell silent, watching the blip inch closer. "I don't think we can outrun them, based on their speed," Yongchen said, voice low. "And for all we know, they could be armed."

"If they are, do you think we could throw off whatever torpedoes they have?" Ricardo asked.

Yongchen shook her head. "I wouldn't bet on it."

"Then let's play dead."

Play dead? Before Roscoe could ask what Ricardo meant, Yongchen flicked a few buttons, then buckled her seatbelt; everyone else grabbed the nearest pipe, handle, or rung. Roscoe barely found his grip before hearing a *whoosh* above and a mechanical whirr below.

"Skegs and depth charge deployed," the pilot whispered. "Everyone hold on."

Water sloshed around them as the ballast tanks filled, and the sub began a slow, level descent before bucking violently from stern to bow. One screen showed a cross-section cutaway graphic of the *Lautaro*. The space between its inner and outer hulls changed color—they had filled with water—and two spindly legs unfolded from the underside.

The sub lurched to port; water sloshed out of the galley's wall gardens. Padre Petí made the sign of the cross, then stared at the floor. Roscoe remembered all the lab equipment below and started to speak, but Ricardo silenced him with a raised finger.

"We set off a depth charge to mimic the sound of a sub imploding," Ricardo whispered. "Now, we drop to the seafloor and act like a wreck."

Roscoe watched the numbers spin inside the sub's old-fashioned depth gauge, then felt a gentle bump—signaling they had reached the bottom. One by one, the screens and lights around them winked out, leaving only a single button glowing red on Yongchen's control console, bathing the bridge in its faint light.

"We have to turn everything off?" Roscoe whispered.

Ricardo nodded. "Sound travels far underwater. And we know they're listening."

Roscoe pointed at the dark sonar screen. "How will we know when they're gone?"

"If we stay quiet, we should be able to hear their propellers."

They waited, minutes seeming to last hours. Just as Roscoe opened his mouth to ask how much longer, bubbles gurgled and machinery whirred above them.

"Shit," Yongchen muttered. "They're purging their airlock."

"Why?" Roscoe asked.

"They think we're a salvage job now," Ricardo whispered. "They're preparing to send in divers."

"Send out another depth charge," Gabriel suggested. When the crew turned to him, he added, "So they think we still have live ordinance on board and aren't worth the risk."

"That could damage us!" Wangari hissed, her whisper sharp with alarm. "Or worse, they could retaliate."

"What have we got to lose?"

The crew traded tense looks, then turned to Ricardo. After a moment, he nodded. Yongchen activated her phone's LED light, found a switch, and flicked it. More bubbles rose, and Roscoe braced himself just before another blast tilted the sub. Silence returned, broken only by a new gurgle outside—one with a different beat and pitch.

"Sounds like they're leaving," Yongchen breathed.

When the sound finally faded, she pushed the glowing button on her console. Lights blinked on, and the sub hummed back to life. The crew squinted against the sudden light as the *Lautaro* began to rise. Roscoe stared at the sonar screen, waiting for the *Dönitz* to reappear. It didn't. They were alone.

Yongchen leaned back in her chair, letting out a shaky breath. "Closest call I've ever had."

"Indeed," Petí said, his voice low. "And never with such precious cargo."

Once the sub returned to cruising depth, Petí and Chip headed to the lab to examine that "precious cargo." Roscoe's curiosity could wait while he savored his rewards—a five-minute hot shower and the best StemSteak the ¡Salud! Specialty Food Co-Op had to offer.

"You better eat all of it, weón," Evangelina said as she set the plate before him. "I put off stress-testing my totoras to grill this for you."

Roscoe didn't leave a scrap, marveling at how he'd endured Spigot's bland galley fare. Then, he made his way down to Petí's lab, no longer worried about disturbing him at work.

The space had survived the evasive maneuvers unscathed, and the cooler sat open on the workbench beneath the Sacred Heart of Jesus painting. Beside it sat the box-like metal scoop that had been mounted underneath the *Hamza*. It was still clamped shut, but a small hole had been drilled into its side, letting Chip insert a probe.

"How's it going?" Roscoe asked.

"The water inside's fresh," Chip said, "so we were at least at the right spot."

"God's gotten us this far," Petí said, "I pray He'll help us find the microbes."

Roscoe, Chip, and the Sacred Heart of Jesus painting watched as the priest drilled a second hole into the scoop. Chip eased a pipette into it and drew out more water. Scum and silt swirled inside the tube.

"Looks just like diarrhea," Chip observed wryly. "That's the sign of a good sample."

Petí sat at an ancient microscope while Chip released a few droplets onto a slide the priest had prepared. Petí placed it under the lens and pressed a button.

The microscope whirred, and the three of them watched a nearby monitor. At first, the screen only showed white. Then, blotches emerged. Gradually, the image resolved into writhing sacs nested together—some cradling dark knots, others extending thin tendrils into the liquid. They wriggled into and out of view.

"Looks like your typical seafloor microbial community," Chip said.

Petí nodded. "Nothing groundbreaking at first glance. We'll need to sequence their DNA back in Griqua Tierra. We have no equipment for that on board."

"Well, in the meantime, we can at least isolate a few specimens for analysis." Chip took a fresh pipette and stuck it back into the metal box. This time, though, the plunger jammed as he drew it back. He scowled, pulling harder.

"That's ... odd. Pipette's stuck on something."

Chip swiveled the pipette around the hole until he found an angle that let him dislodge the obstruction. He pulled out a pebble, brown with gray splotches, about half the size of one of Evangelina's strawberries.

Petí leaned in, holding a jeweler's loupe to the rock. "Basalt."

The two scientists looked at the pebble, then at each other. Chip spoke first.

"You don't think ..."

"Of course I do!" Petí flashed a yellow grin. "Quick—reimmerse it."

Roscoe watched Chip drop the pebble into a test tube, using the pipette to submerge it in more scummy water. He capped the tube and lowered it into a rack on Petí's workbench.

"Um, why do we care so much that it's basalt?" Roscoe asked.

"Because Southern Ocean basalt is a time capsule for ancient life," Chip explained, holding up the test tube. "That rock has microscopic cracks inside. Some of those cracks have clay, and that clay's a great place for bacteria to live."

"Very old bacteria," Petí added, grinning again. "Perhaps bacteria not yet known to science. Bacteria with all kinds of unknown properties."

Chip finished the thought. "Like maybe the ability to desalinate seawater."

"But—hang on," Roscoe said, "I thought you said microbial desalination doesn't work anymore because of everything we've done to the oceans."

"Pollution and acidification kept *geobacter* bacteria from desalinating seawater," Chip corrected. "Those were the bacteria the old desalination cells used. But maybe these chemical changes, combined with whatever's on the floor of Yule Bay, kicked these guys into gear." He tapped the test tube. "Maybe, somehow, these basalt pebbles have become new microbial desalination cells."

"Maybe," Petí said. "We'll need to get this sample back to Griqua Tierra for further testing to be sure."

"And don't forget," Chip said, "StarCross is still planning to nuke these things in a few weeks, unless—"

Petí cut in. "Unless we can prove to the people providing that bomb that they're about to blow up a possible new freshwater source."

Chip leaned against the workbench, crossing his arms. "So, we move to the next phase of our plan. The dye drum's still down there, waiting to release the algae and show the world that there's fresh water. It can transmit video to the sub, and we can send it up to Griqua Tierra on a pirate satellite, and from there to the govellers stateside."

"Sounds too easy," Roscoe said, frowning.

"Because it is." Chip picked up a screwdriver from the workbench and spun it between his fingers. "Think about it—if the only evidence of the dye test is coming from the govellers in America and ... whatever you guys are—"

"StarCross will say it's a hoax."

Petí picked up a few tools scattered on the bench—everything but the screwdriver Chip was toying with—and began returning them to their labeled slots along the wall. "The test has to be picked up by StarCross's own sources," Petí said. "Their StarBuoys."

"Okay, but Chip, you tapped into them before. Shouldn't be an issue, right?" Roscoe asked.

Chip shook his head, handing Petí the screwdriver. "I pulled video from the StarBuoys, sure. But that only worked because of the hearing. I had their undivided attention. We'll need to hijack their feed again."

Pleased his tools were safely stowed, Petí eased into his swivel chair. "Wangari and Gabriel are building a module that can attach to one of Spigot's cables. It'll force a StarBuoy video of the plume site to play in Spigot's drone control room and administrative offices. And we know a way in."

Roscoe thought back to that service entrance.

Chip pressed on. "Yongchen should already have turned us around. We'll get there in about a day."

Roscoe smiled—but just until he realized this whole thing hinged on StarCross's word. "But hold on," he said, his smile fading. "What if they fake their logs? Say the feed's corrupted or doctored."

"Damn," Chip muttered, his grin dropping too. "I'm not sure."

Petí took out his phone and started tapping. "We need to discuss this."

* * *

Fifteen minutes later, Roscoe sat among the plants in the *Lautaro*'s galley with Chip and the rest of the sub's crew—Ricardo, Petí, Gabriel, Wangari, Yongchen, and Evangelina. They were gathered for what the Griquas called a plenary session.

Petí pulled down a screen at the end of the table and projected a photo of the basalt pebbles. "These are the samples Roscoe recovered from the freshwater plume site. We'll need to examine them further in Griqua Tierra, but our working hypothesis is that they harbor microorganisms capable of desalinating seawater."

"If nothing else," Chip added, "we know there's some source of fresh water down there." He then laid out how StarCross had faked recordings and data—at Roscoe's disciplinary hearing. "They would do the same," he said, "if fed video of the freshwater plume."

Roscoe's mood soured. After all they'd been through—the haggling with Whalstone, the narrow escape from Newloon, the sample return mission—could it all be for nothing? StarCross could deny everything.

"Our dilemma," Chip continued, "is getting StarCross to acknowledge that fresh water before they destroy the site, getting one of their biggest customers—the U.S. government—to see it too, and making it impossible for StarCross to deny it. Any ideas?"

The room fell silent. Some crew members furrowed their brows, others studied the table. Roscoe's mind stayed blank.

Wangari stepped up to Petí's laptop and started typing. "We have eighteen hours before we're in position to enter Spigot. No time to waste. I'm starting a quiet plenary now."

"A what?" Roscoe asked.

"It's part of our problem-solving process," she said, opening a file cabinet and pulling out a file. "We let everyone submit anonymized input—stuff they might not want to share out loud." She handed Roscoe a phone. "I know you're used to wristbands, but we still use recycled tech around here," she said. "Let's take fifteen minutes for this one."

The crew turned their backs and hunched over their phones. Roscoe did the same.

The phone's screen displayed a text box with the caption: "Please enter any potential input you do not want to be attached to your name. Submissions are anonymous." A SUBMIT button glowed red beneath the box.

Roscoe didn't see a way to pull this off without sneaking into Spigot's control room to film its workers watching the video. The notion alone made him roll his eyes. He left the box blank.

When the fifteen minutes ended, the screen showed two anonymized suggestions:

- Sneak into Spigot's control room
- Film its workers watching the video

Some jaws dropped. Roscoe's didn't.

"I didn't write this, but it's right," Chip said. "We need proof that they've seen the dye test, that they know there's fresh water down there. Otherwise, they'll just falsify their video logs, play dumb, and say it's a hoax when my bosses confront them with our video."

Wangari scanned the room, nodding. "And it has to be our camera. If we hack Spigot's cameras, they'll just fake the footage."

Chip ran a hand through his hair. "Could you even sneak in, though? Between Roscoe's hearing and the upcoming test, StarCross Security's going to be tight."

"I can signal Tololo," Petí offered. "See if we can get a way in."

"Tololo?" Chip and Roscoe asked in unison.

"A codename," Ricardo explained. "Tololo is our insider. The one who hacked the systems before we did the dye test. Been keeping tabs on Spigot and Jahnford for four years now."

Chip let out a low whistle. "So you weren't just blindly hoping when you gave me that dye. You knew the chance for a test would come up eventually."

"Could Tololo get a video for us?" Roscoe asked.

Ricardo shook his head. "Too risky. His position wouldn't put him anywhere near where the video would be seen, and it could blow his cover. The Council would never approve it. So he can get us in"—his eyes swept the table—"but someone else would still have to record the video."

He called up the second anonymous suggestion:

> Forego dye test; allow nuclear detonation at plume site to proceed. We have the microbes; we can nurture them in Griqua Tierra without exposing ourselves to undue risk.

Murmurs spread as eyes shifted around the table.

Ricardo tilted his chair back. "We already have the microbes."

"We do," Chip said, "but we don't know for sure they'll be as productive outside the plume site. They might require specific pressure levels—or a dense-enough population—to trigger whatever reaction we're seeing."

Pető folded his hands on the table, nodding. "Protecting the site means preserving those conditions, along with more specimens, keeping genetic diversity intact, and letting some microbes remain in their natural habitat. We may need to monitor the site long-term to truly understand them."

"A new species," Evangelina said, her gaze distant—the same look she'd had while tending her totora reeds. "A unique ecosystem, alive and evolving right before our eyes."

"But Evangelina," Ricardo said, voice taut. "The risks—"

"I know the risks, Ricardo!" She scowled, as if she'd just swallowed gritty coffee. "We all know the risks. That's the problem. We focus too much on risks. We need to think about rewards."

"Rewards?" Ricardo rested one forearm on the table, palm up, as if weighing the word. "Evangelina, we're talking about a patch of rocks at the bottom of the ocean that we've already collected a sample from."

She jabbed a thumb behind her, toward the walls of quivering plants. "And these were just reeds from Rapa Nui—plenty of other places too." She paused, all eyes locked on hers. "But my parents smuggled cuttings onto the rescue transport anyway. If they'd been caught, they would've been kicked off for harboring pests."

She leaned forward, voice gaining heat. "But they did it. They thought about how they—and their parents and grandparents—had lived with these plants, used them. They believed someone, someday, would find a way to use them in ways they couldn't even imagine. *That* was the reward they were thinking of."

She sat back down, voice steady but low. "No one thinks that way anymore, except the people who let me study these plants—people on Griqua Tierra." She looked daggers at Ricardo. "*Some* of them, anyway. They still think about long-term rewards—how a few reeds, or a patch of rocks on the bottom of the ocean, might be worth protecting. No one who depends on StarCross thinks that way. We're it."

"I'm it," Roscoe said, almost under his breath.

Heads turned. Roscoe flinched himself, unsure why the heated exchange had drawn out his parents' mantra. He shook it off—he had to explain himself, fast.

"I'll do it," he said, clearer now. "I know Spigot. I know where the control room is. I can find a way in."

"We have some disguises on board," Ricardo said, voice calm as ever, "but let's evaluate this first. Wangari, start a flowchart."

Wangari started typing. A single box appeared on the screen: "Covertly Enter Spigot."

"All right, how could this turn out?" she asked.

"We could ... get the video showing StarCross is about to destroy a freshwater source," Roscoe said. Wangari added his suggestion, branching it from the initial box.

"What else?" she prompted.

"You could get caught," Ricardo said. Wangari typed. The "Covertly Enter Spigot" box sprouted another arrow, one that pointed to a new box labeled "Get Caught." At reading those words, Roscoe felt a phantom wristband squeeze his wrist. Then he remembered how that whole proceeding had ended, and relaxed.

"I'm already blacklisted," Roscoe said. "We'd be back where we started." Wangari typed this in as well.

No one else spoke.

"All right," Wangari said, "let's have another silent input session. Just ten minutes for this one."

When the session ended, the "Get Caught" box had one more outcome: "StarCross Security determines Roscoe is working with Griqua Tierra. Views GT as a threat and takes action."

One by one, the crew members' eyes fell from the screen to the table.

"Well then," Ricardo said at last, "let's send this to the COC's."

"The what?" Roscoe asked as Wangari started typing.

"Councilors-on-call," Ricardo explained. "The co-ops have a lot of autonomy, but if something could blow back on the whole community, they need Council approval."

"That can take a while," Petí added, his eyes fixed on his smartphone, "but there are always three COC's for time-sensitive decisions. They can approve it, escalate it to the full Council, or ask for input from the future-generation ombudsman."

"You think they'll act fast enough?" Roscoe asked. "We've only got a few hours."

Petí shrugged, setting his phone down. "One COC approved the sample collection on her own. We'll see if the one on duty now approves this new plan. Let's just hope the signal relay buoys work."

Ricardo leaned back in his chair. "Welcome to collective decision-making, weón. Real pain in the ass sometimes."

Roscoe managed a half-smile and joined the others at the coffee urn in the galley. He'd just filled his cup when Wangari's laptop pinged.

She rushed back to check it. "We have our decision. Never seen it this fast."

The email appeared on screen, in English and Spanish:

> *The Lautaro Oceanic Shipping and Research Cooperative has the Council's permission to proceed with its proposed covert entry into Spigot. Mr. Slake must agree that, if captured, he will deny any connection to Griqua Tierra. Griqua Tierra will likewise deny any connection to Mr. Slake. If Lautaro decides to proceed with this mission, it must hold another plenary session afterwards to determine the possible consequences of maintaining and cultivating this resource. Please respond to this email with confirmation that Mr. Slake and Lautaro accept these conditions. UC required before proceeding.*

"What's UC?" Roscoe asked.

"Unanimous consent," Yongchen answered. "The margin we need to vote by."

"Do we want a formal vote, or are we all on board as is?" Wangari asked.

One by one, the Griquas raised their hands.

Roscoe drummed his fingers on the table a few times, then turned to Chip. "Guess it's too late to back out now."

"You don't want to let a priest down, do you?" Chip muttered, looking toward Petí, who thumbed through a stack of laminated maps spread across the table. "You might go to hell for that."

"Don't want that."

Chapter 36

Roscoe didn't mind the cold blast from the open submarine hatch this time—it distracted him from the itchy wig and stinging contact lenses that smuggler subs kept for any crew members who might need a disguise. Getting in and out of Spigot seemed like just about the only thing that would make this discomfort worthwhile.

He followed Gabriel and Wangari, both survival-suited but undisguised, through the hatch. A few hundred meters away, the Ross Sea Coast gleamed in the moonlight: a flat plain giving way to a knobbed slope. The red searchlight blinked on, marking their path. Off to the right, Roscoe knew, was Spigot's back door.

The trio piled into an inflatable dinghy, keeping a safe distance from the pier. Gabriel steered them through ice sheets until they finally reached solid ice. Wangari fired a piton gun toward shore and used a winch to drag the dinghy the final few meters. They reached the service entrance without incident. Their first test awaited: Would it be guarded? Bolted?

Wangari pushed—it swung open without a sound. She stepped in first, freeing her braids from her suit's hood. "Looks like Tololo came through."

Gabriel illuminated the interior with a penlight, revealing a UV-ink rectangle on one of the corrugated metal pipes. Scrawled inside it: "el azul."

"Blue cable," Gabriel said. "That's our target."

As Roscoe unbundled himself, Wangari pulled out a tool the Griquas used for precision metal cutting and ran it along the UV pen strokes. Part mini-diamond cutter, part syringe, the tool nicked a groove in the metal, then injected a strain of the Padre's metal-eating bacteria. By the time Roscoe had shed his suit, a neat section of pipe had been cut away. Gabriel grabbed it before it could clatter to the floor. Inside, Roscoe saw a bundle of wires. Thanks to Tololo, they knew the blue one would transmit video from a soldered-on module to Spigot's drone control room.

Roscoe didn't stick around to help attach it. He bolted down the stairs, cracked the door to check for onlookers, then stepped into Spigot's main tunnel. The scene on the sidewalk hadn't changed. No one made eye contact, and no one spoke—both of which worked in Roscoe's favor.

His knees shook as he reached the Drone Control Room and used the wristband "knock" program Tololo had sent. This was the real moment of truth. Would they let him in?

The same stick-thin intern he had seen before answered the door.

"I'm with the nuke team," Roscoe said, flashing a fake U.S. government ID from the spare wristband Chip had given him. The ID photo featured his disguised face. "Here to install some monitoring equipment for the test."

The intern nodded. "Okay. I just need your thumbprint to make sure you have clearance."

Roscoe pressed his putty thumb, etched with Ricardo's print, to her wristband screen. As long as they couldn't tell he was Roscoe Slake, their ruse had a chance.

She creased her brow. "You're not in the system. Doesn't look like you have clearance to be in here."

"I was added to the Argus-3 team at the last minute," Roscoe said, keeping his voice steady. "It's all hands on deck for this operation, and we don't have much time. They said this might happen. Sometimes the clearance log is slow to update."

"Do you have a supervisor I can call?"

Roscoe gave her Chip's wristband number. "While you do that, can I at least get in there and get my tools set up? I won't modify anything yet—I promise. Just want to get ready. We're really on a tight schedule. If I don't get this ready soon, it could be bad for both of us."

She hesitated, looking around. "Okay, sure," she whispered. "Just don't talk with anyone and keep your head down."

That wouldn't be a problem. Roscoe stepped into the Control Room.

It was set up like a lecture hall, with arcs of computer workstations facing a theater-sized screen. It displayed a detailed map of the Ross Sea, a region Roscoe had first seen in the copperplate-printed folds of a two-hundred-eighty-year-old tome.

He found an empty workstation, set down his toolbox, and opened the lid to give the camera inside a clear view of the screen. He pressed the record button. Everything was set. All he had to do was wait.

The engineer seated a few workstations down shot him a quizzical look.

"If anyone talks to you," Chip had told him, "lean into the role."

"I'm with the test team," Roscoe told him. "Just here to install some software and equipment for the test. Is this workstation available?"

"It is now. The guy who sat there offed himself last week."

That comment took the wind out of Roscoe—not only because he was at Hamza's old workstation, but because he recognized the voice: Darren. What was he doing here? Roscoe thought he was in Filtration—had he been reassigned? He deepened his voice, hoping Darren wouldn't recognize him. "Oh, uh, I'm sorry to hear that." He pretended to search his toolbox, angling his face away. "Don't mind me."

He pulled out one tool at a time, stealing glances at the screen and trying to steady his nerves. What was taking Wangari and Gabriel so long? Had the video plug-in failed? Had they been caught? Or was something else going wrong?

He almost jumped when the intern walked up behind him.

"Mister Whalstone, I spoke with your supervisor. The U.S. government has cleared you, but you're not cleared on StarCross's end. I can't let you start until you are."

"Their deadline will be their downfall," Chip had explained. "As a federal employee, trust me; when people are pressed for time, passwords, verification, and all that security bullshit goes out the window. Milk that for all it's worth."

Roscoe sighed dramatically. "Look, I understand it's not protocol, but can't you stretch the rules just this once? Like I said, we're on a super-tight deadline, and if I'm not able to get this installed, we might not be able to do the test."

The intern opened her mouth to respond, but her face went dark as the big screen displaying the Ross Sea map went black. Moments later, it lit up with underwater video footage.

This was it. Wangari and Gabriel had attached the module. Everyone stared at the seafloor. Would the test work?

The intern hesitated, then turned back to Roscoe. "Look, you've put me in a bind here. I don't want to fuck up the test, but if I break protocol—"

"What the hell is that?" a voice called out.

They both turned toward the voice. An engineer near the front of the room was staring at the screen. In the middle of the image—at a point less than a meter from the dye barrel's nozzle—an electric-blue ribbon had appeared. It fanned upward, lighting the seafloor like a piped-in Milky Way.

"Looks like some kind of bioluminescent algae," a different voice suggested.

"But where?"

Several tense seconds passed. "That's ... that's the blast site. Yule Bay."

"Okay, why are we looking at this? Do those things live down there?"

Now came the most dangerous part of Roscoe's mission.

"I know there are some species of bioluminescent algae down here," he said, deepening his voice, "but they need low salt content in the water. Can someone do a quick salinity reading? Or check how the sonar's deflected?"

Sounds of keystrokes filled the room. Then Darren spoke, his voice tight with disbelief.

"That—that water's fresh. There's a freshwater plume down there!"

Roscoe fought back a grin.

Another engineer started typing. "Let's see if we can get an image from another StarBuoy camera."

The projector screen went black, then showed another image—same glowing ribbon, different angle.

"Can someone check that water?" an authoritative voice shouted.

The answer came quickly, from someone across the room.

"It's fresh, boss. Only seen sonar interference like this where glaciers are calving."

"Are you sure?"

"I'd drink it, boss! At least if there weren't any algae in it."

A nervous hush followed, until Darren broke it.

"Shit. Hamza told me about this. Said something about a dye test that would reveal fresh water on the bottom of Yule Bay. Went to a disciplinary hearing where it was supposed to happen. Didn't pan out then, but it sure looks like it has now."

Thanks, Hamza, Roscoe thought. Because his friend had spread the word, more evidence of the plume was now safely recorded on his hidden camera's memory chip. And others were beginning to understand what it could mean.

"Could be a big deal for keeping production in the Goldilocks zone," someone added.

The intern beside Roscoe tore her attention away from the screen. "Anyway, as I was saying—"

"No worries," Roscoe cut her off, quickly gathering his tools. He pressed a button inside the box—sending Wangari and Gabriel the agreed-upon start-packing-up signal—and snapped the lid shut. "I'll come back later."

He headed for the service entrance, mimicking the dour expressions and unassuming shuffles of the others.

A StarCross Security jitney raced down the tunnel, sirens blaring, and screeched to a stop outside the control room. They wanted to hide it, Roscoe knew—to erase all knowledge of the test. But they didn't know that it had already been captured in high definition by the camera in Roscoe's toolbox. He forced himself to act natural.

The moment he reached the stairwell, though, he ran—taking the steps two at a time. Wangari and Gabriel had left the service door open, and his lungs burned with cold, dry air by the time he reached the top. Wangari had already unplugged the video module. While she patched the cut pipe with super glue and spray paint, Gabriel plugged the toolbox's port into a tripod-mounted communications laser and aimed at the *Lautaro*.

Roscoe didn't wait. He shoved his legs into his suit and wrestled the sleeves over his arms, fingers stiff as he fumbled with the zippers. The cold bit deeper with each second he spent exposed.

A red dot flashed on the horizon, followed by a soft ping from the toolbox.

"Video received," Gabriel whispered.

No time to celebrate. Wangari hit the pipe with a final spray of paint, hiding the repairs as best she could. Gabriel and Roscoe stashed the last of the gear, and they hustled out the service entrance, hauling the dinghy back to the water's edge.

As Gabriel motored back through the sheets of ice, every jolt against the hull rattled Roscoe's nerves. He gripped the toolbox with one hand and the dinghy's rope line with the other, watching the *Lautaro*'s conning tower inch closer. After what felt like an eternity, they pulled alongside. Chip leaned out the hatch and flashed a thumbs-up.

"Transmission received—the govellers have the video."

Roscoe's chest loosened, but only a little. They'd done all they could to stop the test. It was out of their hands now.

Chapter 37

Collective decision-making remained a pain in the ass.

Roscoe had returned to the *Lautaro* and enjoyed another five-minute shower as the sub turned back north. Then he headed to the galley for the Council-required second plenary session—to decide what to do with those microbes. Evangelina set out a bowl of berries to share. They didn't last long.

To Roscoe's chagrin, Chip kicked off the session by playing his secret video from the Control Room. Everyone laughed at Roscoe's prevarications and the Spigot employees' realization of what they were witnessing. Despite himself, Roscoe couldn't help but laugh along.

"Thanks to Roscoe," Chip said as the lights came back on, "we have confirmation that there's fresh water on the ocean floor—and that Spigot knows it. I've sent the video to my bosses in Minneapolis for their"—he made air quotes—"'information as they coordinate operations with Spigot and negotiate water purchases.' TBD if they'll call off the nuke test. The ball's in their court on that."

"Have you told them about what we found down there?" Petí asked, concern in his voice.

Chip shook his head. "That's still our secret. All I said is that we're still examining the sample. Which is technically true."

"But we have a potential freshwater source," Ricardo said. "A valuable one at that. We need to evaluate our options. Wangari, call up the flowchart."

Wangari typed on her laptop, projecting the chart and zooming in on the box with Roscoe's optimistic prediction: "Mission successful on all counts; proof of dye test secured and shared with U.S. government; new hypothesis for freshwater source developed and plan for further study determined."

"Now we need to figure out where we go from here," Ricardo said. "Since we're no longer racing the clock, I expect the COC will want to loop in the entire Council. They might even want to run it by a neutral third party—maybe someone in another co-op—to identify additional options and outcomes. But first, we need to develop our own courses of action."

"It sounded like we'd already decided," Roscoe said. Though he was a newcomer, he felt the risk he'd just taken had earned him a voice. "We take this back to Griqua Tierra and figure out how those bacteria—or whatever they are—desalinate water."

"That's one option," Ricardo said, voice heavy with skepticism. He nodded to Wangari, who added a new box to the flowchart: "Return sample to Griqua Tierra; analyze further."

Ricardo leaned toward Roscoe. "What do you think the outcomes of that would be?"

Roscoe paused, caught off-guard. "Well ... Griqua Tierra could have a bargaining chip—a way to desalinate water. Governments might come to them instead of StarCross."

Chip's voice turned dour. "We don't know that. These bacteria might not be scalable. They might need something unique to the seafloor. We might just have rocks."

While they spoke, Wangari added two new branches to the "Return Sample" box: "Griqua Tierra acquires valuable new source of water" and "GT does not."

"Even if it's a valuable water source," Ricardo added, "it might bring us other troubles. StarCross has missiles, surveillance ... all the necessary tools to protect their monopoly."

"And if we have a person inside Spigot, so could others," Yongchen said. "New Swabia, for instance. If StarCross knows about us, so could they."

The blasts of the submarine's decoy depth charges rung in Roscoe's ears as Ricardo nodded grimly. "We could find ourselves with multiple targets on our backs."

"Not if we use this discovery to get defenses from a government," Roscoe suggested.

"Maybe," Ricardo conceded, "but the Council's been talking about militarizing for years. So far, no majority's been willing to support it. I don't know if they'd go for that now."

"What about keeping it secret within Griqua Tierra?" Petí offered. "Evangelina, do you think this could improve our agricultural output?"

The agronomist shook her head. "Water isn't our biggest constraint in Griqua Tierra. Sunlight's a bigger problem in a glacial valley. Fertilizer too. Harvesting ammonia from urine before recycling has worked well on the subs, but scaling that up is the next big hurdle. Only then could we consider more water-intensive crops."

This new detail about the sub's food and water escaped Roscoe's notice. He had risked his life to get these samples. That contribution had now been whittled down to three boxes branching off from the "Valuable new source of water" possibility. One said, "Outside commercial interest in GT's water," but the other possibilities were bleak: "Little or no short-term agricultural gains"; "StarCross seeks to eliminate competition"; "GT forced to seek protection from outside / consider militarization."

"What else could we do if we don't take these samples back?" he asked, leaning over the table in a defensive crouch. "Throw them overboard?"

Ricardo shrugged. "Sure, that's another option."

Roscoe watched, aghast, as Wangari added another box to the flowchart, branching off from the original "Mission Successful" box: "Return samples to seabed."

"Then we're pretty much back to where we started," Chip said. "StarCross might lose its nuke and axe Jahnford for missing or ignoring that freshwater source, but so what? StarCross will know it's down there. Even without nukes, I bet they can find other ways to destroy it."

More boxes appeared on the screen.

Then, with a perverse thrill, Roscoe found a hole to poke in this plan. "If we do that, Griqua Tierra might need weapons anyway."

Chip shot him a strange look.

"StarCross agents probably saw us get on this sub back at Newloon, remember? They might know we got away."

Chip tilted his head back and forth, considering. "Or they could suspect something and cut off water to the Chilean government until they take the settlement out."

Ricardo cut in. "That's one risk we probably don't have to worry about. Griqua Tierra isn't in Chile—or any other country." He tensed, his eyes darting to the others, before continuing. "Our territory's at the end of a fjord that used to be covered in ice. The frontier between Chile and Argentina was never officially demarcated there. Now, both countries' govellers are afraid they'll wind up violating the Updated Terms of Service if they assert their claims." Wangari kept typing, slotting their comments into still more boxes. "All right. Silent input time, two minutes."

Ricardo handed Roscoe a phone with the same anonymous-input screen he'd seen before. Soon, Chip and the others were all focused on their phones. Some just stared at their screens; others rubbed their temples in thought. Only Evangelina seemed to be pecking out an entry. Roscoe couldn't think of anything else to add.

The two minutes passed in silence. The screen went blank.

"Looks like we have just one other entry," Wangari said. "Risk regardless of next steps: StarCross will retaliate against Spigot junior employees and/or Newloon residents for allowing RS to escape; risk increased if microbes shared."

Ricardo and Petí grimaced; Roscoe did the same, remembering the fires burning through Newloon and StarCross Security vehicles racing toward the Control Room. If one of StarCross's main two products came under threat, what kind of message would it want to send to those closest to the source?

Wangari added another box to the flowchart. "All right, let's let the Councilors-on-Call decide."

With a few more taps, the flowchart disappeared and the lights came back on.

"Now what?" Roscoe asked.

"The COCs will evaluate these options," Ricardo said. "They might run them by a third party in another cooperative or in the civil service to see if they can come up with additional outcomes. Then they'll give us our marching orders."

Roscoe squeezed his toes in frustration. Another verdict awaited—a decision that would shape the future of everything they'd done so far. No one else seemed too concerned. Gabriel, Ricardo, and Yongchen rose to get coffee.

The response came before they had even reached the urn.

"Return sample to Griqua Tierra without vote," Wangari read off her laptop. "Consider mission results Top Secret until further notice."

She looked around the table. "Has anyone else gotten a Top Secret directive from the Council before? Is that even something we do?"

No one answered, and she closed her laptop.

That ended the plenary session. Ricardo, Evangelina, and Gabriel went for coffee. Wangari crossed the room to Yongchen and gave her a kiss. Roscoe and Petí stayed seated, staring at the table. One by one, the crew drifted back to their stations, leaving Roscoe and Chip alone.

Roscoe allowed himself a grin. "Work hasn't gone to waste just yet," he said.

Chip grinned back. "Oh, just you wait. Bet there'll be more debate when we get back. And don't forget—science could screw us over again."

Chapter 38

H.M.S. *Erebus*
Off the coast of Victoria Land
February 1841

As the ships sailed north, Yule joined the crew in savoring one last look at the peaks of Victoria Land.

More than two weeks had passed since Yule had slipped the envelope under the door to the Great Cabin, then lain awake, tormented by the thought that he might have just doomed himself. The following morning brought an answer.

A whistle blast summoned the crew to attention.

"Each man on this ship has proven his worth this past month," Ross announced. "We have journeyed farther south than any human being before and have added a vast southern continent to Her Majesty's domains. Alas, this ice barrier has proven an insurmountable obstacle to the South Magnetic Pole. We shall, therefore, return to Hobart and try for the pole again next summer."

The men cheered. Any reprieve, even for a single season, was welcome news. It doubtless helped that Ross had spliced the main brace and ordered more coal for the heating apparatus.

Yule had more to record as the ships headed north. The names Ross had given this landscape on the voyage south had sought to honor the expedition's benefactors: Victoria Land for their sovereign; Royal Society Range for the group that had commissioned their journey; Admiralty Range, Minto Peak, Franklin Island, and even Coulman Island for Ross's father-in-law.

On the voyage back, Ross instead named features for his crew members. Francis Crozier, captain of the *Terror*, was honored with a cape just west of the two volcanoes they had discovered; Archibald McMurdo, the *Terror*'s First Master, received a bay just to the east; Edward Bird, the *Erebus*'s First Lieutenant, received a small cape at the volcanoes' base. Even Tucker, the *Erebus*'s functioning drunk First Master, earned an inlet beneath the Admiralty Range.

"Remind me what we've named that one, Yule?" Ross asked, pointing at a low, wide bay off the port side.

Yule raced below decks, consulted the remark-book, and returned to report that it was unnamed.

The captain nodded stiffly beneath his Welsh wig. "What shall we call it, then? McCormick Bay, perhaps, for our chief surgeon?"

The surgeon, who had already been granted a cape near Possession Island, was within earshot. "You already put my name on this shore once. May I suggest Yule Bay for our navigator—if he doesn't object?"

Ross gave another stiff nod. "Yes, we did give Tucker that inlet. Yule, please go record this location as Yule Bay."

"What about Hooker?" Yule heard himself say, more angrily than he meant. Ross's eyes narrowed between his scarf and Welsh wig. Yule quickly added, "He collected specimens throughout so much of our voyage."

Ross glared at Yule another instant. Then he pointed ahead, at a cape just south of the bay's entrance. "Very well, name that Cape Hooker."

Yule hurried back to the Great Cabin to record these two features in the remark-book. Hooker sat at his desk, engrossed in adding observations to the papers that Yule had returned weeks before. He barely seemed to notice Yule's presence. Sensing it was best not to disturb him, Yule quietly departed—but then remembered the attestation that lay in his bunk, still waiting to disgrace the brave young surgeon.

He tucked the angle-book under his jacket and returned to his bunk. Sweating inside his foul-weather gear, Yule grabbed the pail full of basalt pebbles from Franklin Island. The attestation was still there, alongside the remnants of the insurance policy he would need to cancel as soon as they reached Hobart. Burning the papers or tearing them into the wind might draw notice; hiding them risked their eventual discovery.

Yule studied the pail more closely. True, the Earl of Minto had ordered them to "preserve all such specimens of the animal, vegetable, and mineral kingdoms" collected during the voyage. But McCormick had shown no interest in these particular basalt stones since they had left Franklin Island. Most of his time had been consumed with shooting and skinning the Antarctic bird life. Their absence, Yule decided, would not be noticed.

A door's creak startled him. Hooker stepped past his bunk, leaving the Great Cabin empty. Now was his chance. Yule grabbed the pail, scurried to the cabin, and opened a window. Leaning out, he held the pail over the track of water the ship had carved through the pack ice. Then, he let it go.

Chapter 39

Ross Sea Coast
Antarctica
July 2123

The sub crew members returned to their posts. Chip and Petí went back to the lab, while Roscoe went to get more coffee. He'd managed just one sip when Chip's shout echoed up the stairs.

"What the hell is that?"

Hurrying down, Roscoe found that Petí and Chip had opened the metal scoop, spilling its contents into a large plastic basin. A mound of silt and pebbles now surrounded a rusted metal pail, slightly squashed and big enough to hold maybe two or three cups. A tongue of chalky rock poked out from the pail's rim. Petí broke off a fragment with gloved fingers and held it under his jeweler's loupe.

"Salt," he said. "Precipitating out from desalination."

"So that's what it was," Roscoe muttered. Both scientists turned to him.

"When I was down there and I pulled the lever to drop the scoop, I heard a grinding noise—metal on metal. I guess that's what it was."

"Dropped overboard by a ship, perhaps?" Petí mused, picking up the pail. More stones and silt tumbled out as he turned it. The two scientists rinsed it with a hose, then shined a flashlight inside.

"What the—" Chip stopped midsentence and looked at Roscoe. "Hey man, I think we need your expertise here."

Baffled, Roscoe stepped around the basin and took the flashlight. Inside the pail's base, he didn't see metal—he saw wadded paper, soaked and pressed against the bottom, covered in minute script. Much of it was illegible, but here and there, numbers and capital letters stood out, oddly familiar.

"It's from the Ross Expedition!" Roscoe exclaimed. Petí and Chip stared, bewildered. "Spigot had me looking through their journals and logbooks. I swear I saw the same handwriting in their remark-book. I don't know how, but it's the same."

Petí scratched his head. "Perhaps they dropped this pail overboard. But why fill it with rocks?"

"You said those rocks are basalt, right?" Roscoe asked. "Maybe they were samples from Franklin Island. They wrote about basalt there, and I read that they sent a boat ashore to collect samples."

Chip nodded slowly. "Maybe. But where'd the microbes get their food from? Seafloor basalt microbes we know feed on stuff that drifts down. If these guys lived above the waterline, what sustained them?"

Roscoe hesitated but then spoke. "They also found guano on Franklin Island. Thought they could ship it to Australia as fertilizer. Maybe that was it?"

Chip chuckled, shaking his head. "Bird shit? That could've done it." He looked back into the basin. "So they just happened to drop their samples overboard, and this pail just happened to land in the right spot so enough rocks would scatter over the ocean floor—so that when the ocean chemistry changed enough to let them desalinate seawater, they could do it at scale, and we'd be able to pick it up—and we'd leave enough rocks behind so that we could pick it up." He shook his head. "Damn, talk about a lucky break."

Petí smiled. "Or a blessing."

Chip tilted his head, considering. "Yeah ... or that."

Chapter 40

London
December 1847

Walker summoned Yule with a brief note. "Gift for you. Come by print shop when you have a chance." Yule wondered how Walker had found him at this boarding house—he had been in London less than a week—but he set out right away.

First Master Henry Braddick Yule had spent the past three years gathering depth soundings and theodolite readings along the tamer shores of the Thames Estuary. The *Erebus* had barely docked before he was assigned to this new task aboard the H.M.S. *Porcupine*, one of the new paddle-wheel steamers the Admiralty had commissioned during the Antarctic expedition.

Yule would take it over the poles or a coaling station. The expedition's great promise—a model of global magnetism that would reveal a ship's location by compass bearing alone—remained elusive. Ships still needed first and second masters to navigate them.

He had been glad to put the Antarctic behind him, though many could not. The Admiralty and Hydrographic Office were still digesting all the information he and Tucker had gathered under Ross. Their retreat from the ice barrier that first summer had not ended the expedition. The *Erebus* and *Terror* spent another winter in Hobart—where Yule learned Aspley had burned down his office and fled, becoming what locals called a "bushranger" to escape various creditors. The ships spent two more summers seeking the South Magnetic Pole, again without success. While Ross never brought the ships so close to destruction as during that first summer, his disappointment was clear as they sailed back to England.

That disappointment vanished upon their return. Despite failing to reach the pole or revolutionize navigation, the expedition had brought back a wealth of scientific discoveries. Yule had watched from afar as Ross knelt for his knighthood and later pored over the ship's remark-books at the Hydrographic Office while preparing his memoir.

The significance of their findings had already been grasped. At the Admiralty, Yule's fellow officers were starting to call the waters they had sailed—between Victoria Land and the great ice barrier—the Ross Sea.

Now, Walker's shop had printed a map that brought it all into sharp focus.

The printed sheet showed the ice barrier, the Victoria Land coast, and the tracks taken by the *Erebus* and *Terror* in 1841 and 1842. Yule's eyes traced the path of that first summer, recalling their first brush with the pack ice, Hooker's fall on Franklin Island, the awe-inspiring sight of Mount Erebus, and the ice bay from which they had barely escaped. From there, the expedition's path curved eastward and disappeared off the map.

"This is a gift from our shop," Walker said. "We are printing these maps to accompany Ross's memoir of the expedition, including all the names he bestowed upon the landscape."

The Victoria Land coast was thick with names on this map. Near the bottom, Yule saw "Cape Hooker," and, just above it, "Yule Bay."

"Something history will remember you by!" Walker said, beaming. "Your very own bay in the Antarctic. Right next to a cape named for that up-and-coming botanist."

Yule studied the map in silence. He had fallen out of touch with Hooker since their return to England. The assistant surgeon had never spoken of what Ross had done to him—or of those terrible days when their captain seemed bent on sailing into oblivion. Now, the only evidence of those events lay at the bottom of a bay that bore Yule's name.

"Tell me," Walker asked, "what does the bay look like?"

"It's ... it's a pleasant place," Yule answered. "Not as remarkable as some of the wonders we saw, but I'm honored it bears my name." He shook the mapmaker's hand. "Well done."

Yule had just left Walker's shop when a familiar voice called out. "Yule!"

He turned and saw McCormick—though it took a moment to recognize the surgeon in his haggard state. His face was gaunt, his expression weary, as if he hadn't slept in months.

They shook hands. "Doctor McCormick! Are you well?"

The surgeon shook his head, looking down at his feet. "The news from Ireland keeps getting worse—hunger spreading across the island. Terrible business, and Her Majesty's role in it all ..." He shook his head harder and forced a smile. "I shan't trouble you with the details. Let me call on Mister Walker and join you for a walk."

After collecting his map, McCormick strolled with Yule down Albemarle Street. "Have you heard Ross is setting sail again?" the surgeon asked.

"No. Where?"

"The Northwest Passage, in search of Franklin."

Soon after returning from the Antarctic, the Admiralty had given the *Erebus* and *Terror* a new mission: charting the Northwest Passage, the last great unexplored sea route, through the Canadian Arctic. Ross, the natural first choice to lead the voyage, had claimed his seafaring days were behind him. Instead, the honor went to John Franklin, the "oaf of a governor," recently returned from Van Dieman's Land. He captained *Erebus*, with Francis Crozier again captaining the *Terror*.

The ships had sailed in spring of 1845 and had not been seen in over a year. Fears for the crew were starting to grow.

"Do you think the expedition is safe?" Yule asked.

McCormick sighed. "I cannot say. Franklin is more of a fool than Ross—older, and less fit—but he's explored the Arctic before. From what I've heard, that's his true element, not some governor's post in a place like Van Dieman's Land. And the ships were fitted with locomotive engines and propellers before they sailed for Canada. So they are not at the mercy of the winds and currents as we were."

Yule thought back to the *Erebus* trapped in the ice bay, to the terror he felt as he swung a pickax and prayed the ice would weaken just enough for the sails to pull the ship free.

"Steam would be quite an asset near the poles," he replied. "They'll be able to break through pack ice we never could."

"On the other hand," McCormick said, "they could charge into pack ice that even steam cannot break. They might forget their limits."

"The Admiralty thinks they're in grave enough danger to warrant an expedition?"

McCormick shook his head. "The Admiralty still considers them safe. Lady Jane Franklin has organized a private search. She insisted Ross lead it."

"I thought Ross had retired from polar voyages."

"That's what he said. Somehow, Lady Franklin changed his mind. Maybe rumors of his recklessness on the *Erebus* that first summer had reached her in Van Dieman's Land, and she used them against him."

"How?"

"Guilt," McCormick answered without hesitation. "The nuns at my school always pressed us further by reminding us of the atonement we owed the Lord."

Yule fell silent, thinking back to the young woman who had taken on her husband's work with such ease in Van Dieman's Land. Questions swirled in his head.

What "guilt" was McCormick referring to? Was it simply Ross's near-suicidal pursuit of the South Magnetic Pole, or was there more? Had Lady Jane learned of the insurance policy filed against Ross with Aspley? Did she suspect his men hated him? Had she somehow learned what Ross had done to Hooker? Should Yule tell the surgeon now?

First, he decided to test what McCormick already knew.

"What do you think of that choice?"

"As insufferable as Ross is, he knows polar seas better than any man alive," McCormick said. "And I will admit, he seemed more cautious after the trouble we had near the Great Barrier our first summer. As much as it pains me to admit it, he may be the best hope those men have." He smiled briefly. "After all, Ross never ate his boots."

Yule said nothing further.

Epilogue

Southern Ocean
Antarctica
July 2123

Roscoe lingered on the platform behind the *Lautaro*'s conning tower, savoring the peach sky after months of blackness.

"Mind if I join you?"

Roscoe turned to see Chip leaning on the railing beside him. It was July 31—the date the blast had been scheduled. But the submarine's sonar showed no patrol subs or no-sail zones. The Southern Ocean lay calm, calm enough for the *Lautaro*'s crew to go topside.

The sun wouldn't rise over the Ross Sea for a few more weeks, but the *Lautaro* had voyaged far enough north to catch the first twilight Roscoe had seen in months. Most of the crew had retreated indoors after a few minutes in the cold, but Roscoe stayed behind, his suit's hood loosely draped over his head.

"Makes a hell of a difference, doesn't it?" Chip asked, nodding toward the horizon. "Full-spectrum lamps just don't cut it." He pulled up a message on his wristband. "Says here the nuclear test's been called off," he said, using air quotes. "Determination that the requested warhead is not suitable for undersea detonation."

"They're still buying WECs from StarCross, though?"

Chip nodded. "No govellers will give up their water supply over one video. But it gave them pause before they traded nukes for water."

"You think these microbes will give people an alternative to Spigot?" Roscoe asked.

Chip smiled. "Too early to tell. It's going to take way more research to find out what these things are and what makes them tick. So far, they've stumped the guy who's bred bacteria that can eat metal and algae that glow in fresh water." He cracked his knuckles through his gloves.

"Any idea how long that research will take?"

"Nope," Chip said. "We've just built an incubator that mimics the pressure and chemistry down there. Based on the salinity readings, they seem pretty happy so far, but figuring out what they are and scaling up production? I wouldn't hold your breath. And even if they're scalable, Griqua Tierra will decide whether to share." He shifted, pushing another floating wristband message in front of Roscoe. "StarCross is definitely spooked, though. Check out this out—Tololo forwarded it to the crew."

Roscoe scanned the text:

> *Dear Spigot family,*
>
> *We would like to bid a bittersweet farewell to our friend and CEO, Grei Jahnford. After ten years of visionary leadership, Mr. Jahnford has decided to step down to spend more time with his family and church.*
>
> *In a statement, StarCross President and Chairman—*

Roscoe swiped the screen closed. "Guess Jahnford's prayers weren't answered."

Chip raised an eyebrow. "Prayers?"

"Remember what you told me? You thought Jahnford was praying that the freshwater plume wouldn't get discovered on his watch. He knew it'd look bad if people realized he was selling water while a free source was next door. Guess he was right."

"Yep," Chip said, grinning. "Guess whatever God there is isn't on his side." He reached into his coat and pulled out a flask. "Dry ship or not, if Petí gets communion wine, I should get one flask of McMurdo vodka."

He raised it toward the horizon that now separated them from Spigot and a CEO who was packing his bags. "To Jahnford's end." Before taking a swig, Chip added, "And to Hamza."

Rosco accepted the flask. The vodka burned as it went down. One mouthful of the potent brew had him looking at the submarine's wake, wondering about the ripple effects of their mission.

The mere chance that these microbes could produce fresh water, upsetting StarCross's precious Goldilocks production rate, had convinced StarCross to fire an executive and cost it some of humanity's most powerful weapons. What other problems might it cause for their stranglehold on water, and how far would they go to suppress it?

And what about that scrap of paper in the pail? Could it somehow upset the Revelators, those fanatics who revered people like Ross?

Chip interrupted Roscoe's thoughts with more good news.

"There's a new job waiting for you in Griqua Tierra."

Roscoe turned, intrigued. "What kind of job?"

"Councilor-on-Call says it's top priority. When we get up there, their Civil Service's Library Division wants you to help decipher what that paper inside the pail says."

"I'll drink to that," Roscoe said, taking another swig. Then a thought struck him. "So, I'll be doing the same job as in Spigot."

Chip shook his head. "Not even close. Griqua Tierra's library isn't a dead-end job like in Spigot. When a co-op or the Governing Council needs some thorny problem solved, they go to the Library. A lot of Tololo's intel ends up there. And they waived the probationary period for you. They want you, man."

Roscoe's gratitude felt real now—but he decided to push his luck anyway. "Do you think Griqua Tierra will have room for Hamza's parents? They were hoping Hamza would get them out of their Naurutown. This place sure sounds like an improvement."

The scientist gazed into the waves, tilting his head back-and-forth in his familiar "I'm thinking" motion. "It can't hurt to ask." After a pause, he gave Roscoe an odd look. "What about your parents? Were they counting on you too?"

"Oh yeah, they were." Both his post-hearing anger at his parents and his older dreams of getting them off-world seemed to lie back in Spigot's Archives, relics of bygone days. All the space they'd taken up in his mind had gone empty, leaving him numb. "Dunno if I'd want to bring them down, though." When Chip made the same nasty-sip face Evangelina had during their meeting, Roscoe decided to steer the conversation elsewhere. "Why did the library people say they wanted me?"

"Apparently Tololo said you'd be perfect for the job."

"Tololo?" Roscoe asked, startled. "How does he know me? Do you know who he is?"

Chip shook his head. "Ricardo won't tell me. Just said Tololo's been transmitting old archives. Evangelina thinks it might help her research. She mentioned some botanist named Hooker." Chip snorted.

Roscoe chuckled too—but not at Hooker's name. "I think Tololo's a 'she,' Chip."

The hatch creaked open before he could explain.

"Shit!" Chip hissed, snatching the flask from Roscoe and tucking it in his pocket.

Ricardo appeared, holding his phone. "Message for you, Roscoe," he said.

"A message?" Roscoe repeated.

"Surprised us too," Ricardo said. "It came through a pirate satellite. We had to send it up to the Library in Griqua Tierra for decryption." He held out his phone. "You recognize the sender?"

Roscoe took the phone and shared the screen with Chip:

Roscoe—

Nice work. Greenland's helping me out with some stuff—it'd be great to have you on board too. Can't share more until we meet in person. If you ever want to meet up, go to

Shiduri's. Order a Blood Falls Red Ale and an Elephant Island IPA. Tell her you're meeting with someone about researching Kropotkin's theories on the subglacial lakes. She'll take care of the rest.

In solidarity,
Finn Smalls

Roscoe and Chip looked at each other, then southward, toward the horizon, the thawing continent beyond, and whatever waited for them back there.

Author's Note

From 1839 to 1843, the H.M.S. *Erebus* and *Terror* charted the Antarctic coast and the Southern Ocean under the command of Captain James Clark Ross. The expedition failed to achieve its principal objective—planting the British flag on the South Magnetic Pole—but the Ross Expedition, along with the concurrent U.S. Exploring Expedition commanded by Charles Wilkes and a French expedition led by Jules Dumont d'Urville, helped fill in the blank spaces at the bottom of humanity's maps.

These voyages remain most closely associated with the men who led them. But their true contributions took the form of data collection and survey work by the likes of Henry Braddick Yule and Charles Tucker, and the specimens and observations gathered by Joseph Dalton Hooker, Robert McCormick, and their counterparts on other ships. The Antarctic came into focus for the first time thanks to this patient, methodical, and often unglamorous work—work that continues today, as Antarctica remains the only continent reserved for science.

I sincerely hope that this remains the case and that a future like the one I've written remains fiction.

Each named sailor in the chapters about the Ross Expedition was a real member of that voyage. Their personalities—and those of the other named characters—are largely figments of my imagination. So is Ross's abuse of Hooker, Yule's treasure hunt, and his life insurance policy on Ross from a fictitious Lunk Aspley. Hooker did fall overboard during the expedition's landing on Franklin Island, but the extent of his illness afterward is also fictitious. However, the dates of each port of call are accurate.

Michael Palin's book *Erebus* was an invaluable starting point for my research—one I'd recommend to anyone interested in learning more about the remarkable travels of that hardy bomb vessel. We are also fortunate that no StarCross-like entity has come along to lock up the records of that expedition. The memoirs, journals, and records of Ross, McCormick, Hooker, and other expedition members remain freely accessible in various online databases. My verbatim quotations from these texts, and the map Roscoe found in the Archives, are cited below:

Chapter 4

Earl of Minto's instructions:

Ross, James Clark. *A Voyage of Discovery and Research in the Southern and Antarctic Regions, during the Years 1839–43*. London: John Murray, 1847, pp. xxii-xxviii.

Chapter 7

Ross Sea map:

Ross, James Clark. *A Voyage of Discovery and Research in the Southern and Antarctic Regions, during the Years 1839–43*. London: John Murray, 1847.

Chapter 18

"From 19 January … South Magnetic Pole!"

Palin, Michael. *Erebus: One Ship, Two Epic Voyages, and the Greatest Naval Mystery of All Time*. Vancouver, Canada: Greystone Books, 2018, p. 90.

Chapter 22

"Ah! Old boy, if I put my hand on it, the body must follow."

Robertson, J. "A Few General Remarks on the Antarctic Continent, Discovered by Captains Ross and Crozier." *The Tasmanian Journal of Natural Science, Agriculture, Statistics, Etc.*, vol. 2, no. 6, January 1843, pp. 45–61 at 51.

Chapter 26

"Your former letters … scenery delightful."

Hooker, Joseph Dalton. Received by Lady Maria Hooker, June 6, 1841. Joseph Hooker Collection. https://jdhooker.kew.org/p/jdh/asset/1702.

About the Author

P. Finian Reilly studied history at the University of Chicago, then got a different kind of education by working as a local newspaper reporter in Montana. In that job, he learned how to drive a motorboat alongside a burning lakeshore, interview anti-government militia leaders, and appreciate just how complicated humanity's relationship with the natural world can be. He earned his J.D. at Georgetown University Law Center, and now works as an environmental attorney in New Jersey. *Ice's End* is his first novel.

ACKNOWLEDGMENTS

Many people helped bring *Ice's End* to publication. First, I have to thank my longtime editor and friend, Gwen Florio. Gwen has taken many chances on me over the years. As editor of the *Missoulian*, she hired me to cover a chunk of Montana larger than several states and sharpened my writing and reporting skills in countless ways during my two years on that beat. When I asked her—as the only novelist I knew—for fiction-writing advice, her first words were, "Be a lawyer." She nonetheless read and edited several drafts of this novel and kept me sane through the publication process.

Adrian Horton, another dear friend from my time in Montana, did the same. We worked side by side in our first jobs out of college, covering local news around Glacier National Park for *The Daily Inter Lake*. Remarkably, that experience didn't deter Adrian from agreeing to edit the early drafts of *Ice's End*, and giving me encouragement that kept me going through months of revisions and rejections.

I'm deeply grateful to everyone else who took the time to read earlier drafts of this novel, and to give feedback and encouragement: Sabrina Lourie, Scott Altman, James Schadt, Deniz Demirci, Elaine Yao, Emily Mahapatra, Valeria Stutz, and, of course, my parents, Michael and Elaine Reilly. *Ice's End* is a much better story for all your input.

Special thanks to Mike Lucibella, former editor of *The Antarctic Sun*, for reading it with an Antarctic eye and ensuring that I got the details of the Ross Sea Coast right. I'm also grateful to Professor Bethan Davies for answering my questions about the area's glaciers.

Thanks to Steven Long, publisher of 12 Willows Press, for taking a chance on this novel and giving it several rounds of excellent edits, and to the entire 12 Willows team for doing such a great job with its production.

Finally, I have to again thank my parents, Michael and Elaine Reilly—along with my brother Keelin, my sister Melina, and my sister-in-law Emmeline—for all their support and encouragement over the years.

P. Finian Reilly
April 2025

www.ingramcontent.com/pod-product-compliance
Lightning Source LLC
Chambersburg PA
CBHW030628230626
47082CB00023B/167